THE FORBIDDEN FIANCÉE

BY
SARA ORWIG

MILLS & BOON

Published in Great Britain 2014
by Mills & Boon, an imprint of Harlequin (UK) Limited,
Eton House, 18-24 Paradise Road, Richmond, Surrey, TW9 1SR

© 2014 Sara Orwig

ISBN: 978-0-263-91468-9

51-0614

Harlequin (UK) Limited's policy is to use papers that are natural, renewable and recyclable products and made from wood grown in sustainable forests. The logging and manufacturing processes conform to the legal environmental regulations of the country of origin.

Printed and bound in Spain
by Blackprint CPI, Barcelona

Sara Orwig lives in Oklahoma. She has a patient husband who will take her on research trips anywhere, from big cities to old forts. She is an avid collector of Western history books. With a master's degree in English, Sara has written historical romance, mainstream fiction and contemporary romance. Books are beloved treasures that take Sara to magical worlds, and she loves both reading and writing them.

With thanks to Stacy Boyd,
Allison Carroll and Maureen Walters.
And with love to David and all my family.

One

In the small town of Verity, Texas, when the door to the Texas United Western Bank opened, Jake Calhoun's breath whooshed out as if a fist slammed into his gut. Through the years he had imagined this moment, yet he had thought it would never take place. Now every vivid detail became etched in his memory.

Across the street Madison Milan stepped into the September morning sunlight and glanced around. Sunshine glinted on her thick brown hair that was pulled back and tied with a red scarf. Dressed in jeans, a red shirt showing beneath her open denim jacket, with loafers on her feet, she answered a greeting of someone who passed her.

The shock of finally seeing her rocked him. She was not a figment of his imagination. She was real, alive and only two hundred yards away. Anger surged in his bloodstream, swiftly replaced by desire, intense, hot and startling. Gone was the momentary jolt of finally facing her,

replaced by scalding memories. How could he feel desire?
The hurt had been so deep, and so long ago.

The memories bombarded him, quick and relentless.
She was the most fun female in the junior class, the pretti-
est football queen ever and had the best-looking legs of any
Verity High cheerleader. But now that girl was gone. In her
place stood a beautiful woman. Everyone who passed her
on the street acknowledged her and she responded with a
smile; some stopped to talk. He wondered if she had such
a constant stream of people greeting her every time she
came to town. Right now a tall, thin cowboy took his turn
chatting with her and she smiled up at him.

Jake's emotions warred over the conflicts that rocked
him. On the one hand, he wanted to take her family ranch
from her and destroy her. After all, she was a Milan, as
deceptive, deceitful and out for Calhoun blood as any other
Milan in her family. At the same time, she was beautiful,
sexy and the most desirable woman he had ever known.

She had been only a girl when he had gotten the closest to her. They had met in high school and the attraction
had been hot and instant. He'd been the quarterback of the
football team and she'd been a cheerleader.

His unwanted longing grew stronger, stirred by memories that made him weak in the knees. Memories of her
soft lips and hot kisses, her silky hair that hung to her waist
then, her laughter and boundless energy, her soft curves
against him when they danced. The lightning flashes of
memory continued to pound him: how they each fought
the attraction because of the feud that raged between their
families; their first kiss; the first time they made love—
the first for her ever. The recollections were so vivid they
seemed recent instead of thirteen years ago. She had married the year she had graduated from college and the union
had lasted two months. Since that time she had remained

single—he knew that much about her—and it was long enough ago to be significant now.

She was probably as competitive in business now as she had been years ago in sports.

He brought himself back to the problem at hand. He wanted to talk to her, but he hadn't figured on a steady stream of locals who paused to chat with her.

From the background information his staff had put together he knew she usually drove a white four-door pickup to town. He'd spotted it two blocks farther west down Main Street in front of the grocery, and now he wondered if he should wait at the truck for her.

When she turned to walk in that direction, he crossed the street, lengthened his stride until he was half a block behind her. She entered the hardware store and he followed her inside. In minutes he found her in front of the paint section. As he approached her, his pulse quickened.

Madison Milan selected tubes of paint for her next art project, searching for the perfect shade of burnt umber. Out of the corner of her eye, she saw someone moving along the aisle toward her. When she saw who it was, she froze. Her heart missed a beat and then thudded. Anger swept over her, an intense, scorching fury that shocked her because she had convinced herself she had gotten over the past. This was the drawback about moving to the ranch after her parents gave it to her. She had come every fall and late spring for the past three years, being careful to avoid Verity as much as possible just to avoid running into Jake. This was the moment she had hoped would never happen. At the same time, an unwanted streak of desire heightened her fury. She didn't want to feel desire when she encountered Jake Calhoun.

He had grown taller. His shoulders appeared broader.

He had filled out and he was even more handsome. He wasn't the nineteen-year-old boy she remembered.

How had he found her? She hadn't noticed him on the street. Or was this coincidence? She didn't think it was.

He stopped only feet away and she hoped he couldn't hear her pounding heart.

"'Hello' seems a little ridiculous," he said, his voice deeper than she recalled.

"'Goodbye' is sufficient. I don't care to talk to you or anyone from your company about drilling on Milan land. I don't care to talk to any Calhoun. End of discussion."

She started to turn away and he placed his fingers lightly on her forearm. It was a feather touch, barely discernible, certainly not actually detaining her, but she stopped instantly and a current sizzled from that faint contact. She stood immobile, bound by a nonexistent hold and intense dark brown eyes.

"It isn't about drilling."

"You're not dredging up the past, are you? I definitely don't want to hear about that."

"No, I'm not," he said, suddenly looking hard, angry and withdrawn. A muscle worked in his jaw. His reaction startled her because she was the injured party, not Jake. Why was he angry? Instantly she blocked the question. She didn't want to know what he thought or felt about that time in their lives. She tried to focus and pay attention as he continued.

"This isn't the place to talk, but…it's about a shoot-out between our families long ago on your land and the old legend of buried treasure. I think you'll be interested, so at least listen and don't miss out on something we both might want."

Surprised, skeptical, she suspected he was fabricating a tale about the ancient incident as an excuse to talk to her and to get on her land. It would be another deceptive Calhoun trick to steal something from a Milan. Their families had been feuding since their first respective ancestors had settled here in the days after the Civil War. She didn't figure the feud would end with them.

"I don't believe you and I don't trust you," she said, barely able to speak above a whisper and sounding unconvincing even to herself. How could he turn her to mush by his mere presence and one look from his dark eyes?

"Madison, at least listen and then make your decision. This is important. Let's meet where we won't be constantly interrupted. Come to dinner at my ranch. Or let me take you to Dallas to dinner. Whatever you want. Just somewhere quiet and private and on neutral ground. This concerns your family, too."

"Hi, Jake," a female voice behind him said as if giving emphasis to his request. He turned slightly and faced another local.

"Hi, Becky," he said, greeting a friend he had known since sixth grade.

Becky Worthington smiled broadly, looking back and forth between them and then focusing on Jake and stepping closer to him. "Nice to see you. You don't come into town often, do you?"

"No, I'm rarely at the ranch because I'm in Dallas a lot of the time and traveling some of the time."

"You should come to town and see people once in a while. Stop in and say hey. I still work at TBC bank, which, of course, I think is the best bank in town," she said, giggling.

"I'll try," Jake stated.

Becky looked back and forth between them. "I didn't mean to interrupt," she said and disappeared around the corner of the aisle from the direction she had come.

When she was out of earshot, Madison resumed their conversation. "An evening out with you? I don't really think so. Everything has been said between us that can be said."

"Far, far from it. You should hear me out. You'll be surprised, Madison. If you're not, tell me and I'll stop talking and go."

She could feel the clash of wills as she shook her head. "Whatever ploy this is, I'm sure a Calhoun itching to drill on Milan land is behind it."

"I want that, too, but it has nothing to do with this. I'm after something else and I think you'll be interested to know about this, too."

"If that's the case, tell me now."

He shook his head. "This is not the place. We were just interrupted, and we will be again. And anyone standing in the next aisle can overhear us. I don't want that and I don't think you will, either. Just go to dinner with me. It's not that big a deal. I can take you home whenever you want."

"Eating out around here won't be one degree better than talking here."

"We won't eat in Verity. We'll fly to Dallas and get a private corner. We won't see people we know. We won't be overheard. I'll bring you home whenever you say. Just trust me, you will not regret listening to me."

Debating what to do, she stared at him. There was no way a Milan could trust a Calhoun—that had been proven to her in a devastating way. She couldn't imagine one thing he could want except to make a pitch to let him drill on her land and she was not going to do that no matter what he said or offered. She couldn't think of another reason he'd want to talk to her. Yet, surely he knew better than to tell her he had another reason and then talk about leasing land. Dinner would be over before it started. But she had to admit she was intrigued. What did he know that she didn't that concerned her ranch?

"All right, Jake. This better be good."

"Spending an evening with me is that bad?" he asked without a change of expression, reinforcing her opinion that he could be highly deceptive.

"I'm equally shocked you want to spend any time with me."

"This will be good, Madison. I'll come by to get you a little before seven Sunday night. Thanks. Absolutely no talk about drilling. I promise."

"I know how much your promise is worth," she couldn't keep from saying. She saw the flicker in his eyes and saw that hardness return to his expression, puzzling her. She turned her back on him and walked away, aiming to complete her purchases and get away from him.

She had intended to get two small brushes, but she wanted out of the store away from Jake more than she wanted the brushes. She had tried to put him and the past out of her thoughts, to stop remembering or hurting. She wished she could have faced him without any reaction instead of this heart-pounding longing. She wished the memories hadn't tumbled back into her thoughts as clearly as if they had parted months ago rather than over a decade ago. Instead, seeing him caused all the old pain and anger to return, as well as the intense physical reaction. He was still the best-looking man she knew. In spite of her hurt and fury, he still set her heart racing.

Suddenly she wanted to go back and cancel the evening with him. Her art career had succeeded beyond all her hopes and expectations. She was constantly busy with what she loved to do. She had remained single because there had been so little time for her personal life and her brief marriage had been disastrous from the first moment. Jake, she knew, was still single, which didn't surprise her. He wasn't the marrying type.

She didn't want to spend a whole evening feeling the way she did now—hurting, drowning in memories of a wedding day that never happened. Memories tore at her heart and fueled an ever-simmering rage when she thought about him. She didn't trust him in the slightest. For a little over one year in her life she had gone against all her family's warnings about the unscrupulous Calhouns and she had trusted Jake. Because of that mistake, he had broken her heart. One thing was certain—no matter what excuses Jake presented, she would never let him drill on Milan land.

She hurried out of the store, striding quickly to her truck, planning to forgo her grocery shopping. She wanted to go home to the Double M Ranch, away from town and any chance of encountering him again. She had been careful, coming to town only once a month, usually getting someone else to pick up groceries and supplies. She would go back to that routine. How she wished she could just as easily obliterate all memories of Jake Calhoun.

Instead, the memories poured over her in a deluge. Growing up, because of the century-and-a-half-old family feud, she never spoke to any Calhouns, but she had been aware of Jake from her first year in high school. They were three years apart in age, but two years in school because she had been tutored at home on the ranch when she was little and when she had started school they'd placed her in the fourth grade instead of the third.

Her first close encounter with Jake had been at a school party in the gym to get everyone acquainted. For one of the dances they had two large circles of kids—boys in the outside ring, girls on the inside. They walked in a circle to a drumbeat until the band began to play, then the boy and girl facing each other danced until the music stopped and everybody resumed walking in a circle to get a new partner.

When the music started, she had been facing Jake. "No. Not a Calhoun," she had said loudly enough for him and everyone around her to hear. She had stepped close to the boy next to him, leaving Jake to the girl next to her. Everyone knew about the feud, and besides, the girl had been a friend and hadn't cared because Jake Calhoun was older, on the football team, well-known and popular.

The next time he passed her at school he walked up close and said, "Thanks for changing partners so I didn't have to." Madison had just continued on her way, wondering if he really would have grabbed a different girl in front of all the other kids. The rest of her freshman year she had never spoken to him again and he didn't speak to her, but she noticed him and he always glanced at her. She had thought it was a pity he was a Calhoun because he was the best-looking boy in the high school.

In her sophomore year, she became a cheerleader. At a game, Jake had come out and was headed to the bench on the sidelines where she had been standing.

"Hi, snooty Miss Milan," he said quietly without even looking at her as he passed her.

She had turned to look at him. "Hi, yourself, wicked Mr. Calhoun," she said, and to her surprise, he grinned. He had gone on to the bench, but the next Monday at school as she moved between classes, her path was blocked. "Hi, again," he said. "Scared to speak to me at school where one of your brothers will see you?"

"I'm not scared of my brothers. I just don't particularly want to speak to a Calhoun. You've got brothers in school, too."

"What about your parents?"

"My parents will never know. Dad's busy with his work and Mom has a social life."

"I know your dad is a Dallas judge. Does he commute?"

"No, he and Mom live in Dallas during the week. My brothers and I didn't want to leave Verity High so our grandparents are living at the ranch with us."

"So we can't be together in Dallas or out here. Okay, after school, meet me by the Dumpsters. I'll pick you up and we'll go to Lubbock and get ice cream, if you're not scared to risk it."

"Why would I want to go out with a Calhoun?"

"Same reason I want to go out with one particular Milan. Scared?"

"No, I'm not scared of you. What about football practice?"

"I'll tell Coach I've got an appointment in Lubbock. Maybe I will have one if you'll say yes."

She still remembered the thrill over the prospect of going with him. For one moment she thought of all the warnings to stay away from the Calhouns and never trust one. As she looked into his dark brown eyes fringed with thick black lashes, she took a deep breath.

"I'll meet you," she said and from that encounter on, she thought he was the most exciting boy she had ever met. They worked out an arrangement with their two best friends. Her parents thought she was dating Steve Reynolds, someone they had no objection to. Jake's parents thought he was dating Marilee Wilson. He would pick up Marilee, and Steve would pick her up. Then they'd meet and trade places. She would spend the evening with Jake while Marilee and Steve did the same. At the end of the evening, they would meet, trade places and go home.

Their secret dates ended when her brother Tony saw her in Lubbock with Jake. She still recalled how horrified she had been when they fought, leaving Tony with a bloody nose and Jake with a black eye and a bruised cheek. The fight that followed at home with her brother had not been physical, but just as painful, as they didn't speak to each other for weeks. Tony informed the other brothers. Each brother had reacted in a way typical of his personality—Wyatt talked to her seriously in his quiet manner, warning her never to trust a Calhoun because she would get hurt. In hindsight, she should have listened. Nick laid out a grim scenario that she had dismissed as his gloomy dislike of the Calhouns.

She'd disregarded her brothers' warnings. The year she'd dated Jake had been the best one of her life. The man could dance, and they'd had such fun. And he could kiss. With Jake, she had made love for the first time.

While they dated Jake made plans to attend Mississippi State after high school graduation. She could not stop recalling the day they planned to elope. She had dressed in jeans and a T-shirt, the same as every other Saturday in her life, but she'd already had a bag packed. It held a knee-length white silk dress, veil and matching pumps, and a lace nightgown that she could recall with total clarity. Later, after her family had gone, she had deliberately taken them to the patio and burned them in a metal wastebasket, standing by with a hose in case the fire got out of hand. She could still recall standing there and crying. Jake had just disappeared out of her life without a word to her. The next morning she had driven to Rocky Creek, stepped out of the car and thrown her one-carat engagement ring into the creek. She never saw Jake Calhoun again.

Shaking off the painful memories of the past, Madison tried to focus on the chore for the day—the latest painting that she had been commissioned to do for a Dallas oil magnate's office. But she couldn't stop thinking of Jake.

Work on the painting went slowly that week, and she found her thoughts constantly looking ahead to Sunday and their dinner date. Curiosity about why he wanted to talk to her nagged at her. He had to have a good reason. She knew it wasn't a ploy to get with her. And she most definitely didn't want to get with him.

A little before seven on Sunday night she waited in the library of the ranch, which gave a view of the drive to the front. She wore a dark blue dress with a deep V neckline. The dress was straight, clinging to her figure, the narrow skirt ending above her knees. With her hair pinned up on her head, she hoped to look remote, cool, self-possessed. She was still amazed she was going to dinner with Jake. And then she watched him step out of the limo and head for the house. At the sight of Jake, her heartbeat pounded.

She was going out with him again.

Two

The sun was on the horizon when Jake stood at her front door and listened to chimes. He had rarely set foot on this ranch because they would not run the risk when they had been dating in high school. Even when her parents were away, her siblings were around, or the ranch hands, who would have reported back to her dad.

He and Madison had had secret meetings occasionally on the boundaries of their ranches, but those were rare.

He looked at the house as if seeing it for the first time. The Milan family home was different from most ranch homes in the area. The stately Georgian with white Corinthian columns looked like it belonged in the Deep South. Two giant oaks framed the house but outside the fenced, watered yard were smaller, less majestic mesquite trees and cacti. The fine home stood on a working ranch that had prize-winning cattle and probably lucrative oil and gas reserves in the ground.

He stepped up to the door and took a deep breath. An

evening with Madison. He couldn't believe this was actually happening. He still expected her to try to back out, but he knew once they were on their way, she would be committed. Frowning, he pushed the doorbell and listened to the chimes. Had she backed out, standing him up now in a tiny effort to retaliate for their wedding years ago?

Their wedding. The familiar, burning anger started in the pit of his stomach. He didn't want to think about that time in his life or recall anything connected with that day. *Keep this business tonight,* he told himself. Present his case, feed the lady and whisk her back home. He suspected he was going to have to use his best powers of persuasion, but he had an ace in the hole that he hoped would capture her interest and make her agree to his plan. A twinge of guilt rocked him for the secret only he, his parents and his brothers knew. Clamping his jaw closed, he shifted his weight as he reached again for the bell. The door swung open and his breath left him.

Looking sophisticated and breathtakingly beautiful, the woman he faced was stunning. Momentarily, another twinge of guilt stabbed him, but he shoved it aside. Recalling dealing with Pete Milan, the ever-smoldering anger threatened to make him lose his relaxed demeanor. With an effort Jake pushed aside any thoughts about her dad.

"You look beautiful," he said.

"Thank you," she replied quietly, but she didn't look happy about his compliment.

"Shall we go?" he asked.

"This better be good."

"I wouldn't be doing this if I didn't have to," he said softly as she turned away to pick up a jacket. She scowled at him, so he knew she'd heard him. She punched in an alarm code and stepped outside, closing and locking the door behind her.

The driver stepped out of the black limo to hold the door

for her. She climbed into the seat and watched as Jake sat beside her with space between them. He caught another drift of her perfume. It was not a scent he recognized, but it was enticing, filled with the smell of flowers and spice, and a hint of something more.

Jake had been amazed at how much he had thought about Madison all week. He had the detective's information about her, but it had meant little until he was in her presence. He flicked a quick glance over her. She still had the best-looking legs of any woman he knew.

"So where do we get the plane?" she asked as the limo drove away from her house.

"At the Verity airport," he said.

"Your plane or a charter?"

"It's my private jet. We keep company jets in Dallas," he answered as he shifted so he could face her. Her green eyes were on him, steady, veiled, hiding what she felt, but he could imagine her thoughts were as turbulent as his. "Your art career is going well, I've heard."

"I've been happy with it."

"I'm sure you have since that's what you always really wanted," he said, failing to keep a bitter note out of his voice. "I wouldn't think you'd bury yourself out here on the ranch if you have a gallery in Dallas and one in Santa Fe." He kept up conversation but all he wanted to do was look at her. Her green eyes had always captivated him, but now he noticed so much more—her flawless skin, her full lips that he wanted to kiss. He almost groaned as he made an effort to look away. "I'm surprised you like it out here."

"I grew up here. I'm used to it," she remarked, giving him a glance. She seemed more poised, controlled than she had before. "This way I can live in more than one place. I come out here to paint so I won't be disturbed. In town there is something constantly going on or people dropping by. Mom and Dad gave the ranch to me three years ago.

My brothers have their own places. I'm here in the fall until Christmas and I come back in May. The rest of the time I'm in New Mexico or sometimes in a condo in Dallas. Where are you most of the time—here on the ranch?"

"No. I'd prefer the ranch, but I'm based in Dallas, where the home office for the energy company is. I'm seldom here because of taking care of business. By the time I'm forty, I hope to retire and be a full-time rancher because that's what I love."

She nodded and became silent, looking out the limo windows. The airport was on the east side of Verity and they drove through the wide main street that had once been a dusty cattle trail before the town sprang up. They left the shops and stores, passing the oldest homes in the town, two blocks of wooden Victorian-style homes, some single story, some two or three stories tall, still occupied and taken care of with flowers and the oldest trees in Verity in the yards. Then they reached a tall Victorian house in a block by itself, the last before leaving Verity. She looked at the familiar sight, a wooden three-story surrounded by a three-foot wrought-iron fence and a front gate hanging on one hinge. Windows had been broken out. Weeds and high grass filled the yard, while the two tall oaks by the house were overgrown with vines. Without thinking she glanced at Jake.

"There's the Wrenville house. Remember when you and Wyatt and two other football players went out at night to search through the house?" Madison asked.

"Like everyone else, we didn't find anything and got chased out by the sheriff. I don't think anyone today has much interest in the place."

"You and I have ancestors that were killed there—both in love with Lavita Wrenville according to the legend. Her father drew his weapon and all three men were shot and killed, but it was never clear who shot the other," she said.

"Before she died, Lavita said that one of them lived long enough to tell her who shot who. According to legend, she wrote it down and hid it before she died. I wonder if we'll find anything when 2015 occurs."

"Your brother will know before anyone else. By 2015, there may not be many who care. According to the legend, the city can do what it wants with the house and property in 2015. I heard that's why your brother is sheriff. So many people wanted him to run because he's so honest and everyone trusts Wyatt. He'll be sheriff when they can finally tear down the house and look for the letter," Jake stated.

"I think the reason they wanted an honest man is more because of the part of the legend that says Lavita died a very wealthy woman and her money is hidden somewhere in the house," Madison remarked. "If Wyatt finds anything, he'll turn it over to the city and make public which man shot the others.

"I'd like to hear what happened. Did the Milan shoot the other two? Did the Calhoun? Or did her father shoot both of the men who wanted to marry his daughter?" she said.

"Or," Jake said, "they all could have fired their weapons at the same time and then fired again. It never was made public how many times each man was shot."

"I'm surprised the townspeople didn't insist," Madison said.

"The Milans and the Calhouns were even more influential and powerful in those days than now," Jake said. "If they didn't want the killings made public, they wouldn't have been. And Lavita could have been the one who kept it all secret. We'll know someday. Twenty-fifteen approaches."

She shivered. "I don't know why you and Wyatt decided you wanted to search for an old letter about killings in another century or even for a mythical fortune."

"We were kids," he said. He smiled. "Your brother

doesn't scare easily. We were just curious and we both wanted new, fancy cars."

She became silent again, not mentioning that she had been scared for both Jake and Wyatt that night. Looking at the house now, she wouldn't want to hunt for an old letter or even a fortune in there.

"Jake, we'll have a quick flight to Dallas. Why not talk about what you want on the plane? There's no possible interruption there."

"That sounds agreeable. The weather's good and it should be a smooth flight." The sun had reached the horizon when the plane lifted off the runway, but once they were airborne and headed east there was more light as they chased the sinking sun.

"Might as well enjoy happy hour while we fly. What would you like to drink? We stock a full bar."

"Any chance of conjuring up a raspberry tea?" she asked.

He told the flight attendant what they wanted to drink and shortly, the man reappeared with a tall, chilled glass, which he offered to Madison, and a beer for Jake. When they were again alone, she sipped her drink and smiled. "You have the formula—this is delicious."

"Glad you like it."

Madison leaned back in her chair. "Let's cut to the chase, Jake. There's no need for polite chitchat—why do you want my land? For what possible reason would you expect me to invite you onto the ranch?"

Her eyes were wide, green and thickly lashed, and he was mesmerized. A streak of sunlight streamed through the window, bathing her cheek in golden light, highlighting her fully rosy mouth. He inhaled deeply and then realized she was waiting for him to answer her question.

"This goes back generations before Lavita Wrenville.

This was the earliest Milans and Calhouns. You know there's a legend of hidden treasure on your ranch."

"That old tale went around the family before I was born," she scoffed, sitting back and shaking her head. "All of us looked for it. I've heard men from a couple of past generations were supposed to have searched endlessly. No one has found anything and most of us came to the conclusion long ago that it was merely a myth."

"Still, it persists though all the generations."

"Just try to get a kid to stop looking. Tony and his friends have probably dug up a total of a dozen acres with all their hunting for gold. Look at you and Wyatt, hunting for Lavita Wrenville's fortune, which might not ever have existed."

"I can imagine. I've hunted with my brothers on my side of the boundary that divides our adjacent family ranches. Since part of the boundary line is the river, the boundary keeps changing slightly. Going back to my great-great-grandfather Henry Calhoun, there was a sketchy map. No one in our family ever had interest in sharing it with anyone in your family. I'm guessing that maybe in the early days one or more family members offered to make a deal and split, but your family member refused."

She smiled and his heart turned over. Desire heightened and he suddenly wanted to see her laugh, to hold her, dance with her—to have the past vanish. That wasn't going to happen.

"So you have a map." She shook her head. "I didn't think there was a shred of truth to the legend."

"Occasionally, legends are built on something—maybe not always exactly the way it's stated in the legend, but something caused the legend to spring up."

"It's hard to believe there is a treasure hidden on our ranch."

"That's not so far-fetched. There was a lot of lawlessness in the early days, train robberies, later bank robberies. People just hiding something. This is a vague, damn poor map and has never made any sense to anyone in my family. I don't think it will to you, either, but you know your land better than any outsider."

"All these years. Why would your family even have a map?"

His gaze ran over her features, her skin that looked soft, flawless. He wished she had worn her hair down.

"No one can answer that one. The map may be bogus, although it has been in the family for generations. I'd bet that someone or maybe several in my family have tried to sneak onto Milan land to find the treasure."

"I'm sure you're right there. Why wouldn't they? These ranches are big with wide, open land. Someone could easily search without anyone knowing about it." She sipped her tea and shook her head. "So there's really a map. All these years, actually all my life, I've heard the legend and heard various relatives talk about searching for it, but by the time I was grown, I just figured it was a tall Texas tale with nothing to it." She sat back, smiling at him. "So you want permission to come on our land to search for the treasure."

"That's not all." As her big green eyes focused so intently on him, he forgot the map, the treasure and his whole purpose for the evening. He wanted to close the last bit of distance between them, place his hand behind her head, wind his fingers in her hair and pull her closer to kiss her.

"There's more?" she asked, looking at him with curiosity in her expression.

Desire raged in him, blatant and hot, until he remembered their past and then anger returned, smothering his feelings for her. He inhaled deeply, looked away and focused on his purpose.

She leaned closer. "So what else is there, Jake? What

else besides a map have you kept secret all of these years and never told me when we were so close?"

"At the time we were in high school, we talked about it. It was mysterious and exciting to speculate about the legend, even though neither one of us believed it. Of all the people in both families, you and I seemed the most willing to forget the feud."

"Yes, and I know we both thought the idea of a hidden treasure was exciting. I'm surprised you didn't tell me about the map then."

"I didn't know it then. There's a rule in our family—no one gets told about the map, and sworn to keep it in the family, until he or she is twenty-one years old."

She laughed, a soft sound that played havoc with his insides again and made him forget what he was after.

"That's probably why your family has kept it secret all these years. Kids talk."

"Probably," he said, smiling at her. "When you heard the legend, did the version you heard mention a shoot-out?"

"Yes. I heard there were Milans and Calhouns who would discover each other searching for the treasure and the Milans would run the Calhouns off our land."

"Did you ever hear if any were killed?"

"Yes, but truthfully, I was a kid and didn't pay that much attention to talk about someone who had lived generations ahead of me and who I never knew."

He sipped his beer before he continued. "According to the Calhoun version of the legend, wherever the treasure is buried, your ancestors and my ancestors had a gun battle. Two Calhouns were killed and three Milans. They're buried in shallow graves where they had the gunfight. This goes back to the first generation of each family to settle here and it was before both families had their own cemeteries. Now we have our own burial ground and I imagine you do, too."

"Yes, we do."

"I want the bones of the Calhouns brought home. Hopefully, we'll find the treasure, which is yours since it is on your land."

"You want bones," she said, frowning slightly. "You could search every day for the next ten years and never find graves or bones or treasure, if it even ever existed. I can't imagine that's what's behind this dinner," she said, beginning to sound angry.

"Just one more thing besides the bones. There's supposed to be a deed one of our ancestors was carrying. It was a deed won in a poker game. According to the story my family tells, the deed gives the Calhouns rights to a large part of the McCracken place to the east of us all along the border of his ranch."

"A deed to the McCracken land," she said, staring at him while she seemed lost in thought. "If that exists, it's worth more than any treasure you could possibly dig up."

"Jeb McCracken is mean and ornery and has fought with every neighbor," Jake replied.

"That includes my family. There are people in town he's aggravated. He's left unpaid accounts all over this county and he's spent more than a few nights in jail for brawls on the weekend in town. No one would regret seeing you get a chunk of that property." She stared at him with a speculative curiosity in her eyes. "My ancestors are supposed to have been in that gunfight, also. Suppose we find the deed with my ancestors. Are you still going to claim it?"

He gave her a faint smile. "Not if their name is on the deed or it's in a bony skeleton hand."

She had to smile then and he felt another punch to his insides. Her smiles and her laughter had always been his undoing. He ached to reach out and touch her.

"I have no intention of searching long. I want you to look at the map I have and see if you can recognize anything. You probably have aerial photos of your land, all sorts of photos. If anything seems likely, then I'd like a chance to see if the deed exists, see if a treasure is buried with them and get my ancestors' bones to take back for a proper burial. I have time in my life for that now and it would please my grandfather."

She laughed softly, shaking her head. "You don't seem the type for this. Why do I feel as if I better look at this from all angles, that you're up to something—like surveying my land to drill for oil or gas?"

"All I want is what belongs to the Calhouns—namely my ancestors' bones and the deed to the McCracken land if that exists. I'm not going to do any surveying, I promise you."

"According to the old legend, the treasure is what caused the feud in the first place. Your great-great-great-grandfather and my great-great-great-grandfather came out here after the Civil War. What I've always heard is they found gold in a deserted house in Tennessee during the war. Later, my relative stole away your relative's fiancée right before the wedding and that's when the feud started. Then they fought over the gold and the woman they both loved, but a Milan killed a Calhoun, so the Calhouns rode in at night a week later and burned down a house, killed a Milan and carried off the woman in question, adding to the anger between the two families. The fight has continued until present day. I guess we have a truce of sorts now."

"That matches what I've always heard about the beginning of the feud," he said. "That and when they fought, there were several Milans and several Calhoun brothers, plus an uncle."

She shifted, recrossed her legs, distracting him totally. She sat quietly, so he remained quiet, letting her think about what he had said. She turned to the window and his gaze traveled slowly over her. She was twisted slightly in her seat, the neckline of the blue dress gaping a fraction, revealing the full rise of her breasts, her skin pale and creamy. The temperature in the plane jumped and he wiped his brow as images of long ago tormented him. Her waist was as tiny as ever. How well he could remember the feel of her in his hands. He had to stop thinking about the past, had to avoid erotic memories that set his heart racing.

Jake remembered her dad and that last night before he was going to elope with her, and the tantalizing memories vanished, replaced by anger, dulled by the passage of years, but still there.

She turned back while he was still looking at her neckline. She shifted slightly. "Jake, I have to think about this. We'll be in Dallas before long, so we might as well go to dinner. I'll consider your request and by this time tomorrow, I'll give you an answer."

"That's great, Madison," he said, feeling a stab of satisfaction. He was certain she wanted to discuss his proposal with her brothers. He hoped not her father.

Their pilot announced they were approaching Dallas and as they lost altitude, the sun was low on the horizon. By the time they were in the limo on the way to the restaurant, darkness had set in.

In a short time they were seated in a darkened corner table in a small private room. Lights were low, music from the piano player in another room was muted.

"So you got a private room for us. I didn't know there was any such thing for just two people. I'm impressed."

"That's one reason I like this place. There are only three of these rooms." He paused when their waiter arrived to take drink orders.

"Little chance of interruptions here by people who know either of us," she said as soon as they were alone again.

"That's right. You can barely see your hand before your face, much less who else is in the restaurant. Do you still like fried chicken better than anything else?" he asked, looking at a menu. He glanced up at her.

"No, like so many other things, my tastes have changed. I see lobster on the menu—that's what I'll have."

"Excellent choice. I'll have the steak," he said, watching her while she had her head bent slightly over her menu. The candle flickering in the center of the table highlighted her shiny brown hair and rosy cheeks. Again, he wished she had worn her hair down the way he liked it best. He should forget what he liked best about her and leave anything personal a closed subject.

In minutes the waiter returned. He uncorked a bottle of white wine, gave it to Jake to taste and then poured two glasses after Jake's approval.

As soon as they were alone, Jake raised his glass. "Here's to finding the treasure."

With a faint smile, she touched his glass with hers and heard the faint clink of crystal before she sipped. "That's a safe, innocuous toast," she said.

He smiled in turn. "I thought so."

"I'm still thinking about your request."

"If I'm successful, you'll get your treasure, I will find a deed and get the bones of my ancestors for a proper burial. We both win."

She tilted her head to study him, sipping her wine while she sat staring. "Why do I feel there is more to your request than you're telling me? I find it a little difficult to trust you. You better not have manufactured this map yourself."

He held on to his temper. "My dad took the map to someone in Chicago who could tell him the approximate age. It dates back to the mid-nineteenth century. That's good enough for me. I'll give you a copy of the letter and you can contact the people in Chicago yourself."

"I'd like to see the original map. Will it disintegrate if it is handled?"

"Not if it's handled carefully and you don't intend to pass it all around. But you don't get it until we have a deal."

"You don't trust me," she said, bitterness filling her voice and anger flashing in her eyes, for an instant igniting his own fury, which he banked immediately.

"Should I?" he asked, trying to curb his feelings and get back to amicable dealings with her.

"Of course. You did at one time," she reminded him sharply. Looking away, she took deep breaths. Spots of red were high on her cheeks. She sipped her wine and gradually her breathing went back to normal before she faced him again.

He'd give her time to think it all over; he just hoped the flare of animosity hadn't killed the deal. Again, he had a flash of guilt for what he had kept from her. But then he thought about her father and stopped worrying about the secret he harbored.

Madison ate in silence while she mulled over his proposition, studying it from every angle because she didn't trust him. She suspected he wanted badly to drill on her land and she wondered how much of wanting his ancestors' remains was because he wanted to lease part of her ranch. Why hadn't this come up years earlier or with some other Calhoun? And a deed and map? She had never heard of either one. Were they both hoaxes so he could get on her ranch? She wondered what was behind Jake's request. She couldn't keep from feeling that it was something to do with wanting to drill on their property.

What did she have to lose? That's what she couldn't figure. So he saw her land up close—she was certain he'd seen aerial photos because they were in the county records and on the internet. If he found the treasure, he had said she could have it. He simply wanted his relatives' remains and the deed if there was one. While part of any ranch around here, including the McCracken place, would be a real asset, he would have to fight McCracken to get it.

She couldn't believe a deed and his ancestors' remains could be all there was to his request.

She glanced at him to find him watching her. His thickly lashed midnight eyes were seductive, mesmerizing. And guileless. He looked honest, trustworthy, open—all good qualities, yet she couldn't believe the proposition was simply what he was telling her and nothing more.

Caught in his steady gaze, she forgot the legend, the treasure and the proposition. Instead she remembered Jake's eyes filled with passion, a silent emphasis to what he did with his hands and his body. She had loved him deeply.

Instantly she broke off that train of thought and tried to think about her schedule tomorrow, his proposition, anything to escape memories that twisted a knife in her heart.

No matter how she turned his request in her mind, she couldn't think how there could be an underlying motive and anything else for him to gain without her knowledge if she said okay to him.

"If I say okay to your proposal," she asked him, "what are you going to do? Go out there with your shovel and start digging around?"

"Of course not," he replied, smiling, his smile giving her heart a squeeze. He was so incredibly handsome and appealing and a smile made him doubly so. "I'll get a crew from my ranch hands—not too many—about five. I want you to study the map and see if you can narrow down the location. There is no earthly way I can. You know your land, and if you don't, one of your brothers should."

"I'm no geologist. Suppose I can't tell anything?"

"Then you and I will work on it together, but I'll bet you'll look at the map and come up with some possibilities for the area."

She thought about what he was telling her as she put

down her fork, her appetite suddenly gone. She wondered what she could do to make sure she didn't get cheated.

"You didn't eat much," he observed a few moments later.

"It was delicious, but I don't eat much most of the time and I've been busy thinking about your proposition."

"Take all the time you need. You don't have to give me an answer tomorrow night for that matter. I can wait. Want to go dance?"

"No, thanks," she replied, smiling at him. "This is sort of a business dinner and I have no interest in dancing. Too much on my mind. I'd step on you," she added, broadening her smile.

"I wouldn't mind, but we can sit out the dancing." He leaned forward, reaching across the table to take her hand. The instant her fingers touched his warm ones, she couldn't get her breath. The air around her heated and her body tingled. That slight contact sizzled from her head to her toes and then settled low in the center of her being, a hot torment that made her ache to be in his arms and brought back memories of Jake holding her close, kissing her passionately, making torrid love to her that drove her wild.

"Truce?" he asked and she barely heard what he said as she stared at him. Something flickered in the depths of his eyes and for one brief instant, his fingers tightened around hers and his thumb ran over the back of her hand.

"You always did have the smoothest skin ever," he whispered, his voice husky, a thick whisper, while his eyes blazed with such hot desire that she felt as if she would melt. At the same time, she wanted him to pull her toward him, to take her on his lap while he wrapped his arms around her and kissed her senseless. Closing her eyes momentarily, she tried to stop thinking about the past with him, the love she had thought they had shared. Love that he had smashed the way someone would break a crystal goblet by throwing it down.

She yanked her hand free and looked away, gasping for breath and hating that she had lost control so obviously that he could not avoid knowing exactly what she was feeling and thinking. He could see how much he could still affect her and she hated it.

"I guess we have a truce," he said. His voice was raspy and she realized she still had an effect on him, too, giving her both satisfaction and annoyance.

"Truce for now," she replied without looking at him.

"When you're finished, we can head home. You can think about what I've offered."

She nodded. "Then I'm ready to go back," she said, wondering if they would say goodbye at her door and if she turned him down, if they wouldn't see each other again. She didn't care and she wasn't too interested in accepting his proposition, except there were possibilities that would be good for her family.

She continued to think about all he had told her while he paid the bill and they returned to the airport. They barely talked, which seemed so odd in some ways. Long ago, she could talk to him endlessly and never tire of it.

Finally, as they flew back to Verity, she turned to him. "I think I would like to have our ancestors' remains have a proper burial, also. If you remember, I've always been interested in our family tree and our history. The treasure—that seems a tall tale to me, but who really knows? It's a generous offer to turn the treasure over to me if we find one."

"Somehow, I think we might be more likely to find bones than treasure. If we do find treasure, that's a good payment for your agreement to this," he said. His long legs were stretched out in front of him, his booted feet near her. When they had boarded the plane, he had shed his jacket and tie and unbuttoned his collar. He looked relaxed and he still appeared open and straightforward, but she couldn't shake the feeling that in some way, he was slipping something past her.

After another lapse of silence between them, she sat up straighter and turned slightly to face him. He sat watching her.

"If we do this and do find bones, how will we know whose bones are Milans and whose are Calhouns?"

"Take them to the county medical examiner. We can get some kind of DNA test and they can sort out the two families."

She nodded. "That sounds reasonable. And I walk away with the treasure?"

"Absolutely."

She lapsed into more silence before she broached the topic. "I know you want to lease some of my land for your energy company. Why not go elsewhere? It's a big world."

"So it is, but your land looks promising and is an area that we think may be a big play. It's also cheaper and easier for us because it's close to our headquarters. Labor is available here. Trained men who do this if we need to hire more. It's dollars in the bank instead of going off a long distance."

"That sounds reasonable. Suppose we put a high, high price on this."

"You can price yourself out of the market, but energy companies, I think, are generous when they want something. Are you going to give us a chance?" he asked, looking at her and smiling, making her heart turn over again. Longing swamped her again. Too easily he could trigger those feelings.

"Don't push me, Jake," she said and he became silent again.

She thought about his original offer, still trying to look at it from all possible angles. When they stopped in front of her house, the driver came around to hold the limo door. Jake accompanied her to her door.

"Want to come in a few minutes? Would your driver mind?"

"No, he'll wait. He's getting paid for whatever he does."

She unlocked the house and turned off the alarm. "We'll go into the study," she said, glancing at Jake to see him looking around.

"I forgot—you've never been inside this house. Seems ridiculous in some ways, but understandable in others. My ancestors would be turning over in their graves if they knew I'd invited a Calhoun inside."

Jake smiled again. "I still feel the feud is arcane, ridiculous. Come into the present."

"I agree, but we decided long ago to stop fighting it," she said. As he walked beside her, he looked around. "Is any of this art hanging on the walls yours?"

"Not in the hallway, but in here it is," she said, leading him into a study that held a large wet bar. "The painting over the mantel is mine," she said and he crossed the room to look at the large painting of a field of bluebonnets, a tall oak in one side of the field and a stream running through it. "You're not a contemporary artist. This is a beautiful painting and you're very good."

"Thank you. The painting on that wall by the window is mine, too," she said and he crossed the room to look at the painting of three horses in a field, a cowboy holding the reins and standing by one. "That's good, Madison. Very impressive. I can see why you've been a success."

"Thanks. Would you like a drink?"

He shook his head. "No, thank you. Let's just talk."

She motioned with her hand. "Have a seat," she said, sitting and crossing her legs, pulling her skirt to her knees and catching him watching her.

"I've been thinking about this all evening, Jake," she

said slowly, watching him intently. "I will in fact give you a final word tomorrow night...." She wouldn't commit until she talked to her brothers; after all, she had to protect Milan interests. "But I'm thinking about accepting your proposal." She speared his eyes with her own. "Under one condition."

Three

Jake tried to avoid showing any emotion, but his heart-beat sped up and he had a flash of satisfaction. She was going to agree to let him on her ranch. He barely paid attention when she said she had a condition. He couldn't imagine anything she could come up with that would stop him from accepting.

"Sure. Let's hear it," he said.

"I want to take a couple of my ranch hands and accompany you."

As if cold water had been poured over him, his enthusiasm chilled. "You don't trust me? Madison, if I surveyed your land, it wouldn't get me any further with you on signing a lease," he stated, sitting up straight in the chair. "I don't intend to survey, but why would you want to go with me?"

"First of all how would I know if you found the treasure if I wasn't along, except pure trust that you would inform me about it? That isn't going to happen," she said, her voice sounding cold and harsh, something he had never heard from her before.

"I expected you'd want one person to go with us—I figured one of the men who works for you. There's no reason for you to go with us and it would be a waste of your time to have to sit and watch us dig."

"You said nothing about someone who works for me going with you."

"That's your decision."

She faced him, looking calm and composed again, the flash of anger gone. She shook her head. "That's my condition. Take it or leave it. I go or you don't."

He stared at her a moment and then shrugged. "Sure, come along. If you think it over tonight and still want the same agreement, that's fine. You have yourself a deal," he said, holding out his hand. "If we find the treasure, you get it. I get my ancestors' remains. We'll just have to see if we do find a deed, what it says and who the land goes to. You go with me to search for the treasure."

She placed her hand in his to shake while she smiled at him. "Deal."

Her hand was warm, soft, and when they looked into each other's eyes, he realized it might be torment to work with her beside him every day. He released her hand and the moment was gone, but it had dampened some of his enthusiasm. He didn't want to get emotionally involved with her again and he didn't like this constant flashback to that time in his life when she meant everything to him.

"I can go in tomorrow and clear my calendar. I don't think we'll search for more than a week, but I'll clear my schedule for two weeks just in case. I can be ready to go Tuesday. What about you?" he asked.

"My time is my own. I think it would help if you would give me a copy of the map and let me study it. We need to have an idea where to go before we start. If you can send me an electronic copy of the map tonight when you get home, I can start studying it. Then tomorrow night, if you'd like, you can come over and look at maps of the ranch with me. You're a geologist—I'm sure you can figure out some things from those photos of the ranch."

"Sure. That'll be good. I've already scanned in the old map, so I can send it easily."

"Good. We'll get started tonight."

"You're going to lose a lot of time to work on your art."

She shook her head. "No, I won't. I'll take my sketch pad with me—because I don't intend to dig. You're the one so eager to do this."

"You're the one who will benefit from it if we're successful," he reminded her. "But you don't need to dig so much as one shovelful of dirt."

He stood. "I'll go home and send you a copy of the map. Give me about an hour."

At the door he paused. "Thanks, Madison, for agreeing to let me do this. Hopefully, it will be a productive venture."

"I hope so. Thanks for dinner," she said, following him into the hall.

"I'll call you when I get home," he said, walking away, aware she stood on her porch and watched him. As the limo pulled away, she still stood on the porch—a small figure in the moonlight.

They were going to search for the treasure together. Not what he had expected, but it was okay. The main thing was she had agreed to let him look. He hoped he succeeded in finding everything he was searching for. Again, guilt assailed him, but all he had to do was think about the day he had planned to elope with her. As he rode, he pulled out his phone to call his brother Josh, but there was no answer.

He didn't want to call Mike this late because Mike had a two-year-old son and he would be in bed.

He called Lindsay next to tell her. His sister was jubilant over his success with Madison.

After finishing his call with Lindsay, he thought about Madison. Was she looking forward to the search? He knew she hadn't accepted because she wanted to be with him. It had been obvious that tonight had been a strain on her and she disliked being with him.

He didn't understand the anger he had glimpsed in her eyes a few times. Why was she angry? She had done what she had wanted to do and put her career first. He shrugged, refusing to worry about it. It no longer mattered. He was honest enough with himself to admit it still hurt sometimes but he had put it in perspective and moved on.

As they reached the back door of his ranch house and his chauffeur stopped the limo, Jake opened the door. "Thanks, Chauncy," he said, tipping his chauffeur in spite of the generous salary he paid.

"Night, Jake," Chauncy said, following his boss's orders for informality when it was only the two of them. Chauncy drove on to the garage to park the limo and go to his spacious apartment over the six-car garage while Jake entered his house.

In a short time he called Madison to tell her he had sent the map copy. Their conversation was brief and then she was gone.

Then he spread the maps on a table in his study and compared the ancient one with the one he had of Madison's ranch, which was an aerial view. He had already picked out what he thought the most likely places to search, but he wanted to see what she chose. He could hardly believe it. He'd wanted to do this for a long time and now it was finally going to happen. Adrenaline pumping, he could barely contain his excitement. He had energy to burn, so turning off the light in the study, he went to the gym to work out. If all went well, he was in for some hard physical labor in the coming week.

Monday morning Jake flew to Dallas and went to his downtown office on the twentieth floor of Calhoun Energy. His office was half the floor with a reception room, his private office with its own entrance, the executive conference room, a room with a bar, a bathroom and a small workout room. On the floor above were two penthouse apartments with terraces.

Before Jake could call, Josh phoned and said he was on his way up. Jake was glad Josh was in town. Even though he had an investment in Calhoun Energy, he had his own hotel business and was gone more than he was in Dallas. In minutes his brother came striding into his office. His straight dark brown hair was neatly combed and he looked every inch the successful hotel mogul with his gold cuff links catching the light as he swung his arms. The gray suit and matching tie provided contrast for his brown eyes and dark looks.

"Good morning. How did it go last night?" he asked, sitting in a leather chair facing Jake, who leaned back in his chair behind his desk. Morning sun slanted through the floor-to-ceiling windows behind him.

"Excellent. I have permission to search on her ranch."

"Hot damn! That's perfect. So she bought it. Any stipulations?"

"Yes, she had one. The hitch you predicted," he said, thinking each sibling reacted in a customary way and Josh was the cynical, study-all-angles-first brother.

"She wants someone from her ranch to go along," Josh surmised.

"She does. More than one. In fact, she's going with me."

"Uh-oh," Josh said, narrowing his eyes. "Do you think she wants to renew old times?"

"Not even remotely. She doesn't trust me and she wants to see for herself."

"She's going to join you if you dig for buried treasure?" Josh asked, making a tent of his fingers in front of his chest. One booted foot rested on his knee.

"No, she won't dig. I'm guessing that she'll watch or sketch while she waits. Whatever she plans to do, she is definitely going with me."

"Don't ever trust her."

"I don't think you need to give me that advice," Jake answered.

"I suppose not. So what happens if you find something and she's there?"

"The treasure is hers as we planned. We get the remains. If any remains are Milans, she can have them."

"What about the deed? If it's there, she'll see it."

Jake nodded. "If it's buried with the treasure, yeah. If we find it, she's going to want to see it. At that point, I'll drop the part about the McCracken land because she'll know that I knew all along if there was a deed to land, it was Milan land."

Jake sat forward in his chair. "You know, I wonder if it's a tall tale—that our ancestor won part of the Milan ranch in a poker game and the deed was buried with that treasure."

"You'll have to take on about the bones of our ancestors like they mean the world to you."

"I'll worry about Madison. If that deed exists, I want it. According to what we were told, the deed would give us Milan land all along our border and that would be fabulous."

"I think so," Josh said, his brown eyes twinkling. "You'd

get revenge for old man Milan telling you that you couldn't marry Madison, to never go near her again."

"I don't care about revenge. That's the past. If we have a deed to part of their ranch, I want that Milan land. We're not the only company going after leases there," Jake said, knowing that all his siblings owned shares in Calhoun Energy, just as he had an investment in Josh's company.

Josh ran his fingers through his hair that sprang away and curled in a tangle. "Have you called everyone to tell them?"

"Yeah, I called you, too, and no one answered."

Josh grinned. "I got your text. When you called, I was with…a friend."

"The redhead?"

"No, she's gone. Sandy is a brunette. You'll meet her, maybe. Or maybe not."

He paused as they heard voices outside the office and he watched their oldest brother, Mike, and their sister, Lindsay, appear from his private entrance.

"Good morning," Mike said, standing and gazing at his brothers with wide dark brown eyes. Locks of his curly black hair fell slightly on his forehead. He shed his brown leather jacket, draped it on a coatrack by the door and hung his brown broad-brimmed hat on the rack.

"Come in and sit. Where's Scotty?" Jake asked about Mike's two-year-old.

"Home with Mrs. Lewis."

"Lindsay, I didn't expect to see you this morning."

"I had to get some supplies and Mike talked me into coming. This is great news."

"Madison was suspicious of my motives at first, but then she bought it and said that I can look for the treasure," Jake explained and all three siblings cheered. "You two have a chair," Jake said and Mike sat in the other leather chair while Lindsay took a wingback.

"And Madison thinks the deed gives you land from the McCracken place?" Mike asked.

"Right," Jake replied. "From what I've always understood, until now, no one outside our family knows about the deed."

"Thank heavens," Josh remarked.

"Madison's going with me on the dig. That's the only way she would agree."

"That's bad news," Lindsay remarked, frowning. "You can bet her brothers will be thinking up ways for her to take advantage of this. She'll try something sneaky."

Mike shook his head and rolled his eyes. "She wants to get back together with you."

"No, she doesn't," Jake answered. "Madison doesn't trust me to tell her if I find the treasure. It's that simple."

"Watch her. I don't think it will be that simple," Mike said. "I agree with Lindsay. Don't ever trust a Milan," he said and Jake's eyebrows arched.

"What happens if you do find the deed?" Lindsay asked.

"I show it to her and claim the land."

"You can just act surprised there really is a deed," Mike said. "She can't blame you for feeling uncertain about it."

"I won't need to act," Jake remarked dryly. "I will be as surprised as hell if we find a deed or anything else. I don't really think that legend is true."

"Something got it started and it makes sense. You know our ancestors shot and killed Milans and Milans shot and killed some of our ancestors, which is part of what started the feud," Josh said.

"A woman got it started. She planned to marry a Calhoun and ran off with a Milan," Mike reminded them.

"You know Madison doesn't trust you," Josh remarked.

"I don't really care," Jake replied. "If there is a deed and that deed will stand up in a court of law, then part of the Milan ranch is ours. Maybe the best part of the Milan ranch." All were silent a moment and Jake figured the others were thinking about the prospect of owning part of the Milan ranch just as he was.

"What a deal," Josh stated, his brown eyes on Jake. "This may get the old feud fired up again."

"I hope we're all more civilized today than to go shooting at each other," Jake said. "We may start searching tomorrow. I'm going to her house tonight to look at aerial photos of her ranch and hear her theories on where to look. I sent her a copy of the map last night."

They speculated on where the digging would take place, as they had all studied the map and the aerial photos of the Milan ranch.

"All we can do is wait and see," Mike said. "Call one of us each night and give us a report and we'll call the other two."

Jake agreed.

"That old legend," Lindsay remarked. "It would be funny if it turned out to be true."

"It sounds likely to me," Mike added, glancing at the others.

"I go back and forth about it," Jake said. "I first heard it from Grandad. He said a Calhoun had a box of gold and he was trying to get away from robbers—"

"It might have been just the reverse," Mike said. "The Calhoun ancestor may have been the robber trying to escape a posse."

"They've also said the shoot-out was over a Calhoun's fiancée who ran off with a Milan and they had the shoot-out over her," Mike stated.

"That's what Grandad always said. He said the Calhoun got her back because he killed the Milan," Jake said. "The deed was won by a Calhoun from a Milan and was supposed to say clearly that the land belonged to the Calhouns, and the deed was with a box of gold coins."

"The ranch boundaries we have now weren't clear back in the time that shoot-out happened, but that started the feud," Mike said. "Myth or truth? Maybe we'll finally find out with our generation.

"I'd like to come with you," Mike added, "but I think it would cause trouble with Madison Milan to have two Calhouns."

"No," Jake replied. "She won't want the Calhoun brothers going along, or our sister."

"Frankly, I don't want to go," Lindsay said.

Josh stood up. "I've got to go. I leave for L.A. in a few hours. Good luck, bro," he said, looking intently at Jake. "Sorry, but I don't think you'll find anything. If a treasure is on that ranch, it's a needle in a haystack."

"I'll text all of you each night."

"Good," Mike said, standing with the others. "Good luck to you."

Jake gave him a thumbs-up. He watched as his siblings left and then he sat, turning his chair to look out over Dallas while he thought about the old legend and the Milan ranch. Was it really true or was this a wild-good chase? If there was a buried treasure, was there any hope of them finding it? Actually, it might be buried on Calhoun land because to all his family's calculations it was close to their boundary. Through the years there had been plenty of searching on the Calhoun side, but to no avail.

He thought again of Madison, remembering her perfume, the way the blue dress had clung to a figure that still took his breath away. She was a beautiful woman, poised and confident now. He hadn't slept well last night with her filling his dreams. Memories of making love to her had plagued him, waking him, leaving him hot, sweaty and wanting her, something he didn't want to feel. They had been kids when they had thought they were in love.

What had been a significant difference at nineteen and

sixteen no longer mattered at thirty-two and twenty-nine. When he looked back on it now, he had to admit that they had been too young to marry, but at the time it hadn't seemed that way.

Because of Pete Milan's heavy-handed manner, Jake had never thought about the man being right until the past few years. All he could remember was her father warning him to get out of Madison's life and disclosing that she had already accepted his offer to open art galleries for her and get her showings in the best exhibitions in the Southwest and along the West Coast—if she would call off the wedding. Her father's promise had probably saved her several years of struggles and had made her a legitimate working artist. Evidently that was what she'd wanted the most. More than him. Jake had known instinctively that his own dad would have agreed with Pete Milan and said they were too young to marry; his mother never liked any of the Milans anyway.

He thought again of Madison, remembering holding her soft hand last night when they had the handshake on their agreement. Could he work with her and keep his hands to himself and resist flirting with her? Did he really want to resist? Was she still off-limits to his heart? Wisdom answered yes. She obviously didn't feel kindly toward him or want to recall the past. What would it be like to be with her every day for the next week or two?

Madison bent over the map and aerial photo spread before her as she made notes. For several hours she'd tried to focus her thoughts, but too often she realized she was staring into space, lost in thought about Jake and their time together last night. She had been shocked at how handsome he looked—far more than when he had been nineteen years old. Worse, he was even more appealing to her as a man than he had been as a teenager.

She had never known if her parents had any inkling of the depth of her feelings for Jake Calhoun. It didn't matter now.

One time their foreman, Charley, had come around the garages and seen her in her car at midnight. He had asked if her parents knew she was out and he had told her to go back inside. She had gone back, climbing in through her open bedroom window and sitting there, watching in the dark until she saw Charley disappear into the bunkhouse. She had climbed out again and taken a truck, driving across the ranch in the moonlight to meet Jake. That had been one of the last times they had been together before the night they had planned to run away and get married.

For days she had wondered if Charley had ratted her out to her dad, but when nothing happened, she decided he had not. Charley had always kept an eye on them for her dad, especially the boys, and she never liked Charley because of it, although now that she was grown, she understood why he had. She'd never even told Jake about the incident because it hadn't seemed that important.

How in love she had been with Jake! She had thought he was the most wonderful person she had ever known. She remembered his dark brown eyes last night and her racing pulse when she had caught him looking at her lips while desire blazed in his eyes. What was it going to be like to work with him every day for the rest of the week? Could she hold up her end of this expedition?

She thought about crossing the porch with him last night when they had come home after dinner. If he had taken her into his arms to kiss her, would she have stopped him? Breathless, she thought about Jake's kisses. Would she have been able to stop him?

Tonight he would be in her house to look at her photos and maps. Could she eat with him tonight, work with him and still resist him?

This morning she had called the man in Chicago who had validated the map. He had searched his records, finally calling her back and telling her the map was authentic. The thought of seeing the actual map that was a tie to her past was exciting.

She had sent a text to all her brothers about the search. Tony had called immediately after he received the text, which was typical because he could be impulsive. Nick's call had come later in the afternoon after he had thought things over. Wyatt had needed the most time to think it all over, as he tended to view everything more objectively than any other family member.

Tony had started arguing instantly. "I don't think you should go. I should. You can't trust Jake Calhoun, or any Calhoun about anything. You should know that. I'll call him."

"No, you won't," she'd said patiently. "Just wait. I'm taking two men with me and we'll watch all the time to see what is going on."

"Don't do it. The Calhouns are up to something."

She had argued with Tony for half an hour before she finally got him to promise to stay out of it until she asked for his help.

Wyatt and Nick had been easier, but the message had been the same—they didn't trust a Calhoun. She had promised them both she would be careful and she'd keep all her brothers informed of what was happening. She had promptly put them and their warnings out of her mind. She could take care of herself and her ranch.

She looked down at the map again, even though she had it memorized by now.

Would the map really help them? She thought of all the warnings and pushed aside her worries. Men who had worked for them for years would be with her, so there was nothing to worry about.

Except maybe falling in love with Jake Calhoun all over again.

The thought came unbidden. No, she assured herself, she would not fall in love with him again. Still, a nagging doubt tormented her. Jake still set her pulse racing and the slightest contact with him was electrifying. For the next few days she would be with him from sunrise to sundown.

Why hadn't he married? Was he wondering the same about her? Regardless, she intended to guard her heart. She suspected he wouldn't want to fall in love again any more than she did.

She forced herself to get back to her notes. Promptly at six, when she had told him to appear, the doorbell rang. She opened the door and looked into Jake's dark brown eyes before his gaze drifted slowly to her toes and back up again, taking in her jeans and plaid shirt, and making her tingle all over.

"You look gorgeous," he said in a husky voice.

She was thinking the same about him. He wore a navy Western shirt, boots and tight jeans. He had a wide-brimmed tan Stetson on his head, creased in the familiar local style. He held a brown leather briefcase.

"Thank you. Come in," she said, stepping back. "Let's get something to drink and then go look at the map and pictures I have. I have a casserole in the oven and we can eat whenever we want."

"Show me the way," he said. "I wonder how long it will take me to get accustomed to entering this house and not feeling as if I'm committing a crime."

She smiled. "You shouldn't feel that way now."

"This was the forbidden palace. Any of your family around tonight?"

"No. They're in Dallas. They're rarely out here except at Christmas when we all get together. Even our Christmas celebration has been in Dallas the last few years. I'm sure you see my brothers some because they're around. Nick has a home in Dallas, Wyatt has a home here in Verity and Tony lives on his ranch. We all have our own ranches now, but only Tony lives on his year-round."

"Sure, the illustrious sheriff of Verity, Wyatt Milan. I see Tony sometimes in Verity or at rodeos. Your brother Nick is probably too busy trying to become president someday."

She laughed. "He would like to be, but right now, he's too busy being a state representative."

They stopped in the kitchen to get drinks. As he helped, she caught him watching her. His gaze made her heart beat faster and she wondered again how she would get through the next few days, or weeks, working with him.

"Let's go to the library," she said and when he walked beside her, she was aware of him, close, almost touching her.

"Madison, I'm sorry about your sister-in-law."

Madison nodded. "Thanks. That car wreck was a tragedy. In public Nick does fine, but he's had a hard time dealing with the loss. He was so excited because she was expecting."

"That must have been rough."

"You've had your own losses. I'm sorry about Mike losing his wife to cancer. At least he has his son."

"That helps, and keeps him busy. It's been hard for him trying to be both mom and dad for Scotty."

"That's tough and so sad."

"Mike's happy with his nanny and Mom comes to stay sometimes for a month at a time, so that's helped him. The baby is a cute little fella and that cheers him up. He tries to stay upbeat because of Scotty."

"Do your brothers know what you're doing?"

"Oh, yeah. I don't think they really expect much to

come from it. This isn't the first search for that fabled buried treasure."

"I know. It'll probably be another wild-goose chase, but the map is fascinating. I'm anxious to see the actual map. It gives a little more validity to the legend, but finding something buried anywhere on this ranch is kind of mind-boggling."

Carrying her tea while he carried a beer, she led the way to the library, a large room filled with floor-to-ceiling shelves of books and pictures.

She stopped at a long table filled with maps and photos. "Those are aerial photos, but over here are satellite pictures," she said, waving her hand and moving to a computer and an iPad toward one end of the table. "You can see these photos better and move around or expand them. Look at whatever you want."

"This is impressive," he said as he bent over one of the aerial pictures. "I haven't seen this one."

"No, it's not out there for the public. That's one of our pictures. Look at the map and then look at the aerial photo and the satellite maps of the ranch. Maybe you can find some landmarks in them that are similar." She glanced up and saw him staring at the open neckline of her shirt. Self-conscious, she wanted to reach up and button one more button, but she didn't want to draw that much attention to herself. His eyes met hers and she was ensnared in his dark gaze, desire filling her as she stared at him. Realizing what was happening, she looked away. To cover the flush that heated her cheeks she pointed to the aerial photo.

"Look at this, Jake."

He shifted his attention to the papers on the table and while he studied them, she looked at his profile. He was clean-shaven, his thick black hair combed neatly. Jake's lashes had a slight curl over seductive dark eyes that could hide his feelings easily. The past few moments had shaken her. Desire had overwhelmed her, and he had felt it, too. She hoped that didn't happen again during the coming week. She had to go with him. No way would she trust him even if she had her men go with him.

As she studied him, she knew the week or weeks ahead would be a strain. It would help if he hadn't gotten more appealing through the years. He was breathtakingly handsome. Did other women see him that way, or was it just an effect he had on her?

Jake sat in front of the wide-screen computer to look at a satellite map.

She stepped closer to sit near him so she could look with him. As she did, their shoulders brushed lightly, the slightest touch, but she was acutely aware of the contact. She forced her mind back to the screen.

"These maps should help in our search," he told her. "I've studied the old map off and on through the years. In my judgment, it looks as if the location is along the banks of Rocky Creek." He picked up his briefcase to set it on his knees to open it. "I brought the original. I got it out of the vault."

"That's exciting, Jake," she said in anticipation.

He removed a box with a glass front. Inside was the yellowed, torn and wrinkled map. He opened the box and lifted it slowly, gently, his well-shaped hands holding it gingerly.

"Maybe you should leave it in there and we'll just look through the glass," she said, though she wanted desperately to hold it herself.

"No. We can see it better this way."

"Jake, can I touch it? It's a connection to my first Texas ancestors."

"Hold out your hands," he ordered. When she did, he carefully placed it into her open hands, his warm fingers brushing hers. The contact of their hands made her forget the map for a few seconds as she looked up at Jake. He sat so close, and as she looked into his dark eyes she felt a flash of longing.

"Thank you," she said, the words coming out in a whisper. She remembered the fragile map and looked at it, drawing a deep breath. "Jake, this feels like a tangible tie with the past."

"I hope it's a damn tangible tie to a real buried treasure."

She examined the map, thinking about the ancestor who had carried it. "This is fantastic. It makes me wonder about those early-day Milans. If there is a treasure, was it ill-gotten gains, or gold that had been acquired legitimately?"

"We'll never know the answer to that one."

"Here. You can have it back."

"Just place it close here where I can compare it with the satellite map that shows everything the most clearly." Jake studied the computer and she looked at a picture that showed her ranch, all the trees, bushes, the house and other buildings and roads. He adjusted the map on the computer and pointed to a place with his finger. "I want to compare this stretch along Rocky Creek. There are some trees on the map, but trees die or are cut down. New trees crop up beside them. I don't think we can go by the trees on the map."

"Probably not," she said, placing the antique map gingerly near the computer. He moved so close his arm brushed hers. He reached into his briefcase to retrieve a flashlight. "Can you hold this?"

She took the flashlight and he turned back to shift the map, moving it slowly and carefully. The additional light showed the map more clearly.

"Now look—these circles—it's printed here, I think, 'rocs.' Look at this aerial picture along the creek bank."

"There are rocks, but there are about a dozen more places along the banks where there are rocks on both sides."

"Yes, but look. The creek curves here in the picture," he said, pointing. "The creek curves here on the map. It looks like the same place," he said, leaning closer to the table.

"That's true, but then look here." She pointed farther up on the screen. "Here's where I thought it looked most like the electronic copy of the map you sent me. There are rocks, the creek curves just slightly around a sandbar, but in all these years the creek could have swallowed up the sandbar. You see what I mean?" She looked around to catch him studying her so intently she forgot the map momentarily. He drew a deep breath and turned back to the map.

"That's a possibility." He let out a heavy breath. "I never expected this to be easy. People have been hunting for that treasure all my life and probably since the late nineteenth century."

"Maybe you should sit and study these maps while I get dinner on the table. After all, this is the first time you've seen these photos of the Double M Ranch."

"Sure you don't want kitchen help?"

"I'm sure," she said, leaving Jake looking at the computer screen, pausing at the door to look back at him. Light shone on him, giving midnight glints to his black hair. Was she going to be able to work with him without rekindling feelings she didn't want? Some feelings had already ignited. And that's what scared her.

While she got drinks and dinner on the table, her thoughts stayed on Jake.

When she returned to call him for dinner he shook his head as he stood. "I've found four likely places so far. We'll both look after dinner. I have the feeling the longer we look, the more places we'll find," he said, walking beside her to the kitchen.

"That does smell good," he said and she smiled.

"A simple dinner—baked tilapia on angel-hair pasta

with artichoke hearts and sun-dried tomatoes. I have a sauce for the fish or lemons."

They entered the kitchen, which had glass-fronted cabinets built in the late 1900s when the original part of the house was constructed.

"Nice kitchen," he said, looking around.

"All the equipment is about three years old, which was the last remodeling. It is a nice kitchen. I've grown up in it and I love it, high ceilings and all."

He held her chair and she was acutely conscious of every brush of his hands, every look he gave her. What did she still feel for Jake? She didn't want to answer her own question. A week ago, she would have told herself that she had no feelings for him, but after being around him, responding to him in startling ways, she had to admit that she was still attracted to him.

"We have some fancy homemade garlic bread."

"Did you do all this?" he asked and she shook her head.

"I'd like to say yes, but I didn't. Jessie Lou cooks for me now and Harriet cooks for the men. Dad deeded this ranch to me. He and Mom don't care to stay here at all any longer. I inherited the staff, too, so Ethel still cleans three days a week and her daughter comes once a week to help. Ethel and Jessie Lou still live here on the ranch and Ethel's husband still works, too."

"I don't know about the cleaning, but you have the best cook possible."

"I think so. Jessie Lou isn't here tonight, but she was here until five. She and Harriet are still both wonderful cooks. Some things don't change."

"I remember some great picnics we had where you brought something Jessie Lou made."

She smiled. "Remember her chocolate cake that got ants all over it? You said you weren't giving your slice up to a bunch of ants and juggled the cake around to let some of the ants run off and then ate it, ants and all."

She laughed while he grinned and shrugged. "And you were so afraid I had ants in my mouth that you wouldn't let me kiss you that afternoon or that night."

As she laughed, his grin widened and her heart turned over. Desire flared to life, a hot torment that made her want him badly. She should never have opened the door on memories of fun times with him. She looked down at her plate. Her appetite had fled and she tried to think about something besides Jake.

"We had fun," he said quietly and there was silence that stretched between them. She didn't want to look up and meet his probing dark eyes because he always saw too much of her. He could hide his feelings better than she could.

"I guess we should each pick the places we want to look and list them," he said briskly to her a few moments later. They were back in the present and she tamped down the memories that threatened her heart.

He sipped his iced tea. "Did you get over your fear of snakes?"

"No, I did not. I still won't swim in Rocky Creek."

"How are you going to go traipsing around out there? You know we have an abundant snake population."

"You said you're bringing some men. I'll have two, plus you and me. We ought to make enough noise to scare the rattlers away. And if we don't, I also figured that one of you will have a pistol."

"One of us will. I keep one in the pickup."

"There," she said, smiling at him. "You can kill a snake if we encounter one."

Through dinner they discussed the search and when they had finished, they sat sipping more tea, talking about the treasure. "We better look at the maps," Jake said. "I'll help you with the dishes."

"No need. I'll just put the leftovers in the fridge and rinse our dishes for the dishwasher. You go back and keep looking."

"I'll do the cleaning and you go look," he countered. "You've never had this chance with the actual old map and it is clearer than the copy. I insist," he said, taking dishes from her and blocking her path.

"So I see you are as stubborn as you used to be," she said.

He smiled. "Just as stubborn as you. Some things don't change."

She realized they were getting back where she didn't want to go. Her smile vanished as she returned to the table to push in her chair. "Let me put up the leftovers," she said, picking up the pasta bowl. He took it from her, his hands closing over hers. Startled, she looked up at him and drew a deep breath.

"It's all yours," she said and left quickly. Desire ignited each time they made contact. Sometimes when they were close she caught him looking at her with a gaze that clearly conveyed he wanted her.

She hurried out of the kitchen, feeling him watching her walk away. How would she get through being together with him every day for the next week or two? This wasn't working out the way she had imagined.

Four

She pored over the maps swiftly and stuck by the list she already had. She wanted to finish and get him out of the house.

When he joined her, she showed him her list, pointing out each place and waiting while he looked. Jake got a legal pad from his briefcase, turning to look at her while he held both of their lists.

"We have three places that are the same, so those will go to the top of the list. Your first choice is my second, so we'll put yours first because you know your ranch better than I do."

She marked the three locations on each map. "Look at our other choices so we can decide and get them listed."

She pulled her chair close to his, far more aware of him beside her than the map in front of her. "I think my number four should be next."

It took another hour to get everything listed and finally

he stood and put away the original old map in its glass box and then into his briefcase.

"Jake, I hope we find something," she said, walking him to the door. "I don't care about the money so much, but if the treasure exists, it's a tie to the past. I'm sure it's true that there was a gunfight and both families had members killed. We do need to give those bones a burial place." She stepped out onto the porch with him. The September night was cool, the black sky dotted with twinkling stars. "Thanks again for letting me see the original map. I'm fascinated by it."

"You're a romantic," he said in a deep voice. He stood only inches from her and his dark eyes were shadowed. She had an urge to step into his arms and raise her face for a kiss, but she fought it and moved back.

"Can you be here about six in the morning? We can get started early and get out on the ranch by the time the sun rises."

"Sure. We'll be here. Want me to get lunch packed?"

"No, Jessie will do it each day. See you in the morning."

"Thanks for dinner, Madison."

"You're welcome," she said, thinking how polite they were being with each other. Better that than the flashes of scalding longing to be in his arms and make love again. She stepped back and watched him walk away. As soon as he drove out of sight, she went in and closed up, setting the alarm on the grounds around the house.

The next morning she was on the driveway with her two men and a nearby pickup packed with gear and food. The outside lights were on because it was still dark, without even a hint of the dawn to come.

It had taken her an hour to dress this morning. She had tried to avoid thinking about Jake, but whatever she selected, she thought about wearing for him. She finally decided on a long-sleeved blue Western shirt, jeans, boots and a brown wide-brimmed hat. Her hair was in a thick braid down her back. A tingle of excitement made her edgy. She couldn't wait to get going and start the search. It wasn't about the gold. Honestly, if he had said he wanted half, she would have agreed instantly. It was about the tie to the past and the Milans who had lived generations ago. It would mean the legend was a true accounting of events of the past, which she hoped it was.

She spotted headlights coming up the ranch road. When they drove into the light she saw two pickups. Jake drove his big black pickup with someone seated beside him and two in the backseat. Another red pickup followed with two men.

Jake stopped and climbed out, slamming the door and striding toward her. His black Western hat sat squarely on his head and his tight jeans emphasized his small waist and long legs. He wore a navy-and-red-plaid Western shirt and looked filled with energy because of the spring in his step.

"Good morning."

"Morning, Jake," she replied. "This is Darren Hopkinson and Stoney Rassmussen. Darren and Stoney, meet Jake Calhoun."

The men shook hands. "We're ready," she said.

"It's your ranch, so you lead the way and we'll follow," Jake suggested.

"Sure. Let's go," she replied and they parted to get into their trucks.

She turned down a dirt path that ran past houses, outbuildings, the ranch office, corrals, barns, sheds. Finally they left the graveled road and took a dirt road in the opposite direction, bumping over rocks and dips in the road, running over weeds that grew in the center between the ruts.

She knew where she was going and could have driven it with her eyes closed. She had learned to drive on these ranch roads. She glanced in the rearview mirror and saw Jake's black pickup behind her, the third pickup coming last. From the list they had selected, they had mapped out a plan to start on the north side of the creek and search eastward. They both agreed that the map looked as if the treasure had been buried along Rocky Creek.

By dawn, they had reached the trees and in a short time approached the only bridge over Rocky Creek on the Double M Ranch. Trees lining the creek bank blocked the sunlight so the vehicles still had on headlights. Madison reached the creek first.

"Miss Milan," Stoney said beside her. "Wait. Look at the bridge."

She stopped the truck, her headlights illuminating the far end of the bridge. One of the tall cottonwoods lining the creek had fallen on the end of the bridge, preventing any vehicle from crossing.

"Nobody's said anything about a tree falling on the bridge," she said, turning to look at Darren and Stoney, who both shook their heads. Switching off the motor, she stepped out while Stoney and Darren followed her. Jake stepped out of his truck.

"We can get that tree moved out of the way. It'll just slow us down, but it's not going to stop us," Jake said. "All the men come with me and we'll move it."

"We'll cut it up later and get it out of here," she said, looking around. "What could have caused that tree to fall? It looks healthy and there hasn't been a storm recently. That tree hasn't been down long," she said more to herself than anyone else.

She waited in the truck and in minutes the men all returned. Stoney and Darren climbed into the truck while Jake stopped beside it. "Someone cut that tree down so it would fall on the bridge. There's someone who doesn't want us hunting for this legendary treasure."

Startled, she stared into his dark eyes. "That's foolishness. That was a temporary setback and it won't stop any of us. Who would do that anyway?"

"Not my family," he answered. "We have too much to gain. Just be careful. That may merely be a warning."

She shivered and looked at the tree that had been pulled away from the bridge.

"We'll go ahead as we planned," she said.

"Why don't you let me drive around you and cross the bridge first? No one will drown if the bridge collapses, but it won't be fun to go into the creek in one of these trucks. Let me see if anyone tampered with the bridge."

"Very well, but I'm not scared to go first."

"I'll go." He left and climbed back into his truck. He drove around her and she followed, letting him get completely across before she followed.

Within ten minutes he switched off the engine and parked. She pulled up beside him and the last pickup stopped. Men climbed out while Jake joined her.

"This is our first stop. Now you call the shots. What do you think? Look here or start walking?" she said.

He studied his map. Bits of sunlight slipped between leaves and branches, highlighting his raven hair. "Gather round," he said to the others.

The day was warming and because of rains farther north, the narrow stream gurgled and splashed over rocks nearby.

"Before we start, I want to talk to all of you," Jake said. He pushed his hat to the back of his head and the broad Western brim framed his face.

"Myth or truth, we're going to try to find the legendary treasure. If we find any gold or even just bones that are remains from a gunfight, everyone will get a bonus of five thousand dollars—Milan hands and Calhoun hands alike—from me."

Jake paused as the men grinned and applauded.

"You'll have earned it. This will be tedious work. If we find nothing, you'll get a thousand dollars above your regular salary just for volunteering for this."

Again the cheers and applause caused Jake to wait. "Okay. Madison and I have been over the maps and this is the area we picked to start. We're just going to spread out and start digging along Rocky Creek this morning. Good luck and let's dig."

Jake was a take-charge person—she had known that back in high school when she'd watched him on the football field as quarterback. They had both been in the math club and he had been president, taking control of the meetings and being decisive when problems arose. She had been vice president and she could remember some clashes they'd had, too.

Jake turned to her. "You might as well do what you want—look on or sit it out, but if you sit, watch out for snakes."

"Sure, Jake," she said, pulling out her map. She began to move up the creek, but after a few feet saw a likely spot. She sat on a rock and studied her surroundings, the mesquite, cactus, small plants and, at the water's edge, grasses and weeds.

Jake walked up and sat beside her. "What do you think?"

"Now, I'm not so sure."

"It's a start. You can stay right here."

"I'm getting my sketch pad." She stood to follow him but slipped on loose rocks. Instantly his strong hands closed around her waist and held her. She grasped his arms to steady herself and then looked up into his brown eyes, her breath shortening as his gaze lowered to her mouth and her lips parted.

She stood there, immobile, aware of his hands on her,

of hers holding him, and of how close they stood. Would he kiss her? Her eyes widened before she stepped away quickly. "Thanks for keeping me from going into the creek," she whispered, not knowing what else to say to him.

He nodded, but didn't respond.

Shaken more by Jake's hands on her than by almost falling, she moved away, walking a few yards upstream before she stopped. He stood watching her.

Maybe coming along hadn't been a good idea, after all, she thought. Yet she knew she was the only one who could deter Jake if he wanted to do something that none of the people with Milan interests thought he should.

Moments ago her body had blazed with desire. She had wanted his kiss. That's what had shocked her the most. Over eight or nine years ago, she had thought she was completely over him, no longer feeling a vestige of attraction or love for him. She had thought she'd put him away with childhood memories, boxed up and stored as a keepsake of a long-ago phase of her life. She'd thought she'd blocked him out of her mind. Well, she had been wrong. Obviously. In one moment with his hands locked around her waist, she had wanted to wrap her arms around his neck, step close and kiss him.

She couldn't trust Jake. She would never trust him. Right now, he could be up to something. He could have offered to let her have the treasure so she couldn't see that he had any hidden agenda or ulterior motive.

It would take a long while and lots of time together for him to win back her trust. If he ever could.

She got out her pad and sketched for about two hours, but then laid aside her pencils.

Feeling a need to stretch her legs, she started moving away the rocks that would have to be relocated before anyone could dig in this area. She hadn't moved more than half a dozen rocks when Jake's hand closed on her wrist.

Startled, she straightened to face him. "What?"

"Stop. You don't need to be doing heavy labor."

She laughed and pushed tendrils of hair from her face. "I'm all right. I'm not fragile."

"You'll be surprised what will hurt in the morning if you keep that up. Leave this stuff to us. You can break out the lunch shortly back at the trucks or we can drive up here."

"This land is too rough for that."

"No, it's not. That's what our trucks are built to do. Come on, we'll go get two of the trucks." He took her arm to steady her over the rugged terrain and she went with him, again aware of his fingers on her arm. This time he seemed oblivious of the contact, which helped a degree.

At the trucks he opened her door. "This time let me lead. You follow me."

Jake held the door for her and she climbed in and he took the lead pickup. When they reached the place where three men were digging, they parked.

"Go back to your digging," she said. "I'll get lunch ready."

She washed her hands from a jug of water she had brought for that purpose. Opening the back of both pickups, she spread out Jessie Lou's sandwiches, chips, and opened the coolers filled with ice, pop and water. She set out two homemade apple pies and a container of whipped cream, then rang a small bell to call everyone.

Jake and the men grabbed the camp stools he had brought or sat on nearby logs or rocks. Jake came to sit beside her on a slab of sandstone.

"So far, it's a bust. The only progress is that we can eliminate this area."

"You said that you didn't expect this to be easy," she

stated. "We're just getting started. Over the generations my family has scoured this part of the ranch for the treasure, although I don't think they went along the creek a whole lot because creeks move as years pass, which means, in some spots, the treasure could possibly be in the bottom of the creek."

They ate and went back to work. She cleaned and put away leftovers, finally finishing and pulling on her gloves to move some more small rocks again. She picked up one and a thin snake slithered away, trying to get beneath the adjoining rock. She cried out with fright and yanked it up by the back end, swinging it and throwing it toward the creek as fast and as hard as she could.

She heard laughter and turned to see Jake not far away. "I believe you've gotten over your snake fears."

"No, I haven't," she snapped, "and stop laughing. That wasn't funny." She shivered. "I couldn't do anything else to get it away from me. I can't kill one."

"If you'd waited a second, I would have killed it," he said, grinning. "Good toss, by the way. Looked like a copperhead, though. I should tell you they don't usually travel alone."

She shivered again. "I'm taking a break," she said, turning her back on him to walk to the truck and climb inside. She glanced back to see him still grinning, making her even angrier. She hated and feared snakes as much as ever. When she had grabbed it up, she hadn't stopped to think. She just wanted it away from her. She had to admit she was ready to call this quits and leave her ancestors' bones where they had been buried in the 1800s. She was too aware of Jake. Being close to him was beginning to awaken feelings she hadn't had for years, feelings she thought she was over and didn't want to have again. She was hot and tired already from moving rocks. She thought back to the pre-morning hours. Had the tree blocking the bridge been a warning? She couldn't imagine who would do such a thing or why. Her brothers didn't want her doing this, but they wouldn't stoop to cutting down a tree to achieve what was only a temporary delay.

She wanted to be back at the house painting and enjoying her quiet life. From the moment Jake had appeared in the hardware store, he had done nothing but stir up trouble for her.

Later in the afternoon Jake dug in the shade of a cottonwood at the edge of the creek. He had shed his shirt and the muscles in his back rippled as he worked. He was muscular, strong, and she could recall the feel of his bare back as she'd run her hands over him, kissing him. He had been a tall, lean, bony teen then. Now he had filled out, become a man.

The temperature had risen and she was hot, but the heat of the day wasn't her problem. It was the memory of being locked in his arms, naked, her body held tightly against his. She could recall his hands moving over her, caressing her. She didn't want to remember, but the sight of him shirtless triggered the memories with a clarity that surprised her. "Jake," she whispered and then clamped her mouth shut.

She didn't want to get to the point where she longed to have the past repeat itself. If every day of this search would be like this, she would have to quit because this was bringing torment into her peaceful life.

She shifted to watch him dig. He was forming a large, shallow hole. He stopped and glanced around as he wiped his brow, and when he saw her watching him, he leaned on the shovel and simply stood there openly staring at her. She wondered what he was thinking.

He didn't say anything, and after a few moments he went back to work.

They worked until dusk and then they all climbed into

SARA ORWIG   71

the pickups to drive back to their ranches. At her house,
Jake stopped to talk to her. She thanked the men with
her and then stepped out of her pickup to wait while Jake
parked and climbed out.

"Jake, you still have a long drive to get home. Why don't
you tell the men to bring clothes tomorrow and bunk down
here and you can stay up here at the house? We have room."

"If you're sure, I'll take you up on it and I think they
will, too. If anyone doesn't, he can drive his own truck.
Are you going again tomorrow?" he asked.

"Of course," she replied even though she had been on
the verge of canceling for the past four hours.

"I'll see you in the morning, then," he said, standing
with his hands on his hips, staring at her. She wondered
what was going through his thoughts because he looked
on the verge of saying more to her. Instead, he got in his
truck and drove off.

She wanted to shower and to change clothes before she
ate the dinner Jessie Lou had ready for her to reheat. As
Madison emerged from the shower, her phone rang and
she answered to hear her father's voice.

At first they talked briefly about nothing in particular
and then he said, "I hear you allowed Jake Calhoun to dig
on our property today."

Startled that he knew, she realized one of the ranch
hands must have informed him. All of them knew about
Jake because she had asked for two volunteers to go with
her. "Yes, I did. I told all my brothers. Jake has a map that
seems authentic."

"Aren't you running some risks by letting a Calhoun
traipse all over our ranch?"

"It's a calculated risk, I guess. But if we find the treasure I get it."

"So what does he get?"

"His ancestors' remains." She heard her father's derisive grumble and she continued, "Plus there may be a deed giving them McCracken land from a poker game."

There was a moment of silence. "Be careful, Madison. You can't trust him one inch. I think you're foolish to allow this, and if I were you, I'd call the deal off tomorrow. The treasure won't be worth whatever he's up to. You can believe that he is up to something more than wanting his ancestors' remains and an old deed that might not ever stand up in court."

"I'll be careful," she said patiently, wishing he hadn't found out and hoping he didn't hear about the felled tree on the bridge. "I have Darren and Stoney with me. We'll be careful and they've been warned to watch him and his three men."

"You think about what I've said—you should just run him off."

"He's shared his map with me because I said he could do this. It will be brief, probably three or four days."

"Be very careful. You should know you can't trust him in any way."

"I'll be careful. Don't worry."

"That goes with being a dad," he said. "Think about what I've said and tell him you've changed your mind. No good can come of this."

"All right."

"Take care of yourself."

"I will. Thanks, Dad," she said far more cheerfully than she felt. As they said goodbye, she stared into space, seeing Jake's dark eyes and remembering moments during the day. Was there a reason to be suspicious? Was he truthful or deceitful? Had she been taken in again? And which person had reported to her father? Someone left behind, or Darren or Stoney?

In all of this, just who could she trust?

* * *

As Jake returned from dropping the men off at the bunkhouse, he saw a familiar pickup heading toward his back door. He got out of the truck and waited while his younger sister pulled up beside him and got out.

"Hi. Did I come at a bad time?" she asked.

"Never," he said, smiling at her. Six years older than Lindsay, he felt like a second dad to her. He watched her walk through the gate—the only blonde Calhoun as well as the only blue-eyed Calhoun, but she had the Calhoun bone structure, their height and their deep love of ranching.

Her sandy-blond hair was in a thick braid that hung over her shoulder.

"I had an errand anyway, so I swung by. I thought you'd be back and I wanted to see how the search went today."

"Come in and we'll have a beer while I give you the details. But I can tell you right now, we didn't find any treasure, bones or deed."

"You're just getting started."

"Thank you for being kind enough to keep from telling me I'm on a hunt that is hopeless."

She grinned. "I'm glad you're doing it. It would be fabulous if you found the deed. That would be sweet revenge and serve the Milans right for all the things they've done."

"Let it go, Lindsay."

"I can't let it go with Tony Milan. If I ever catch him on my ranch I've got buckshot and I intend to let him have it."

"Lindsay, listen to me. Don't do it. I don't want to bail you out of jail over something stupid like that. Take him to court—follow legal channels against trespassing. Don't go off half-cocked and do something you'll regret."

"Then he needs to stay off my ranch."

Jake caught her shoulders and turned her to face him. "I mean it. Don't get yourself in trouble over a Milan."

"Sometimes, Jake, you are such a wet blanket," she said, wriggling out of his grasp.

"Yeah, well, dealing with me is still a whole lot better than standing up in front of Judge Milan."

"Judge Milan is in Dallas and he would have to recuse himself. Don't get your coattails in a twist. I won't go after Tony with buckshot, but he can be really annoying, and at the last horse auction, he was there and outbid me for a horse I wanted and— Don't you smile. When he trespasses, I can't call the sheriff because the sheriff is his brother. Sheriff Milan is not going to do one thing to harm his brother."

"No, he probably won't. Why is Tony trespassing?"

She sighed. "He has when one of his animals gets into my pasture. We had a fence go down and his stock overgrazed that section before I found out—"

"He has to get his livestock back, Lindsay. You don't have a case. Cut him some slack. I just want you to be protected. Don't give the sheriff an excuse to cause you trouble."

"I hope you find that deed and it gives you acres and acres of Milan land."

"You're too bitter, Lindsay. You're the youngest Calhoun, but you sound like Granddad."

"Tony Milan is like a pesky fly you can't swat. Enough about them. Tell me about today." Her long legs kept pace with him as they went to Jake's back door and entered the house.

"I have to shower, Lindsay," he said as they walked down the hall to the kitchen. "I'm filthy and hot."

"Sure. Go shower. I'll get the beers."

He left, hurrying to shower quickly and dress. He didn't want to keep her waiting and he was ready to sit and relax.

He found her on the patio. With the setting of the sun the weather had cooled. He had enough lights to illuminate his patio and enough of the kinds of plants and lights to repel bugs.

He sat half facing her. "I'm ready for that beer."

"You talked Madison into letting you search for Calhoun ancestors' bones. How was it today when you had to go with her?"

"It was fine. We can both keep the old anger and ill feelings in check. We've had a lot of years to get accustomed to the idea and to practice."

"You haven't been around her during that time. You haven't even spoken to her since that night her dad threatened you."

"No, I haven't, not until this past week. We didn't find anything today, but we're just getting started and I'm hopeful there's a thread of truth to the old legend."

"It could be true in every way and a big treasure could be buried on their ranch, but finding it may be impossible after all these years. Especially if it is buried around Rocky Creek the way you think it might be. Creeks change course over the years, unfortunately."

"I'm hopeful, and with her men and mine, we've got a large enough crew to cover a good-size area."

"Well, I'll keep hoping." She sipped her beer and gazed at his pool.

"How's the ranch?" he asked, always slightly amazed by his baby sister buying a sizable ranch and then running it herself. She had a fine foreman, but Lindsay did a man's work daily on the ranch. All of them had a strong love of ranching, particularly Mike and Lindsay, who lived all the time on their ranches.

"Everything is fine."

"Good deal. I'll put steaks on the grill if you'll stay."

"Sure. Let me help," she said, getting up to walk to the kitchen with him.

They talked about ranching all through dinner and as

soon as she put the last dish in the dishwasher she turned to him.

"I'd better go now. I know you've probably got emails and texts and things to answer since you've been away from the office so long. You'll be up and going early tomorrow, I guess."

He nodded. "Be glad to have you stay."

"Thanks but I've got to go."

He walked beside her to her car.

"Good luck with this, Jake. I sure hope you find that deed."

"I do, too. I'd like to face Pete Milan with it. I'll have to settle for handing it over to his daughter, but the judge will hear about it. If we find it," he added.

She slid behind the wheel and he closed her door.

"Thanks for coming by. It's always good to see you, Lindsay."

"Send me a text if you find anything."

"I will. All of you will get one. I dug as much and as fast as I could today and I will again every day. This is our chance to hunt for that deed."

"Night, Jake. Thanks for the steak."

He stepped back from the pickup and watched her drive out of sight, the red taillights disappearing around a curve, before he turned to go into the house.

He wanted to look once more at the maps and aerial photos. He hoped they weren't missing the right location. He longed to get the deed and get some Milan land. It would be payback, but also, it might be a dandy place to drill.

He thought about Madison. Part of him hadn't ever gotten over her. He still couldn't view her the way he did other women he had dated and then told goodbye.

This opportunity had come when he didn't have a woman in his life. Maybe that heightened the impact of seeing her. In spite of all his hurt and anger over the years, she still made his heart pound and he had to battle desire.

She still felt something, too. It was obvious. She wasn't happy that she did. That was also obvious. Anger simmered in her constantly, little flares of it showing, although he thought they both were doing a commendable job of being civil to each other.

He wanted her, wanted to kiss her, to seduce her. In spite of his fury, his body still responded to her.

Could he seduce her and then walk away? Perhaps the anger would enable him to do that. Time would tell.

Her room was still cloaked in predawn darkness when her cell phone rang. Madison reached for the phone and groaned. She ached all over.

"Good morning." Jake's voice was cheerful, filled with eagerness and energy, and she wanted to hang up on him. "Are you going today?"

"Yes," she mumbled and heard him chuckle.

"A little sore?"

"Yes, I am." She made an effort to try to stay awake.

"I hate to say, 'I told you so.' I can give you a rubdown if you want me to come early this morning."

"No," she said, coming more awake. "How can you be so cheerful?"

He laughed softly. "I'll see you in a little while."

She switched off her phone and sat up, groaning and rubbing her shoulder. "Ugh." She could imagine Jake arriving looking fresh and energetic and eager to go. With a whimper she stepped out of bed. The smell of coffee was faint and she guessed Jessie Lou already had breakfast ready. Moving carefully, Madison headed to her closet to get her clothes for the day.

When she entered the kitchen, more tempting smells

filled the house. "Good morning," she told Jessie Lou, who turned and pushed glasses up her nose with her wrist.

"Morning. This is an early start."

"Everything smells good."

"Help yourself. I'll cut and toast some of my bread and get you an egg right away. There's orange juice."

"I told Jake he and his men could stay here tonight. He accepted the offer and he'll be here for dinner."

"I'll be glad to see him."

"Can't say the same for my family. Dad already called to tell me I'm making a mistake," Madison said as she poured a glass of orange juice.

"Your dad dislikes the Calhouns in a giant way and he doesn't trust any of them."

"He feels strongly about the Calhouns, that's for sure."

"The judge had a run-in with them when he was young. He and Jake's dad both bid on all that land that Lindsay Calhoun has now. Mr. Calhoun won. The judge has never forgiven him."

"That's too bad Dad didn't get the land because it adjoins Tony's ranch. I don't even remember."

"You were away in college."

Madison tilted her head. "You know what happened. Do you think I shouldn't have let him on the ranch?"

"It's not for me to say. I haven't seen Mister Jake in a long time. I'll tell you after I see him. I suppose I will see him since you asked him to stay here. I always liked him until he up and hurt you," Jessie Lou said, staring up at Madison through wire-rim bifocals.

"That's in the past," Madison replied. "What about the lunches? Can I help you with them?"

"Everything is packed in the picnic basket or the big cooler. You have another cooler for water and a cooler of bottled drinks," she said, turning off the stove and spooning the scrambled eggs onto a plate, which she handed to Madison.

"Thanks, Jessie Lou," Madison said, getting her toast and sitting to eat breakfast. Jessie Lou had already placed a bowl of sliced strawberries, kiwi and blueberries on the table. Madison glanced at the clock, wanting to be ready when Jake arrived.

She ate quickly and got showered and dressed. An hour later she watched him emerge from his truck.

To her annoyance he looked just the way she had expected. Sexy and handsome in his Western shirt, tight jeans and Stetson. His stride was long and brisk.

"Good morning," he said. "You don't look as if you suffered any from yesterday."

"I'm great," she said, smiling at him while hoping she really looked that way. "Ready to go?"

"Absolutely," he replied. "You lead the way again."

"Sure. According to our plans, we'll move along the same side of Rocky Creek today."

"See you there."

She watched him walk away, her gaze running across his broad shoulders, down to his narrow waist and long legs. Even with all the cowboys, he stood out because he was the tallest and the best-looking and had a manner about him that conveyed his confidence. She realized how long she'd stood watching him and climbed into her truck where Darren and Stoney waited.

The day was a repeat of the previous one except for the slight differences of lunch and she didn't encounter a snake.

Jake dropped the men at the Milan bunkhouse and then drove to her house. She stood waiting at the back gate, holding it open.

He picked up a satchel he had brought and locked his

pickup. He waved the bag. "I assume the invitation still stands?"

"Of course. Jessie Lou is cooking and I think she stayed this late just to say hello to you."

"Can't wait. She is one fine cook," he said, closing the gate behind them. "You need your latch fixed," he said, jiggling the gate.

"I know. I'll show you where you can put your things and where you'll be staying. Come on." His wavy hair was tangled and he hung his hat on the rack in her back entry-way as he came in.

Enticing smells of baking bread and a pot roast min-gled in the air. They entered the kitchen and Jessie Lou set a covered bowl on the counter, turning to smile at Jake.

"Mister Jake, I think you've grown even taller."

Jake gave her a big smile. "Jessie Lou, it's good to see the best cook in the state of Texas. I haven't forgotten a single meal of yours."

She giggled and her blue eyes sparkled. Her mass of hair was always caught up and tied behind her head with curls springing free all around her face. Madison realized that Jake hadn't seen her since her red hair had turned white. She still had her freckles and still was short, thin and wiry in spite of all her wonderful cooking.

"How have you been, Jessie Lou?" Jake asked.

"I'm fine and you look mighty fine, too."

"I do all right. How many grandkids?"

She beamed. "I have sixteen grandchildren and four great-grandchildren."

"No way—you don't look a day older."

"Then you need to see an eye doctor soon. My hair is white now."

"Prematurely, and it becomes you. Thanks for cook-ing dinner tonight. I can't wait and it smells marvelous."

"I'm glad you're here," she said, glancing briefly at Madison. "Now this world seems right again."

Jake grinned. "After dinner I'll tell you if you still have the magic touch in your cooking. We're searching for buried treasure, but I think the real treasure is right here in the kitchen."

She giggled and turned to stir something cooking on top of the stove.

"Would you like a cold beer or some tea or pop?" Madison asked him.

"The cold beer," he said and she retrieved one from the fridge.

"I for one would like to shower and clean up before dinner," she said. "Then I'll have a glass of wine."

"Good plan."

"I'll show you where you will stay while you're here," Madison said. "We'll be back, Jessie Lou," she stated, leading him out of the kitchen. "There's a guest suite right down the hall and my suite is upstairs." She led him into a sitting room in his guest suite.

"If you need anything, just text me. I think you'll find towels and most everything you need." She glanced down at the satchel he carried. "That's not a very big bag. If you need anything we may have some new shirts that will fit you. Look in the dresser drawers and help yourself. There aren't any extra jeans, though, and I'm afraid I can't furnish you with underwear."

"That's all right. I won't wear any," he answered. Although he didn't smile, she knew he was teasing.

"Yes, you will," she answered recklessly. "You used to wear underwear."

"Well, if you're real curious, you can always find out tonight," he said and this time there was a twinkle in his eyes and she realized she had started this. They were flirting and getting on dangerous ground. She did not want to flirt, have fun or get emotionally involved with him ever again.

"I think I started something that has to end now," she told him. "See you in the kitchen or thereabouts. If I'm not there, step outside on the patio."

"Sure," he said, giving her a curious look.

She hurried away, feeling her skin tingling. She fought the urge to turn around to see if he was still standing there watching her because she had not heard him move. She went around a corner and let out her breath. "Don't flirt with him," she whispered to herself.

She picked up a glass of ice water and went upstairs to her suite to shower and change. She swiftly washed and combed out her hair, blow-drying it and straightening it so it fell over her shoulders and down her back. She pulled on jeans, a blue knit shirt and sandals and went to the kitchen to see about the dinner that Jessie Lou was getting ready.

"Ah, you look pretty now," Jessie Lou said, smiling at her before turning back to continue stirring gravy in a pan on the gas stove.

Soon Madison heard boot heels and in seconds, Jake entered. He looked as energetic and virile as he had early this morning. When her insides clutched, she hoped she didn't have any visible reaction to the mere sight of him.

His gaze drifted over her. "You look great. You don't look as if you could have been climbing around the creek bank since sunrise."

"Thank you. I definitely feel as if I have been."

He wore a short-sleeved navy knit shirt tucked into his jeans. "It felt great to get the shower. Jessie Lou, this is the best-smelling kitchen ever. Whatever you're cooking, I can't wait."

She giggled, looking at him intently as she grinned. "I hope you like it. It's not quite ready yet."

"We'll wait until you say it's time," Jake answered as she turned back to her cooking.

Madison poured glasses of wine that they carried to the patio. They sat only ten minutes before Jessie Lou appeared. "It's on the table," she announced.

They came in to eat and Jessie Lou untied her apron. "Everything is on the table and the pie is on the counter. I'll be going now and please leave the dishes. I'll get them in the morning."

"That'll be fine. Thank you so much," Madison said.

"It was good to see you," Jake told the older woman. "And thank you for this dinner and double thanks for the pie."

Jessie Lou giggled and smiled. "You haven't eaten a bite yet."

"I know."

She giggled again and turned away, disappearing into the utility room. In minutes the back door closed and a lock clicked as she left the house.

They helped themselves to the pot roast with thick brown gravy, fluffy white rolls and creamy mashed potatoes sprinkled with tiny bits of green chives. Slender green asparagus had been steamed along with slices of carrots.

"She is still the best cook ever," Jake said as he ate. "This roast is tender and delicious."

"I have to agree," Madison said. "I'm lucky to have her because some of her children want her to come live with them."

"I would, too, if she were my mother."

"You just want a cook."

"Have you ever seen her without a smile?"

"She can get angry," Madison said, remembering when she had to tell Jessie Lou that Jake had left her on her wedding day. Jessie hadn't been smiles then and she had held Madison when she had cried, something her own mother hadn't done. Jessie Lou had kept shaking her head and repeating, "I would never have thought him to be mean like that."

Madison realized Jake was talking to her and focused on him, forgetting Jessie Lou and letting Jake charm her through dinner.

They sat on the patio until long after dark had come and the outside lights and pool lights came on automatically.

By ten o'clock, Madison was thirsty.

"Would you like iced tea, or wine, beer…or whiskey? What would you like?" Madison asked him.

"I'll just take another cold beer," he said, getting up to follow her into the kitchen. "I have some cashews we can have with our drinks," she said, standing on tiptoe, trying to reach a bowl on a high shelf. "I want this bowl—"

His hands closed on her waist to move her away. She turned abruptly.

"I'll get it," he said, but when she faced him, he inhaled and stood still. His dark gaze enveloped her and she couldn't get her breath. All she could think was that he looked as if he intended to kiss her. Her heart drummed a pounding rhythm and she couldn't move, not her hands from his arms or her eyes from his gaze. His glance lowered to her mouth and she leaned toward him. His fingers wound in her hair while his other hand slipped around her waist and pulled her against him.

The moment she pressed against him she was lost. She wanted his kiss in spite of the constant smoldering anger that flared up anytime she was reminded of the past. At that moment she couldn't move away if her life depended on it.

Desire blazed in his eyes. "Damn, Madison," he whispered, scowling. He wound his fingers in her hair and pulled slightly so she had to turn her face up.

His mouth came down on hers hard, his tongue thrusting deep into her mouth and then stroking hers slowly, teasing.

She moaned while her insides knotted with longing. His arm tightened around her waist while he bent over her, tasting, branding her with his possessive kiss. She wasn't aware of wrapping her arm around his neck until she was clinging tightly to him. He was solid, muscled, much more so than she remembered. His kiss was stormy and passionate. She kissed him back as if she had been waiting for this moment since the night he'd walked out on her, jilting her the day she had expected to be saying her wedding vows.

When he leaned over farther, she held him tightly, kissing him in return, unable to resist winding her fingers in his hair. Her heart pounded harder, louder, and a moan escaped from deep in her throat. Her flesh heated, burned, ached for his touch. The anger, the hurt and pain and dreadful memories all were replaced by desire.

Her world narrowed until there was only this man, this kiss. She poured herself into the kiss, taking everything she'd missed all these years. Jake slid his mouth from hers, hungrily nipping at her lips, her ear, her throat. Like a dying man she gasped for air. The cool air was like a blanket over a flame, smothering her ardor. As it rushed into her heated lungs, she realized what she was doing. She broke away, stepping out of his embrace and gasping for breath.

"I never meant for that to happen," she said. She ran from him, picking up her wine and heading into the adjoining family room that overlooked the patio and pool and gardens.

She stood looking at the blue pool, trying to get her breath and ignore the overpowering longing that shook her. Torn between wanting him and hating her loss of control, she sipped the wine. She thought she was over wanting him, beyond responding to him. His kiss shattered that illusion. She didn't want to yearn for his kisses, to ache to be held by him.

He didn't want it, either. She had heard the whispered expletive before he kissed her. Should she tell him to get out and go back to his ranch or to the bunkhouse with his men? She was tempted, but she didn't want him to know that she cared that much, that the kiss had rattled her that badly.

Making an effort to pull herself together so she could overlook and make light of the incident as if his kiss had not disturbed her and meant nothing, she took deep breaths.

She heard him moving around in the kitchen and when she turned he was standing in front of her, with his beer and the cashews in the bowl he had gotten from the cabinet.

He placed the bowl on the coffee table and they sat on opposing couches, neither speaking for a moment. She sipped her wine and tried not to watch him. She was unsuccessful. Jake looked relaxed, his long legs stretched out, crossed at his ankles. He didn't look as if he felt any inner turmoil or was racked with desire. Was he making an effort as much as she to appear indifferent or did he really feel that way?

She would never have an answer. Her insides churned. The kiss had stirred too many old feelings that she had thought were gone forever. She wanted to fling accusations at him and ask him why, but she wasn't going there. She intended to avoid a confrontation with him. She didn't want him to realize how much she still hurt over what he had done.

Instead, she talked about the fruitless search they'd endured this second day. It was the most innocuous topic she could think of. Imagine that, she thought. The generations-old feud that had involved murder and deception was a *safe* topic. But then anything that didn't involve his kiss was safe.

"I still think we're searching in the right area, but I also am aware that we could be on the wrong side of the ranch or it could be on your ranch," she said, hating the huskiness in her voice. She cleared her throat.

"That would be a hoot if both families had spent well over one hundred years searching and digging on the wrong ranch."

"It wouldn't be funny to some members of our families. Not to the ones who searched so much and so hard."

"No, it wouldn't. I hope we're not doing that."

"There's always a strong possibility that your old map and the legend, the rumors, everything might all just be a hoax."

"I have to at least try to find where they had the gunfight. That part of the story sounds like something that actually occurred." As they sat there talking about the day, she said the right words, responded to his comments in the right manner, but her errant thoughts betrayed her. Nothing could keep her mind from wandering back to the kiss. It had taken hold of her and wouldn't let her go. His kiss had opened a door that she had kept closed since high school. Desire simmered in her, but anger was bubbling inside her and she just wanted to end this night before she said things to him she shouldn't.

She stood up abruptly, cutting off what he said and she didn't hear. "I'm turning in. It's been a long day."

He stood, too, with his hands on his hips. His gaze lowered to her mouth and tingles disturbed her. She turned and left the room before her anger spilled over. Drawing in deep breaths, she reached the stairs…but there she lost the battle raging inside her. She turned and went back.

He stood much as she had left him except he was by the windows with his back to her. She wondered if he was actually looking at the pool or lost in thought.

"Jake," she said, crossing the room to stand near him

as he turned to face her. She couldn't control her fury any longer.

"I think I've waited long enough. Why did you walk out on me when we were supposed to run away and get married?"

Five

He narrowed his eyes while anger stabbed him. "Madison, you know damn well why I did. What are you up to now?"

"No, I don't know why," she snapped. "I'm not up to anything. I want an explanation."

He stared at her. As rosy spots flushed her cheeks, her fists clenched at her sides. Shock buffeted him. "I never doubted your dad for one minute. I called and you didn't answer."

"I didn't get any call from you," she said, frowning. "What are you talking about my dad? He didn't have anything to do with that night."

"The hell he didn't. And I did call you and you didn't answer."

"I was home waiting for you," she said in a strangled voice filled with anger.

"Don't put on an act with me," he snapped in disgust.

Why was she doing this now? He had never known her to lie to him.

"What I'm feeling is no act. I'm as truthful right now as I can possibly be."

"I called repeatedly and never got anyone."

"My dad? I sat beside the phone and never got a call from you. You're lying, Jake," she said, grinding out the accusation.

Fury made him shake. He closed the space between them and wound his fingers in her hair to turn her head up so he could look directly into her eyes. "Your dad told me that you had agreed you would not run away and get married. You agreed not to elope when he offered to put two hundred thousand dollars into a bank account for you and it would be your money for college and later. He offered to jump-start your art career and get you in the best galleries in Texas and on the West Coast if you would not get married."

All color drained from her face and she narrowed her eyes. But anger blazed in him, hot and ferocious, because she obviously had taken the money, later got help with her art career and agreed to what her father wanted.

"Yeah, you did," he spat out. "You wanted money more than wanting to marry me." He pulled her closer, his grip tighter on her hair. "I don't know why you started this charade, but it's a damn poor one. There's no need to dig up our past. Not now."

She jerked her head away from him. "Let me go," she snapped and he turned her loose. He strode across the room, wanting to get away from her before he said hurtful things that he'd regret. She had started this and now it was like a monster within him; he had to get away before it broke free. He reached the door before her voice stopped him.

"My dad gave me that money for college and he wanted

to help me get my art career started," Madison said stiffly. "He didn't do it to get me to call off our wedding."

Jake stopped and turned to face her again. She hadn't moved, just stood where she had been. "It didn't have anything to do with you. He told me he had opened an account for me, that he hoped I took only what I needed and perhaps a little for extras, but kept most of the money intact so I would have it when I got out of college. It had nothing to do with you or with marrying you. Absolutely nothing."

"The hell it didn't. It was a payoff. He flat out told me that he offered it to you and told you to make a choice between me or the money."

"He would never do any such thing," she said fiercely.

Pain, sharp and intense, stabbed him. Had he been bluffed by her dad? Even worse, had he been gullible enough to believe her father?

"Madison, if you're lying now—"

"I'm certainly not. Why would I? Dad gave me money for college." She frowned and stared at Jake as if she had never seen him before in her life. "My father would never hurt me that way. He wouldn't do such an underhanded thing."

Shocked, Jake stared at her. Her father had lied to him. A man who was a pillar of the community, a leader. Judge Milan had lied to him and to his daughter. And since he was regarded as so ethical and honest, he had expected to get away with the lie.

Rage made Jake clench his hands and grind his teeth. How much Pete Milan must have laughed to himself at how easily he had put that over on the two of them.

"My dad would never have hurt me like that," she repeated, her voice shaking with anger. "I don't know what you hope to gain."

"Your dad did exactly what I said he did. The judge had a reputation for honesty. Everyone in the county trusted him. I trusted him. If you're telling me the truth, I was suckered in, a gullible kid that he easily manipulated."

"I don't believe you," she said. Her fists clenched until her knuckles turned white, and the color in her cheeks now suffused her entire face. "My father would never, ever hurt me like that. He would have come to me and tried to talk me out of eloping." She shook her head as she frowned. "There's no point in going over all this. We'll finish our hunt and then I hope I never see you again," she said sharply. She spun around to hurry out of the room and he let her go.

He stood there, shock and rage warring within him alongside disbelief and acceptance. Had her dad tricked him into believing she had taken the bribe? Or would she not admit the truth—that she'd taken the money and the promise of a boost in getting her art shown instead of marriage?

If he believed her now, it would be the second time he had been taken in by a Milan. No, he wasn't going to accept her explanation. It had been a payoff, pure and simple. She had to have known the conditions and agreed to them. How else would she have not figured out what her dad was up to?

Jake's fists clenched until he realized what he was doing and opened his hands. If only they could find the treasure, the bones and the deed. He would be happy to flash the deed in her face and take her land from her.

He strode to the suite she had given him and slammed the door, standing in the center of the living area to take in deep breaths and blow them out. He had to get out and move, to work off his fury and frustration.

He left again, heading outside to jog down the ranch road toward the highway. He swore quietly when the back gate stuck and made a mental note to repair it when it was daylight.

Though he jogged faster, the memories of that fateful night caught up with him. In his mind he relived the painful hours when he'd called her repeatedly and no one had answered until he finally gave up and stopped calling. "She's lying," he mumbled to himself. Why hadn't she answered the phone if she had been so innocent?

Darkness enveloped him even though the moon shone bright. She had to know that she couldn't hide the truth or keep saying that he had never called her.

When he ran back to the ranch after his third circuit to the highway, he returned to his suite to shower. Afterward he hurried to the library to spread out the maps and papers to look again for a likely place for the hidden treasure and deed. One thing was certain: he would never get another chance to search after this one.

If he found a deed to part of her ranch, it would help ease his anger and regrets. No matter what happened, he would never be able to forget her.

Jake looked on the new day as another day of opportunity. He dressed quickly and left his room.

As he entered the front hall, tempting smells of hot bread and steaming coffee enticed him. He followed the scents into the kitchen and saw her seated in the breakfast area, with her back to him. He looked her over, taking in the snug jeans that fit her sexy backside and long legs. She wore her brown boots and a long-sleeved green shirt. Her hair was in a ponytail, tied with a green scarf, and he remembered when she had worn ponytails as a high school cheerleader.

Helping himself, he carried his plate of scrambled eggs with fresh basil, toast and a bowl of berries to the breakfast area. "May I join you?"

"I'm finished," she said, standing and picking up her plate that still had a lot of food on it. "Here's the paper."

He caught her wrist. She stopped instantly, her eyes narrowing. "What?"

"Let's try to get through the rest of this week in a civil manner the way it has been between us. Then we'll go our separate ways and probably avoid seeing each other for years again." He wanted to stand, move close and be more commanding in his request because his patience was frayed and she was obviously holding her temper in check.

"Of course," she said, jerking free, but annoying him because he would have released her anyway.

He watched her hips as she left the room until he realized what he was doing and looked away. Why did she still attract him? After last night he didn't want to be around her, yet physically, he was as attracted to her as he had been when he had been an eighteen-year-old the year they started dating.

Memories tugged at him of her leading cheers, dancing and jumping, turning flips, smiling with her ponytail swinging behind her or bouncing with each step. He had been so in love, he wouldn't have thought he would ever get over wanting her. Now all he felt was anger and lust.

He ate in silence, looking at the paper, but still lost in thought about her. When it was almost time to leave, he got up, chastising himself. There should be only one thought in his head. Finding that deed.

Madison came down the stairs and saw Jake getting ready. His brown wide-brimmed hat was squarely on his head, his gloves were half tucked into his hip pocket next to the pocketknife she knew he always carried. She walked in silence beside him until they reached the back door. As she started to punch in the code for the alarm, Jake stepped in front of her to block her.

Furious, she lashed out at him, "What do you think you're doing?"

Jake stood too close, his proximity disturbing her. Her heart raced and in spite of all the anger she felt, there still was a running current of awareness of him as an appealing man. How could she be furious with him and want him so badly?

More than ever, he towered over her, seeming inches taller than he had been when they had dated. In spite of his appeal, she wanted to get away from him and never see him again. She wanted him out of her life so she could forget him forever, instead of being in constant turmoil and having a reaction to his mere presence.

"Before you spend much time being even angrier with me than before, why don't you ask your dad what ultimatum he gave me? Just ask him what he told me you had agreed to do. While you're at it, ask him what threats he made, too."

She shook with anger and clenched her fists. "You're saying my father threatened you with physical harm?"

"No, more like financial problems. He had the power. You ask him what threats he made. And you should know me well enough to know that I would never make any such statements to you if they weren't true. I've never lied to you, Madison," he said, his dark brown eyes holding fiery anger that seemed to match what she felt.

She glared back at him another few tense seconds before he stepped away. She punched in the alarm and as he reached around her to open the door, she stepped outside without looking back. Adding to her anger, she had been aware of brushing her shoulder against him, of his arm almost touching her as he held the door.

She climbed into her truck and watched him walk to his in his long-legged stride that covered the ground swiftly. He was a tall, handsome rancher, his boots adding to his height. He was also a powerful energy mogul from an old-moneyed family. There was no way her father could have done anything to really hurt him financially.

When everyone was ready to go, she took the lead again. It was an effort to think about the coming day and searching for a buried treasure that most likely did not exist. She wanted this search to be over and done and was tempted to give it up now, tell him to get off her land and let it go.

He would accuse her of giving her word and permission and then backing out of it because of spite. He'd be right, and she didn't want to stoop to spite. His confrontation before they had left her house worried and shook her. Jake had never lied to her until that night, when he hadn't shown up after asking her to elope with him.

Otherwise, he had always been honest with her, and she had always trusted him. Her father had kept his bargain— from the time of her college graduation, she had risen to prominence in the Western art world, having showings in the most ideal galleries for her work and then opening her own successful galleries. She had a name and a following early in her career. If Jake was telling the truth, she had achieved it all at the cost of the love of her life.

She couldn't believe her father would ever stoop to doing what Jake accused him of. Never. He was a judge, had been a banker, was trusted and respected by family, friends and people from all over the state of Texas. There was no way he could have done what Jake had said. Her insides churned. How could Jake accuse her father of doing those things and then tell her to ask her father?

Maybe Jake was counting on the fact that he knew she would not ask her dad.

Then again, if there was no truth in what Jake said, he wouldn't push her to quiz her father.

The more she thought about it, the more concerned she became. She looked in the rearview mirror and saw Jake at the wheel of the truck behind her. Was he telling the truth? Knowledge of her father made her say no to her question instantly. Knowledge of Jake yielded an affirmative answer. Lost in thought, she hit a rock and the truck bounced badly. "Sorry," she said to Stoney and Darren, her passengers.

Embarrassed, she glanced in the rearview mirror to see Jake avoid the rock.

When they reached the place where they would leave the trucks, she retrieved her hat and her backpack, and turned to face Jake, who approached her. He had left the motor running in his truck and the door open and she wondered why.

"I studied the maps again last night and there's another place I want to look that isn't far from here, in an arroyo that may no longer exist. I'll go by myself so as to not waste everyone's time, but I thought you might want to send one of your hands with me."

All the time he talked, she looked at his lips and remembered his kisses. Realizing what she had been doing, she looked away.

"Stoney, do you mind going with him?"

"'Course not. Be glad to. Maybe I can help."

"I'll show you the map and what we're looking for," Jake said as the two men walked away.

She wondered how late he had sat up studying the map and if he had been unable to sleep because of the harsh words said between them. As she retrieved a shovel from the truck, she glanced back to see Jake turn around to head back the way they had come and she wondered where he was going. She would ask Stoney tonight.

The men who worked for her had been with them for a long time and were as familiar with the ranch as she was.

She wouldn't have a chance this week to go to Dallas to see her parents. It would have to be next week when the search was over and Jake and his men went back to the Calhoun ranch. Not by any stretch could she imagine her father threatening Jake. She couldn't imagine a threat that Jake would have responded to at nineteen. It all was impossible, but she had to know and the sooner, the better.

She realized she was supposed to lead the way and without Jake she would have to give everyone orders, including the men from his ranch.

She tried to focus on where she had intended to start digging today and realized she must have walked right past the place because she had been so lost in thought over Jake.

Embarrassed, she stopped to look around and turned to Darren. "Sorry, but I think we have to turn back. I think I've passed where we should start digging today."

"Whatever you say. We'll follow you."

Feeling the heat rise in her cheeks, she headed back to walk toward where they had parked. In minutes she held up her hand and everyone stopped.

"This is the area for today and all of you have a rough map of where you'll look."

The men fanned out to where each one thought he was supposed to search. She studied the copy of the map she had marked and moved closer to the creek. She began to dig and in seconds Russ, one of Jake's men, blocked her way. Pausing, she looked up at him.

Stocky with sandy hair that seemed to be swallowed up by his oversize hat, Russ faced her. "Ms. Milan, you don't need to dig. We'll do that."

"I can dig with the rest of you."

He shook his head. "My boss will have my neck if I let you dig. May I use your shovel?"

She didn't want to argue with him because his intentions were nice and she didn't want him in trouble with Jake, although at this point, she didn't care for Jake to have any say about how she lived her life. Handing Russ her shovel, she walked over to start moving away a pile of river rocks.

She watched Russ dig swiftly, moving more dirt faster than she had been able to do. She really wanted to find the treasure, the bones and be done with this.

If they didn't find the treasure and bones, Jake would never be satisfied and she could imagine that he would think she would continue searching without him after this week or two.

By the end of the day, she was exhausted. She had moved smaller rocks so others could dig, trying to concentrate on the physical labor and forget the fight with Jake. By quitting time, she was worn out. When her cell phone jingled and she heard Jake's voice, her heartbeat quickened. She still reacted physically to him in the same manner she had before their fight.

"Ready to head back?" he asked. "It'll be dark before we get there."

"Yes. We're leaving now. We'll meet you at the house."

He clicked off without a goodbye. She didn't want to spend the evening with him and intended to get something to eat and take it upstairs. At some point in the course of the day she'd made the decision to drive to Dallas tomorrow and talk to her father so she could settle this once and for all.

She refused to contemplate how it would be if Jake had been truthful. She had believed, loved and relied on her dad all her life. Her parents had done so much for her, she couldn't imagine her father doing anything to hurt her and to threaten Jake.

When they arrived at the house she went inside without waiting for him. She didn't want to be with him another minute. Nor did she want to hear about his day. If he had found anything significant, he would have told her or Stoney would have.

When she reached the back gate, the latch stuck. Determined, she jiggled it and tugged at it. He came up beside her. "Let me try," he said.

"I can't remember to have that fixed. We can go to a side door."

"I'll fix it as soon as I can. In the meantime—" He jumped over the fence, clearing the gate and landing on the other side. Before she realized what he intended, he turned, his hands closing on her waist, and he lifted her up and over the gate easily.

She grabbed his upper arms, feeling the flex of solid biceps. Startled, she looked at him and he gazed back into her eyes and the moment changed. The anger and arguments no longer held meaning. For an instant, he held her, and as she clung to him, she remembered his kisses while sparks ignited her desire.

Setting her on her feet, he released her, leaving her bereft. "I'll fix that damn latch," he said, heading for the house.

"Jake, wait," she called as she caught up with him. "I'll get Terry to fix the gate. I'll call him tonight."

"Forget it. I'll do it after dinner when it's cooler." They walked toward the back door together.

"Jessie Lou said she left dinner in the oven. Whenever you eat, you can just put any leftovers back in the oven." She wanted to make it clear she didn't intend to eat dinner with him.

"Fine," he said, holding the door for her after she unlocked it. As she switched off the alarm, he passed her.

"Jake," she called. When he turned around she said, "I'm going to skip the search tomorrow. All of you can go ahead. I'll be in touch by cell phone."

"Going to Dallas?" he asked, looking down at her.

Surprised he had so easily guessed she wanted to talk to her father, she nodded. "Yes. I want to know the truth. The trip will take most of the day."

"We'll get along and your hands will be with us so they can report back to you on everything we do," he said in a tone dripping with sarcasm. He started to walk away and then he paused. "You can fly in my jet. I'll tell my pilot. It'll save you the long drive there and back."

"Thank you, but I can drive," she said, wanting to avoid letting him do anything for her.

"Don't be ridiculous. This is no trouble. What time do you want to leave?"

"About nine in the morning," she said after a moment's hesitation, deciding it was silly to turn down his offer when it would save her hours of driving. "I'll have to see him after his work and I want to stop to see my brother because I haven't seen Nick for a while."

"Going to see the politician, Representative Milan. How's he getting along?"

"Nick keeps really busy. It's been hard for him losing Karen and the baby. They were both so excited over the prospect of a baby."

"Yeah. It was a drunk driver if I remember reading about it."

"Yes. All three were killed. After the accident Nick poured himself into politics and he's more interested in Washington now than he was before."

"What about Wyatt and Tony? More political aspirations?"

"Not at all. Until the town gets full rights in 2015 to the Lavita Wrenville house, Wyatt will stay sheriff of Verity County. Sometime in the not too distant future, Wyatt will return to ranching."

"And Tony got a law degree, didn't he?"

"Of course, but no one will pry Tony off the ranch. He hung a shingle out at the ranch for one year to pacify Mom and Dad and then tossed it aside. He said that should take care of the family superstitions."

One of Jake's dark eyebrows arched higher. "How so?"

"You've forgotten. We not only have the legend of the buried gold at the family ranch, but there's an old Milan legend that all male Milans have to go into the field of law or be doomed. They've all gone to law school."

Jake shook his head. "That's superstition. No one's doomed if they don't get into the field of law, practicing or enforcing it or, I suppose in Nick's case, creating laws. I can't imagine they are doomed if they choose another profession."

"That's what Tony thinks."

"So now you have what—four lawyers in your immediate family? One is a judge. One is a sheriff. One is a legislator, a representative to the Texas legislature, and one is a retired lawyer after one year of practice who is a rancher and does the rodeo circuit. One out of five couldn't stand the law profession—that's not bad."

"My dad loves being a judge. Ditto Wyatt being a sheriff. He's a natural for that job. I'm sure Nick will be in Washington, someday, but he would like nothing better than to be a full-time rancher."

"I can understand how he feels," Jake said.

"Tony makes no bones about it. My grandmother, Mom and Dad, Nick, they all browbeat him into getting that law degree. He has a double major—law and animal husbandry. He spent one year satisfying those members of the family and that's the last he's opened a law book or anything else regarding law unless he's had to for his ranch business. He is one hundred percent cowboy."

"I envy him."

"Anyway, I'd like to see Nick, maybe have lunch with him and go spend some time with Mom before Dad gets home," she said, realizing her anger was fading slightly the longer she stood and talked with Jake.

"Drive to the airport in Verity and get the flight there. A limo will be waiting when you get to Dallas."

"Thanks."

He shrugged.

She still didn't want to eat with him. If he had lied in any manner about her dad, she would stop this search for treasure and tell Jake to get off the ranch and not return. She suspected each one had his own version of the story, but if Jake had lied, she didn't want to deal with him five more minutes. She couldn't imagine he was right, but the nagging doubt persisted because he had been convincing.

Washing her hands, she got her dinner, serving herself to a pot of steaming chili and tamales, taking only one tamale and covering it with a little chili. She had lost her appetite. She poured ice water and carried her dinner to the study, closing the door to avoid Jake and eat alone.

First, she phoned her parents and talked to her mother before talking to her dad to ask if they would be home late tomorrow afternoon. Her mother was eager to see her and told her to stay as long as she could.

Next she called her brother Nick and they agreed to meet for lunch. She hurt for him when she broke the connection. It had been almost two years since the car wreck, but the loss was not one Nick could ever completely get over.

Madison carried her dishes to the kitchen and was relieved to see Jake wasn't there.

Would she regret learning the truth? Either way, she would be hurt and angry.

It would be another sleepless night, but by this time tomorrow, she would have some answers to her questions about Jake.

Six

She entered the kitchen by seven and Jessie Lou turned to greet her, her eyes filled with curiosity. "Jake has already left for today."

"I'm going to Dallas to see my folks today."

"Ahh. That will be good," Jessie Lou said and turned back to the pie crust she was making.

Madison stared at Jessie Lou, realizing while she kept quiet and in the background, she saw and heard a lot.

"Jessie Lou, Jake told me he didn't walk out on me on our wedding day because he didn't want to marry me. He said he was told to."

With deliberation Jessie Lou washed her hands, dried them and then turned to face Madison. For once, the woman had lost her smile. "Then it probably is time for you to find out the truth."

"Do you know it?" Madison asked because she had always felt as close to Jessie Lou in some ways as she did her mother.

"No, I don't. I've just always wondered. I think it's good that you go."

Jessie Lou's answer shook Madison because she had expected to have the cook tell her she was being foolish to even think about questioning her parents.

"I can't believe my dad would do anything to hurt me," Madison whispered, but Jessie Lou heard her.

"Well, it's time you know. You and Jake were very young. Very young."

"You do know something."

Jessie Lou shook her head. "No. I would have told you as badly as you were hurt. Maybe not right away, but I never would have waited all these years and let the hurt fester in you the way it has. I see the way the two of you look at each other. It's time the truth comes out."

"I can't believe it."

"It's best to go ask because now you'll wonder until you do." She turned back to the pie crust.

Madison had lost her appetite and carried her dishes to the counter. Jessie Lou looked at her. "Are you all right?"

Madison nodded. "I think so. I'm going to get ready to go. Jake is letting me fly in his plane. His pilot will be waiting."

Jessie Lou nodded. "I will be thinking about you— both of you."

Feeling far more worried, Madison left to get dressed.

At eleven, she rode in a limo to a restaurant in Dallas where she told the driver she would call him when she needed him again. She hurried inside the glass-enclosed round building. In the lobby Nick stepped up to greet her and give her a light hug. Three inches over six feet tall, Nick oozed personality. He was a politician through and through and she had heard their dad talk to Nick about a presidential run someday. She couldn't imagine, yet Nick had won every race he had entered from Most Popular Boy in the Sixth Grade to his reelection to the Texas legislature.

Gold cuff links complemented his tailor-made white shirt. He wore a brown suit and a dark brown tie. Whether it was a working day or not, Nick was always camera-ready.

His dark brown hair was the color of hers and his eyes were blue. There the similarity ended because his face was longer, his hair wavy, his nose had a slight crook from being broken playing football in a neighborhood game. Nick had perfect, snowy teeth, along with a smile that probably helped him win votes. People had always liked him and he seemed full of life, able to enjoy himself more than most people. Every day was an adventure for him and she had often been amazed by his perpetual optimism and energy. He had changed after the loss of his pregnant wife and their baby, but to her relief his cheerfulness was beginning to return to him.

Hugging her, Nick smiled as he stepped away. "Thanks for calling. I'm glad to see you. I've got a table waiting."

They looked at their menus briefly, ordered, and while they waited, he smiled again. "I saw you drive up. So what's the deal with the limo? The art must be doing extremely well."

"Jake Calhoun let me fly in his private jet today and he arranged for the limo. That's his chauffeur."

"After the heartbreak Jake caused you, I don't see why you agreed to let him search on your ranch."

"I still think of it as the family ranch, even though Dad has put it in my name. It would benefit us, too, if Jake finds anything. Today, some of our men are with him, so he's not out there looking without Milan interests being protected. And I've gone with them every day until today."

"When we were at Verity High, I liked Jake, but after

what he did to you, I haven't trusted him or wanted to be around him or have any dealings with him."

"Sounds funny, coming from you, because you're always friendly to him," she said, unable to argue with him. "You're always friendly with everyone,"

He grinned. "I want to keep those votes coming." His smile vanished. "Kidding aside, you said he's giving you the treasure if you find it—I think that's suspicious. Why is he being so generous? I don't believe for a second he's interested in his ancestors' remains. It's not like remains that need to be returned to a sacred tribal burial ground."

"I told you he's hoping to find a deed giving him a bit of the McCracken ranchland."

"Sounds fishy to me, Madison." He shook his head, unconvinced. "Be careful. If you find remains, you won't know whose they are. Could have been a posse after a Milan or a Calhoun."

"Well, if we find bones, we'll get a forensic specialist to identify them and any Milan bones will get a proper burial in our Milan cemetery."

Nick's blue eyes rested intently on her. "Keep me posted and watch Jake. I wouldn't trust him one second."

"I will. How are you doing, Nick?" she asked, suddenly eager to change the subject.

"Busier than ever," he replied. "People are sounding me out about running for a U.S. Senate seat."

"That would be fantastic. I'm thrilled for you," she said and for an instant saw a slight frown crease his brow, but then it was gone. "You don't want to do that?"

"We're a long, long way from me having to make that decision, but yes, I'd like to. In a way, I hate to get so far from Texas and the ranch, but politics is my life and if I really get a chance for this, I'm taking it."

"Of course you should," she said. "Your life revolves around politics." While they were served, they remained silent. She watched as a tossed salad was placed in front of her and then a waiter placed a hamburger in front of Nick.

"Do the folks know you're letting Jake dig on the ranch?"

"Of course. Someone, maybe Charley, keeps Dad posted and Dad has already called to try to talk me out of letting Jake search. So far it's been as useless and hopeless as when y'all dug for that treasure when you were kids."

Nick grinned. "We imagined finding a big trunk filled with gold. We never gave a thought to ancestors' bones and knew nothing about a deed."

"We'll see. You can always come join us."

He laughed and she smiled because she knew his schedule kept him busy every minute, which was what he wanted. She was certain he was trying to occupy his time so he wouldn't have a chance to think too much about his loss.

She chatted and ate, finishing and sipping iced tea until Nick glanced at his watch. "I'm sorry. I have to get back to the office. I have an appointment."

"It's been good to see you. I need to call the limo," she said as they stood to walk out. She put away her phone. "He's already here and waiting. Want a lift back to your office?"

"No, thanks. I drove myself." Nick smiled at her. "Thanks for having lunch with me."

"Thanks for taking me," she replied. "You take care of yourself, Nick."

"You, too. See you soon," he said.

He followed her until they were almost at the limo. "Shall I tell the chauffeur to drive carefully?"

She grinned. "You? My brother who got into trouble for drag racing?"

He laughed and shrugged. "I'm grown up and responsible now." He smiled at her and walked away as she climbed into the limo for the ride to their parents' home.

It wasn't too long until they reached the gated community where mansions started above one million in price. The well-landscaped grounds had tall oak trees along the wide, winding drive to the house while giant magnolias grew between the oaks.

Like the house on their family ranch, this was another Georgian redbrick with white Corinthian columns. Two beds of red and yellow hibiscus bloomed on either side of the front porch. She used her key to unlock the front door. A small shaggy brown dog stood in the foyer wagging its tail.

She hurried inside, stopping to pet the happy dog. "Hi, Prissy," Madison said, scratching the dog's head. "Where's your family?"

The little dog danced around her as Madison searched for her parents, finding them in the study, her father playing with another brown dog, her mother holding a laptop. The moment she saw Madison, she smiled and came forward to hug her.

Catching a whiff of her mother's rose perfume that she had worn as long as Madison could remember, Madison felt foolish for even coming because she couldn't imagine that her father had done anything to hurt her or that her mother would allow him to.

Even after the hug, her mother's beige silk blouse and matching silk slacks did not have a wrinkle. Madison had always thought her mother was a beautiful woman and at fifty-two, Evelyn Milan still looked beautiful to Madison. Her short brown hair was perfectly styled.

"Well, look who's here," her dad said as he came to hug her. Twelve years older than her mother, her dad's life revolved around law and being a judge. Even in his aged brown slacks, a white dress shirt and a favorite brown cardigan he looked imposing and judicial. He had never had to raise his voice to get Madison or Nick or Wyatt to obey him when they had been children. Only Tony had been the wild one who could sometimes wear their father's patience to the breaking point.

Madison kissed both parents and sat to talk to them, bringing them up to date on the search for the buried treasure. Her father sat listening quietly, which she knew meant he was thinking.

"I've always heard about the gun battle and that members of both families were killed," he said, "so it's logical their bones are out there somewhere if they weren't carried off by animals."

"Pete, that's gruesome," Evelyn Milan said, shivering.

"It's the truth. I can imagine someone from each family returning to bury their own dead. That part of the tale I've always thought was true. As for a buried treasure—who knows? Could have been or might be pure myth. It might be as little as two or three gold coins. And he didn't ask you to split the booty with him?"

Madison shook her head. "No, sir. He said he didn't want the treasure, whatever it is, just his ancestors' bones."

"That's generous," Evelyn said.

"I don't think he believes there is really any treasure and it's an inducement to get me to agree to this," Madison explained.

"That makes sense," Pete said. "I imagine he's done plenty of looking on his side of the boundary when he was a kid. Besides, you said there might be a deed giving the Calhouns some McCracken land?"

"Yes, that's what Jake is hoping to find," she replied.

"Madison, be careful. I don't trust the Calhouns. There may be more to this than we know."

"I know he wants to lease the land and he wants the mineral rights. I think he intends to drill gas wells. I've gotten several calls from energy companies, geologists. I told you a while back, Dad, for right now, I'm talking to three companies to see which one will be the best deal for us. None of them belong to Jake. I'll let you know before I do anything. I want you to approve."

"Thanks, that's very nice, Madison. I'm sure Mom and I will be happy with whatever you decide."

"I don't know that I'll make any decisions before your trip, but I'll keep you in the loop." Her parents were leaving in November to go to Paris, Switzerland and the Italian coast. Her aunt Edna was staying at the house to watch the dogs. "Is there anything I can do while you're gone?"

"Thank you, but no, Madison," her mother answered. "If there is, we'll let you know."

"You should have a wonderful trip." They spent the next half hour talking about the upcoming vacation and their plans.

"Mom, I have a legal problem I need to discuss with Dad. Would you excuse us? I think this will bore you terribly."

"Of course. And you're right—I don't need to hear a legal problem unless *you're* in trouble with the law."

Smiling, Madison shook her head. "Hardly. Old stuff and nothing illegal."

"I'll give you an hour and then I'll be back. That's long enough for legal talk," Evelyn said as she left the room, taking the dog with her. Madison followed her to the door.

"Thanks, Mom. I'll come get you," she said, closing the door after her mother had walked away. She walked back across the room to face her dad.

He sat in his favorite chair with his feet propped on an ottoman, his feet crossed at the ankles. He looked relaxed, friendly, supportive, but a glance into his alert blue eyes and she knew he was paying attention and ready to listen.

She wanted to catch him off guard, hoping to be able

to tell by looking at him if he had been honest in what he had said to Jake.

She pulled a wingback chair close to the ottoman to face him.

"What's happened, Madison?" he asked.

She leaned forward, placing her hands on his knees. "Dad, when I was in high school, I was going to elope with Jake Calhoun. He never showed up. Why?" Her heart pounded hard. She had never questioned her father before. As a child she had thought every word he said was the absolute truth and the way things should be. She had always obeyed, never rebelled; when he wanted her to do something, she had always done it unquestioningly.

His expression never changed. There was not even a flicker of an eyelid, yet she knew something was wrong. Her dad had waited too long to reply. She couldn't get her breath and her head swam.

Jake had been telling the truth.

She gulped for air.

"Madison, are you all right? Do you need to lie down?"

She shook her head, but she couldn't get her breath. She closed her eyes and held her head in her hands, gulping for air while her whole world shifted and changed.

The father she had always implicitly trusted had deceived and hurt her. Jake had walked out because of her father.

"Dad, how could you have done that to me?" she said between her gasps for air. Jake had been right. That was all she could think. And she hadn't believed him at all. "I didn't think you would ever hurt me like that," she whispered, staring at him while hot tears spilled from her eyes.

"Madison, I love you and I did it for you. You were way too young to get married then."

"There were so many other ways to handle it that wouldn't have hurt us that badly." Her father's betrayal had caused a lasting hurt that might be with her all her life. "I've been so awful to Jake and accused him of terrible things."

"First of all, he's a Calhoun and this family would never accept him. His family wouldn't accept you. Second, both of you were children and you were way too young and immature to go into marriage. I see too much suffering and unhappiness. I couldn't let you throw away your future."

"Why didn't you talk to me? I've always done what you wanted."

"You have, but you were growing up and getting more headstrong. Your elopement would have divided both families and brought that old feud back to life, stronger than it had been in over a century. Those who sided with you and were ready to end the feud would have split with those who would have opposed you and felt you betrayed your family. Some family members would never have recognized you as part of the family again."

"Did you physically threaten Jake?"

"I did bring some pressure to bear because Jake would understand that kind of threat."

Shock gripped her as she stared in silence.

"Honey, I'm sorry. Maybe you and Jake would have worked things out and been happy the rest of your lives, but the odds were not on your side. And neither of you had your education completed. You hadn't even finished high school."

"I don't know you. I don't know how you could have threatened Jake and gone behind my back to be cruel and deceitful," she said, feeling her pride in him and her high regard for him crumble.

"I wasn't exactly happy about it, but I had to stop both of you. I didn't even know you were seeing each other until Charley saw you climbing out and leaving the ranch. I started asking quietly and it didn't take long to find out."

She covered her eyes and cried quietly. "What you did was so awful and hurt badly all these years." She looked at him. "I've always trusted you totally, but I never will again."

"I hope you do. I hope you fall in love and marry, and if you do and have your own children, you will see that in life you have to make tough decisions. I know few people who haven't had to face them with their children. Then maybe you'll understand."

"I'll never understand you threatening Jake. I can't understand you being underhanded. If you had come to me and said we couldn't marry, I would have argued, but I wouldn't feel this dreadful deceit. If you had said, 'You can't elope. I'll annul it,' you know I would have done what you wanted even though I wouldn't have liked it."

"You might have, but Jake wouldn't have been so obedient to me, a Milan. Besides, I didn't know how much influence he carried with you. Honey, I apologize," he said. "Maybe I didn't handle it right. But babies don't come into the world with instructions on how to raise them, you know."

"I sat by the phone all that afternoon and evening and Jake never called, but he told me he called repeatedly. Why didn't I get his calls?" she asked, ignoring his apology that came way too late and only because she asked.

He looked away and ran a hand through his hair. "It was the weekend. I had the calls forwarded to the line in my toolshed. It simply rang and no one answered. On Monday I switched it back."

"Did Mom know?"

"Partly. She didn't want you to marry a Calhoun and she wanted me to stop you. She didn't know exactly how I did so." He looked at her, and his shoulders somehow didn't seem quite so broad. "I'll call Jake and I'll try to talk to him. Being a Calhoun, he will probably always hate me and I may have added years to this archaic feud."

She tried to take in her father's explanation, painful though it was. But one thing didn't make sense. "I didn't get him when I called him. You couldn't change his phone."

"That was the one thing I worried about, but by the time you tried to call him, he had already left town. I knew his folks were out of town that weekend and all his siblings were furious with you."

He sat forward and reached out for her, but she pulled back. "I'm sorry, Madison, but I still feel it was for the best, and at this point in your life, I'd think you'd agree. You have a marvelous career in art, a field that is difficult and competitive. You and Jake are free to marry now and if you don't want to now, my guess is that a marriage at sixteen and nineteen would not have lasted anyway."

"If I had called him right after talking to you, I might have learned the truth."

"It was a chance I had to take. But I thought I'd made him so angry with you, that he wouldn't have taken your call or believed anything you said. I'm amazed he tried to call you. If you had gotten through, then I would have tried other ways to stop you and I would have called his parents to intervene. I don't think the two of you could have fought both families."

Each revelation made her pain deepen. "All these years I thought he just left me waiting with no explanation," she said, thinking about Jake and the intervening years.

"Jake went home, packed and left for college that afternoon, way, way early. I had someone check on him."

She fished a tissue from her pocket and wiped her eyes, standing and turning away from him. The tears wouldn't stop. When she thought how furious she had been with Jake all these years, her stomach churned.

"Dad, for thirteen years I have been angry with Jake.

I've shed a million tears over his walking out on me. I married someone I didn't love just to get back at Jake—"

He stood in front of her. "I was afraid of that. Madison," he said, frowning and looking more worried than she had ever seen him look, "your mother and I were afraid you were doing that, but we hoped the marriage would work out and you would find happiness. Will was a nice fellow and quite acceptable to the family."

"Our marriage was dreadful."

"That's behind you now. I'll call Jake and talk to him. I owe you both that much, but if I had it to do over, I probably would do things the same way. I don't think I could have stopped the two of you otherwise."

"There had to have been better ways to handle it and you could have been honest. That's what I'm having a difficult time with." She walked away from him. "It's going to take me a while to get accustomed to all this. I would never have believed you could have done such a thing if you hadn't told me yourself."

"I apologize, Madison, and I hope someday you'll understand and you'll forgive me. But let me ask you something. Do you think you would have been the artist you are today if you had run away and married Jake?"

Startled, she turned to look at him and thought about the years and the work, the hours she had poured into her art career, especially after being so hurt.

"Maybe not, Dad, but a career doesn't trump love."

"You wouldn't have had this wonderful success," he replied solemnly.

He reached out to hug her, but she stood stiffly. He released her and stepped back. "I love you, Madison. Always remember that. I'm human and not infallible in spite of being a judge. And judges may be the worst with their own families."

From out of nowhere a thought struck her. She remembered the tree across the bridge on the ranch. "Dad, someone cut down a big cottonwood and it blocked the bridge over Rocky Creek. Did you have anything to do with that?"

He shook his head. "I don't even know where you're searching. Trust me, I haven't been out on the ranch sawing down big trees."

Before she could answer, there was a light knock at the door and the door opened. Evelyn thrust her head into the room. "Ready for company yet?"

"Sorry, Mom," Madison said. "I have to go. I should get back to the ranch so I can hear how the men did today." She cast a glance at her father. "We're finished here."

Her mother studied her intently and gave her dad a penetrating stare. Madison wanted out before her mother realized the problem and they started discussing it all over.

She felt she had to get out or suffocate. She needed fresh air and to get away by herself for a while before she went back to the ranch to face Jake when he returned tonight. Jake had been right all along. She hurt all over for what her dad had done. She felt betrayed, hurt and filled with regret. She owed Jake an enormous apology.

Her folks followed her out to hug her before she left. When her dad hugged her, he brushed her cheek with a kiss. "You just remember always that I love you. That's always my motivation."

She nodded and turned away.

"Madison," her dad said and she paused to turn back. "Be careful. I don't think Jake can really care that much about his ancestors' bones. He's still a Calhoun and he's got a reason to want revenge."

"I'll be careful," she said stiffly. The chauffeur held the limo door for her and she climbed in. She didn't look back as the limo drove away. She didn't want to cry in the limo so she fought tears and emotions that rocked her.

She was still in shock, reeling and adjusting to seeing a side to her father that was tough and hard, a side she had never seen before.

Tonight she had to apologize to Jake. She thought of all his pent-up anger. He had never told her about her dad until now. What had her dad threatened to do to him that had scared Jake off? He didn't scare easily and he especially wouldn't as a nineteen-year-old. There had been something. Some kind of leverage. Her dad had been a powerful attorney back then with a lot of influence. At one time he had been with the district attorney's office before she had even started school. They were wealthy, influential. Her mother was also from an old Texas family.

At the same time, Jake's family could match them in power and wealth, and the Calhouns were an old Texas family with roots that went back to the 1800s.

It wouldn't have mattered, though. Jake would never have had any help from his own family because some of the Calhouns still hated the Milans with a vengeance. Jake's mother was one—she had never spoken to Madison or any other member of the Milan family that Madison knew about. His grandparents disliked Milans also, but she suspected the animosity worsened steadily with each previous generation. Lindsay Calhoun would not speak to any Milan and Tony's fights with Lindsay as his neighboring rancher were notorious.

Madison wanted the truth, all of it. She felt dazed, shocked that her own father had been the one to destroy her plans to marry Jake.

If she had confronted her father back then, would he have admitted what he had done?

She would never have an answer to that question.

Frowning, she stared out the limo window, but she

didn't see the surroundings. She saw Jake's angry dark
eyes. His anger ran deep and now she could understand it.

They would all get in about dark and she had to be
ready to face him.

The minute she entered the kitchen her eyes met Jessie Lou's and Madison was swamped by the emotional
upheaval of the day. She couldn't control her feelings as
tears spilled down her cheeks.

"Jessie Lou, Dad admitted everything Jake accused
him of doing. All these years—" She couldn't talk. And
then Jessie Lou's arms wrapped around her and she clung
to Jessie Lou to cry.

"You finally know. I always thought Judge Milan might
have been behind whatever happened. He's very close to
Charley and Charley keeps an eye on you for your dad.
Charley has never liked Jake."

Madison stepped back. "Charley? Yesterday someone
cut a big cottonwood so it fell on the bridge and blocked
the way. Jake and the men moved it, but it gave us a delay.
Do you suppose my dad told Charley to try to interfere?"

Jessie Lou stared back with a slight frown. "I'd be careful around Charley."

Madison cried, trying to get control of her emotions.
Finally she wiped her eyes. "I was just so shocked that
my dad would do something like that and not be open and
honest about it."

"You're his daughter. He thought he was protecting
you."

"Instead, he hurt me badly and I feel terrible for the
hateful way I've treated Jake all these years."

"It's over now, I'd say," Jessie Lou said. "I have dinner
all fixed and I think I will go along and leave you two to
discuss the past with no interference. I won't be here until
after lunch tomorrow because I have a dental appointment

in Lubbock in the morning, so you should have the privacy you need to talk this out."

Madison wiped her eyes and tried to smile. "Thank you. I'm going to shower and get ready. Jake will be here by dark."

Jessie Lou nodded and patted her shoulder. "You'll both be better off now that you can clear the air between you."

Madison nodded, but she wondered if they could ever get back even some of the friendship they once had. "I'll get ready for Jake."

Jake glanced at his watch as he walked toward the Milan ranch house. He was tempted to go on home, but staying here was easier and they could have slightly more time each day to hunt. The days were flying past and his options dwindled with each one. They hadn't found anything. Madison would never give him another chance so he wanted to find the deed this week.

He was hot, dusty and disgusted that they didn't know any more about a buried treasure than they had when they started. He wondered how it went with Madison and her dad. He hated Judge Milan and would be more than happy to take a big chunk of the judge's ranch from him. And if he did find treasure and a deed and got the land, he was going to go tell the judge himself. How sweet that would be. Madison had no idea how harsh her father could be or what he had really done in the past. Would Judge Milan lie to his daughter now? If he did, could Jake ever convince her otherwise? Soon they'd part again and he didn't expect to see her after they did.

Jake rang the bell at the locked back door.

In minutes the door opened and she stood in the shadowy interior. She stepped back. "Come in."

He entered and paused. Her hair was down, hanging loosely over her shoulders and framing her face in a brown cascade that was longer than he had guessed. She had on makeup and a short-sleeved hot-pink cotton dress with a scoop neck that revealed her curves and took his breath away.

"You look gorgeous," he said, his voice raspy, lust consuming him. For a few seconds he forgot where she had gone today or why or the harsh differences between them when he had last seen her in the morning.

"Come in. Would you like a beer before dinner?" she asked.

"Sure," he thought he answered. He couldn't be sure; all he could think about was how much he wanted her. He watched her walking ahead of him, saw that familiar little sway of her hips that had stirred him plenty of times and did again now.

She turned and gave him a look filled with curiosity. "Jake? Are you all right?"

"I can't stop looking at you," he admitted.

She smiled, but it was cool and brief and he had a feeling she didn't really feel like smiling, but was merely being polite. He thought about her trip to Dallas and was curious because she didn't give a hint of what had happened or what she felt.

He followed her and watched her get his beer and a tall glass of ice water for herself. He sipped and lowered the bottle.

"That's really good," he said, but he looked at her as he spoke and he was thinking about her, not his beer.

"Do you want to talk now or get cleaned up?"

It took a second for her words to register. He stared at her. She looked cool, clean, sexy. He wanted to touch her.

"I need to clean up first because I'm covered in dust. I'll be back shortly. Don't go away. Don't change."

This time she did smile. "I won't do either one. See you soon."

"You sure will," he said, hurrying out of the room. Curiosity consumed him. He couldn't read her reaction, but he was beginning to hope her father had confessed to the truth. Jake had never expected him to, but if Pete Milan had lied about what he had done, Jake didn't think Madison would have let him in her house now.

Jake lengthened his stride. He wanted to find out what had happened and how she had reacted.

Madison watched him go, thankful she'd had an effect on him. She wanted to leave him dazzled. Time was when she could do so without much effort. That was no longer true. He seemed so angry sometimes when they had been together that she had wondered if he even liked her anymore.

She had talked to Jessie Lou about dinner and she had made appetizers and dessert. Jessie Lou had great-looking steaks ready to grill so Madison hoped he liked dinner.

It was another half hour before he reappeared and now she felt desire blaze as she looked at him. His hair was neatly combed, the ends still damp near the collar of his Western shirt. His jeans hugged his strong legs.

"Do you want another beer? I have some appetizers I made. We can take our drinks and appetizers to the family room or we can sit outside."

"Beer and family room sounds good to me."

He helped as she retrieved a plate of imported cheeses and fancy crackers. They carried them to the family room and set them on a table. Dreading the next hour, but knowing it was long overdue, she turned to face him, meeting his gaze.

As Jake sipped his beer, he noticed she appeared worried with a slight frown on her brow and her fingers locked together tightly in her lap. He had a swift rush of satisfaction.

"Your dad must have admitted what he did," he said.

Standing, she faced him while her frown deepened. She shivered and stepped away as if she had to move around. In seconds her eyes met his. "Jake, I'm so sorry."

Her eyes filled with tears, but he couldn't feel sorry for her. He merely nodded. "Apology accepted, but you're not the one who should be apologizing."

"I didn't know my dad was capable of what he did. I didn't dream he would ever do such a thing as threaten you and I didn't think he would do something that would hurt me so badly. I had no inkling that he was behind your disappearance. Not a clue. Why didn't you tell me?"

"Your dad must not have confessed everything. He told me to pack and go to college early, to get away and to stay away from you. He threatened me if I didn't."

"Threatened you with what?" she asked, her voice barely above a whisper.

"He would do everything he could to ruin my future. He would try to make life difficult for me if I lived around here. He listed several possibilities. Frankly, I didn't think my family would have protected me."

Shaking her head, Madison placed her hand over her eyes. He didn't think it was an act. Madison had always been sincere with him. Tears filled her eyes and he could see her struggle for control.

"I don't even know my own dad and that's dreadful. And I know you're right—you couldn't turn to your family for help."

"No, I couldn't," he said, standing and stepping closer to face her. She wrung her hands. He was certain she wasn't even aware of what she was doing. "Some members of my family hate all Milans. They would have been as bad as your dad. I knew that at the time. We were on our own in too many ways and we got caught."

"I feel terrible that I was angry with you." The tears spilled over, running down her cheeks. "I always thought you walked out on me."

"I was angry because I thought you would rather have all he offered instead of me. We had been so in love, Madison. But he was so emphatic that it was your wish and since it was, he was warning me to leave you alone and stay far away. If I didn't, he would let my family know."

She wiped away the tears but they wet her cheeks again quickly. "Sorry. I can't control my emotions. I'm still shocked. I wouldn't have ever believed my father capable of hurting me or being so cruel if I hadn't clearly heard him admit it today. Jake, I'm just terribly sorry I've been mean to you. You didn't cause it any more than I did. I wish you had called me and told me everything."

"I couldn't get through to you, remember?"

"My dad told me about that. He had the calls sent to the phone line in his toolshed on the ranch. I never knew you tried to call."

"I can't believe I was so gullible, either." Jake shook his head. "But even if we had managed to elope, with your dad's power and influence he would have found a way to separate us and have the marriage annulled."

"You had a scholarship to play football in Mississippi. I thought if we had married, and I had gone with you, they wouldn't have brought me back." She looked at him, raising her chin.

They stared at each other and his gaze ran over her features again, sliding down to her low neckline and tempting curves. His gaze returned to her mouth. He didn't know what his feelings were for her, but he knew he wanted her. He wanted to make love to her. She was no teenage girl anymore. She was a grown, intelligent woman who could make her decisions with far more judgment and clarity.

He set his beer on a table and closed the space between them. As he approached her, her eyes widened. Her lips parted as she took a deep breath.

"Jake?" she asked breathlessly.

Seven

Jake leaned down to cover her mouth with his own. His arms tightened around her and he leaned over her.

Madison pressed against him, standing on tiptoe to kiss him passionately.

"Jake, forgive me," Madison whispered, pausing a moment.

"It's in the past, Madison," he replied. "Let it go because it's over and can't ever affect us again unless we let it."

"I was as mean to you as my dad," she said, feeling agonized as a deep frown furrowed her brow.

"Forget it now," he ordered. "You didn't know and I couldn't fight your family and mine. We wouldn't have been able to stay together because you were underage. The main thing is now you know I did not deliberately hurt you."

Madison pulled his head down to kiss him. She wanted him with all the longing that seemed to have built through the past empty years. She wanted to love him and be loved by him, mindlessly, not thinking about yesterday or tomorrow, just to love him once again for what had been taken from them. She wanted to forget and replace the past with memories of today.

She kissed him passionately, winding her fingers in his thick hair, relishing touching him, thinking he was still the most exciting man she had ever known.

While she kissed him, she leaned away a fraction to undo the buttons on his knit shirt. Her hands went to his belt and she unfastened the heavy buckle he had won in a rodeo.

With shaking fingers she tugged his shirt swiftly from his jeans. He released her to yank his shirt over his head and toss it away.

While he slid the zipper down the back of her dress, he watched her. She glanced up and the blatant desire in his brown eyes made her weak-kneed.

As she started to move closer again, he held her away. "Wait," he commanded. He slipped her dress off her shoulders and when he let it fall, she stepped out of it. His gaze roamed over her slowly, a tantalizing perusal that she knew was the precursor to his caresses. She inhaled, tingling, wanting to grab him. Instead, she clung tightly to his upper arms as he unfastened her bra and tossed it aside.

"Jake," she whispered as he cupped her breasts. His hands were warm, rough, calloused from the days of digging and moving rocks, heightening sensations as he caressed her so lightly, his thumbs circling her nipples with feathery touches that set her on fire.

She repeated his name, loving the feel of it on her mouth, just as she relished the feel of his hands on her breasts. She closed her eyes and moaned with pleasure. One hand continued to caress her while his other hand peeled away her lace panties, letting them fall around her ankles so she could step out of them.

He bent to take her nipple in his mouth, his tongue replacing his thumb and driving her wild.

She held his shoulders tightly, tension mounting, desire a raging fire, while uppermost in her mind was the knowledge that she was being loved by Jake. Nothing would ever give them back the lost years, but right now, in this moment, he was making love to her. At last, she could freely make love to him in return, to try in this way to convey her regrets and long-ago feelings for him that had remained part of her life even when he had gone.

"Jake, there's never been anyone that it's been the same with," she whispered. She opened her eyes to unfasten his jeans and push them off his narrow hips.

As her gaze ran over his chest, she inhaled deeply, wanting him with a building desperation. She didn't think she could wait as long as he could hold out and continue the foreplay that built flames into a raging inferno of need.

"I don't know how to make it up to you," she whispered, looking up at him.

His lips were red from her kisses and his eyes still filled with naked desire.

"You can keep trying," he whispered, kissing her breast and making her forget conversation.

She knelt to caress and kiss him, hoping to stir him to the heights where he had already taken her. She wanted him to remember this night, to know she had regrets and was trying to make it up to him. She wanted to make up in a tiny measure for lost years of loving between them.

His fingers tangled in her hair while she stroked and kissed him until he caught her beneath her arms and raised her to her feet. He swung her into his arms and carried her to his bedroom. Setting her on her feet beside the bed, he yanked back covers and then placed her on the cool sheets.

He stretched beside her, kissing her and caressing her while he held her. In minutes he moved over her, rolling her over and kissing her slowly, a hot torment as his tongue teased and desire built even more.

"It's been so long," she whispered.

"Too long, Maddie."

A thrill spiraled from her head to her toes. *Maddie*. That's what he had always called her before, but never once since he had been back. She wanted to hear him say it again, and again.

"Jake, make love to me. It's been so long." She pulled him to her, lost in desire, but then she remembered. "I'm not protected."

He moved away, stepping off the bed to retrieve his jeans, and came back with a package. She watched him slip on the condom, looking at his strong hands that she remembered so well.

Her gaze inched over him slowly, taking in his strong thighs with short brown hairs sprinkled over them, his thick rod that was ready, his virile body, muscled, fit and vital, energy radiating from him.

His dark brown eyes studied her as much as she studied him. Locks of his black hair fell on his forehead. He was handsome, exciting, sexy, marvelous. His kisses and lovemaking could rock her and touch the core of her being, an intimacy that she treasured.

Once, she had loved him with all her heart. So much had happened between them and she had harbored bitter feelings for so long, she didn't know what she felt now except passion and lust. She wanted his hard body against her, his thick manhood inside her, filling her, driving her over a blinding edge.

"Jake, let's make love," she whispered again.

"We are, darlin'. Maddie, you're the most beautiful, exciting woman I've ever known," he whispered and came down to cover her mouth with his before she could answer him. He entered her slowly, driving her wild as he pulled away for seconds and then claimed her again.

She held him tightly while she kissed him possessively, thrusting her tongue deep over his and clinging to him.

He eased into her and withdrew slowly, setting her on fire and then repeating his thrusts. Her hips arched against him, her legs pulling him closer as they wrapped around his narrow waist and held him tightly.

Sweat dotted his forehead as he continued to move with slow deliberation, holding off while building her need, until she didn't know what she was saying to him, what she was feeling except the desire to cling tighter, move faster.

When his control snapped, he thrust quickly and she rocked with him, rising and crashing over the edge. She cried out with eagerness, climaxing in a release that dazzled her.

Rapture spilled over her along with joy because he was in her arms, loving her and sharing the most intimate moments. He shuddered and pumped with his own release, gasping for breath.

Afterward, he showered kisses on her, making her wonder if he truly felt such closeness and tenderness for her or if it was merely a response to his own satisfaction.

In some ways now, she felt she knew so little about him. They had grown up and been apart all these years. They had both lived in anger and bitterness toward the other, so she didn't have the closeness with him that they had shared as kids.

She stroked his damp back, running her fingers along the strong column of his neck and then through his hair. She held him to her, welcoming his weight, his closeness.

He rolled to his side, taking her with him, and he smiled at her while he held her. "This is the best, Maddie."

Another thrill rocked her. She liked having him go back to the old nickname that only he had ever called her. "It seems right to be together and in some ways it wipes out the empty years between then and now," she said.

"Your dad cheated us of a lot of time together. No one will ever know if he was right or not and I suppose if I had a sixteen-year-old daughter, I might stop her from marrying, too. That's young, Maddie, even though we didn't feel it at the time."

"We'll never know, Jake. If we had married then, we'd probably have four or five kids by now and I wouldn't have had an art career."

"It's in the past. There's no use speculating and thinking about the 'what ifs.'"

She gazed beyond him, thinking about what he just said, to forget their love and their times together and what they had planned. Had tonight been purely lust for both of them? What did she really feel for him and what did Jake feel for her?

She couldn't answer her questions, but she suspected that he was no longer in love. They were basically strangers now. Sadness filled her and she ran her hands over him, unable to get enough of touching him. The memories of making love long ago were to a different person—a boy. Now he was a man and physically, as well in other ways, he had changed. She had, too. Maybe what they once had had been lost forever.

She tightened her arms around him and pressed against him, holding him tightly. For right now, she was satisfied. They had shared a closeness that was good and the anger and bitterness between them no longer existed. That had to be better.

"You used to talk more than you do now," she remarked.

He smiled, twisting to look at her. "Another change. I've been alone so long, maybe in some ways, I'm all locked up inside myself. I still say life has changed. Just keep on with taking one day at a time."

They both became silent and she wondered what thoughts ran through his mind. Had too much bitterness passed between them for them to rekindle a relationship?

Physically, it would be no problem, but there was far more to it than a physical relationship. They had lost the joy they once shared. She remembered her father's warning to be cautious about Jake, that he might want more from this treasure hunt than he had indicated.

At the thought of her father, she recalled her afternoon visit with him.

"It won't mean anything to you," she told Jake, "but my dad apologized to me for what he did."

"That's nice for you, but it doesn't change a thing."

"I know, but I'm glad he did and glad he feels some remorse."

Jake toyed with her hair and remained silent. "You're a beautiful woman."

"Thank you."

They gazed into each other's eyes. Desire stirred and he leaned closer, his gaze drifting to her mouth. She couldn't get her breath. She wanted his kiss, needed him just as if they had never made love. She turned her face up to him and then raised her lips to kiss him.

His arms tightened around her and he turned on his back, pulling her on top of him. Her hair fell around her face as she kissed him and passion rekindled.

It was like that throughout the night. He held her in his arms and they made love often, as if they could never get enough of each other.

In the morning he worshipped her body once again, then, afterward, he held her close. "Shall we call off the search today and stay in bed?"

Smiling, she ran her finger along his jaw. "We'll go and then tonight, as soon as Jessie Lou leaves, we'll have the house to ourselves. How does that sound?"

"Okay, but staying in bed and making love all day sounds better."

She laughed and stepped out of bed, taking the sheet with her. "I'm off to shower upstairs in my own bathroom."

"Do you realize I have never even seen that sanctuary of yours upstairs? You have never invited me up for so much as a peek."

She turned to reply to him, but her answer was momentarily forgotten. He had propped up the pillows and lay against them. A light blanket was pulled across his lap and his hands were behind his head as he looked at her.

Her mouth went dry and she wanted to go back and kiss him again, feel the reassurance of his strong arms around her. She worried that when she walked away, she was going to lose him again.

He sat up slightly and lowered his arms. "Maddie? You look upset. What is it, hon?"

She walked back to him, to sit on the side of the bed and kiss him. He wrapped his arms tightly around her, pulling her onto his lap as he kissed her. He was aroused again, ready to love. She kissed him passionately, slipping her arms around him, wanting to hold him against her heart.

She leaned away finally, pulling the sheet back up. His searching gaze went over her face while he combed her hair from her face with his fingers. "What is it?"

"I've found you again. I don't want to lose you a second time."

For a moment he frowned and then he smiled and hugged her. "You're not going to lose me. Not anytime soon." His voice lowered, took on a husky whisper. "If we stay in bed all day, you'll feel more reassured."

He was teasing, making light of the moment to cheer her or to allay her fears or to just put her off. She didn't know what he felt. She gathered the sheet, stood and turned. "I'll still go shower and start breakfast." At the door she turned back. He sat on the side of the bed, the blanket across his lap. It was obvious he was aroused. His hair was a tangle and he had a dark stubble of beard on his chin.

"And tonight you can come up and see my very private bedroom."

Smiling, she left the room and quickly climbed the stairs. The sooner they got going, the sooner they'd get home. She couldn't wait to share her bed with Jake.

As she dressed, she glanced out the window and saw Charley pause in front of the garage door. He glanced around. He had a gas can in his hand. He stepped inside the garage and closed the door quickly.

She wondered what he was doing. She yanked on her clothes and raced down the steps and out a side door, running to the garage.

She opened the door carefully, trying to avoid noise, and slid inside. The light was on and she could smell gasoline.

She tiptoed toward the truck she had been taking each day. Charley stood waiting while gas drained into the can he had been carrying.

"Charley, what are you doing?"

He whirled around and took a deep breath. "You have water in your gas tank. The last gas we got had water. I'm draining the vehicles."

She stared at him and shook her head. "You work for me now."

"I'm trying to take care of your truck. You'll use it today. I'll fill it with good gasoline."

She stared at him, hanging on to her temper. "My dad has hired you to cause trouble for me, hasn't he?"

Charley's lips clamped together and his face flushed.

"You work for me now. Make a choice. You either give me your loyalty or you get another job. You no longer work for my dad. You cut the tree, or had others cut it and place it on the bridge, didn't you?"

He stared at her without replying.

"You don't even have to answer. Pour my gas back into my truck unless you've put something in it. Which is it? Do you work for me or my dad?"

Silence stretched between them as he shifted from one foot to the other. "Your dad thinks Jake Calhoun is up to no good and using the search for a reason to get on Milan land. You know your father has your interests at heart."

"Charley, who are you going to work for?"

Another silence stretched between them. "Your father said I could come to work for him in town anytime," Charley finally replied. "He needs a handyman and caretaker and he said he can keep me busy. I'm getting older and some of the men don't like what I'm doing. I'll pack and go to work for your dad."

"Good enough. I'll have a check ready for you at the end of the day and you can get your things and leave when you're ready."

He nodded. "He always said this was in your best interests."

She didn't reply. "Have you done anything else to hamper our search?"

"No. I remember when you were born. We go back a long way. Your father's intentions are good."

"Get my truck ready to go," she said, trying to hang on to her temper because her real anger was with her dad.

She turned and left, hurrying back to the side door. She decided to say nothing to Jake until the search was over and Charley had gone. Jake might not be as kind.

After breakfast they left for another day of searching that turned out to be as fruitless as all the previous days of looking.

When they arrived back at her house, she glanced at Jake. "I heard from Wyatt today. He's stopping by and

Tony is with him. Do you care if I ask them to stay for dinner?"

"Of course not. I'll be glad to see Wyatt. I see him around town, but we just say hello and keep going. I don't know Tony as well, but we've met. Do they know I'm here?"

"Yes, they do."

"I know Tony does not like the Calhouns at all and I'll have to admit, my sister is pretty rotten right back at him."

Madison smiled. "I know. I told him no fights. Wyatt is always too closed up and in control to ever lose it and get in a fight. Besides, you and Wyatt played football together and you both did well with the other's help."

"That's for sure. He made me look good and vice versa."

"Maybe he wants to talk about the old football games you played. You two helped carry that team to some championships. The quarterback and the wide receiver. You were a good match."

"Wyatt was a fantastic receiver. He should have played pro longer than two years."

"He didn't like being away from his ranch. He could afford to turn down football so he did. And even though he probably will be glad to see you and reminisce about the glory days, I think he's coming by to check you out and see what you're up to on this hunt. They may want to see the map. Now that I think of it, I should have called them because they know the ranch better than I do."

"I'm guessing football might not be the only topic," Jake said with a harsh note. "Your dad probably wants *Sheriff* Milan to ask me a few questions."

"Maybe, but if Tony starts the questioning, it will be purely what Tony is wanting to know and nothing more. He's too involved in his ranch to care about gold or bones."

Jake smiled. "Gotta love the cowboys. I saw where Tony won a bareback bronc event recently."

"His office at his ranch is filled with his trophies and he has belt buckles galore."

"Tell them to come on. I'll be glad to see both of them. And I don't mind answering Wyatt's questions. Wyatt's a good guy."

"I think so. I like my brothers—most of the time."

Jake grinned. "The same with my siblings. Lindsay can be a brat, but she's growing up and she's turning into a damn good rancher. We're all scattered and now that our folks are retired and living in California, we don't get the family together as often as we used to."

"Us, too," Madison agreed. "And my brothers probably call me a brat, too. Although Tony can be the real brat. Wyatt was just born grown. He's always been responsible and levelheaded and the most take-charge one."

"Good to have one in every family."

"Spoken like the man who's the one in his family," she remarked with a grin.

He smiled back at her as they approached the rear of the house and saw her two brothers sitting on the porch. "Your brothers may have beaten us here, but I'm getting a shower."

"Amen to that one and I think they'll want us to shower."

"Yeah, it's been a hot, dirty, unsuccessful day."

"Maybe we can do something about that later," she teased.

"I'm holding you to that one," he said. "And getting to visit the inner sanctum on the second floor."

"Of course. I'll try to wear something special."

"Something really special would be maybe a handkerchief."

She laughed and he grinned. "You're laughing, but I mean it," he added.

As they approached her two brothers, she reminded

him, "Shower quickly and get in there to talk football. I'll let Jessie Lou know there will be four for dinner."

On the porch Tony had his tan hat pushed down above his eyes and was seated with his booted feet perched on the railing. Wyatt sat the same way, his brown hair showing from beneath his black Western hat. His badge was on his shirt while his firearm was out of sight, but she was certain it was on his hip.

Both of them remained seated until she and Jake reached the top step. Wyatt unfolded with a lazy motion and a slow grin, his six-foot-five-inch frame stretching over Tony, who was only an inch over six feet. Wyatt was the oldest and the tallest sibling. He grinned as he extended his hand to Jake.

"Good to see you again, Jake. You don't come to town often."

"No, I don't. It's good to see you."

Madison greeted her brothers as Jake shook hands with Tony.

"We have to clean up before we can socialize, so you two will just have to get a beer and find a comfortable spot to wait," Madison said as they walked through the back entryway. All three men removed their hats and hung them on a large hat rack inside the door.

"I take it you haven't found any buried treasure yet," Tony said, curiosity in his blue eyes that were flecked with green.

"No. Not a thing," she replied.

"I'll show you two the old map I have," Jake said. "You both know this land, probably as well as Madison."

"Better," she said. "There are extra copies of the map in the library."

"I've got mine right here," Jake said, fishing a copy from his hip pocket to hand it to Wyatt. "Look at that and see what you think."

"Will do," Wyatt answered. "But first things first. Let's find the fridge and get a beer. Then I'll look at your map. As kids, Tony and I spent plenty of time digging for that damn treasure."

"Have you had this map all these years?" Tony asked.

"Yep, my father and grandfather had it," Jake replied. "It's been passed down through generations. I suppose Madison told you I want to see if we can find where the gunfight was and have our ancestors' bones moved to the family cemetery and given a proper burial with a marker. No one thought about bringing the bones back until last Christmas when we got to talking about it and that's what brought this about. That and a deed. In our family, it's always been said there was a deed that gave some Mc-Cracken land to the Calhouns, over where the ranches border each other."

"That would be worth a search. Far more than any legend about a treasure, I'd think," Tony said.

"I agree," Jake replied. "I had some time on my hands and I figured I had put this off long enough." He nodded to her two brothers. "For now, though, I'm going to shower. We can talk about the map when I get done. Meanwhile, you guys go study it," Jake said as he headed for his suite.

"We'll be in the library," Wyatt replied.

Madison took her time to shower and change, expecting the three men to pore over the map and the aerial photos and discuss the best places to search. Maybe *argue* about the best places. All three were strong-willed, take-charge men.

Only one of those men dominated her thoughts right now. She couldn't stop thinking of Jake and the night that awaited them. As if a dam had broken, she was swamped by a running current of desire. Desire she no longer fought.

Beer in hand, Jake went to meet the two Milan brothers. As soon as he entered the library, he joined Wyatt and

Tony at the table with the pictures spread before them and a map on the computer.

Wyatt wasted no time with small talk. "There's one spot we agree on," he said, pointing to the map. "Then we each have places the other doesn't have. See this outcropping and this rock formation?"

Jake studied the drawing. "Yeah. Madison and I couldn't decide what that was—it doesn't exactly look like rocks. It almost looks as if they were trying to draw a steer— maybe to represent a herd of cattle."

"I don't think so," Wyatt said. "When I was ten years old I remember where they were going to build a line shack for ranch hands to have a place to stay out on the ranch. There was a rock formation that looked like a snowman. I was a kid and wanted to save it. Dad said that it would fall apart anyway, so I watched them blow it up, but I think I remember where it was."

"Come with us, Wyatt," Jake said. "Both of you if you want," he added, glancing at Tony.

"I can't this week. I have some appointments and need to be in Lubbock for a court case that involves several counties," Wyatt replied.

"I can't, either. Maybe later if you don't have success," Tony added. "Look, I think this resembles your map," he said, pointing to another place on the map on the computer and placing the map on the photo.

"I hope you've found better places than I did." At the sound of Madison's voice Jake turned to see her walk into the room.

When he did, he forgot the map and the treasure. All he could focus on was Madison in cutoffs. Her long legs were fabulous, muscled enough to be shapely, lean enough to be sexy. He remembered them wrapped around him last night.

He wanted to untie the scarf that held her hair and peel away her blouse.

As much as he wanted to hear Tony's and Wyatt's thoughts, he hoped they ended their visit quickly and left him alone with Madison.

It was an effort to turn his attention back to the map and he tried to listen to Tony, who was talking and pointing. Madison came to stand beside him, moving into a space between Wyatt and him.

Jake could detect the scent of her perfume, reminding him of moments last night when they had made love and he caught whiffs of her perfume.

He couldn't resist just a glance at her. Once again his mind betrayed him and he was flooded with memories of last night, her warm, soft body in his arms, her luscious curves that took his breath. Would old feelings rekindle now that they both knew what had happened and who was really to blame?

"What do you think, Jake?" she said, turning to look up at him.

The only thoughts he had were on making love to her. He tried to pick up the conversation because all three Milans stared at him.

"Your brothers have some new ideas about this. They think Rocky Creek cut an entirely different path, farther to the west," he said, hoping that wasn't a repetition of whatever had just been said.

Jake leaned over the photos, and pointed out places to Madison that Wyatt and Tony had picked.

"Some of these aren't anywhere near the creek," Madison said. "I think the map looks as if there is a creek running through it."

"I don't think this line is Rocky Creek. I don't think it's a creek at all, or if it is, it dried up years ago," Wyatt said.

"It looks like a creek," Madison said, leaning closer.

"I agree with Madison," Tony said. "But I also agree with Wyatt that it may have dried up before 1900."

"We'll hunt in different places tomorrow—away from Rocky Creek—and see what we can find," Jake said.

Madison stepped back. "While y'all hash over the possibilities, I'll see if Jessie Lou needs help with dinner."

"Good idea," Tony said, patting his flat stomach.

"Tony, you eat like a nineteen-year-old. Constantly," she added and he grinned, flashing straight white teeth. "I'll let you know when it's ready," she said and left the room.

After dinner everyone thanked Jessie Lou. She stayed in the kitchen to clean while Madison and the men returned to the library, once again studying pictures and the copies of the map. Jake thought it was a good idea because he wanted to go over the map carefully with each of them.

"Look. I haven't attributed any significance to these small circles," Wyatt said. "I figured it was rocks or just circles. They don't look like something that would indicate buried treasure. At first, I didn't even notice them and then I thought they looked like doodling, maybe to throw someone off, but they could have some purpose."

All three Milans bent over the map on the table and Jake's gaze ran over Madison's back and down over her bottom. He wanted to reach out and touch her. He longed to untie the scarf that held her hair behind her head and let her hair fall free around her face.

Jake picked up the copy of the map and looked at it. "Tough part will be finding where this is as well as whatever it is. If that isn't Rocky Creek, all we can do is look to see what else you think the circles might depict."

"Try the places we've suggested," Wyatt said.

"Frankly, I think the buried treasure is just a crazy myth," Tony said. "I'll be shocked if you find anything."

"You may be right," Jake replied, "but I've thought about this off and on the past couple of years. Right now I have some time when I can get away, so I'm glad the Milans are letting a Calhoun onto their land," he said, smiling at Madison, who smiled in return.

"Let us know how it comes out," Wyatt said, heading for the back door.

Madison and Jake followed. Wyatt and Tony each put on his hat and on the porch, Jake shook hands with first one and then the other.

"Thanks again for not objecting to my search."

"You're agreeing to give us the treasure if you find it and we'll get our ancestors' bones, too. Sounds like a good deal to me," Wyatt said, his blue eyes searching Jake's.

"Right. I hope to find the deed that gives us some Mc-Cracken land. He won't miss it. He has a big ranch."

"Well, I better get on home," Wyatt said.

"I have to go, too," Tony said. "I'm going out tonight."

As the brothers went down the porch steps, Jake and Madison stood at the top step watching them go. Jake wanted to drape his arm around her, but he fought the impulse.

As soon as they stepped inside, he reached behind him to close the door and lock it and then he turned to face her. She had walked away a few steps.

"Madison, come here," he said in a deep voice.

She turned and he didn't wait for her. He closed the distance between them and took her into his arms.

Eight

Madison's heart skipped a beat and she drew a deep breath. She was in Jake's arms—where she'd fantasized about being all night. More than anything she wanted his kisses. Right now. She gave no thought to the future, to a relationship with him; she thought only of this moment. She felt desire and a need to wipe out the years of bad feelings between them. "I want to forget," she said, looking up at him. "I want our loving to destroy the bad memories, the anger and hurt for both of us."

"Yes," he agreed. "In some ways, it's as if we just met and in some ways, it's as if I've known you forever."

Before she could answer, he leaned closer and his mouth covered hers, making her forget conversation.

She tightened her arms around his waist, holding him close, kissing him passionately in return, her heartbeat racing. Desire swept through her as she ran her hands over his back and then tugged his shirt out of his jeans.

Clothing was an unwanted barrier. While he continued

to kiss her, he picked her up and carried her to his bedroom, where he stood her on her feet.

"Jake," she whispered, stepping back to unbuckle his belt, wanting to make love while at the same time wanting to prolong the kisses and caresses for hours. It was Jake she was making love to and that seemed the best thing possible and so incredibly right.

They made love all through the night and when she woke right before dawn, she found herself lying against him, their legs entangled, her head in the hollow of his shoulder, her hair spread over his shoulder, arm and chest. Jake held her with one arm and combed long strands of her hair from her face. Rising on his elbow, he tucked her against him and smiled down at her while he continued to comb her hair from her face in slow, feathery strokes that made her tingle.

"You are so beautiful, Maddie."

"Thank you." She smiled sleepily. "You're the only person who has ever called me Maddie. I like it."

"Good. You were right, what you said. Making love to you does help soften the past. It's a rediscovery of you, but we're both different people now. You can never get back the past."

"I know you can't," she said. "We can't go back and pick up from where we were."

He shook his head. "No. We can start from here and see where we go, and so far, it's good."

They were both quiet, her thoughts in turmoil over the revelations and changes, the emotional upheavals again in her life. What did she feel for Jake now? Would she ever rekindle the feelings she'd had for him?

She couldn't answer her own questions. There had been so much hurt and anger between them; once that was gone, what did they have? In some ways she barely knew him. Their lives had gone separate ways.

She sat up and pulled a sheet beneath her arms, turning to look down at him.

"I've decided we'll talk to you about leasing land on my ranch."

For a moment he was silent while his eyes narrowed. "All right. I'll let someone know. We'll set up an appointment with you."

He pulled her down again beside him. They were both silent and she suspected the moment had changed for him as much as it had for her.

"Thanks for the change of heart."

"Now that I know the truth, why wouldn't I talk to you about leasing our land? Our lives have had another monumental change."

He drew her close to hold her and they were both quiet. Finally she moved away and again pulled the sheet under her arms. Holding it close, she stepped out of bed. "Today is Sunday and I'll go to church. You and the guys can search. I don't care. I told Stoney and Darren to go to church if they want."

"I'll go home and regroup, then. That's what my guys did last night."

Smiling, she walked out of the room, aware of his gaze still on her and the questions still in her mind. She didn't know the answers. All she knew was she didn't want to lose him a second time.

Upstairs, she gathered fresh clothes and went to shower, moving routinely, her thoughts still wrapped up in Jake and the changes that had transpired. Already, she wanted to get back with him and she wanted more of his kisses and lovemaking.

Jake showered, shaved and pulled on fresh clothes. All the time he dressed he thought about Madison and her willingness to talk to his company about leasing Milan land.

He sent a text to Lindsay and to his brothers to tell them about the change in events. He also explained that he had told Madison the truth and she had flown to Dallas to confront her father and the judge had verified it.

Lindsay answered promptly with a brief text: Hooray!

He got a congratulatory one from Josh, while Mike urged him to get a lease signed soon.

He glanced out the window, but instead of seeing the land spreading away from the house, he saw her green eyes and lush body. What did he really feel for her?

He couldn't answer his own question. Lust was paramount now. Already he wanted to make love to her again. He couldn't get enough of her, and her appetite for lovemaking seemed as insatiable as his, which made him desire her even more.

He combed his hair and went to find her.

On Monday they spent another day searching and finding nothing except dirt, roots and rocks. At the house, Jessie Lou had the night off, and Jake had agreed to grill steaks.

Madison turned when she heard Jake enter the kitchen and her heart missed a beat. His black shirt emphasized his muscles and his dark eyes and hair, his broad shoulders. She thought about their lovemaking and fought the urge to go kiss him.

"Want a drink?" she asked instead.

"I'll get a beer. I'll pour wine for you."

"Just a small glass, thanks. I have the steaks ready for you to grill." They got drinks and he carried the steaks outside. While they waited for the grill to get hot, they sat with their drinks.

"Whenever you want, we can set a time to discuss leasing land."

She was surprised. "Don't you need to look it over first?"

He shook his head. "We're far more familiar with this ranch than you'd guess. Several ranches around here, in fact. Geologists have studied this area off and on through the past three years. This isn't the only likely spot, but it's a choice one."

"My, oh, my. I knew nothing about that."

He smiled. "Enough about business. You look great," he said, pulling his chair close to hers and holding her hand. "I want to take you out soon. Some night when we haven't spent a day digging and searching for treasure."

"Name the time." She grinned as she said, "We'll start all sorts of rumors the first time we're seen together. Has word gotten back to your parents in California?"

"Not yet, but I imagine it will by tomorrow from Lindsay."

"Lindsay," Madison repeated his sister's name. "I'll bet she's not one bit happy. Lindsay does not like the Milans and I'll have to admit that Tony probably makes things worse."

"That he does. I know that for a fact. Don't pay any attention. She'll be friendly if I am." He paused to raise her hand and brush a feathery kiss on her palm. His breath was warm, his kiss making her tingle. She drew a deep breath and wanted to be in his arms. He looked up into her eyes while he continued to hold her hand.

"You're definitely hungry?" he asked in a raspy voice.

"I'm famished," she whispered, looking at his mouth. He wanted to make love. His dark eyes conveyed his desire and she responded. Her body grew warmer, and she wanted to step over and sit in his lap. "Jake, we should eat," she whispered.

"Come here, Maddie," he said, taking her drink from her other hand to set it on a table. His fingers tightened around her hand and he tugged lightly. She stood and he pulled her closer, down to his lap, where he wrapped his arms around her and kissed her.

In minutes she pushed against his chest and sat back. "Jake, we're not wasting dinner." She could barely say the words. She stood and walked away from him.

He followed and stepped to the grill to put the steaks on.

"I'll get the rest of the dinner on the table," she said, going inside. She inhaled deeply, trying to cool herself, to get through dinner before it got burned or wasted, but she couldn't stop thinking about afterward and making love the rest of the night. Once again those nagging questions bombarded her, questions about a potential relationship with Jake, about a future. She banished them from her mind and glanced outside to see him standing in front of the grill while a dark cloud of smoke rose and dissipated into the air. Jake was incredibly handsome. It was difficult to think about dinner when all she wanted was to go back to bed.

The steaks were thick, juicy, delicious, but after a few bites her appetite vanished.

"You'll go back to Dallas soon, won't you?" she asked him. "I've been told you're rarely at the ranch."

"That's right. I'd like to be here, but I'm too busy. I've blocked out this week and next week. How long are you here on the ranch before you'll go to New Mexico?"

"I go after Christmas to New Mexico and come back here in late spring for about a month."

"Any chance you'll stay in Dallas some of that time?"

"Maybe," she said, smiling at him.

"I want to see you after this search is over."

"I'd like that," she replied. They gazed in silence at each other. She could see desire in his dark eyes while all she wanted was to be in his arms.

"I don't think you're any hungrier than I am," he said.

"I seem to remember that I was promised a visit to your suite upstairs, but that's never happened."

She stood and he came to his feet at the same time. "That's because we never get that far when heading to a bedroom. C'mon. I'll show you around my digs."

Smiling, he joined her, draping his arm across her shoulders and pulling her close against him. She was aware of his height, his warmth. She tingled with anticipation and fought the urge to stop to kiss him now.

"When I'm in Dallas or farther away and I call you, I want to be able to envision you in your room. Right now that's a blank."

"So you're going to call me?"

"Yes, I am," he said, turning her to face him as they stopped at the foot of the stairs. "I want to see where this is going." His gaze roamed over her features. "We're not the same people we were and we have a lot that has happened between us."

"In some ways we hardly know each other at all."

"That's right, but what I know, I like," he said, his voice getting husky and her heartbeat quickening while her gaze went to his mouth.

"That tour upstairs is going to have to wait a little longer," he whispered before he leaned down to kiss away her reply.

Over an hour later they were still in the bed in his suite. They were lying facing each other and she loved the feel of him toying with long strands of her hair.

"You know, Maddie, I haven't even seen your artwork except the few pictures you showed me downstairs. You're a famous, successful artist but I've always ignored your publicity. You must have other artwork here. You must have a studio somewhere in this house, too. By the way, I haven't seen the whole house, either."

"I think it's your fault that we have limited our seeing the house to the kitchen, the family room, library and your bedroom."

He grinned, flashing snow-white, even teeth. Locks of his dark hair fell over his forehead. "I want to see your bedroom and your studio."

"Then I suggest we get dressed and you keep your hands to yourself and I will try to do the same."

"Keep your hands to myself?" he said.

"You know what I meant." Aware of his steady gaze, she stepped out of bed and began to pick up her clothing. "I will go up and shower and you come up when you're ready."

"Or we could save time and shower here and both go up together."

"I don't really think that would be a time-saver at all. See you upstairs," she said as she left the room.

She showered, dressed in cutoffs and pulled on a bright pink T-shirt. As she brushed her hair, she heard a light knock.

"Anybody home?" Jake stood in the doorway. He was barefoot, wearing jeans and shirtless.

"Oh, honey," she said, crossing the sitting area to him to wrap one arm around his waist and run her hand over his muscled chest. "I would never keep a handsome man like you out," she drawled in a sultry rasp.

He grinned and started to lean down to kiss her. She moved back. "I'll give you the tour first," she said, taking his hand and walking into the hall. She released his hand to wave her fingers. "To the east is the wing with three bedrooms and one smaller bedroom suite. Here in the center of the house…" She glanced at him and momentarily lost her train of thought. Jake had stepped back, leaning one shoulder against the wall with his feet crossed and a hand on his hip while his gaze roamed slowly over her legs.

She tingled and forgot the tour. Her mouth went dry and the temperature around her spiked. "Jake, you're not paying attention," she whispered.

"Oh, I'm paying real close attention. Those are the best-looking legs in Texas and that is saying a lot."

"Thank you, but I believe you're ready for glasses. I can't live up to that description," she said, crossing the distance to him. "Do you want the tour or not?"

He looked down at her, his gaze going to her mouth, and her heart skipped a beat. She tightened her arm around his waist, turning her face up slightly.

"Yeah, give me the tour," he replied and his voice was as raspy as her own.

Surprised, because his words did not match his actions, she waved her hand in a semicircle. "Here in the center are two large bedroom suites. One was my parents' all the years we were growing up and they still stay there if they come to visit me." She moved on to another bedroom suite. "I have taken this one because it's so large and more convenient than being in one of the wings. Now to the west wing," she said, facing west. "There are four more middle-size bedroom suites. One was mine growing up, one was Wyatt's, one was Nick's and one was Tony's. Although Nick rarely sees his ranch, they all have their own ranches now and my dad deeded this one to me. Nick prefers Dallas and Austin. I think he keeps his ranch for an investment."

"You said they gave you the ranch three years ago?"

"Yes, after they started living in Dallas so much. I was out of school and beginning to do well with my painting and Dad said he was giving me the ranch partially because of the success I had made of my art. He helped the others buy their ranches."

"Did it ever occur to you that he might have been so generous to make up for what he did when you were going to elope?"

Startled, she stared at Jake as she shook her head. "No. No, I don't think so."

Jake looked around, dropping the subject.

"Down this hall past the bedrooms is a large room I've had converted into a studio," she said, leading him into a room that had tables, two oversize sinks, easels, racks with brushes and tubes of paint. Canvases, some finished, some in various stages from pencil sketches, were on easels, propped on the floor and hanging on the walls.

He walked over to look at them. "You're really very talented," he said. "I'm impressed."

"I'm glad," she said, smiling at him. "Now, back to my suite." She took his hand and they entered her suite, where she paused to look around.

She glanced at the familiar surroundings of the sitting room, the red, white and green decor, the antique mahogany furniture, the polished plank floor with a thick red area rug in the center. He followed her to an adjoining room, where she held out her hand, waving toward the bedroom.

She walked inside with him, where the same red, white and green decor was used. A four-poster mahogany queen-size bed stood in the center of the room. As she turned to say something to him, the words never came. Looking at her mouth, Jake stepped close to slip his arms around her.

As his lips covered hers, her heart thudded. She wrapped her arms around his neck and held him tightly, wanting his kisses as if it were the first time he had kissed her. She wanted to make love, to hold and kiss him. Even more, she wanted to get to know him again.

They made love long into the night.

By then she had decided she would lease the ranchland to him. She suspected it would be a very good deal for her and would top the other offers they had had.

Other decisions weren't so easily made. Would they fall in love again? Had she already and didn't realize this was the real thing? She was uncertain, something that thirteen years ago she wouldn't have thought possible. She had been so wildly in love with him then. Now she was scared to let go and she didn't know what he felt.

As she ran her fingers lightly over his chest, she kept telling herself one thing: time would tell.

On Tuesday Madison returned to the search with the men. She took a sketch pad and drew while the men dug, pacing off a grid that she and Jake had planned and drawn.

Following her brothers' suggestions, they had moved away from the creek and were in an arroyo that was dry. They worked in the sun and even though it was a fall day, the temperature was in the nineties and Jake's shirt was plastered to his body. She still wanted to come along, in case they found something, but now that she trusted Jake and had no worry about him deceiving her, she decided this would be the last day she would go with them.

When they broke for lunch they went back to where they had parked the trucks in a grove of acacias along the creek to keep the vehicles in the shade.

She sat eating a sandwich with Jake. He had brought a fresh cotton shirt and pulled it on. It was unbuttoned, the shirttail hanging out over his jeans.

He hadn't shaved this morning and had dark stubble on his jaw. His hair was in a tangle with ends wet from his sweat. In spite of the dust, sweat and stubble, he looked sexy and appealing and she thought about the evening, looking forward with anticipation.

"I need to go home and get some other boots tonight. I forgot to bring them this morning. Come home with me and we'll eat there. You've never been in my house."

"All right. Are we coming back to mine or staying at yours?"

"Stay at mine tonight, Maddie," he said, his gaze stirring a sizzling current, making her wish the afternoon would not be so long.

"You have a deal, but I'll need some clothes. What about stopping at the house when we go back and letting me pick up a few things?"

He nodded. "Sure. You're the first woman to stay there, you know."

"That surprises me. You were so eager to marry. I'm surprised you haven't had a serious relationship, let alone that you're still single."

"I've been busy and there never has been anyone I've been that serious about. And I got burned badly, so I've skirted around serious romantic entanglements."

"I married out of spite."

"I always wondered if you were as in love with him as we had been," Jake said quietly.

"Not ever. It was a dreadful mistake that I knew I was making and I got out of it early on because it was messing up Will's life."

"Damn," Jake said quietly, setting down his half-eaten sandwich. "I hope you told your dad."

"I did and he looked pained and said he was afraid of that. It's over and done and I'm sorry if I hurt Will. I wasn't thinking clearly and I was so angry with you at the time."

She met Jake's level gaze. "I hate that," he said and she shrugged.

"As you would say, it's over. Forget it."

His gaze shifted beyond her while he seemed lost in his thoughts for a moment. "That's true," he said and picked up his bottle of water to take a long drink. He waved the bottle at her. "This is the best part of lunch."

"It'll be hotter this afternoon."

"We can swim when we get to my house."

"Sure," she said, smiling at him. He had been about to

take a bite of sandwich, but he lowered it and looked at her with raised eyebrows.

"You have something else in mind when we arrive at my house?"

"You don't?"

He grinned. "I wish we were alone now."

"I promise you, it would not do you any good out here with the ground full of cactus pines, cockleburs and snakes possibly crawling past. Not ever."

"There's a challenge if I ever heard one."

She pointed a finger at him. "Well, we're not alone, so forget it. Eat your sandwich and look forward to finishing here for today."

"Oh, I am looking forward to it," he said in a husky, seductive drawl while his gaze roamed slowly from her head to her toes, making her tingle in its wake. "It's going to be difficult to concentrate on digging holes in the ground this afternoon. My thoughts will be elsewhere."

"It doesn't take great powers of concentration to dig," she said, smiling at him. When he gave her a sexy grin, she began to count down the hours.

In the hot afternoon sun, Jake dug, thinking the treasure could be buried at her ranch house for all they knew. He paused, leaning on his shovel while he glanced at Maddie, who sat with her head bent over her drawing pad while she sketched. Where were they going with their relationship?

She didn't seem to have an answer any more than he did. Sex was hot, the best, and he couldn't get enough of her, but did it go deeper than that? Was he so blinded by desire that he couldn't even perceive the depth of his feelings for her? Did he care if they walked out of each other's lives when this search was over?

He cared about that. In fact, he wanted her to move in with him, but it was a purely lustful longing. He didn't feel the way he had at nineteen—as if she was necessary for his life to continue. At that age he couldn't imagine life without her. They were teenagers and both wildly in love in the way that only teens could be. It had been intense, dramatic and youthful, a love that had been totally entwined with hot sex that she experienced for the first time in her life.

Her father had turned his world upside down. Jake still didn't like to think about how badly it had hurt to lose her.

What about now? He needed to get a reading on what he felt for her, because she would walk out of his life again soon and there might not ever be another chance. Was it going to hurt to tell her goodbye?

With the hot sun beating down on his shoulders and back, he stood looking at her. The thought of her going her own way made his stomach churn. Their time together was coming to an end and he didn't want it to—but was that love or just lust?

From what she had said to him, she was as uncertain as he was about the extent of her feelings. He envied the certainty he had felt at nineteen, never questioning if he truly loved her enough to want to spend the rest of his life with her. He had been so sure and it had taken a lot of pain, time and anger to kill those feelings.

Common sense said to step away, get the physical relationship in perspective and see how he felt. That was common sense, but it didn't appeal to him.

He fished out his phone to call his ranch to tell his cook to put out two steaks for him to grill, and to fix the rest of the dinner and put it in the refrigerator for tonight. He returned to digging, thinking about Maddie and their lovemaking last night and looking forward to tonight. There had never been any woman in his life he had felt so strongly about as he had Maddie. That made him search his feelings now more than ever. If they really fell in love, surely they would each recognize it.

As he dug it dawned on him that if they found the deed, he would have a dilemma—all the more reason to decide soon what his feelings were for her. Now that she would let him lease her land to drill, the whole reason for searching for the deed had vanished.

He didn't want to hurt her. That was one certainty in his life. For Maddie's sake, he would never take any of the Milan land. When he'd thought it would affect her dad, he'd wanted to take it and enjoy every minute when he could tell Judge Milan that part of his ranch now belonged to the Calhouns. That would be sweet revenge. But the ranch was now owned by Maddie. Taking part of it would hurt her, so he wasn't going to do it. He didn't really think the deed existed anyway. With the lack of success they had been having, he figured the old legend was just a tall Texas tale and nothing more.

He couldn't wait to get to the ranch, clean up and enjoy the evening with Maddie.

By Wednesday, Jake's hopes had plummeted. Monday he would be in Dallas, back in the corporate life. When would he see Maddie once he was in Dallas or traveling and she was out here at the ranch?

He loved being a rancher, loved everything about the cowboy life and living on the ranch. The quiet was something he occasionally had to come home and enjoy. But he had only days left.

He plunged the shovel into the hard earth and tossed a shovelful of dirt to one side. "Your ranch looks as if an army of gophers have taken over," he said to Madison, who sat on a nearby rock and sketched.

Once again they were near Rocky Creek. They were in the shade of another grove of trees, digging in ground slightly less packed, and she had found a rock where she could sit and draw.

"What do you say to us stopping at four today? If we haven't found anything by then, I'm giving up for today. We have tomorrow to try one more time. Tomorrow I'll pay the guys a bonus for helping this week—yours and mine."

"You don't have to do that. I can pay the ones who work for me."

He shook his head. "No, this has been my project from the start. It's like chasing rainbows. I insist."

She shrugged. "Okay. Thanks. That's nice." His gaze raked over her. She was dressed to be out on the ranch—boots, jeans, long-sleeved cotton shirt and a broad-brimmed tan Stetson that looked as if she had had it since high school.

"Back to quitting at four. Let's go home, get dressed and let me take you to Dallas tonight to dinner, maybe dancing. I have a home in Dallas and we can just stay in the city. We've earned a night out. Will you go with me?"

A big smile broke out on her face that made his heartbeat quicken. She was irresistible to him when she smiled. "You have a deal," she said.

"Great. Think you can be ready to go by six?"

"Oh, yes. Easily."

"Half past five?" he asked and she thought a moment before she nodded.

"That's it, then," he said. "If I can get home, shower and get back. If not, I won't be much later than that, but I'm definitely aiming for half past five."

"I can't wait. I haven't been out to dinner and dancing with an exciting, handsome man in way too long."

"I hope not since you were sixteen."

She laughed and his grin widened.

"It was a little later than that, but it was not in the past few months."

"Not what I wanted to hear."

"Forget it. I'm going with you tonight."

"So you are and I can't wait." He wanted to chuck this whole search and head home now, but this was next to the last day he could devote to this, so he would stay until four. He jammed the shovel into the ground to get another scoop of dirt and scraped something hard.

Nine

Madison heard the metallic click of Jake's shovel striking something and looked around. She stood up from the rock and walked closer to watch, her eyes meeting Jake's.

"Keep your fingers crossed."

Jake turned to call two of the closest men. "Stoney, Russ, can you come here?"

Both of them came with shovels in hand.

"I've hit something. Help dig here so we can get to it quicker."

They joined him, digging, and Russ struck something after the third shovelful of dirt.

She stood in silence watching them uncover what looked like a piece of battered and scratched black metal. In minutes they began to enlarge the hole. The more dirt they removed the better she could see a large metal box with handles on each side and a smaller handle in the center of the top. Excitement gripped her along with curiosity, far more to see if the legend was actually true than to expect any real treasure.

Soon dirt was dug away from the box and Jake leaned down to pick it up. The other two men bent over to help. Her excitement mounted when it was obvious that the box was heavy. Because it was below them in the ground, it was awkward to grasp, and required all their strength to lift it out unless they dug a larger hole.

Jake called over his shoulder and the other men came to see as Jake and Russ set the box on the ground. She noticed a keyhole on the front of the box. When Jake tried to open it, the lid didn't move.

"It's locked," he said, looking around for a rock. "We're not digging for a key," he remarked. Someone handed him a rock and Jake grasped it to swing hard. After the third hit, the lid budged a fraction. Jake opened it and sunlight glinted on gold coins.

The men broke out in applause.

Madison could barely believe her eyes. "You found it!" she exclaimed.

"That legend was true," Jake said. She could see the surprise on his face and she knew how he was feeling. He'd heard it all his life and had searched for it many times on the Calhoun ranch before trying the Milan ranch.

He picked up a coin and turned it in his hand, standing to show it to Madison while they both peered at it.

"It's from 1849. One side is a Liberty head, and the other is an eagle," Jake said, reading and turning the coin. It's a five-dollar gold coin. I'll be damned," he said, still turning the gold coin in his hand.

"Since you said the treasure is mine," Madison said, "I think everyone here should have ten coins." The men grinned and cheered and told her thanks.

"And you'll still get your bonus," Jake added.

Madison picked up a handful of coins to pass them out. "I'll have this appraised and find out what these are worth."

"I'm keeping mine," Stoney said. "Eighteen forty-nine was a long time ago."

Others agreed as they looked over the coins, turning the gold in their hands.

"This means the remains of our ancestors may be buried in this vicinity," Jake said, looking around. "I'll drive the truck up here and we'll lock this up in the truck. I don't know anything about old coins, but these are in good shape. I have a feeling they're worth a fortune—as long as they're real, and I think they are."

Jake gave orders about where to dig to search for the bones. As the men dispersed, he walked to Madison. "I'll go get the truck and one of them can help me load the box." He shook his head. "I'm still in shock that the legend is true."

"Jake, when we get that back to the house, I want you to take half the treasure. We don't know who that chest really belonged to, and some members of your family may want to keep the coins just because of the historical value. Those coins are part of the Old West, part of early-day Texas and part of our families' histories."

"I think you better reconsider your generous offer. Your brothers may not be happy if you give half away. I get along with Tony, but he doesn't like Calhouns."

"Tony doesn't begin to compare to Lindsay's dislike of Milans," she added. "The family feud lives on in those two."

"Our folks, also. And grandparents even more."

"I don't care who agrees and disagrees."

"That's generous, Maddie," he said. "But if you want to wait to talk to your family—"

"I'll talk them into accepting it," she said. She looked

around the site. "I hope we find the remains and I know you want the deed."

"Yeah. See you in a few minutes." She watched him stride away, his long legs covering the distance until he climbed into his pickup and drove toward her with the truck bouncing over the rough ground.

She couldn't stop her thoughts from returning to a few moments ago. When he'd opened the box, her first reaction was surprise that the legend was true. The thought that immediately followed was a sinking realization that Jake might possibly walk out of her life. Again.

Everything inside her felt squeezed and hurt. The reason for his presence in her life had ended. But she wasn't ready to say goodbye.

Over an hour later, Darren called out to Jake, "Mr. Calhoun, come look. I think I may have found some bones."

Madison had heard Jake instruct the men that they were not to disturb any bones they uncovered, but to wait and let the medical examiner tell them what to do. To her relief, that was what Darren was doing. While Darren stood leaning on his shovel, she hurried to catch up with Jake to go down to the creek bank.

"I hope we can tell whether these are human bones or animal bones," Jake said. "This is a grim discovery, but if it's our ancestors' remains it will be good to get them buried in a proper place."

She stood beside Jake and looked at a large bone. "I don't know much about bones, so I don't know whether it's from a human or not."

"Well, we'll find out from someone official," Jake said, then he turned to Darren. "Just keep looking carefully and see if you can find some more bones here."

She walked away from them, going back to get her sketch pad, but she couldn't take her eyes off Jake. He was strong and fit, sexy. She wanted to hold him and kiss him and she wanted them to make love far more than flying to Dallas for dinner and dancing. She wondered if she could get him to change the plans.

Now they had found the gold and the bones. Her time with Jake was over. She would go back to her artwork and he would return to Dallas and his energy business that probably caused him to travel often.

She didn't want to say goodbye to him. The mere thought of not seeing him hurt deep in her soul. The more time she spent with him, the more she wanted to be with him and the more she wanted him in her life. Permanently in her life. She had no idea how Jake felt and she wasn't going to tell him because he might not feel as strongly.

She was in love with him. It went beyond the love-making, beyond carnal desire. She loved him. Maybe she always had and there was never anyone else and never would be.

What if Jake didn't feel that way and walked out?

She couldn't answer her question, and she hoped she'd never have to.

Later, as they drove to Jake's ranch after having stopped at her house so she could pick up her things, she turned to face him. She placed her fingers lightly on his warm thigh. Instantly, his hand covered hers. "Jake, it's getting late. Let's just go to your ranch tonight instead of Dallas."

"Really? I don't want you to be disappointed if you had your heart set on Dallas, but truthfully, I'm glad to hear you say you'd rather stay here."

"It'll be a lot better. Frankly, I want to open the box and look at the gold. Besides, I can think of more fun ways to spend the evening than going to Dallas."

He glanced at her and then turned his attention to the highway. "When we're home, I'll show you what I've been thinking about all day long."

"You've been thinking about those gold coins," she said, smiling at him.

"Not nearly as much as making love to you," he said in a husky voice. "Just shower while I shower, wrap in a towel and I'll be ready and waiting."

"I figured we'd eat dinner, look at the coins and let our families know and *then* we would spend the rest of the evening in the best way possible," she said softly, stroking his thigh.

He covered her fingers again and held her hand against his leg. "Save the caresses for when we're home. I might wreck the truck."

She laughed softly and started to move her hand away, but his fingers tightened, holding her hand on his leg.

"When we get home, I'll take the box inside. Later tonight, much later, we can count the coins, but I agree we should let our families know. This is a big deal for us. That old legend was the truth—I'm still shocked. Deep down, I really didn't think we would ever find anything. Now we'll have to try to identify whose remains we have. We may not know all of our earliest ancestors who came to Texas."

"I know some of mine, but I don't know how they can specify which ones they might be."

"They should be able to decide which are Milans and which are Calhouns from our DNA, I'd think. I'll call tomorrow and see what to do with the remains."

She turned herself in her seat so she could face him. "This has been a most amazing day. Wyatt will probably want to come by tomorrow and see the coins."

"My whole family will come see them so we're telling them too late tonight for anyone to come to the ranch. I want you to myself with no interruptions."

"I'll get my brothers to come get the coins and take them to the bank. I'm sure word will travel about them and we need to get them secured tomorrow."

"I can do it for you if you'd like."

"Thanks, but I promise you, my brothers will be happy to take mine for me." She couldn't contain the grin that overtook her. "This is so exciting. It isn't the money as much as the link with the past."

"It's a link, but those coins may be worth a lot. It may surprise you."

She realized that an awful lot was surprising her these days.

She turned to look out the window then as they neared Jake's ranch. She glanced out at mesquite and cactus, an occasional acacia or a tall cottonwood. When they reached the entrance to his ranch, the gates were open. He drove across the cattle guard and headed down a graveled road.

Happiness filled her because she was with him and they would soon be alone for the evening. She studied his handsome profile, his straight nose and firm jaw, his prominent cheekbones. Always by the end of the day his black, wavy hair was in a tangle and stubble was beginning to show on his jaw.

She wanted to unbuckle her seat belt, scoot close to him and put her hands on him, but she controlled the impulse. They were almost to his ranch house. Soon she would be able to do what she wanted with him.

The road was winding and seemed long, but finally he drove to the back, parked and handed her a ring with keys. "You unlock the door and I'll give you the alarm code so you can switch it off. I'll carry the gold. It'll help if you'll hold the door."

"Sure you don't want me to help you?"

"No. I got it."

He climbed out and picked up the metal box. She closed the door and rushed ahead to get the back door unlocked. The alarm beeped as she held the door for him and he hurried past her. She punched in the code before the alarm went off, then locked the back door and turned to go look for Jake.

His home was far more ranch style than her parents' elegant house, and it looked comfortable and inviting. She found him in a spacious family room with a beamed ceiling and brown leather furniture. He had set the box on the floor, removed the lid and stood looking at the gold coins. All she could think was that it meant she would see the last of him.

He turned as she walked up. Slipping his arm around her, he pulled her close against his side. "Finding this was like finding a needle in a haystack. It's thanks to your brothers. That location was Wyatt's suggestion."

"It's great, Jake. I'm thrilled."

He looked down at her, tilting her face up to his. "I'd say let's shower together, but I'm really grubby. C'mon. I'll give you a room and we can get cleaned up. I meant it when I said you don't have to wear anything except a towel. That would suit me just fine. That would be even better than that box of gold coins."

Smiling at him, she wanted to pull his head down and kiss him, whether they had cleaned up or not. Her smile faded because desire made her heart pound. She gazed intently into his thickly lashed brown eyes and then she looked at his mouth.

His expression changed. Stepping closer, he slipped his arm around her waist to draw her close against him. "I'm dusty and sweaty."

"I don't care," she said, thinking he was appealing and sexy. With a moan, wanting him with all her being, she wrapped her arms around him and kissed him passionately. She poured her feelings into her kiss, all her longing, all her love for him that had returned full force if it had ever really gone at all.

His hand unfastened her buttons and yanked off her shirt. He had already tossed his aside.

With shaking fingers she undid his belt and jeans. Clothes and boots were tossed away. She could think only of Jake, wanting him desperately, feeling as if she might lose him again. He released her a moment to get protection and then he pulled her into his arms again.

While he kissed her, he picked her up and she wrapped her legs around him. Holding her tightly, he let her slide down so he could enter her, fill her. She was wrapped around him, kissing him as if it were her last time with him.

He thrust deep and fast, pumping his hips. Tension built, a physical need that swept her. He groaned while he kissed her, the sound muffled deep in his throat.

She cried out with her climax. "Jake!" she gasped. "I love you." She whispered the words, meaning them with all her heart, mindlessly lost in the moment as ecstasy and relief poured over her.

He slowed while she draped herself on him. "Jake," she whispered. She showered kisses on his face and throat, not caring about the salty taste of him. She held him tightly with her growing fear that when she let go of him sometime soon, he would be gone forever.

She finally slipped down, placing her feet on the floor, still holding his shoulders.

"It'll be better next time," he said. "We'll take a long time. You'll see." He leaned down to brush kisses on her mouth, her throat.

"It was perfect this time," she whispered before turning away to gather her clothes.

His fingers closed over her wrist. "Come on. I'll show you where a shower is."

He took her down a hall and into a spacious bedroom with polished oak flooring, a sofa, a desk, a big-screen television and a king-size bed. There was a big wooden rocker in the room along with a full-length mirror.

"Right through there is a shower and there should be fresh towels for you. I'm just across the hall."

She nodded and watched him as he left.

Would he disappear out of her life again soon? She intended to see that he didn't.

She showered, washed and dried her hair, and wrapping herself in a thick, pink towel, she went to find her clothes. When she opened the door and stepped into the hall, the bag she had brought from the ranch was waiting outside the door. Smiling, with a glance at the closed door across the hall, she gathered her things and went back inside, closing the door.

Shortly she was dressed in red slacks and a red short-sleeved shirt with flip-flops on her feet. She let her hair fall freely across her shoulders.

She left to find Jake, discovering him in the kitchen. She walked into the room with a high-beamed ceiling, a copper pot rack hanging over the center island workstation, cherry cabinets and stainless-steel appliances, making for a far more up-to-date kitchen than the one on the Milan ranch.

Jake had his back to her while he placed twice-baked potato halves to warm in the oven. He turned and stopped, his gaze roaming over her appreciatively and making her want to be in his arms again.

He crossed the kitchen to her and rested his hands on her hips. "You look too composed and refreshed. We may end up right back in bed."

"I'm not going to argue with that," she said, wrapping her arms around his neck, standing on tiptoe to brush his lips with hers.

His arm tightened around her waist, pulling her tightly

against him while he captured her mouth. With a pounding heart, she kissed him as if they hadn't just made love.

Finally he released her. "I'm fascinated with the old coins," he said.

"The coins are exciting." She didn't add that they weren't as exciting to her as he was.

She could swear his eyes were almost twinkling, and he looked like a kid at Christmas when he asked, "Want to go count them now?"

Seeing his excitement, she agreed.

"There's no way to know which family the gold belonged to," she said, following him into the family room. Jake set his drink on a table, hunkering down to tilt the metal box to dump out the coins.

She sat on the floor across from him and gold coins spilled out, sliding and building into a stack until some came to rest on her crossed feet. She could see inside the open chest and there was a small metal box in the bottom. She reached inside to take it out. "Jake, look. Here's something else," she said, raising the lid to see a folded paper inside.

She picked it up.

"Maddie, let me see that," he said, but she had already started unfolding it with great care.

Ten

"Maddie—" Jake said, stretching out his arm to take the paper from her, but she twisted out of his reach as she began to read.

"'To whom it may concern. Having just lost in a game of chance with cards, a gambling game, I hereby pay in gold one half of my debt to Reuben Calhoun.'" Her mouth went dry and her heart began to pound, but she continued with the note.

"'For the other part of my debt I deed a ten-acre strip of land from the west boundary to the east boundary, along the entire north side of my property, to Reuben Calhoun.' It's signed 'Mortimer Milan.'"

"Maddie, wait a minute—" Jake ordered.

Hurting again as she had so long ago by his actions, she turned to look at him. "This is a deed for part of our ranch to go to the Calhouns. There are witnesses. It's dated 1887." She stared at him while pain squeezed her heart.

"You were after this deed all along. That's why you said I could have the gold if we found it."

Angry, feeling betrayed all over again, she stood and flung the ancient paper at him. "Answer me. You knew about this deed, didn't you?"

"Listen to me." He stood facing her. "Yes, I knew about it."

Closing her eyes, she rocked on her heels as if he had physically hit her, only the blow was to her heart.

"Maddie, I don't want it now."

She opened her eyes. "I don't believe you. You set this all up to see if you could find the deed and have that much of our ranch because that's where you want to drill.

"Don't lie to me, Jake," she demanded, her face flushing. "That's why you wanted to look for the treasure, not for your ancestors' remains. Answer me. That's why you got into this search, isn't it?"

"Yes, it was in the beginning because we were still angry with each other. Maddie," he said, walking around the gold between them.

She was shaking as she faced him and she stepped back to avoid his touch. "Take the property. You succeeded completely and you've made a fool of me in doing so."

Closing the distance, he grasped her shoulders and held her. "Listen to me. I don't want it. I wouldn't think of hurting you that way. Not now."

"I don't believe you," she said, his deceit turning her to ice.

He leaned down and caught up the letter and the deed that was rolled up, tied with a strip of leather with writing on the outside of it.

He handed her the deed. "This may be the real thing and the only copy. Who knows. I'm sure it's the first deed to this land." He held up the letter and tore it in two.

Stunned, Madison watched him. "What are you doing?"

"I would never hurt you deliberately."

"Your family knew you were doing this in hopes of finding the deed, didn't they? They'll expect that land to go to them."

He caught her wrist and picked up the two pieces of the letter. "Come here," he said, taking her into the kitchen. Still shocked by his tearing up the letter, she followed and watched as he opened a drawer to get a box of matches, striking one. Standing over the sink, he set fire to the lower part of the two strips of paper. He glanced at her as the paper burned brightly.

She could only stare at the flames engulfing the letter as it swiftly disappeared. He dropped the remains into the sink before they burned his hand and she watched them curl into black cinders with a plume of fading gray smoke.

"There is no evidence of any change in the Milan deed now," he said.

Momentarily speechless, she stared at him. "Why?" she whispered, unable to get the word out clearly. She gulped for breath. "You did all that searching for the treasure just to get that letter."

Jake stared at her, his own thoughts in turmoil. "I love you," he said, declaring it as if more to himself than her. "Maddie, I just realized that I'm in love with you," he said. He stepped closer to take her in his arms. He felt dazed, but he couldn't bear to hurt her and he realized he did not want to lose her a second time.

"I promise you, I will not take your property and neither will my family. First of all the letter has been destroyed, so now no one can use it. Second—I wouldn't let them take your property if they tried. Third—no living person knows about that letter except the two of us."

"Your family will ask you. Tell them the truth, Jake."

"They'll understand why and if any of them don't, so be

it. If we get into it about the land, I can pay them for their share. I don't care. I love you with all my heart. Maybe I always have deep down. There's really never been any other woman I've been deeply interested in since high school. I love you," he declared again.

Would she accept what he was telling her? He hoped he'd proved his feelings for her. Hoped she realized that to do what he had just done, he had to love her deeply.

He searched her eyes for a clue to her feelings, and saw all the hurt vanish faster than the letter had, replaced by a shimmering glow. Tears spilled down her cheeks as she reached for him, and he gasped for the breath he'd been holding.

"Oh, Jake," she said, "I love you with all my heart. I thought I was losing you again. And I misjudged you again—I'm sorry."

"Shh, Maddie. Originally, I was searching for that deed to wave it in your dad's face. Sorry." Jake pulled her into his embrace, wrapping his arms around her while he lowered his head to kiss her.

In minutes he picked her up, carrying her to his bedroom, yanking back the covers on the bed and then pulling her into his arms to kiss her again. He had a lot to prove to her, yet again.

Later, Madison lay beside Jake with his arm around her. She shifted and turned to look at him and he rolled on his side to face her. "What?" he said.

"Won't your family be terribly unhappy with you?"

"For burning the letter? I don't think so. We're all well-fixed. We don't need to take part of your land. You've told me I can lease a piece of your land or present you with an offer and you'll listen."

"Yes, but you'll be paying the Milans for the lease.

That's different from you owning the land," she said, thinking about what he had just said to her.

He propped his head on his hand to look at her. "I love you, Maddie. I've been searching my feelings, but when you got so angry, I was afraid I was going to lose you again. I don't want that to happen. I want you in my life all the time. This week has been the best week of my life since I was a teenager. The love we had then has gone because it was different. We were kids and I'll have to admit, maybe your dad was right about us being too young to marry. He just went about keeping us apart in a terrible way."

"I know he did, Jake. I have never known that side of my dad. I didn't dream he was capable of doing something so hurtful."

"It's over. We've got now," he said, hugging her and shifting so he could kiss her.

"Maddie, I heard an 'I love you' from you earlier tonight, didn't I?"

She raised her head and met his gaze, and now she wasn't afraid to admit it. "Yes, you did, because I do. I've realized that I love you."

"I love you, too," he said, hugging her. He leaned back and propped his head up. "I want to take you out tomorrow night. We haven't had a fair chance with all that's been happening. Will you go to dinner with me tomorrow night?"

"I would love to go to dinner with you," she said, smiling at him.

"Perfect. We need a fun night out."

She snuggled against him, feeling as if her life was back on an even keel and good once more, finally. In her mind she could hear Jake saying "I love you" again and again.

Thursday night she stood in front of her mirror, checking herself over far too many times to keep track. She wanted to look her best for Jake. He had seen her in her jeans and cutoffs, out hunting treasure all day with him.

She was dressed in a red sleeveless dress with her hair falling free the way he liked it. She had diamond stud earrings in her ears and high-heeled red pumps that matched her knee-length dress. She was eager to be with him, and when she heard the door chimes, she flew to the door.

Smiling, she opened the door to face him and her breath caught in her throat.

Dressed in a navy suit with a white shirt and red tie, he looked more handsome than ever before. His gaze ran over her and the warm approval showed in his dark brown eyes. "You're gorgeous," he said in a husky tone.

"Thank you. Come in and I'll get my purse," she said, stepping back. He entered and waited quietly while she picked up her red purse and joined him.

As they rode in the limo to the airport, he held her hand. "This is the first chance I've had to tell you—I've talked to my siblings about the gold and invited them out Saturday night for a cookout. The gold is still in my vault at the ranch, so I'll show them my share."

It wasn't so much the gold that had her worried. "Have you told them about the deed?"

"Yes, and nobody raised an objection. They're okay with the whole deal."

"I can't imagine. Especially your sister."

"Lindsay surprised me a little because she was willing to accept whatever I decided."

"That's great," Madison said, unable to imagine Lindsay Calhoun yielding so gracefully to her brother's wishes where it involved a Milan.

"I've thought about it and I'll be happy to invite your family, too, on Saturday if they want to come."

"My brothers are fascinated and amazed that we found the treasure."

"I still am. I never really expected to find anything."

"I didn't, either."

"Maddie, there's something else. While I was at my office today, your dad called me. He said he wants to talk to me. He asked for an appointment to come to my office, so we have one tomorrow afternoon at four."

"I hope he apologizes, although he can't really undo what he's done," she said, looking at Jake and wanting to kiss him. She couldn't get enough of him and now that they had both said they were in love, her feelings for him seemed to strengthen steadily. She reached out to hold his hand. He smiled, giving her hand a light squeeze.

"I'll let you know about your dad. Now enough about the family. Let's think about us. Although if I think about you too much, we may have to cut short this evening by quite a bit."

Laughing, she hugged him. She felt giddy with love for him.

They flew in his jet to Dallas, where they went to an elegant new restaurant on the twenty-fifth floor where the view overlooked the city. Jake ordered wine for them, and after it had been tasted, approved and poured, he asked her to dance.

She stepped into his arms and was carried back to high school, to being young, carefree and so in love with him. She looked up at him, smiling, winding her arms around his neck.

"This is good, Jake. I didn't expect to ever be dancing with you again."

"I agree. It's very good."

They danced a slow number, next a fast dance and returned to their table. They sipped their wine and he gazed at her over candlelight. "How did it go when you took in the gold?"

She smiled. "You know who did it. Wyatt came in his

sheriff's car to take it to the bank. Nick and Tony were with him and they all had to see the coins. I told them each to take ten home for now. They were amazed that the coins really existed, but none of us knows who the Milan was who was named Mortimer. Some of our property goes back that far, but the Double M was named for Michael Milan."

"Did you tell any of them about the letter and the deed?"

"Yes and they're all three shocked that you burned the letter. They were impressed by your generosity, that's for certain, and maybe that made a dent in the old feud. At least for Wyatt and Nick. My brothers are really surprised to find the treasure actually existed, as well as the deed, and I think they're as fascinated by the coins as I am. Now the coins are deposited safely in the Bank of Verity," she said, smiling at him.

"Good place for them to be."

When the small band started the next song, she recognized the ballad as the one they called "our song" when they had been in high school.

Still in his arms out on the dance floor, she looked up at him. "Did you ask them to play that song?"

Jake smiled. "Yes. I wanted to see if you remembered."

"I remember so much," she said. "That was a special time in our lives." She danced with him, holding him close as joy bubbled inside because she was in his arms and he seemed as happy as she.

Later, after dinner, he took her to his house in a gated area in a new suburban section, set back on a landscaped lawn. Her gaze roamed over the two-story Colonial that was large but not the mansion she guessed he would have. Inside he showed her the downstairs, after which they sat in the large family room, where he stepped behind the bar to pour nightcaps and then returned to sit with her on a dark brown leather couch.

He shed his coat and tie, unbuttoning the top buttons of

his shirt while she watched him. "Keep going," she said when he stopped, and he grinned at her as he took her drink from her hand and set it on a glass coffee table. He reached into his pocket and sat beside her.

"Maddie, will you marry me?"

As her heart thudded, she flung her arms around his neck. "I love you, Jake. Of course I'll marry you," she cried, joy bringing tears of happiness to her eyes.

He leaned back. "Hey, don't start crying."

"I'm so happy," she said, watching as he took her hand and slipped the ring on her finger.

"I love you and I'll try to always make you happy," he said.

"Jake, this is beautiful," she said, looking at the large diamond, surrounded by an intricate design of smaller diamonds. "This is just gorgeous. And it fits." She looked up at him and could see the love she felt mirrored in his eyes. She threw her arms around him to hug him while she kissed him.

In a few moments he paused to face her again. "I should tell your dad, and I will, but there's no way I'm asking for his permission."

She laughed. "No, you're not. You don't even have to tell him. I will. Some of the Milans and Calhouns are going to have to start speaking to each other now that they will be in-laws."

He grinned. "They'll adjust. I don't care what they do, really. I love you and that's all that really matters to me. And please, my big request is let's not wait forever for a wedding."

"Suits me fine," she answered, looking at her ring. "Jake, this is the most beautiful ring I've ever seen."

"You might be exaggerating there, but I'm glad you're happy with it. Ahh, I love you, darlin'. With all my heart, forever." He drew her into his embrace again and kissed away her reply. Finally, she looked up at him.

"Jake, we're going to have to tell our families. I'm too excited to wait even though it's kind of late. Tony is just going to have to adjust to having a Calhoun for a brother-in-law."

"I don't know whether he can stop fighting with Lindsay long enough to try to be friends. And I will have a talk with Lindsay about her attitude. Mike's another one."

"We should call your parents first. I barely know them."

"Doesn't matter. Everyone can get to know each other. We're the ones getting married and that's all that's really important. They should act civil to each other through the wedding."

She laughed. "I can't stop laughing. I feel giddy with happiness. Get your phone and let's start calling. I'm telling Tony first and then Wyatt and Nick if we can find him."

Jake picked her up and placed her in his lap, holding her and smiling at her. "This is going to be so good, Maddie. We have a lot of years to make up for."

She felt a warm glow of joy as she wrapped her arms around his neck and smiled in return. "You're going to have to put up with my art and with me traveling to New Mexico, though for much shorter trips than I'm used to. For now, I'd like to keep the gallery I have there. It helps that I have good people running it."

"Sure, just like you'll have to put up with my traveling. I promise you, though, I've always had a schedule and I intend to retire from that business in about ten more years to be a rancher all the time. This is what I love."

"We'll work it all out." She held his jaw to get his full attention. "Jake, we've lost a lot of years together. I want your babies, a family. Soon. How do you feel about it?"

He smiled at her and leaned forward to kiss her lightly.

"I think that's great. We both grew up in families with several kids. That's what I want, too, Maddie."

They kissed, long and deeply, a kiss that to her was a promise and a physical bonding that reflected the feelings in her heart. When she leaned away, she looked up.

"I love you more than I can ever tell you or show you. It'll take a lifetime."

"I feel the same way, and right now, I feel like the luckiest man on the planet."

She laughed. "That's an exaggeration, but I'm glad you feel that way. This is wonderful, Jake, and no one will stop us or interfere this time. This wedding will set a record for how fast it gets planned."

"They sure won't stop us and fast is great."

"Jake, I'm going to become a Calhoun. Mercy!"

He grinned, kissing her cheek. "You will be the most beautiful Calhoun to ever be in the family. You'll be a good influence on the Calhouns for sure, and maybe this may be the death knell for the feud."

She sat up and reached for her phone. "I'm calling Tony."

"I'm going to ask your brothers to be groomsmen."

"That's nice, Jake. Then I should ask Lindsay to be a bridesmaid, but I think she'll turn me down." She shook her finger at him. "And don't you browbeat her into accepting."

"Fine," he agreed, feigning a sheepish face. "Whatever you want. Just as long as you pick a date tonight before we call everyone." He found the calendar on his phone.

"We could have a Christmas wedding."

Jake groaned. "You're not listening to me. I said you couldn't make me wait. How about a September wedding?"

"This month?" She laughed. "That's impossible."

"Are we going to have our first fight?"

"Absolutely not. I promise very soon—I'll aim for setting a record for planning a big wedding."

"I'm anxious. I can't wait. Ahh, darlin', I've waited too long in the past. I can pay for the wedding and I can afford to pay rush rates."

"You don't have to pay for the wedding. Dad owes us this. And we will have a rush job. But a deluxe one," she said.

Jake grinned and shook his head. "Why do I think this wedding is going to cost the judge a small fortune?"

"I meant it when I said Dad owes us. Think of the biggest church in Dallas and let's rent the whole country club for the reception. If we can't get it on short notice, we'll go elsewhere."

"Maddie, let it go. We don't need a whole country club," he said, chuckling.

She studied the calendar. "Okay, this is almost humanly impossible for a big wedding, but we can do it if we pay extra for services. How about the first Saturday morning in October?"

"Ahh, that's my darlin'. I'd prefer this weekend, but the first Saturday in October isn't bad. Do you have any druthers for a honeymoon?"

"Only with you," she said, smiling.

"Great. Now for the phone calls. We have a wedding to plan."

"An expensive wedding," she added, laughing with him.

Epilogue

Madison stood with her arm linked through her father's as they stood in the vestibule of the church. She could see Jake, tall and handsome, waiting for her at the altar. The men in the Milan and Calhoun families were handsome. Her gaze ran down the line of eight groomsmen, which included her brothers as well as Jake's.

The problem person had been Lindsay, who had coolly and politely turned down Madison's invitation to be a bridesmaid. Jake had insisted there were no hard feelings over her rejection, but Madison wondered. She suspected Lindsay would not speak to her tonight, because she usually didn't speak if they encountered each other in Verity.

Madison didn't want a hostile bridal attendant, even if she was her future sister-in-law, so she was not unhappy to have Lindsay turn her down. The bridesmaids were all her friends plus a cousin and a relative Madison had always been close friends with.

Jake had the same sort of arrangement because he had a cousin as a groomsman. Friends and cousins served as ushers for Jake and she had friends and cousins who would be at the guest register.

Her father squeezed her hand, getting her attention. "Madison, I know I've told you this a hundred times, but I'll tell you one last time—I'm sorry you and Jake were hurt," her father said. "I wish you all the happiness possible now."

"Thank you," she said, gazing into his blue eyes and knowing it was time to accept his apology and forgive him. Glancing at Jake, her thoughts changed to when they could get away from their reception for their honeymoon.

Soon the bridesmaids began their walk down the aisle. With a fanfare of trumpets, violins started the wedding march as the wedding planner cued Madison and her father to walk down the aisle.

Her gaze flew to Jake's and she never saw anyone else while she walked slowly beside her dad. With each step her happiness grew. She would finally marry Jake. It seemed right and so long awaited.

When his dark brown eyes met her gaze, she was eager to repeat her vows and become Mrs. Jacob Calhoun.

Finally they reached the altar and Jake came forward. She didn't even hear her father's reply when he released her hand and Jake's fingers wrapped around hers as he stepped to her side. He looked down at her and smiled, enveloping them both in their own world on the best day of her life.

They repeated vows, prayed, listened to solos and finally they were introduced to the guests as Mr. and

Mrs. Jacob Calhoun. To her delight, she had just become Jake's wife.

They rushed back up the aisle and out to go around and come back for pictures.

In an empty hallway Jake halted to draw her into his arms. "I love you, Mrs. Calhoun."

She smiled at him. "I hope you do half as much as I love you."

He kissed her hard, possessively, and she returned his kiss, looking forward to their wedding night and every night thereafter.

The reception was at the country club. The train to her white satin designer dress had been removed, leaving her in a strapless sheath. Her hair was swept in an updo, and she had already shed her veil.

The crowd spilled outside onto the veranda. It was a sunny, warm fall day in Dallas and children of guests played on the lawn.

All afternoon while she talked to guests, Madison was aware of Jake in various parts of the room or out on the terrace.

Occasionally, she would lose sight of him, but then she would spot him again.

It was late afternoon and she was talking with some friends when Jake walked up to take her arm. "If you ladies will excuse us, someone wants to see Madison."

They moved away and he headed toward the kitchen door.

"Where are we going and who wants to see me?" she asked, smiling to friends as she passed them.

"I want to see you in the worst way and we are going to a waiting limousine. Your maid of honor, Carol, is waiting in the kitchen to get your bouquet to toss it in your place if you can forgo the thrill of throwing your bouquet."

She laughed. "I can, but now Carol doesn't have a chance to catch it."

"I believe the lady is already wearing an engagement ring on her finger, so I don't think she needs to catch the bouquet. Are you arguing about leaving with me now?"

"Not one word," she said, grasping his hand and moving ahead of him. They entered the kitchen while the staff smiled and waved to her. If she passed close to any of them, she thanked them for their help.

Jake held the door and they stepped to the delivery drive behind the kitchen. A high fence surrounded the area with thick shrubbery along the fence to hide the back door.

A sleek black limo waited and a chauffeur held the door for them, closing it behind them once they got in. In seconds he pulled the limo away.

Turning to her, Jake took her into his arms. "Mrs. Calhoun, how I've waited for you to be my bride." He kissed her, a long kiss that she wanted to never end.

His jet waited and by nightfall they were in a penthouse in New York. She briefly saw the balcony and the city lights, but then she was in Jake's arms and the world was forgotten.

She pushed the jacket to his tux off his shoulders and tossed it onto a chair. In the plane she had changed from her wedding gown to a knee-length pale blue silk dress. Jake's fingers moved deftly at the back of her neck and she felt cool air as he pulled the zipper down slowly and then pushed the dress away. He held her away from him so he could look at her for moments.

"You're beautiful, Maddie. I love you more every day."

She stepped into his arms and stood on tiptoe to kiss him, holding him tightly. Jake leaned over her, wrapping his arms tightly around her. "I love you, darlin', with all my heart."

Joyously, she kissed him, certain this tall, handsome Texas rancher was the love of her life and always had been.

* * * * *

"Look, Ava, I know we were never the best of friends..."

Even if we were—for one night, anyway—lovers, Peyton couldn't help thinking. Hoping she wasn't thinking that, too. Figuring she probably was. "But I obviously need help with this new and improved me, and I'm not going to get it from some total stranger. I don't know anyone here who could help me except you. Because you're the only one here who knows me."

"I *did* know you," she corrected him. "When we were in high school. Neither of us is the person we were then."

There was something in her voice when she said that that made Peyton hesitate. It was true he wasn't the person he'd been in high school; Ava obviously still was. Maybe the adult wasn't quite as snotty, vain or superficial, but she could still put a guy in his place. She was still classy.

She was still beautiful.

She was still out of his league.

MY FAIR BILLIONAIRE

BY
ELIZABETH BEVARLY

MILLS
BOON®

Published in Great Britain 2014
by Mills & Boon, an imprint of Harlequin (UK) Limited,
Eton House, 18-24 Paradise Road, Richmond, Surrey, TW9 1SR

© 2014 Elizabeth Bevarly

ISBN: 978-0-263-91468-9

51-0614

Harlequin (UK) Limited's policy is to use papers that are natural, renewable and recyclable products and made from wood grown in sustainable forests. The logging and manufacturing processes conform to the legal environmental regulations of the country of origin.

Printed and bound in Spain
by Blackprint CPI, Barcelona

Elizabeth Bevarly is a *New York Times* bestselling, RITA® Award nominated author of more than seventy novels and novellas who recently celebrated the twenty-fifth anniversary of signing her first book contract—with Mills & Boon! Her novels have been translated into more than two dozen languages and published in more than three dozen countries, and someday she hopes to visit all the places her books have. Until then, she writes full-time in her native Louisville, Kentucky, usually on a futon between two cats. She loves reading and movies and discovering British TV shows on Netflix. And also fiddling around with soup recipes. And going to farmers' markets with her husband. And texting with her son, who's at college in Washington, DC. Visit her website at www.elizabethbevarly.com or find her on Facebook at the Elizabeth Bevarly Reader Page.

For David and Eli.
Thanks for always having my back.
I love you guys. OXY.

One

T. S. Eliot was right, Ava Brenner thought as she quickened her stride down Michigan Avenue and ducked beneath the awning of a storefront. April really was the cruelest month. Yesterday, the skies above Chicago had been blue and clear, and temperatures hovered in the high fifties. Today, gray clouds pelted the city with freezing rain. She tugged her scarf from the collar of her trench coat and over her head, knotting it beneath her chin. The weather would probably ruin the emerald silk, but she was on her way to meet a prospective vendor and would rather replace an injured scarf than have the perfect auburn chignon at her nape get wet and ragged.

Image was everything. Bottom line. That was a lesson life hammered home when Ava was still in high school. April wasn't the only thing that was cruel—teenage girls could be downright brutal. Especially the rich, vain, snotty ones at posh private schools who wore the latest designer fashions and belittled the need-based-scholarship students who made do with discount-store markdowns.

Ava pushed the thought away. A decade and a half lay between her and graduation. She was the owner of her own business now, a boutique called Talk of the Town that rented haute couture fashions to women who wanted only the best for those special occasions in life. Even if the shop was operating on a shoestring and wishful thinking, it was starting to show a profit. At least she looked the part of successful businesswoman. No one had to know she was her own best customer.

She whipped the scarf from her head and tucked it into the pocket of her trench coat as she entered an elegant eatery. Beneath, she wore a charcoal-gray Armani jacket and trousers, paired with a sage-colored shell she knew enhanced her green eyes. The outfit had arrived at Talk of the Town just this week, and she'd wanted to test-drive it for comfort and wearability.

As she approached the host stand, her cell phone twittered. It was the vendor she was supposed to be meeting, asking to postpone their appointment for an evening later in the week. So Ava would be on her own for dinner tonight. As usual. Still, she hadn't taken herself out in a long time, and she had been working extra hard this month. She'd earned a bit of a treat.

Basilio, the restaurant's owner, greeted her by name with a warm smile. Every time she saw him, Ava was reminded of her father. Basilio had the same dark eyes, close-cropped salt-and-pepper hair and neatly trimmed mustache. But she was reasonably certain that, unlike her father, Basilio had never done time in a federal prison.

Without even checking the seating chart, he led Ava to her favorite table by the window, where she could watch the passersby as she ate. As she lifted her menu, however, her attention was yanked away by a ruckus in the bar. When she glanced up, she saw Dennis, her favorite bartender, being berated by a customer, a tall man with broad shoulders and coal-black hair. He was evidently offended by Dennis's suggestion that he'd had too much to drink, a condition that was frankly obvious.

"I'm fine," the man insisted. Although his words weren't slurred, his voice was much louder than necessary. "And I want another Macallan. Neat."

Dennis remained calm as he replied, "I don't think—"

"That's right," the man interrupted him. "You don't think. You serve drinks. Now serve me another Macallan. Neat."

"But, Mr.—"

"Now," the man barked.

Ava's pulse leaped at the angrily uttered word. She'd worked her way through college at three jobs, one of which had been as a waitress. She'd dealt with her share of patrons who became bullies after drinking too much. Thankfully, Basilio and her waiter, Marcus, were on the spot quickly to attend to the situation.

Dennis shook his head at the others' approach, holding up a hand for them to wait. In gentling tones, he said, "Mr. Moss, maybe it would be better if you had a cup of coffee instead."

Heat splashed into Ava's belly at hearing the name. Moss. She had gone to school—long ago, in a galaxy far away—with a Moss. Peyton Moss. He had been a grade ahead of her at the tony Emerson Academy.

But this couldn't be him, she told herself. Peyton Moss had sworn to everyone at Emerson that he was leaving Chicago the moment he graduated and never coming back. And he'd kept that promise. Ava had returned to Chicago only a few months after earning her business degree and had run into a handful of her former classmates—more was the pity—none of whom had mentioned Peyton's return.

She looked at the man again. Peyton had been Emerson's star hockey player, due not just to his prowess, but also to his size. His hair had been shoulder-length, inky silk, and his voice, even then, had been dark and rich. By now, it could have easily deepened to the velvety baritone of the man at the bar.

When he turned to look at Marcus, Ava bit back a gasp. Although the hair was shorter and the profile harsher, it was indeed Peyton. She'd know that face anywhere. Even after sixteen years.

Without thinking, she jumped up and hurried to place herself between Peyton and the others. With all the calm she could muster, she said, "Gentlemen. Maybe what we need here is an unbiased intermediary to sort everything out."

Peyton would laugh himself silly about that if he recognized her. Ava had been anything but *unbiased* toward him in high school. But he'd been plenty biased toward her, too. That was what happened when two people moved in such disparate social circles in an environment where the lines of society were stark, immutable and absolute. When upper class met lower class in a place like Emerson, the sparks that flew could immolate an entire socioeconomic stratum.

"Ms. Brenner, I don't think that's a good idea," Basilio said. "Men in his condition can be unpredictable, and he's three times your size."

"My condition is fine," Peyton snapped. "Or it would

be. If this establishment honored the requests of its paying customers."

"Just let me speak to him," Ava said, dropping her voice.

Basilio shook his head. "Marcus and I can handle this."

"But I know him. He and I went to school together. He'll listen to me. We're...we were..." Somehow she pushed the word out of her mouth. "Friends."

It was another word that would have made Peyton laugh. The two of them had been many things at Emerson—unwilling study partners, aggressive sparring partners and for one strange, intoxicating night, exuberant lovers—but never, ever, friends.

"I'm sorry, Ms. Brenner," Basilio said, "but I can't let you— "

Before he could stop her, Ava spun around and made her way to the bar. "Peyton," she said when she came to a halt in front of him.

Instead of looking at Ava, he continued to study Dennis. "What?"

"This has gone far enough. You need to be reasonable."

He opened his mouth, but halted when his gaze connected with hers. She'd forgotten what beautiful eyes he had. They were the color and clarity of good cognac, fringed by sooty lashes.

"I know you," he said, suddenly more lucid. His tone was confident, but his expression held doubt. "Don't I?"

"You and I went to school together," she said, deliberately vague. "A long time ago."

He seemed surprised by the connection. "I don't remember you from Stanford."

Stanford? she echoed to herself. Last she'd heard he

was headed to a university in New England with a double major in hat tricks and cross-checking and a minor in something vaguely scholastic in case he injured himself. How had he ended up on the West Coast?

"Not Stanford," she said.

"Then where?"

Reluctantly, she told him, "The Emerson Academy here in Chicago."

His surprise multiplied. "You went to Emerson?"

Well, he didn't need to sound so shocked. Did she still look that much like a street urchin?

"Yes," she said evenly. "I went to Emerson."

He narrowed his eyes as he studied her more closely. "I don't remember you from there, either."

Something sharp pricked her chest at the comment. She should be happy he didn't remember her. She wished she could forget the girl she'd been at Emerson. She wished she could forget Peyton, as well. But so often over the past sixteen years, he and the other members of his social circle had crept into her brain, conjuring memories and feelings she wished she could bury forever.

Without warning, he lifted a hand to cradle her chin and jaw. Something hot and electric shot through her at the contact, but he didn't seem to notice. He simply turned her face gently one way, then the other, looking at her from all angles. Finally, he dropped his hand back to the bar. He shook his head, opened his mouth to speak, then—

Then his expression went slack. "Oh, my God. Ava Brenner."

She expelled an irritated sigh. Damn. She didn't want anyone to remember her the way she'd been at Emerson, especially the kids like Peyton. Especially Peyton, period. In spite of that, a curl of pleasure wound through her when she realized he'd made a space for her, however small, in his memory.

Resigned, she replied, "Yes. It's me."

"Well, I'll be damned," he said, his tone belying nothing of what he might be thinking.

He collapsed onto a barstool, gazing at her with those piercing golden eyes. A rush of conflicting emotions washed over her that she hadn't felt for a very long time—pride and shame, arrogance and insecurity, blame and guilt. And in the middle of it all, an absolute uncertainty about Peyton, about herself, about the two of them together. Then as well as now.

Oh, yes. She definitely felt as if she was back in high school. And she didn't like it now any better than she had then.

When it became clear that Peyton wasn't going to cause any more trouble, Dennis snatched the empty cocktail glass from the bar and replaced it with a coffee mug. Basilio released a slow breath and threw Ava a grateful smile. Marcus went back to check on his diners. Ava told herself to return to her table, that she'd done her good deed for the day and should just leave well enough alone. But Peyton was still staring at her, and something in his expression made her pause. Something that sent another tumble of memories somersaulting through her brain. Different memories from the others that had plagued her tonight, but memories that were every bit as unpleasant and unwanted.

Because it had been Ava, not Peyton, who had led the ruling social class at the posh, private Emerson Academy. It had been Ava, not Peyton, who had been rich, vain and snotty. It had been Ava, not Peyton, who had worn the latest designer fashions and belittled the need-based-scholarship students who made do with discount-store markdowns. At least until the summer before her senior year, when her family had lost everything, and she'd suddenly found herself walking in their discount-store markdowns herself. Then she'd been the one who was penniless, unwanted and bullied.

Peyton didn't say a word as Ava studied him, pondering all the things that had changed in the decade and a half since she'd seen him. A few threads of silver had woven their way into his dark hair, and the lower half of his face was shadowed by a day's growth of beard. She couldn't remember him shaving in high school. But perhaps he had, even if that morning when she'd woken up beside him in her bedroom, he—

She tried to stop the memories before they could form, but they came anyway. How it had all played out when the two of them were forced to work together on a semester-long project for World Civ, one of the classes that combined seniors and juniors. Money really did change everything—at least at Emerson, it had. School rules had dictated that those whose families had lots of money must belittle those whose families had none, and that those who had nothing must resent those who had everything. In spite of that, there had always been… something…between Ava and Peyton. Something hot and heavy that burned up the air in any room the two of them shared. Some strange, combustible reaction due to…something. Something weird. Something volatile. Something neither of them had ever been able to identify or understand.

Or, ultimately, resist.

It had culminated one night at her house when the two of them had been working late on that class project and had ended up… Well, it hadn't exactly been making love, since whatever they'd felt for each other then had had nothing to do with love. But it hadn't been sex, either. There had been more to it than the mingling of two bodies. It had just fallen short of the mingling of two souls.

The morning after, Peyton had jumped out of bed on one side, and Ava had leaped out on the other. They had hurled both accusations and excuses, neither listening to the other. The only thing they'd agreed on was that they'd made a colossal mistake that was never to be mentioned again. Peyton had dressed and fled through her bedroom window, not wanting to be discovered, and Ava had locked it tight behind him. Monday morning, they turned in their assignment and went back to being enemies, and Ava had held her breath for the remainder of the year. Only after Peyton graduated and took off for college had she been able to breathe again.

For all of three weeks. Until her entire life came crashing down around her, pitching her to the bottom rung of the social ladder among the very people she had treated so callously before. People whom she quickly learned had deserved none of the treatment she had spent years dishing out.

She turned to Basilio. "I need a favor. Could I ask one of your waiters to run back to my shop for my car so I can drive Mr. Moss home? I'll stay here and have coffee with him until then."

Basilio looked at her as if she'd lost every marble she possessed.

"It's only a fifteen-minute walk," she told him. "Ten if whoever you send hurries."

"But, Ms. Brenner, he's not—"

"—himself," Ava quickly interjected. "Yes, I know, which is why he deserves a pass tonight."

"Are you sure that's a good idea?"

No, she wasn't. This Peyton was a stranger to her in so many ways. Not that the Peyton she used to know had exactly been an open book. He might not have thought much of her kind when they were in high school, and maybe he hadn't been much of a gentleman, but he hadn't been dangerous, either. Well, not in the usual sense of the word. Whatever had made him behave badly tonight, he'd calmed down once he recognized a familiar face.

Besides, she owed him. She owed him more than she could ever make up for. But at least, by doing this, she might make some small start.

"My keys are in my purse at my table," she told Basilio, "and my car is parked behind the shop. Just send someone down there to get it, and I'll take him home. Please," she added.

Basilio looked as if he wanted to object again, but instead said, "Fine. I'll send Marcus. I just hope you know what you're doing."

Yes, well, that, Ava thought, made two of them.

Peyton Moss awoke the way he hadn't awoken in a very long time—hungover. Really hungover. When he opened his eyes, he had no idea where he was or what time it was or what he'd been doing in the hours before wherever and whatever time he was in.

He lay still in bed for a minute—he was at least in a bed, wasn't he?—and tried to figure out how he'd arrived in his current position. Hmm. Evidently, his current position was on his stomach atop a crush of sheets, his face shoved into a pillow. So that would be a big yep on the bed thing. The question now was, *whose* bed?

Especially since, whoever the owner was, she wasn't currently in it with him.

But he concluded the owner of the bed must be a she. Not only did the sheets smell way too good to belong to a man, but the wallpaper, he discovered when he rolled over, was covered with roses, and a chandelier above him dripped ropes of crystal beads. He drove his gaze around the room and saw more evidence of gender bias in an ultrafeminine dresser and armoire, shoved into a corner by the room's only window, which was covered by billows of lace.

So he'd gone home with a strange woman last night. Nothing new about that, except that going home with strangers was something he'd been more likely to do in his youth. Not that thirty-four was old, dammit, but it was an age when a man was expected to start settling down and figuring out what he wanted. Not that Peyton hadn't done that, too, but… Okay, so maybe he hadn't settled down that much. And maybe he hadn't quite figured out everything he wanted. He'd settled some and figured out the bulk of it. Hell, that was why he'd come back to a city he'd sworn he would never set foot in again.

Chicago. God. The last time he was here, he'd been eighteen years old and wild as a rabid badger. He'd left his graduation ceremony and gone straight to the bus station, stopping only long enough to cram his cap and gown into the first garbage can he could find. He hadn't even gone home to say goodbye. Hell, no one at home had given a damn what he did. No one in Chicago had.

He draped an arm over his eyes and expelled a weary sigh. Yeah, nothing like a little adolescent melodrama to start the day off right.

He jackknifed to a sitting position and slung his legs

over the bed. His jacket and tie were hanging over the back of a chair and his shoes were on the floor near his feet. His rumpled shirt and trousers were all fastened, as was his belt. Obviously, nothing untoward had happened the night before, so, with any luck, there wouldn't be any awkward moments once he found out who his hostess was.

Carefully, he made his way to the door and headed into a bathroom on his right, turning on the water to fill the sink. After splashing a few handfuls onto his face, he felt a little better. He still looked like hell, he noted when he caught his reflection in the mirror. But he felt a little better.

The mirror opened to reveal a slim cabinet behind it, and he was grateful to see a bottle of mouthwash. At least that took care of the dead-animal taste in his mouth. He found a comb, too, and dragged that through his hair, then did his best to smooth the wrinkles from his shirt.

Leaving the bathroom, he detected the aroma of coffee and followed it to a kitchen that was roughly the size of an electron. The light above the stove was on, allowing him to find his way around. The only wall decoration was a calendar with scenes of Italy, but the fridge door was crowded with stuff—a notice about an upcoming Italian film festival at the Patio Theater, some pictures of women's clothing cut out of a magazine and a postcard reminding whoever lived here of an appointment with her gynecologist.

The coffeemaker must have been on a timer, because there was no evidence of anyone stirring but him. Glancing down at his watch, he saw that it was just after five, which helped explain why no one was stirring. Except that the coffeemaker timer must have been set for now, so whoever lived here was normally up at this ungodly hour.

He crossed the kitchen in a single stride and exited on the other side, finding himself in a living room that was barely as big as the bedroom. Enough light from the street filtered through the closed curtains for him to make out a lamp on the other side of the room, and he was about to move toward it when a sound to his right stopped him. It was the sound a woman made upon stirring when she was not ready to stir, a soft sough of breath tempered by a fretful whimper. Through the semidarkness, he could just make out the figure of a woman lying on the couch.

Peyton had found himself in a lot of untenable positions over the years—many of which had included women—but he had no idea what to do in a situation like this. He didn't know where he was, had no idea how he'd gotten here and was clueless about the identity of the woman under whose roof he had passed the night. For all he knew, she could be married. Hell, for all he knew, she could be a knife-wielding maniac. Then his hostess made that quiet sound of semiconsciousness again, and he decided she couldn't be the last. Knife-wielding maniacs couldn't sound that delectable. Still, if she was sleeping out here and he'd spent the night in her bedroom, he had nothing to feel guilty about, right? Except for tossing her out of her bed when he should have been the one sleeping on the couch. And except for passing out on her in the first place.

What the hell had happened last night? He mentally retraced his steps from the moment he set foot back on his native soil. Although he'd left Chicago via Greyhound bus more than fifteen years ago, his return had been aboard a private jet. His private jet. He might have been a street dog in his youth, but in adulthood... Ah, who was he kidding? In adulthood, he was still a street dog. That was the reason he was back here.

Anyway, after landing, he'd headed straight to the Hotel Intercontinental on Michigan Avenue. That much Peyton remembered with crystal clarity, because the Hotel Intercontinental was the sort of place that A) he never would have had the nerve to enter when he was a kid, and B) would have tossed him out on his ass if he *had* tried to enter when he was a kid. Funny how they'd had no problem accepting his platinum card yesterday.

He further remembered walking into his suite and tossing his bag onto the massive bed, then going to the window and pushing aside the curtains. He recalled looking out on Michigan Avenue, at the gleaming high-rises and upscale department stores that had always seemed off-limits to him when he lived here. This whole neighborhood had seemed off-limits to him when he was a kid. In spite of that, he'd come to this part of town five days a week, nine months a year, because the Emerson Academy for College Preparatory Learning sat in the middle of it. For those other two days of the week and three months of the year, though, Peyton had always had to stay with his own kind in the rough South Side neighborhood where he'd grown up.

Yesterday, looking out that window, he had been brutally reminded of how his teenage life in this part of town had been juxtaposed to the life—if he could even call it that—that he'd led in his not-even-marginal neighborhood. As much as he'd hated Emerson, it had always felt good to escape his home life for eight hours a day. Yesterday, looking out at the conspicuous consumption of Michigan Avenue, Peyton had, ironically, been transported back to his old neighborhood instead.

He'd been able to smell the grease and gasoline of the garage he and his old man had lived above—and where he'd worked to save money for college when he wasn't at school. He'd heard the police sirens that pelted the crumbling urban landscape, had seen the roving packs of gangs that considered his block fair game. He'd felt the grime on his skin and tasted the soot that belched from the factory smokestacks. And then...

Then had come memories of Emerson, where he'd won a spot on the school hockey team—along with a full scholarship—thanks to his above-average grades and his ruthlessness on the rink. God, he'd hated that school, teeming as it had been with blue-blooded trust-fund babies who were way too rich for his system. But he'd loved how clean and bright the place was, and how it smelled like floor wax and Calvin Klein perfume. He'd liked the quiet during classes and how orderly everything ran. He'd liked being able to eat one decent meal a day. He'd liked feeling safe, if only for a little while.

Not that he would have admitted any of that back then. Not that he would admit it to anyone now. But he'd been smart enough to know that an education from a place like Emerson would look a hell of a lot better on a college application than the decaying public school he would have attended otherwise. He'd stomached the rich kids—barely—by finding the handful of other students like himself. The wretched refuse. The other scholarship kids who were smart but poor and determined to end up in a better place than their parents. There had been maybe ten of them in a school where they were outnumbered a hundred to one. Peyton hadn't given a damn about those hundreds. Except for one, who had gotten under his skin and stayed there.

Ava Brenner. The Golden Girl of the Gold Coast. Her daddy was so rich and so powerful, and she was so snotty and so beautiful, she'd ruled that school. Not a day had passed at Emerson that didn't revolve around Ava and her circle of friends—all handpicked by the princess herself, and all on eggshells knowing they could be exiled at her slightest whim. Not a day had passed that Peyton hadn't had to watch her strolling down the hall, flipping that sweep of red-gold hair around as if it was spun copper…and looking at him as if he were something disgusting stuck to the bottom of her shoe. And not a day had passed when he hadn't wanted her. Badly. Even knowing she was spoiled and shallow and vain.

He opened his eyes. Yeah, he remembered now that he had been thinking about Ava yesterday. In fact, that was what had made him beat a hasty retreat to the hotel bar. He remembered that, too. And he remembered tossing back three single malts on an empty stomach in rapid succession. He remembered being politely asked to leave the hotel bar and, surprisingly, complying. He remembered lurching out onto Michigan Avenue and looking for the first place he could find to get another drink, then being steady enough on his feet to convince the bartender to fix him a couple more. Then…

He tried harder to remember what had happened after that. But all he could recall was a husky—sexy— voice, and the soft scent of gardenias, and a pair of beautiful sea-green eyes, all of which had seemed oddly familiar somehow.

That brought his gaze back to the woman sleeping on the couch. In the semidarkness, he could see that she lay on her side, facing the room, one hand curled in front of her face. The blanket with which she had covered herself was drooping, part of it pooled on the floor. For some reason, he was compelled to move to the couch and pick it up, to drape it across her sleeping form. As he bent over her, he inhaled the faint scent of gardenias again, as if it had followed him out of his memories.

And just like that, he was pummeled by another one.

Ava Brenner. Again. She was the one who had smelled of gardenias. Peyton remembered the night the two of them had— Well, the night they'd had to finish a school project together at her house. In her room. When her parents were out of town. At one point, she'd gone downstairs to fix them something to eat, and he'd taken advantage of her absence to shamelessly prowl around her room, opening her closet and dresser drawers, snooping for anything he could discover about her. When he came across her underwear drawer, he actually stole a pair of her panties. Pale yellow silk. God help him, he still had them. As he'd stuffed them into his back pocket that night, his gaze lit on a bottle of perfume on her dresser. Night Gardenia, it was called. That was the only way he knew that what she smelled like was gardenias. He'd never smelled—or even seen— one before that night.

As he draped the cover over the sleeping woman, his gaze fell to her face, and his gut clenched tight. He told himself he was imagining things. He was just so overcome with memories of Ava that he was imprinting her face onto that of a stranger. The odds of him running into the last person he wanted to see in Chicago—within hours of his arrival—were too ridiculous to compute. There were two and a half million people in this city. No way could fate be that cruel. No way would he be thrown back into the path of—

Before the thought even formed in his head, though,

Peyton knew. It was her. Ava Brenner. Golden Girl of the Gold Coast. Absolute ruler of the Emerson Academy for College Preparatory Learning. A recurring character in the most feverish dreams he'd ever had as a teenage boy.

And someone he'd hoped he would never, ever see again.

Two

"Ava?"

As if he'd uttered an incantation to free a fairy-tale princess from an evil spell, her eyes fluttered open. He tried one last time to convince himself he was only imagining her. But even in the semidarkness, he could see that it was Ava. And that she was more beautiful than he remembered.

"Peyton?" she said as she pushed herself up from the sofa.

He stumbled backward and into a chair on the other side of the room. Oh, God. Her voice. The way she said his name. It was the same way she'd said it that morning in her bedroom, when he'd opened his eyes to realize the frenetic dream he'd had about the two of them having sex hadn't been a dream at all. The panic that welled up in him now was identical to the feeling he had then, an explosion of fear and uncertainty and insecurity. He *hated* that feeling. He hadn't felt it since…

Ah, hell. He hadn't felt it since that morning in Ava's bedroom.

Don't panic, he told himself. He wasn't an eighteen-year-old kid whose only value lay in his ruthlessness on the rink. He wasn't living in poverty with a drunk for a father after his mother had deserted them both. He sure as hell wasn't the refuse of the Emerson Academy who wasn't worthy of Ava Brenner.

"Um, hi? I guess?" she said as she sat up, pulling up her covers as if she were cloaking herself in some kind of protective device. She was obviously just as anxious about seeing him as he was about seeing her.

As much as Peyton told himself to reply with a breezy, unconcerned greeting, all he could manage was another quiet "Ava."

She pulled one hand out of her cocoon to switch on a lamp by the sofa. He squinted at the sudden brightness but didn't glance away. Her eyes seemed larger than he remembered, and the hard angles of her cheekbones had mellowed to slender curves. Her hair was shorter, darker than in high school, but still danced around her shoulders unfettered. And her mouth—that mouth that had inspired teenage boys to commit mayhem—was… Hell. It still inspired mayhem. Only now that Peyton was a man, *mayhem* took on a whole new meaning.

"You want coffee?" she asked. "It should be ready. I set the coffeemaker for the usual time, thinking I would wake up when I normally do, but I don't think it's been sitting too long. If memory serves, you like it strong, anyway."

If memory serves, he echoed to himself. She had brewed a pot of coffee for them at her house that night, in preparation for the all-nighter they knew lay ahead. He had told her he liked it strong. She remembered.

Even though the two of them had barely spoken to each other after that night. Did that mean something? Did he want it to?

"Coffee sounds good," he said. "But I can get it. You take yours with cream and sugar, if *I* recall correctly."

Okay, okay. So Ava wasn't the only one who could remember that night in detail. That didn't mean anything.

She pulled the covers more snugly around herself. "Thanks."

Peyton hurried to the kitchen, grateful for the opportunity to collect himself. Ava Brenner. Damn. It was as if he'd turned on some kind of homing device the minute he got into town in order to locate her. Or maybe she had turned on one to locate him. Nah. No way would she be looking for him after all this time. She'd made her feelings for him crystal clear back at Emerson. They'd only shone with an even starker clarity after that night at her parents' house. And no way would he be looking for her, either. It was nothing but a vicious twist of fate or a vengeful God or bad karma that had brought them together again.

By the time he carried their coffee back to the living room, she had swept her hair atop her head into a lopsided knot that, amazingly, made her look even more beautiful. The covers had fallen enough to reveal a pair of flannel pajamas, decorated with multicolored polka dots. Never in a million years would he have envisioned Ava Brenner in flannel polka dots. Weirdly, though, they suited her.

She mumbled her thanks as he handed her her coffee—and he told himself he did *not* linger long enough to skim his fingers over hers to see if she felt as soft as he remembered, even if he did notice she felt softer

than he remembered. He briefly entertained the idea
of sitting down beside her on the couch but thankfully
came to his senses and returned to the chair.

When he trusted himself not to screw up the question, he asked, "Wanna tell me how I ended up spending the night with you again?"

He winced inwardly. He really hadn't wanted to
make any reference to that night in high school. But
her head snapped up at the question. Obviously, she'd
picked up on the allusion, too.

"You don't remember?" she asked.

There was an interesting ambiguity to the question.
She could have been asking about last night or that night
sixteen years ago. Of course she must have meant last
night. Still, there was an interesting ambiguity.

He shook his head. As much as it embarrassed him
to admit it, he told her, "No. I don't remember much of
anything after arriving at some restaurant on Michigan Avenue."

Except, of course, for fleeting recollections of green
eyes, soft touches and the faint aroma of gardenias. But
she didn't have to know that.

"So you do remember what happened before that?"
she asked.

"Yeah." Not that he was going to tell her any of that,
either.

She waited for him to elaborate. He elaborated by
lifting one eyebrow and saying nothing.

She sighed and tried again. "When did you get back
in town?"

"Yesterday."

"You came in from San Francisco?"

The question surprised him. "How did you know?"

"When I offered to take you home last night, you told

me I was going to have a long drive. Then you told me you live in an area called Sea Cliff in San Francisco. Sounds like a nice neighborhood."

That was an understatement. Sea Cliff was one of San Francisco's most expensive and exclusive communities, filled with lush properties and massive estates. His two closest neighbors were a globally known publishing magnate and a retired '60s rock and roll icon.

"It's not bad," he said evasively.

"So what took you to the West Coast?"

"Work." Before she could ask more, he turned the tables. "Still living in the Gold Coast?"

For some reason, she stiffened at the question. "No. My folks sold that house around the time I graduated from high school."

"Guess they figured those seven thousand square feet would be too much for two people instead of three. Not including the servants, of course."

She dropped her gaze to her coffee. "Only two of our staff lived on site."

"Well, then. I stand corrected." He looked around the tiny living room, recalled the tiny kitchen and tiny bedroom. "So what's this place?"

"It's…" She glanced up, hesitated, then looked down into her coffee again. "I own the shop downstairs. A boutique. Women's designer fashions."

He nodded. "Ah. So this apartment came with the place, huh?"

"Something like that."

"Easier to bring me here than to someplace where you might have to explain my presence, huh?"

For the first time, it occurred to him that Ava might be married. Hell, why wouldn't she be? She'd had every guy at Emerson panting after her. His gaze fell to the

hands wrapped around her coffee mug. No rings. Anywhere. Another interesting tidbit. She'd always worn
jewelry in high school. Diamond earrings, ruby and
sapphire rings—they were her parents' birthstones, he'd
once heard her tell a friend—and an emerald necklace
that set off her eyes beautifully.

Before he had a chance to decide whether her ring-
less state meant she wasn't married or she just removed
her jewelry at night, she said, "Well, you're not exactly
an easy person to explain, are you, Peyton?"

He decided not to speculate on the remark and instead asked about her status point-blank. "Husband
wouldn't approve?"

Down went her gaze again. "I'm not married."

"But you still have someone waiting for you at home
that you'd have to explain me to, is that it?"

The fact that she didn't respond bothered Peyton a
lot more than it should have. He told himself to move
along, to just get the condensed version of last night's
events and call a cab. He told himself there was nothing
about Ava he wanted to know, nothing she could say that
would affect his life now. He told himself to remember
how bad things were between them in high school for
years, not how good things were that one night.

He told himself all those things. But, as was so often
the case, he didn't listen to a single word he said.

Ava did her best to reassure herself that she wasn't
lying to Peyton. Lies of omission weren't really lies,
were they? And what was she supposed to do? No way
had she wanted him to see the postage stamp-size apartment she called home. She was supposed to be a massive
success by now. She was supposed to have a posh address in the Gold Coast, a closet full of designer clothes

and drawers full of designer jewelry. Well, okay, she did have those last two. But they belonged to the shop, not her. She could barely afford to rent them herself.

People believed what they wanted to believe, anyway. Even sitting in her crappy apartment, Peyton assumed she was the same dazzling—if vain, shallow and snotty—Gold Coast heiress who'd had everyone wrapped around her finger in high school. He thought she still lived in a place like the massive Georgian townhouse on Division Street where she grew up, and she still drove a car like the cream-colored Mercedes convertible she'd received for her sixteenth birthday.

He obviously hadn't heard how the Brenners of the Gold Coast had been reduced to a state of poverty and hardship that rivaled the one he'd escaped on the South Side. He didn't know her father was still doing time in a federal prison for tax evasion, embezzlement and a string of other charges, because he'd had to support a drug-and-call-girl habit. He didn't know her mother had passed away in a mental hospital after too many years of trying to cope with the anguish and ostracism brought on by her husband's betrayal. He didn't know how, before that, Colette Brenner had left Ava's father and taken her to Milwaukee to finish high school, or that Ava had done so in a school much like Emerson—except that *she* had been the poor scholarship student looked down on by the ruling class of rich kids, the same way she had looked down on Peyton and his crowd at Emerson.

Sometimes karma was a really mean schoolgirl.

But that was all the more reason she didn't want Peyton to know the truth now. She'd barely made a dent in her karmic debt. Spending her senior year of high school walking in the shoes of the students she'd treated so shabbily for years—being treated so shabbily herself—she had learned a major life lesson. It was only one reason she'd opened Talk of the Town: so that women who hadn't had the same advantages in life that she'd taken for granted could have the chance to walk in the designer shoes of high society, if only for a little while.

It was something she was sure Peyton would understand—if it came from anyone but Ava. If he found out what she'd gone through her senior year of high school, he'd mock her mercilessly. Not that she didn't deserve it. But a person liked to have a little warning before she found herself in a situation like that. A person needed a little time to put on her protective armor. Especially a person who knew what a formidable force Peyton Moss could be.

"There's no one waiting for me at home," she said softly in response to his question.

Or anywhere else, for that matter. No one in her former circle of friends had wanted anything to do with her once she started living below the poverty line, and she'd stepped on too many toes outside that circle for anyone there to ever want to speak to her. Peyton would be no exception.

When she looked up again, he was studying her with a scrutiny that made her uncomfortable. But all he said was, "So what did happen last night?"

"You were in Basilio's when I got there. I heard shouting in the bar and saw Dennis—he's the bartender," she added parenthetically, "talking to you. He suggested, um, that you might want a cup of coffee instead of another drink."

Instead of asking about the conversation, Peyton asked, "You know the bartender by name?"

"Sure. And Basilio, the owner, and Marcus, the

waiter who helped me get you to the car. I eat at that restaurant a lot." It was the only one in the neighborhood she could afford when it came to entertaining potential clients and vendors. Not that she would admit that to Peyton.

He nodded. "Of course you eat there a lot. Why cook for yourself when you can pay someone else do it?"

Ava ignored the comment. Peyton really was going to believe whatever he wanted about her. It didn't occur to him that sixteen years could mature a person and make her less shallow and more compassionate. Sixteen years evidently hadn't matured him, if he was still so ready to think the worst of her.

"Anyway," she continued, "you took exception to Dennis's suggestion that you'd had too much to drink—and you *had* had too much to drink, Peyton—and you got a little…belligerent."

"Belligerent?" he snapped. "I never get belligerent."

Somehow Ava refrained from comment.

He seemed to realize what she was thinking, because he amended, "Anymore. It's been a long time since I was belligerent with anyone."

Yeah, probably about sixteen years. Once he graduated from Emerson, all the targets of his belligerence—especially Ava Brenner—would have been out of his life.

"Basilio was going to throw you out, but I…I mean, when I realized you were someone I knew…I…" She expelled a restless sound. "I told him you and I are… That we were—" Somehow, she managed not to choke on the words. "Old friends. And I offered to drive you home."

"And he let you?" Peyton asked. "He let you leave with some belligerent guy he didn't know from Adam?

Wow. I guess he really didn't want to offend the regular cash cow."

Bristling, Ava told him, "He let me because you calmed down a lot after you recognized me. By the time Marcus and I got you into the car, you were actually being kind of nice. I know—hard to believe."

There. Take *that,* Mr. Belligerent Cow-Caller.

"But once you were in the car," she hurried on before he could comment, "you passed out. I didn't have any choice but to bring you here. I roused you enough to get you into the apartment, but while I was setting up the coffee, you found your way to the bedroom and went out like a light again. I thought maybe you'd sleep it off in a few hours, but... Well. That didn't happen."

"I've been working a lot the last few weeks," he said shortly, "on a demanding project. I haven't gotten much sleep."

"You were also blotto," she reminded him. Mostly because the cow comment still stung.

In spite of that, she wondered what kind of work he did and how he'd spent his life since they graduated. How long had he been in San Francisco? Was he married? Did he have children? Even as Ava told herself it didn't matter, she was helpless not to glance at his left hand. No ring. No indentation or tan line to suggest one had ever been there. Not that that was any definer of status. Even if he wasn't married, that didn't mean there wasn't a woman who was important in his life.

Not that Ava cared about any of that. She didn't. Really. All she cared about was getting him out of her hair. Getting him out of her apartment. Getting him out of her life.

In spite of that, she heard herself ask, "So why *are* you back in Chicago?"

He hesitated, as if he were trying to figure out how to reply. Finally, he said, "I'm here because my board of directors made me come."

Board of directors? she thought incredulously. *He* had a board of directors? "Board of directors?" she asked. "*You* have a board of directors?"

The question sounded even worse coming out of her mouth than it had sitting in her head, where it had sounded pretty bad.

Before she had a chance to apologize, Peyton told her—with a glare that could have boiled an ice cube, "Yeah, Ava. I have a board of directors. They're part of the multimillion-dollar corporation of which I am chief shareholder, not to mention CEO. A company that's named after me. On account of, in case I didn't mention it, I own it."

Ava grew more astonished with every word he spoke. But her surprise wasn't from the discovery that he was an enormous success—she'd always known Peyton could do or be whatever he wanted. She just hadn't pegged him for becoming the corporate type. On the contrary, he'd always scorned the corporate world. He'd scorned anyone who strove to make lots of money. He'd despised people like the ones in Ava's social circle. And now he was one of them?

This time, however, she kept her astonishment to herself.

At least, she thought she did, until he added, "You don't have to look so shocked. I did have one or two redeeming qualities back in high school, not the least of which was a work ethic."

"Peyton, I didn't mean—"

"The hell you didn't." Before she could continue, he added, "In fact, Moss Holdings Incorporated is close to

becoming a *billion*-dollar corporation. The only thing
standing between me and those extra zeroes after my
net worth is a little company in Mississippi called Montgomery and Sons. Except that it's not owned by Montgomery or his sons anymore. They all died more than a
century ago. It's now owned by the Montgomery sons'
granddaughters. Who are both in their eighties."

Ava had no idea what to say. Not that he seemed to
expect a response from her, because he suddenly became agitated and rose from the chair to pace the room.

He sounded agitated, too, when he continued, "Helen
and Dorothy Montgomery. They're sweet little old
Southern ladies who wear hats and white gloves to corporate meetings and send holiday baskets to everyone
every year filled with preserves and socks they make
themselves. They're kind of legendary in the business
and financial communities."

He stopped pacing, looking at something near the
front door that Ava couldn't see. At something he probably couldn't see, either, since whatever it was must
have existed far away from the apartment.

"Yeah, everybody loves the Montgomery sisters,"
he muttered. "They're so sweet and little and old and
Southern. So I'm going to look like a bully and a jerk
when I go after their company with my usual…how
did the *Financial Times* put it?" He hesitated, feigning
thought. "Oh, yeah. Now I remember. With my usual
'coldhearted, mind-numbing ruthlessness.' And no one
will ever want to do business with me again."

Now he looked at Ava. Actually, he glared at Ava, as
if all of this—whatever *this* was—was her fault. "Not
that there are many in the business and financial communities who like me much now. But at least they do
business with me. If they know what's good for them."

Even though she wasn't sure she was meant to be a part of this conversation, she asked, "Then why are you going after the Montgomerys' company? With ruthlessness or otherwise?"

Peyton sat down again, still looking agitated. "Because that's what Moss Holdings does. It's what *I* do. I go after failing companies and acquire them for a fraction of what they're worth, then make them profitable again. Mostly by shedding what's unnecessary, like people and benefits. Then I sell those companies to someone else for a huge profit. Or else I dismantle them and sell off their parts to the highest bidder for a pile of cash. Either way, I'm not the kind of guy people like to see coming. Because it means the end of jobs, traditions and a way of life."

In other words, she translated, what he did led to the dissolution of careers and income, plunging people into the sort of environment he'd had to claw his way out of when he was a teenager.

"Then why do you do it?" she asked.

His answer was swift and to the point. "Because it makes me huge profits and piles of cash."

She would have asked him why making money was so important that he would destroy jobs and alienate people, but she already knew the answer. People who grew up poor and underprivileged often made making money their highest priority. Many thought if they just had enough money, it would make everything in their life all right and expurgate feelings of want and need. Some were driven enough to become tremendous successes—at making money, anyway. As far as making everything in their life right and expurgating feelings of want and need, well…that was a bit trickier.

Funnily, it was often people like Ava, who had grown

up with money and been afforded every privilege, who realized how wrong such a belief was. Money didn't make everything all right, and it didn't expurgate feelings of anything. Sure, it could ease a lot of life's problems. But it didn't change who a person was at her core. It didn't magically chase away bad feelings or alleviate stresses. It didn't make other people respect or admire or love you. At least not for the right reasons. And it didn't bring with it the promise of…well, anything.

"And jeez, why am I even telling you all this?" Peyton said with exasperation.

Although she was pretty sure he didn't expect an answer for that, either, Ava told him, "I don't know. Maybe because you need to vent? Although why would you need to vent about a business deal, seeing as you make them all the time? Unless there's something about this particular business deal that's making you feel like… how did you put it? A bully and a jerk."

"Anyway," he said, ignoring the analysis, "for the sake of good PR and potential future projects, my board of directors thought it would be better to not go after the Montgomery sisters the way I usually go after a company—by yanking it out from under its unsuspecting owners. They think I should try to—" he made a restless gesture "—to…finesse it out from under them with my charm and geniality."

Somehow, the words *finesse* and *Peyton Moss* just didn't fit, never mind the charm and geniality stuff. Ava did manage to keep her mouth shut this time. But he seemed to need to talk about what had brought him back here, and for some reason, she hesitated to stop him.

"The BoD think it will be easier to fend off lawsuits and union problems if I can charm the company away from the Montgomerys instead of grabbing it from them. So they sent me back here to, and I quote, 'exorcise your street demons, Peyton, and learn to be a gentleman.' They've even set me up with some Henry Higgins type who's supposed to whip me into shape. Then, when I'm all nice and polished, they'll let me come back to San Francisco and go after Montgomery and Sons. But *nicely*," he added wryly. "That way, my tarnished reputation will stay only tarnished and not firebombed into oblivion."

Now he looked at Ava as if he were actually awaiting a reply. Not that she had one to give him. Although she was finally beginning to understand what had brought him back to Chicago—kind of—she wasn't sure what he expected her to say. Certainly Peyton Moss hadn't been bred to be a gentleman. That didn't mean he wasn't capable of becoming one. Eventually. Under the right tutelage. Which even Ava was having a hard time trying to imagine.

When she said nothing, he added quietly, "But you wanna hear the real kicker?"

She did, actually—more than she probably should admit.

"The real kicker is that they think I should pick up a wife while I'm here. They've even set me up with one of those millionaire matchmakers who's supposed to introduce me to—" he took a deep breath and released it slowly, as if he were about to reveal something of great importance "—the right kind of woman."

Ava's first reaction was an odd sort of relief that he wasn't already in a committed relationship. Her second reaction was an even odder disappointment that that was about to change. There was just something about the thought of Peyton being introduced to the "right kind of woman"—meaning, presumably, the kind of woman she herself was supposed to have grown up to be—that did something funny to her insides.

He added, "They think the Montgomery sisters might look more favorably at their family business being appropriated by another family than they would having it go to a coldhearted single guy like me." He smiled grimly. "So to finally answer your question, Ava, I'm back in Chicago to erase all evidence of my embarrassing, low-life past and learn to be a gentleman in polite society. And I'm supposed to find a nice society girl who will give me an added aura of respectability."

Ava couldn't quite keep the flatness from her voice when she replied, "Well, then. I hope you, in that society, with that nice society girl, will be very happy."

"Aw, whatsamatter, Ava?" he asked in the same cool tone. "Can't stand the fact that you and I are now social and financial equals?"

"Peyton, that's not—"

"Yeah, there goes the neighborhood."

"Peyton, I didn't mean—"

"Once you start letting in the riffraff, the whole place goes to hell, doesn't it?"

Ava stopped trying to explain or apologize, since he clearly wasn't going to let her do either. What was funny—or would have been, had it not been so biting—was that they actually weren't social and financial equals. Ava was so far below him on both ladders, she wouldn't even be hit by the loose change spilling out of his pockets.

"So what about you?" he asked.

The change of subject jarred her. "What about me?"

"What are you doing now? I remember you wanted to go to Wellesley. You were going to major in art or something."

She couldn't believe he remembered her top college choice. She'd almost forgotten it herself. She hadn't allowed herself to think about things like that once the family fortune evaporated. Although Ava had been smart, she'd been a lazy student. Why worry about grades when she had parents with enough money and connections to ensure admission into any school she wanted? The only reason she'd been accepted at her tony private school in Milwaukee was that she'd tested so high on its entry exam.

How was she supposed to tell Peyton she'd ended up studying business at a community college? Not that she hadn't received a fine education, but it was a far cry from the hallowed halls of academia for which she'd originally aimed.

"English," she said evasively. "I wanted to major in English."

He nodded. "Right. So where'd you end up going?"

"Wisconsin," she said, being deliberately vague. Let him think she was talking about the university, not the state.

He arched his brows in surprise. "University of Wisconsin? Interesting choice."

"The University of Wisconsin has an excellent English department," she said. Which was true. She just hadn't been a part of it herself. Nor had she lied to Peyton, she assured herself. She never said she went to University of Wisconsin. He'd just assumed, the same way he'd made lots of other assumptions about her. Why correct him? He'd be out of her life in a matter of minutes.

"And now you own a clothing store," he said. "Good to see you putting that English degree to good use. Then again, it's not like you actually work there, is it? Now that I think about it, I guess English is a good major for an heiress. Seeing as you don't have to earn a living like the rest of us working stiffs."

Ava bit her tongue instead of defending herself. She still had a tiny spark of pride that prohibited her from telling him the truth about her situation. Okay, there was that, and also the fear that he would gloat relentlessly once he found out how she'd gone from riches to rags.

"Have you finished your coffee?" she asked. It was the most polite way she knew how to say *beat it*.

He looked down into his mug. "Yeah. I'm finished."

But he made no move to leave. Ava studied him again, considering everything she had learned. He'd achieved all his success in barely a decade's time. She'd been out of school almost as long as he, but she was still struggling to make ends meet. And she would consider herself ambitious. Yet he'd gone so much further in the same length of time. That went beyond ambitious. That was...

Well, that was Peyton.

Still, she never would have guessed his stratospheric status had he not told her. When she'd removed his jacket and shoes last night, she had noted their manufacturers—it was inescapable in her line of work. Both could have been purchased in any department store. His hair was shorter than it had been in high school, but he didn't look as if he'd paid a fortune for the cut, the way most men in his position would. He might be worth almost a billion dollars now—and don't think that realization didn't stop her heart a little—but he didn't seem to be living any differently than any other man.

But then, Peyton wasn't the kind of guy to put on airs, either.

When he stood, he hesitated, as if he wanted to say

something. But he went to the kitchen without a word. She heard him rinse his cup and set it in the drainer, then move back to her bedroom. When he emerged, he was wearing his shoes and jacket, but his necktie hung loose from his collar. He looked like a man who'd had too much to drink the night before and slept in a bed other than his own. But even that couldn't detract from his appeal.

And there was the hell of it. Peyton did still appeal. He appealed to something deep inside Ava that had lain dormant for too long, something she wasn't sure would ever be able to resist him. Thankfully, that part of her wasn't the dominant part. She *could* resist Peyton Moss. Provided he left now and never came back.

For a moment, they only gazed at each other in silence. There were so many things Ava wanted to say, so many things she wanted him to know. About what had happened to her family that long-ago summer and how her senior year had changed her. About the life she led now. But she couldn't find the words. Everything came out sounding self-pitying or defensive or weak. She couldn't tolerate the idea of Peyton thinking she was any of those things.

Finally—thankfully—he ended the silence. "Thanks, Ava, for…for making sure I didn't spend last night in an alley somewhere."

"I'm sure you would have done the same for me."

He neither agreed nor disagreed. He only made his way to the front door, opened it and stepped over the threshold. She thought for a moment that he was going to leave without saying goodbye, the way he had sixteen years ago. But as he started to pull the door closed, he turned and looked at her.

"It was…interesting…seeing you again."

Yes, it had certainly been that.

"Goodbye, Peyton," she said. "I'm glad you're—" *What?* she asked herself. Finally, because she knew too long a hesitation would make her look insincere, she finished, "Doing well. I'm glad you're doing well."

"Yeah, doing well," he muttered. "I'm sure as hell that."

The comment was curious. He sounded kind of sarcastic, but why would he think otherwise? He had everything he'd striven to achieve. Before she could say another word, however, the door closed with a soft click. And then, as he had been sixteen years ago, Peyton was gone.

And he hadn't said goodbye.

Three

It wasn't often that Ava heard a man's voice in Talk of the Town. So when it became clear that the rich baritone coming from beyond her office door didn't belong to anyone delivering mail or freight, her concentration was pulled from next month's employee schedule to the sales floor instead. Particularly when she recognized the man's voice as Peyton's.

No sooner did recognition dawn, however, than Lucy, one of her full-time salesclerks, poked her dark head through the office door. "There's a man out here looking for you, Ava," she said, adjusting her little black glasses. "A Mr. Moss? He seemed surprised when I told him you were here." She lowered her voice as she added, "He was kind of fishing for your phone number. Which of course I would never give out." She smiled and lowered her voice to a stage whisper. "You might want to come out and talk to him. He's pretty yummy."

Ava sighed inwardly. Clearly, Peyton hadn't lost his ability to go from zero to sixty on the charm scale in two seconds flat.

What was he doing here? Five days had passed since their exchange in her apartment, not one of which had ended without her thinking about all the things she wished she'd said to him. She'd always promised herself—and karma—that if she ever ran into any of her former classmates from Emerson whom she had mistreated as a teenager, she would apologize and do whatever it took to make amends. It figured that when fate finally threw one of her former victims into her path, it would start with the biggie.

So why hadn't she tried to make amends on Saturday? Why hadn't she apologized? Why had she instead let him think she was still the same vain, shallow, snotty girl she'd been in high school?

Okay, here was a second chance to put things to right, she told herself. Even if she wasn't sure how to make up for her past behavior, the least she could do was apologize.

"Actually, Lucy, why don't you show him into the office instead?"

Lucy's surprise was obvious. Ava never let anyone but employees see the working parts of the boutique. The public areas of the store were plush and opulent, furnished with gilded Louis Quatorze tables and velvet upholstered chairs, baroque chandeliers and Aubusson carpets—reproductions, of course, but all designed to promote the same air of sumptuousness the designer clothes afforded her clients. The back rooms were functional and basic. Her office was small and cluttered, the computer and printer the only things that could be called state-of-the-art. The floor was concrete, the walls were cinder block, the ceiling was foam board and nothing was pretty.

Lucy's head disappeared from the door, but her voice trailed behind her. "You can go back to the office. It's right through there."

Ava swiped a hand over the form-fitting jaguar-print dress she had donned that morning—something new from Yves Saint Laurent she'd wanted to test for comfort and wearability. She had just tucked a stray strand of auburn back into her French twist when Peyton appeared in the doorway, dwarfing the already tiny space.

He looked even better than he had the last time she saw him. His hair was deliciously wind tossed, and his whiskey-colored eyes were clearer. He'd substituted the rumpled suit of Saturday morning with faded jeans and a weathered leather jacket that hung open over a baggy chocolate-brown sweater. Battered hiking boots replaced the businesslike loafers.

He looked more like he had in high school. At least, the times in high school when she'd run into him outside of Emerson. Even in his school uniform, though, Peyton had managed to look different from the other boys. His shirttail had always hung out, his shoes had always been scuffed, his necktie had never been snug. Back then, she'd thought he was just a big slob. But now she suspected he'd deliberately cultivated his look to differentiate himself from the other kids at Emerson. Nowadays, she didn't blame him.

He said nothing at first, only gazed at her the way he had on Saturday, as if he couldn't quite believe she was real. Gradually he relaxed, and even went so far as to lean against the doorjamb and shove his hands into the pockets of his jeans. Somehow, though, Ava sensed he was striving for a nonchalance he didn't really feel.

"Hi," he finally said.

"Hi yourself."

She tried to be as detached as he was, but she felt the same way she had Saturday—as if she were in high school again. As if she needed to shoulder the mantle of rich bitch ice princess to protect herself from the barbs she knew would be forthcoming. She was horrified by the thought—horrified that the girl she used to be might still be lurking somewhere inside her. She never wanted to be that person again. She never *would* be that person again. In spite of that, something about Peyton made the haughty teenager bubble up inside her.

Silence descended for an awkward moment. Then Peyton said, "You surprised me, being here. I came into the shop to see if anyone working knew where I could find you. I didn't expect you to actually be here."

Because he didn't think she actually *worked* here, Ava recalled, battling the defensiveness again. She told herself not to let his comment get to her and reminded herself to make amends. The best way to do that was to be the person she was now, not the person she used to be.

"I'm here more often than you might think," she said—sidestepping the truth again.

Then again, one couldn't exactly hurry the appeasement of karma. It was one thing to make amends for past behaviors. It was another to spill her guts to Peyton about everything that happened to her family and admit how she'd ended up in the same position he'd been in in high school, and now she was really, really sorry for how she had behaved all those years. That wasn't really necessary, was it? To go into all that detail? A woman was entitled to some secrets. And Ava wasn't sure she could bear Peyton's smug satisfaction after he learned about it. Or, worse, if he displayed the same kind of fake pity so many of her former so-called friends did.

Oh, Ava, they would say whenever she ran into them. *Has your poor father gotten out of prison yet? No? Darling, how do you stand the humiliation? We must meet for lunch sometime, get you out of that dreary store where you have to work your fingers to the bone. I'll call you.*

No calls ever came, of course. Not that Ava wanted them to. And their comments didn't bother her, because she didn't care about those people anymore. But coming from Peyton… For some reason, she suspected such comments would bother her a lot.

So she stalled. "We're supposed to be receiving a couple of evening gowns from Givenchy today, and I wanted to look them over before they went out on the floor." All of which was true, she hastened to reassure herself. She just didn't mention that she would have also been at the store if they were expecting a shipment of bubble wrap. She put in more hours at Talk of the Town than her two full-timers did combined.

"Then I guess I was lucky I came in today," he said, looking a little anxious. Sounding a little anxious.

"What made you come in?" she asked. "I thought you were going to be all booked up with Henry Higginses and millionaire matchmakers while you were in town."

He grinned halfheartedly and shifted his weight from one foot to the other. Both actions were probably intended to make him look comfortable, but neither really did.

"Yeah… Well… Actually…" He took a breath, released it slowly and tried again. "Actually, that's kind of why I'm here."

He gestured toward the only other chair in the office and asked, "Mind if I sit down?"

"Of course not," she replied. Even though she did kind of mind, because doing that would bring him closer, and then she would be the one trying to look comfortable when she felt anything but.

He folded himself into the other chair and continued to look uneasy. She waited for him to say something, but he only looked around the office, his gaze falling first on the Year in Fashion calendar on the wall—for April, it was Pierre Cardin—then on the fat issues of *Vogue, Elle* and *Marie Claire* that lined the top shelf of her desk, then lower, on the stack of catalogs sitting next to the employee schedule she'd been working on, and then—

Oh, dear. The employee schedule, which had her name and hours prominently at the top. Hastily, she scooped up the catalogs and laid them atop the schedule, tossing her pencil onto both.

He finally returned his gaze to her face. "The Henry Higgins didn't work out."

"What happened?"

His gaze skittered away again. "He told me I had to stop swearing and clean up my language."

Ava bit her lip to keep from smiling, since, to Peyton, this was clearly an insurmountable problem. "Well, if you're going to be dealing with two sweet little old ladies from Mississippi who are in their eighties and wear hats and white gloves, that's probably good advice."

"Yeah, but the Montgomery sisters are like five states away. They can't hear me swearing in Chicago."

"But if it's a habit, now is a good time to start breaking it, since—"

"Dammit, Ava, I can stop swearing anytime I want to."

"Oh, really?" she said mildly.

"Hell, yes."

"I see."

"And you should have seen the suits he tried to put me into," Peyton added.

"Well, suits are part and parcel for businesspeople," Ava pointed out, "especially those in your position. You were wearing a suit at Basilio's the other night. What's the sudden problem with suits?"

"The problem wasn't suits. It was the suits this guy wanted to put me into."

She waited for him to explain, and when he didn't, asked, "Could you be a little more specific?"

He frowned. "One was purple. Oh, excuse me," he quickly corrected himself. "I mean *eggplant*. The other was the same color green the guys on the team used to spew after getting bodychecked too hard."

Ava thought for a minute, then said, "Loden, I think, is the color you're looking for."

"Yeah. That's it."

"Those are both very fashionable colors," she said. "Especially for younger guys like you. Sounds to me like Henry knew his stuff."

Peyton shook his head. "Suits should never be anything except gray, brown or black. Not slate, not espresso, not ebony," he added in a voice that indicated he'd already had this conversation with Henry Higgins. "Gray. Brown. Black. Maybe, in certain situations, navy blue. Not midnight," he said when she opened her mouth to comment. "Navy blue. They sure as hell shouldn't be purple or puke-green."

Ava closed her mouth.

"And don't get me started on the etiquette lessons the guy said I had to take," Peyton continued. "Or all that crap about comportment. Whatever the hell that is. He even tried to tell me what I can and can't eat in a restaurant."

"Peyton, all of those things are important when it comes to dealing with people in professional situations. Especially when you're conducting business with people who do it old school, the way it sounds like the Montgomery sisters do."

He frowned. "Ava, I didn't get where I am today by studying etiquette books or comporting myself—whatever the hell that is. I did it by knowing what I want and going after it."

"And that's obviously worked in the past," she agreed. "But you admitted yourself that you'll have to operate differently with the Montgomerys. That means using a new rule book."

"I like my rule book just fine."

"Then do your takeover your way."

Why was he here? she asked herself again. This was an odd conversation to be having with him. Still, they were getting along. Kind of. Maybe she should just go with the flow.

He growled something unintelligible under his breath, but if she had to wager a guess, she'd bet it was more of that profanity he was supposed to be keeping under wraps.

His voice gentled some. "All I'm saying is that this guy doesn't know me from Adam, and he has no idea what's going to work for me and what isn't. I need to work with someone who can, you know, smooth my rough edges without sawing them off."

Okay, she was starting to understand. He wanted to see if she could recommend another stylist for him. Since she owned a shop like Talk of the Town, he figured she had connections in the business that might help him out.

"There are several stylists in Chicago who are very good," she said. "Some of them bring their clients to me." She reached for a binder filled with business cards she'd collected over the years. "Just give me a minute to find someone whose personality jibes with yours."

Ha. As if. There wasn't a human being alive whose personality jibed with Peyton's. Peyton was too larger-than-life. The best she could hope for was to find some-one who wasn't easily intimidated. Hmm…maybe that guy who worked with the Bears before their last Super Bowl appearance. He'd had to have a couple of teeth replaced, but still…

Peyton placed his hand over hers before she had a chance to open the binder. She tried to ignore the ruffle of butterflies in her midsection. Ha. As if.

His voice seemed to come from a very great distance when he spoke again. "No, Ava, you don't understand. Anyone you recommend is going to be in the same boat as Henry Higgins. They won't know me. They won't have any idea what to do with me."

She said nothing for a moment, only gazed at his hand covering hers, noting how it was twice the size of her own, how much rougher and darker, how his nails were blunt and square alongside her smooth, taupe-lacquered ovals. Their hands were so different from each other. So why did they fit together so well? Why did his touch feel so…right?

Reluctantly, she pulled her hand from beneath his and moved it to her lap. "Then why are you…"

The moment her gaze connected with his again, she began to understand. Surely, he wasn't suggesting…

There was no way he... It was ludicrous to even think...
He couldn't want *her* to be his stylist.

Could he?

She was his lifelong nemesis. He'd said so himself.
Not to her face, but to a friend of his. She'd overhead
the two of them talking as they came out of the boys'
restroom near her locker at Emerson. The seniors had
been studying *Romeo and Juliet,* and she'd heard him
say that the Montagues and Capulets had nothing on
the Mosses and Brenners. He'd told his friend that he
and Ava would be enemies forever. Then he'd ordered
a plague on her house.

Very carefully, she asked, "Peyton, why exactly are
you here?"

He leaned forward in the chair, hooking his hands
together between his legs. His gaze never leaving hers,
he said, "Exactly? I'm here because I didn't know where
else to go. There aren't many people left in this city who
remember me—"

Oh, she sincerely doubted that.

"And there are even fewer I care about seeing."

That she could definitely believe.

"And I'm not supposed to go back to San Francisco
until I'm, um—" he made a restless gesture with his
hand, as if he were literally groping for the right word
"—until I'm fit for the right kind of society."

When Ava said nothing in response—because she
honestly had no idea what to say—he expelled a restless breath and leaned back in the chair again.

Finally, point-blank, he said, "Ava, I want you to be
my Henrietta Higgins."

Peyton told himself he shouldn't be surprised by
Ava's deer-in-the-headlights reaction. He'd had a sim-

ilar one when the idea popped into his head as he was escaping Henry Higgins's office the previous afternoon. But there was no way he could have kept working with that guy, and something told him anyone else was going to be just as bad or worse.

How was someone going to turn him from a sow's ear into a silk purse if they didn't even know how he'd become a sow's ear in the first place? He'd never be a silk purse anyway. He needed to work with someone who understood that the best they could hope for would be to turn him into something in between. Like a... hmm...like maybe a cotton pigskin. Yeah, that's it. Like a denim football. He could do that. He could go from a sow's ear to a denim football. But he was still going to need help getting there. And it was going to have to be from someone who not only knew how to look and act in society, but who knew him and his limitations.

And who knew his limitations better than Ava? Who understood society better than Ava? Maybe she didn't like him. Maybe he didn't like her. But he knew her. And she knew him. That was more than he could say for all the Henry Higginses in the world. He and Ava had worked together once, in spite of their differences— they'd actually pulled off an A-minus on that World Civ project in high school. So why couldn't they work together as adults? Hell, adults should be even better at putting aside their differences, right? Peyton worked with people he didn't like all the time.

The tension between him and Ava on Saturday morning had probably just been a result of their shock at seeing each other again. Probably. Hey, they were being civil to each other now, weren't they? Or at least they had been. Before he dropped the Henrietta Higgins bombshell and Ava went all catatonic on him.

"So what do you say, Ava?" he asked in an effort to get the conversation rolling again. "Think you could help me out here?"

"I, ah…" she nonanswered.

"I mean, this sort of thing is right up your alley, right? Even if you didn't own a store that deals with, you know, fashion and stuff." *Fashion and stuff?* Could he sound more like an adolescent? "You know all about how people are supposed to dress and act in social situations."

"Yes, but…"

"And you know me well enough to not to dress me in purple."

"Well, that's certainly true, but…"

"And you'd talk to me the right way. Like you wouldn't say—" He adopted what he thought was a damned good impression of the man who had tried to dress him in purple. "'Mr. Moss, would you be ever so kind as to cease usage of the vulgar sort of language we decided earlier might be a detriment to your reception by the ladies whom you are doing your best to impress.' You'd just say, 'Peyton, the Montgomerys are going to wash your mouth out with soap if you don't stop dropping the F-bomb.' And just like that, I'd know what the hell you were talking about, and I'd do it right away."

This time, Ava only arched an eyebrow in what could have been amusement or censure…or something else he probably didn't want to identify.

"Okay, so maybe I wouldn't do it right away," he qualified. "But at least I would know what you were talking about, and we could come to some sort of compromise."

The eyebrow lowered, but the edge of her mouth twitched a little. Even though he wasn't sure whether it was twitching up or down, Peyton decided to be optimistic. At least she hadn't thrown anything at him.

"I just mean," he said, "that you…that I…that we…" He blew out an irritated breath, sat up straighter, and looked her straight in the eye. "Look, Ava, I know we were never the best of friends…" *Even if we were—for one night, anyway—lovers,* he couldn't help thinking. Hoping she wasn't thinking that, too. Figuring she probably was. Not sure how he felt about any of it. "But I obviously need help with this new and improved me, and I'm not going to get it from some total stranger. I don't know anyone here who could help me except you. Because you're the only one here who knows me."

"I *did* know you," she corrected him. "When we were in high school. Neither of us is the person we were then."

There was something in her voice that made Peyton hesitate. Although it was true that in a lot of ways he wasn't the person he'd been in high school, Ava obviously still was. Maybe the adult wasn't quite as snotty, vain or superficial as the girl had been, but she could still put a guy in his place. She was still classy. She was still beautiful. She was still out of his league. Hell, she hadn't changed at all.

"So will you do it?" he asked, deliberately not giving her time to think it over.

She thought it over anyway. Dammit. Her gaze never left his, but he could almost hear the crackling of her brain synapses as she connected all the dots and came to her conclusions. He was relieved when she finally smiled.

Until she asked, "How much does the position pay?"

His mouth fell open. "Pay?"

She nodded. "Pay. Surely you were paying your previous stylist."

"Well, yeah, but that was his job."

She shrugged. "And your point would be?"

He didn't know what his point was. He'd just figured Ava would help him out. He hadn't planned on her being mercenary about it.

Wow. She really hadn't changed since high school.

"Fine," he said coolly. "I'll pay you what I was paying him." He named the figure, one that was way too high to pay anyone for telling people how to dress and talk and eat.

Ava shook her head. "No, you'll have to do better than that."

"What?"

"Peyton, if you want to make use of my expertise in this matter, then I expect to be compensated accordingly."

Of course she did. Ava Brenner never did anything unless she was compensated.

"Fine," he said again. "How much do you charge for your expertise?"

She thought for another minute, then quoted a figure fifty percent higher than what he had offered.

"You're nuts," he told her. "You could build the Taj Mahal for that."

She said nothing.

He offered her 10 percent more.

She said nothing.

He offered her 25 percent more.

She tilted her head to one side.

He offered her 40 percent more.

"All right," she said with a satisfied smile.

"Great," he muttered.

"Well, I didn't want to be unreasonable."

This time Peyton was the one who said nothing. But he suddenly realized it wasn't because he was irritated with their lopsided bargaining—as if Ava was any kind of bargain. It was because it felt kind of good to be sparring with her again. He remembered now how, despite the antagonism of their exchanges in high school, he'd always come away from them feeling weirdly energized and satisfied. Although he still sparred with plenty of people these days, none ever left him feeling the way he'd felt taking on Ava.

"But Peyton, you'll have to do things my way," she said, pulling him out of his musing.

Peyton hated it when people told him they had to do things any way other than his own. He waited for the resentment and hostility that normally came along with such demands to coil inside him. Instead, he felt strangely elated.

"All right," he conceded. "We'll do this your way."

She grinned. He told himself it was smugly. But damned if she didn't look kind of happy to have taken on the task, too.

Four

Scarcely an hour after Ava agreed to be Peyton's makeover artist, she sat across from him at a table in a State Street restaurant. He'd asked her if they could get started right away, since he was eager to get on with his corporate takeover and had already lost a week to his previous stylist. And since—Hey, Ava, would ya look at that?—it was coming up on noon anyway, lunch sounded like a really good idea. After ensuring that one of her morning clerks would be able to pull an afternoon shift, too, Ava had agreed.

As surprised as she'd been by his request to help him out, she was even more surprised to realize she was happy to be doing it. Though not because he was paying her, since the figure she'd quoted him would barely cover the cost of the two additional salesclerks she'd need at Talk of the Town to cover for her. The strange happiness, she was certain, stemmed from the fact that she would finally be able to make amends for the way she had treated him in high school. It was that, and nothing more, that caused the funny buzz of delight that hummed inside her.

Anyway, what difference did it make? The point was that she would be helping Peyton become a gentleman, thereby ensuring he added to his already enormous financial empire. The point was that she would be performing enough good deeds over the next week or so to counter a lot of the mean things she'd said and done to him in high school. And the point was that, by helping him this way, she wouldn't have to bare her soul about the specifics of her current lifestyle. Specifically, she wouldn't have to tell him how she didn't have any style in her life, save what she was surrounded by at work every day.

What would telling Peyton about what happened to her family sixteen years ago accomplish? It wouldn't change anything. Why shouldn't she just do this nice thing for him and make some small amends for her past? No harm, no foul. They could complete the mission, job well done, then he could be on his way back to the West Coast none the wiser.

Yeah. That's the ticket.

She sighed inwardly as she looked at Peyton. Not because of how handsome he was sitting there looking at the menu—though he was certainly handsome sitting there looking at the menu—but because he was slumped forward with one elbow on the table, his chin settled in his hand. He had also preceded her to the table and seated himself without a second thought for her, then snatched up the menu as if it he hadn't eaten in a week. Combined, the actions gave her some small inkling of what his previous Henry Higgins had been up against.

"Peyton," she said quietly.

His gaze never left the menu. "Yeah?"

She said nothing until he looked up at her. She hoped he would realize she was setting an example for him to follow when she straightened in her chair and plucked the menu delicately from the table, laying her other hand in her lap.

He changed his posture not at all. "What is it?"

She threw her shoulders back and sat up even straighter.

"What?" he repeated, more irritably this time.

Fine. If he was going to behave like a child, she'd treat him like a child. "Sit up straight."

He looked confused. "Say what?"

"Sit up straight."

He narrowed his eyes and opened his mouth as if he were going to object, but she arched one eyebrow meaningfully and he closed his mouth again. To his credit, he also straightened in his chair and leaned against its back. She could tell he wasn't happy about completing the action. But he did complete it.

"Take your elbow off the table," she further instructed.

He frowned at her, but did as she said.

Satisfied she had his attention—maybe a little more than she wanted—she continued with her lesson. "Also, when you're in a restaurant with a woman and the host is taking you to your table, you should always invite her to walk ahead of you and follow her so that—"

"But how will she know where she's going if she's walking ahead of me?" he interrupted.

Ava maintained her calm, teacherly persona. "This may come as a surprise to you, Peyton, but women can generally follow a restaurant host to a table every bit as well as a man can. Furthermore," she hurried on when he opened his mouth to object again, "when the two of you arrive at the table, if the host doesn't direct her to a chair and pull it out for her, then you need to do that."

"But I thought you women hated it when men pull out a chair for you, or open the door for you, or do anything else for you."

"Some women would prefer to do those things themselves, true, but not all women. Society has moved past a time when that kind of thing was viewed as sexist, and now it's simply a matter of common—"

"Since when?" he barked. Interrupting her. Again. "The last time I opened a door for a woman, she about cleaned my clock for it."

Ava managed to maintain her composure. "And when was that?"

He thought for a minute. "Actually, I think it was you who did that. I was on my way out of chemistry and you were on your way in."

Ava remembered the episode well. "The reason I wanted to clean your clock wasn't because you held the door open for me. It was because you and Tom Sellinger made woofing sounds as I walked through it."

Instead of looking chagrined, Peyton grinned. "Oh, yeah. I forgot that part."

"Anyway," she continued, "these days it's a matter of common courtesy to open a door for someone—male or female—and to pull out a woman's chair for her. But you're right that some women prefer to do that themselves. You'll know a woman who does by the way she chooses a chair when she arrives at the table and immediately pulls it out for herself. That's a good indication that you don't have to do it for her."

"Gotcha," he said. Still grinning. Damn him.

"But from what you've told me about the Misses Montgomery," Ava said, "they'll expect you to extend the courtesy to them."

"Yeah, okay," he muttered. "I guess you have a point."

"Don't mutter," she said.

He narrowed his eyes at her again. But his voice was much clearer when he said, "Fine. The next time I'm in a restaurant with a woman, I'll let her go first and watch for clues. Anything else?"

"Oh, yes," Ava assured him enthusiastically. "We've only just begun. Once you sit down, let her open her menu first." When he started to ask another question that would doubtless be more about when women had changed their minds about this sort of thing—as if women had ever stopped having the prerogative to change their minds about whatever they damned well pleased—she continued, "And when you're looking at your menu, it's nice to make conversation over the choices. Don't just sit there staring at it until you make a decision. Ask your companion what she thinks looks good, too. If you're in a restaurant where you've eaten before, you might even make suggestions about dishes you like."

He considered her for another moment, then asked, "You're not going to make me order for you, are you? I hate that."

"*I* won't make you order for *me*," she said. "But some women like for men to do that."

"Well, how the hell will I know if they want me to or not?"

Ava cleared her throat discreetly. He looked at her as if he had no idea why. She stood her silent ground. He replayed what he had just said, then rolled his eyes.

"Fine. How...will I know?" he enunciated clearly, pausing over the spot where the profanity had been.

"You'll know because she'll tell you what she's planning to have, and when your waiter approaches, you'll look at her, and she'll look back at you and not say anything. If she looks at the waiter and says she'll start with the crab bisque and then moves on to the salad course, you'll know she's going to order for herself."

"So what do you think the Montgomerys will do?"

"I have no idea."

"Dammit, Ava, I—"

She arched her eyebrow again. He growled his discontent.

"I hate this," he finally hissed. "I hate having to act like someone I'm not."

Ava disagreed that he was being forced to act like someone he wasn't, since she was confident that somewhere deep inside he did have the potential to be a gentleman. In spite of that, she told him, "I know you do. And after your takeover of the Montgomerys' company is finished, if you want to go back to your reprobate ways, no one will stop you. Until then, if you want your takeover to be successful, you're going to have to do what I tell you."

He blew out an exasperated sound and grumbled another ripe obscenity. So Ava snapped her menu shut and stood, collecting her purse from the back of her chair as she went.

"Hey!" he said as he rose, too, following her. "Where the hell do you think you're going? You said you would help me out."

She never broke stride. "Not if you won't even try. I have better things to do with my afternoon than sit here watching you sulk and listening to you swear."

"Yeah, I guess you could get a crapload of shopping done this afternoon, couldn't you?" he replied. "Then you could hit that restaurant where you know everyone's name. Some guy there will pull out your chair for you and do all the ordering. And I bet he never swears."

She halted and spun around to face him. "You know, Peyton, I'm not sure you *are* fit for polite society. Go ahead and bulldoze your way over two nice old ladies. You were always much better at that than you were asking for something politely."

Why had she thought this could work? Just because the two of them had managed to be civil to each other for ten minutes in her office? Yeah, right. Ten minutes was about the longest the two of them had ever been able to be in each other's presence before the bombs began to drop.

Well, except for that night at her parents' house, she remembered. Then again, that had been pretty explosive, too...

"Excuse me," she said as civilly as she could before turning her back on him again and making her way toward the exit.

She took two steps before he caught her by the arm and spun her around. She was tempted to take advantage of the momentum to slam her purse into his shoulder, but one of them had to be a grown-up. And she was barely managing to do that herself.

She steeled herself for another round of combat, but he only said softly, sincerely, "I'm sorry."

She relaxed. Some. "I forgive you."

"Will you come back to the table? Please?"

She knew the apology hadn't come easily for him. His use of the word *please* had probably been even harder. He was trying. Maybe the two of them would always be like fire and ice, but he was making an effort. It would be small of her not to give it—not to give him—another chance.

"Okay," she said. "But, Peyton..." She deliberately left the statement unfinished. She'd made clear her terms already.

"I know," he said. "I understand. And I promise I'll do what you tell me to do. I promise to be what you want me to be."

Well, Ava doubted that. Certainly Peyton would be able to do and say the things she told him to do and say. But be what she wanted him to be? That was never going to happen. He would never be forgiving of the way she had treated him in high school. He would never be able to see her as anything other than the queen bee she'd been then. He would never be her friend. Not that she blamed him for any of those things. The best she could hope for was that he would, after this, have better memories of her to replace the ugly ones. If nothing else, maybe, in the future, when—if—he thought of her, it would be with a little less acrimony.

And, hey, that wasn't terrible, right?

"Let's start over," she said.

He nodded. "Okay."

She was talking about the afternoon, of course. But she couldn't help thinking how nice it would be if they could turn back the clock a couple of decades and start over there, too.

The last time Peyton was in a tailor's shop—in fact, the only time Peyton was in a tailor's shop—it had been a cut-rate establishment in his old neighborhood that had catered to low-budget weddings and proms. Which was why he'd been there in the first place, to rent a tux for Emerson's prom. The place had been nothing like the mahogany-paneled, Persian-carpeted wonder in which he now stood. He always bought his clothes off the rack and wore whatever he yanked out of the closet. If the occasion was formal, there was the tux he'd bought at a warehouse sale not long after he graduated from college. His girlfriend at the time had dragged him there, and she'd deemed it a vintage De la Renta—whatever the hell that was—that would remain timeless forever. It had cost him forty bucks, which he'd figured was a pretty good deal for timelessness.

Ava, evidently, had other ideas. All it had taken was one look at the dozen articles of clothing he'd brought with him, and she'd concluded his entire wardrobe needed revamping. Sure, she'd been tactful enough to use phrases like *a little out-of-date* and *not the best fitting* and *lower tier*. The end result was the same. She'd hated everything he brought with him. And when he'd told her about the vintage De la Renta back in San Francisco and how he'd worn it as recently as a month ago, she'd looked as though she wanted to lose her breakfast.

Now she stood beside him in front of the tailor's mirror, and Peyton studied her reflection instead of his own—all three panels of it. He still couldn't get over how beautiful she was. The clingy leopard-print dress she'd worn the day before had been replaced by more casual attire today, a pair of baggy tan trousers and a creamy sweater made of some soft fuzzy stuff that didn't cling at all. She'd left her hair down but still had it pulled back in a clip at her nape. He wondered what it took—besides going to bed—to make her wear it loose, the way it had been Saturday morning. Then again, as reasons went for a woman wearing her hair loose, going to bed was a pretty good one.

"Show him something formal in Givenchy," she said, speaking to the tailor. "And bring him some suits from Hugo Boss. Darks. Maybe something with a small pinstripe. Nothing too reckless."

The tailor was old enough to be Peyton's grandfather, but at least his suit wasn't purple. On the contrary, it was a sedate dark gray that was, even to Peyton's untrained eye, impeccably cut. He had a tape measure around his neck, little black glasses perched on his nose and a tuft of white hair encircling his head from one ear to the other. His name was the very no-nonsense Mr. Endicott.

"Excellent choices, Miss Brenner," Mr. Endicott said before scurrying off to find whatever it was she had asked him to bring.

Ava turned her attention to Peyton, studying his reflection as he was hers. She smiled reassuringly. "Hugo Boss is a favorite of men in your position," she said. "He's like the perfect designer for high-powered executives. At least, the ones who don't want to wear eggplant, loden or espresso."

Peyton started to correct her about the high-powered-executive thing, then remembered that he was, in fact, a high-powered executive. Funny, but he hadn't felt like one since coming back to Chicago.

"I promise he won't bring you anything in purple or puke-green," she clarified when he didn't reply. "He's one of the most conservative tailors in Chicago."

Peyton nodded, but still said nothing. A weird development, since he'd never been at a loss for words around Ava before. He'd said a lot of things to her when they were in high school that he shouldn't have. Even if she'd been vain, snotty and shallow, she hadn't deserved some of the treatment she'd received from him. There were a couple of times in particular that he maybe, possibly, perhaps should apologize for...

"It's not that your other clothes are bad," she added, evidently mistaking his silence as irritation. "Like I said, they just need a little, um, updating."

She was trying hard not to say anything that might create tension between them. And the two of them had gotten along surprisingly well all morning. They'd been stilted and formal and in no way comfortable with each other, but they'd gotten along.

"Look, Ava, I'm not going to jump down your throat for telling me I'm not fashionable," he said. "I know I'm not. I'm doing this because I'm about to enter a sphere of the business world I've never moved in before, one that has expectations I'll have to abide by." He shrugged. "But I have to learn what they are. That's why you're here. I won't bite your head off if you tell me what I'm doing wrong."

She arched that eyebrow at him again, the way she had the day before at the restaurant, when he'd bitten her head off for telling him what he was doing wrong.

"Anymore," he amended. "I won't bite your head off anymore."

The eyebrow went back down, and she smiled. It wasn't a big smile, but it was a start. If nothing else, it told him she was willing to keep reminding him, as long as he was willing to remember he'd reminded her to do it.

The tailor returned with a trio of suits and a single tuxedo, and Peyton blew out a silent breath of relief that none of them could be called anything but *dark*. The man then helped Peyton out of his leather jacket and gestured for him to shed the dark blue sweater beneath it. When he stood in his white V-neck T-shirt and jeans, the tailor helped him on with the first suit jacket, made some murmuring sounds, whipped the tape measure from around his neck, and began to measure Peyton's arms, shoulders and back.

"Now the trousers," the man said.

Peyton looked at Ava in the mirror.

"I think it's okay if you go in the fitting room for that," she said diplomatically.

Right. Fitting room. He knew that. At least, he knew that *now*.

When he returned some minutes later wearing what he had to admit was a faultless charcoal pinstripe over a crisp white dress shirt the tailor had also found for him, Ava had her back to him, inspecting two neckties she had picked up in his absence.

"So…what do you think?" he asked.

As he approached her, he tried to look more comfortable than he felt. Though his discomfort wasn't due to the fact that he was wearing a garment with a price tag higher than that of any of the cars he'd owned in his youth. It was because he was worried Ava still wouldn't approve of him, even dressed in the exorbitant plumage of her tribe.

His fear was compounded when she spun around smiling, only to have her smile immediately fall. Dammit. She still didn't like him. No, he corrected himself—she didn't like what he was wearing. Big difference. He didn't care if she didn't like him. He didn't. He only needed for her to approve of his appearance. Which she obviously didn't.

"Wow," she said.

Oh. Okay. So maybe she did approve.

"You look…" She drew in a soft breath and expelled it. "Wow."

Something hot and fizzy zipped through his midsection at her reaction. It was a familiar sensation, but one he hadn't felt for a long time. More than fifteen years, in fact. It was the same sensation he'd felt one time when Ava looked at him from across their shared classroom at Emerson. For a split second, she hadn't registered that it was Peyton she was looking at, and her smile had been dreamy and wistful. In that minuscule stretch of time, she had looked at him as if he were something worth looking at, and it had made him feel as if nothing in his life would ever go wrong again.

Somehow, right now, he had that feeling again.

"So you like it?" he asked.

"Very much," she said. Dreamily. Wistfully. And heat whipped through his belly again. She finally seemed to remember where she was and what she was supposed to be doing, because she looked down at the lengths of silk in her hand. He couldn't help thinking she sounded a little flustered when she said, "But you, ah, you need a tie."

She took a few steps toward him, stopped for some reason, then completed a few more that brought her within touching distance. Instead of closing the gap, though, she held up the two neckties, one in each hand.

"I hope you don't mind," she said, "but I'm of the opinion that the necktie is where a man truly shows his personality. The suit can be as conservative as they come, but the tie can be a little more playful and interesting." She hesitated. "Provided that fits the character of the man."

He wanted to ask if she actually thought he was playful, never mind interesting, but said nothing. Mostly because he had noted two spots of pink coloring her cheeks and had become fascinated by them. Was she blushing, or was the heat in the store just set too high? Then he realized it was actually kind of cool in there. Which meant she must be—

"If you don't like these, I can look for something different," she told him, taking another step that still didn't bring her as close as he would have liked. "But these two made me think of you."

Peyton forced himself to look at the ties. One was splashed with amorphous shapes in a half dozen colors, and the other looked like a watercolor rendition of a tropical rain forest. He was surprised to discover he liked them. The colors were bold without being obnoxious, and the patterns were masculine without being aggressive. The fact that Ava said they reminded her of him made him feel strangely flattered.

"I'll just look for something different then," she said when he didn't reply, once again misinterpreting his silence as disapproval. "There were some nice striped ones you might like better." She started to turn away.

"No, Ava, wait."

In one stride, he covered the distance between them and curled his fingers around her arm, spinning her gently around to face him. Her eyes were wide with surprise, her mouth slightly open. And God help him, all he wanted was to keep tugging her forward until he could cover her mouth with his and wreak havoc on them both.

"I, uh, I like them," he said, shoving aside his errant thoughts.

Once again, he forced himself to look at the ties. But all he saw was the elegant fingers holding them, her nails perfect ovals of red. That night at her parents' house, her nails had been perfect ovals of pink. He'd thought the color then was so much more innocent-looking than Ava was. Until the two of them finally came together, and he realized she wasn't as experienced as he thought, that he was the first guy to—

"Let's try that one," he said, not sure which tie he was talking about.

"Which one?"

"The one on the right," he managed.

"My right or your right?"

He stifled the frustrated obscenity hovering at the back of his throat. "Yours."

She held up the tie with the unstructured forms and smiled. "That was my favorite, too."

Great.

Before he realized what she was planning, she stepped forward and looped the tie around his neck, turning up the collar of his shirt to thread it underneath. He was assailed by a soft, floral scent that did nothing to dispel the sixteen-year-old memories still dancing in his head, and the flutter of her fingers as she wrapped the length of silk around itself jacked his pulse rate higher. In an effort to keep his sanity, he closed his eyes and began to list in alphabetical order all the microbreweries he had visited on his travels. Thankfully, by the time he came to Zywiec in Poland, she was pulling the knot snug at his throat.

"There," she said, sounding a little breathless herself. "That should, ah, do it."

He did his best to ignore the last two words and the fact that she had stumbled over them. She couldn't be thinking about the same thing he was.

"Thanks," he muttered, the word sounding in no way grateful.

"You're welcome," she muttered back, the sentiment sounding in no way generous.

When he opened his eyes, he saw Ava glaring at him. Worse, he knew he was glaring at her, too. Before either of them could say anything that might make the situation worse, he went back to the mirror. Mr. Endicott took that as his cue to start with the measuring and adjusting again. He made a few notations on a pad of paper, struck a few marks on the garment with a piece of chalk, stuck a few pins into other places and told Peyton to go try on the next suit.

When he returned in that one, Ava was near the mirror draping a few more neckties onto a wooden valet. Upon his approach, she hurriedly finished, then strode to nearly the other side of the room. Jeez, it was as though anytime the two of them spent more than an hour in each other's presence, a switch flipped somewhere that sent a disharmony ray shooting over them. What the hell was up with that?

This time Peyton tied his own damned tie—though not with the expertise Ava had—then turned for her approval. Only to see her still riffling through some neckties on a table that she'd probably already riffled through.

He cleared his throat to get her attention.

She continued her necktie hunt.

He turned back to the tailor. "This one is fine, too."

Out came the tape measure and chalk again. The ritual was performed twice more—including Peyton's futile efforts to win Ava's attention—until even the tuxedo was fitted. Only when he was stepping down from the platform in that extraformal monkey suit did Ava look up at him again. Only this time, she didn't look away. This time, her gaze swept him from the top of his head to the tips of his shoes and back.

He held his breath, waiting to see if she would smile.

She didn't. Instead she said, "I, um, I think that will do nicely." Before Peyton had a chance to say thanks, she added, "But you need a haircut."

All Peyton could think was, *Two steps forward, one step back.* What the hell. He'd take it.

"I'm guessing that's somewhere on our to-do list?" he asked.

She nodded. "This afternoon. I made an appointment for you at my salon. They're fabulous."

"Your *salon?*" he echoed distastefully. "What's wrong with a barbershop?"

"Nothing. If you're a dockworker."

"Ava, I've never set foot in a salon. A record I plan to keep."

"But it's unisex," she said, as if that made everything okay.

"I don't care if it's forbidden sex. Find me a good barber."

She opened her mouth to argue, but his unwillingness to bend on the matter must have shown in his expression. So she closed her mouth and said nothing. Not that that meant she would find him a barber. But at least they could bicker about it after they left the tailor's.

And why was he kind of looking forward to that?

When it became obvious that neither of them was going to say more, Peyton made his way back to Endicott, who led him back to the fitting room.

"Don't worry, Mr. Moss," the tailor said. "You're doing fine."

Peyton looked up at that. "What?"

"Miss Brenner," Endicott said as he continued to walk, speaking over his shoulder. "She likes the suits. She likes the tuxedo even more."

"How can you tell?"

The tailor simply grinned. "Don't worry," he repeated. "She likes you, too."

Peyton opened his mouth to reply, but no words emerged. Which was just as well, because Mr. Endicott continued walking, throwing up a hand to gesture him forward.

"Come along, Mr. Moss. I still need to pin those trousers."

Sure thing, Peyton thought. Just as soon as he pinned some thoughts back into his brain.

Five

After addressing Peyton's wardrobe and hair, ah, challenges, Ava turned his attention to the appreciation of life's finer things—art, music, theater. At least, that was where she was planning to turn his attention the morning after their sartorial adventures. No sooner did she rap lightly on the door of his hotel suite, however, than did she discover her plans were about to go awry.

"Sorry," he said by way of a greeting. "But we have to cancel this morning. I'm supposed to meet with the matchmaker. I forgot all about it yesterday when you and I made plans for this morning."

Ava told herself the reason for the sudden knot her stomach was because she was peeved at his last-minute canceling of their date. Ah, she meant *plans*. And she was peeved because they were *plans* she'd given herself the day off from work for when she might have saved herself some money instead of paying Lucy overtime.

It had nothing to do with the fact that Peyton would be spending the morning with another woman.

Not that the other woman was, you know, *another woman,* since for her to be that, Ava would have to be the primary woman in his life, and of course that wasn't the case. Besides, the other woman he was seeing today was only a matchmaker. A matchmaker who would be setting him up with, well, *other women.* Women he would be seeing socially. Confidentially. Romantically.

The knot squeezed tighter. Because she was peeved, Ava reminded herself. Peeved that he was messing up their *plans.*

"Oh. Okay," she said, sounding troubled and unhappy, and in no way peeved.

"I'm really sorry," he apologized again. "When I checked my voice mail last night, there was a message from Caroline—she's the matchmaker—reminding me. By then it was too late to call you, and you didn't answer your phone this morning."

He must have called while she was in the shower. "Well, you don't want to miss a meeting with her. I'm sure you and she have a lot to go over before you can launch your quest for Ms. Right."

"Actually, I've already met with her once. We're meeting today because she's rounded up some possible matches, and she wants me to look at their photos and go over their stats before she makes the actual introductions. Maybe we could just push things back to this afternoon?"

"Sure. No problem."

So what if Peyton was meeting with his matchmaker? Ava asked herself. He was supposed to be doing that. Finding an appropriate woman was half the reason he was back in Chicago, and Ava didn't even have to work with him on that part. She only had to make sure he was presentable to any woman he did meet.

She leaped on that realization. "But you know, Peyton, I'm not sure you're ready to meet any prospective dates just yet. We still have a lot of work to do to get you ready for that."

"How much more do we have to do?"

He'd actually come a long way in four days, Ava had to admit. And not just because of his stylish new wardrobe and excellent new haircut—which he had finally agreed to get at her salon, but not after much haggling. Haggling that, in hindsight, hadn't been all that unpleasant, especially when he seemed to be enjoying it as much as she did.

At any rate, his faded jeans and bulky sweater of the day before had made way for expensive dark-wash denim and a more fitted sweater in what she knew was espresso, but which she'd conceded to Peyton—after more surprisingly enjoyable haggling—was actually brown. His shorter hair had showcased the few threads of silver amid the black, something that gave him a definite executive aura—not to mention an added bit of sexiness. Ava's charcoal skirt and claret cashmere sweater set—both by Chanel—should have seemed dressy, but he made denim and cotton aristocratic to the point where she felt like the palace gardener. He was the kind of client that would make a matchmaker drool—never mind the effect he would have on his prospective matches. It was amazing what a little polish would do for a guy.

Then again, it wasn't always the clothes that made the man. What made Peyton Peyton was what was beneath the clothes. And that was something even teaching him about the finer things in life wouldn't change.

Yes, he needed to learn to become a gentleman if he wanted to impress the sisters Montgomery and acquire their company. But there was too much roughneck in him to ever let the gentleman take over for very long.

It was a realization that should have made Ava even more peeved, since it suggested that everything she was doing to help him was pointless. Instead, it comforted her.

Remembering he'd asked her a question that needed a response, she said, "Well, I was kind of hoping to cover the arts this week. And we still need to fine-tune your restaurant etiquette. And we should—" She halted. There was no reason to make him think there was still tons more to do, since there really wasn't. For some reason, though, she found herself wishing there was still tons more to do. "Not a lot," she said. "There's not a lot."

Instead of looking pleased about that, he looked kind of, well, peeved.

"I should go," she told him. "What time do you think you'll be finished?"

"I don't know. Maybe I could call you when we're done?"

She nodded and started to turn away.

"Unless..."

She turned to face him. "Unless what?"

He looked a little uncomfortable. "Unless maybe..." He shoved his hands into the pockets of his jeans, a restless gesture. "Unless maybe you want to come with me?"

It was an odd request. For one thing, Caroline the matchmaker would be curious—not to mention possibly peeved—if Peyton showed up with a woman. A woman who, by the way, Caroline had had no part in setting him up with, so she wouldn't be collecting a finder's fee. For another thing, why would Peyton want Ava with him when he considered a potentially life-changing decision?

As if he'd heard her unspoken question, he hurried on, "I mean, you might be able to give me some advice or something. I've never worked with a matchmaker before."

Oh, and she had? Jeez, she hadn't even had a date in more than a year. She was the last person who should be giving advice about matters of the heart. Not that Peyton needed to know any of that, but still.

"Please, Ava?" he asked, sounding as if he genuinely wanted her to come along. "You know what kind of woman I need to find. One who's just like—"

You. That was what he had been about to say. That was the word his lips had been about to form, the one hanging in the air between them, the one exiting his head and entering her own. Ava knew it as surely as she knew her own name.

After an almost imperceptible pause, he finished, "—Jackie Kennedy. I need to find a woman like Jackie Kennedy."

Oh, sure. As if there were *any* women in the world like Jackie Kennedy. How Peyton could have jumped from thinking about Ava to thinking about her was a mystery.

"Okay, I'll come with you," she said. She had no idea when she had made the decision to do so. And she was even more uncertain about why. What was really odd, though, was how, suddenly, somehow, she didn't feel quite as peeved as she had before.

The office of Attachments, Inc. had surprised Peyton on his first visit. He'd thought a matchmaker's office would be full of hearts and flowers, furnished with overblown Victorian furniture in a million different colors, with sappy chamber music playing over it all. Instead, the place was much like his own office in San Francisco, twenty stories above the city, with wide windows that offered panoramic views of Lake Michigan and Navy Pier, furnished in contemporary sleekness and soothing earth tones. The music was jazz, and the only plants were potted bamboo.

Caroline, too, had come as a surprise that first time. He'd expected a gingham-clad grandmother with a graying bun and glasses perched on her nose, but the woman who greeted him and Ava was a far cry from that. Yes, her hair was silver, but it hung loose and was stylishly cut, and her glasses were shoved atop her head. In place of gingham, she was wrapped in a snug, sapphire-colored dress and wearing mile-high heels that click-click-clicked on the tile floor as she approached them.

"Mr. Moss," she gushed when she came to a stop in front of him and extended her hand the way any high-powered business CEO would. "It is so nice to see you again." Her gushing ebbed considerably, however—in fact, the temperature seemed to drop fifty degrees—when she turned to Ava and said, "Now who are you?"

Before Ava had a chance to answer, Peyton replied, "She's my, ah, my assistant. Ava Brenner."

Caroline gave Ava a quick once-over and, evidently satisfied with his answer, immediately dismissed her. She turned to Peyton again. "Well, then. If you'd like to come back to my office, we can get down to business."

Confident the two of them would follow, she spun on her mile-high heels and click-click-clicked in the direction from which she'd come. Peyton turned to Ava and started to shrug, but stopped when he saw her expression. She looked kind of…peeved. Although that wasn't a word in his normal vocabulary, he couldn't think of any other adjective to describe her. She was looking at him as if he'd just insulted her. He backtracked the last few seconds in his brain, then remembered he'd introduced her as his assistant. Okay, so maybe that suggested she was his subordinate, but he was paying her to help him out, so that sort of made her an employee, and that kind of made her a subordinate. And what was the big deal anyway? Some of his best friends were subordinates.

Anyway, they didn't have time for another argument. So he only gestured after the hastily departing Caroline and asked, "Are you coming?"

"Do I have a choice?" she replied crisply.

He did shrug this time, hoping the gesture looked more sincere than it felt. "You could wait out here if you want."

For a moment, he thought she would take him up on that, and a weird panic rose in his belly. She wouldn't. He needed her to help him with this. He had no idea what kind of woman would be acceptable to his board of directors. Other than that she had to have all the qualities Ava had.

Caroline called back to them, and although Ava tensed even more, she turned in the direction of the matchmaker and began to march forward. Relief—and a strange kind of happiness—washed over Peyton as he followed. Because he needed her, he told himself. Or rather, he needed her *help*. That was why he was glad she hadn't stayed in the waiting room. It had nothing to do with how he just felt better having her at his side. The reason he felt better having her at his side was because, you know, she was helping him. Which he needed. Her help, he meant. Not her at his side.

Ah, hell. He was just happy—he meant *relieved*—that she was with him.

Caroline's office was a better reflection of her trade. The walls were painted the color of good red wine, and a wide Persian rug spanned a floor that had magically become hardwood. Her desk was actually kind of Victorian-looking, but it was tempered by the sleek city skyline in the windows behind her. On one wall hung certificates for various accomplishments, along with two degrees in psychology from Northwestern. Her bookshelf was populated less by books than by artifacts from world travels, but the books present were all about relationships and sexuality.

Instead of deploying her strategy from behind her desk, Caroline scooped up a small stack of manila folders atop it, invited Peyton and Ava to seat themselves on an overstuffed sofa on the opposite wall, then sat down in a matching chair beside it.

"May I call you Peyton?" she asked with a warm smile.

"Sure," he told her.

He waited for her to smile warmly at Ava and ask if she could call her by her first name, too, but Caroline instead began to sift through the folders until she homed in on one in particular.

Still smiling her warm smile—which Peyton would have sworn was genuine until she dismissed Ava so readily—she said, "I inputted your vital statistics, your likes and dislikes, and what you're looking for in a match into the computer, and I found four women I think you'll like very much. This one in particular," she added as she opened the top folder, "is quite a catch.

Very old-money Chicago, born and raised here, Art Institute graduate, active volunteer in the local arts community, a curator for a small gallery on State Street, contributing reviewer for the *Tribune,* member of the Daughters of the American Revolution…. Oh, the list just goes on and on. She has every quality you're looking for."

Caroline handed the open folder to Peyton, who took it automatically. It contained a few sheets of printed information with a four-by-six head shot attached. It was to the latter that his gaze was naturally drawn. The woman was—well, there was no other word for it—breathtakingly beautiful. Okay, okay, that was two words, but that just went to show how amazingly gorgeous and incredibly dazzling she was. Women who looked like her just demanded adverbs to go along with the adjectives. Her hair was dark auburn and pooled around her bare shoulders; her eyes were huge, green and thickly lashed. He didn't kid himself that the photo wasn't retouched or that she would look the same had she not been so artfully made up with the kind of cosmetic wizardry that made a woman look as though she wasn't wearing makeup at all. She was still… Wow. Breathtakingly beautiful, amazingly gorgeous and incredibly dazzling.

"Wow," he said, speaking his thoughts aloud. Well, part of them, anyway. There were some that were best left in his head.

"Indeed," said Caroline with a satisfied smile. "Her name is—"

"Vicki," Ava finished, at the same time Caroline was saying, "Victoria."

The women exchanged looks, then spoke as one again. But, again, they each said something different.

"Victoria Haverty," said the matchmaker.

"Vicki Nielsson," said Ava.

The two women continued to stare at each other, but it was Caroline alone who spoke this time. "Do you know Ms. Haverty?"

Ava nodded. "Oh, yes. We debuted together. But Haverty is her maiden name. She's Vicki Nielsson now."

Caroline's eyes fairly bugged out of her head. "She's *married?*"

"I'm afraid so," Ava told her. "And living in Reykjavik with her husband, Dagbjart, last I heard. Which was about two weeks ago."

"But she gave me an address here in Chicago," Caroline objected, as if that would negate everything Ava had said.

"On Astor Street?" Ava asked.

Caroline went to her desk and tapped a few keys on a laptop sitting atop it. It was then that Peyton realized all the information on his pages was nonidentifying statistics such as age, education, occupation and interests. "Yes," the matchmaker said without looking up.

"That's her parents' place," Ava replied. "She does come home to visit fairly often."

The matchmaker looked at Ava incredulously. "But why would she apply with a Chicago matchmaker if she's happily married and living in…um, where is Reykjavik?"

"Iceland," Peyton and Ava said in unison.

The matchmaker looked even more confused. "Why would she apply with Attachments if she's married and living in Iceland?"

When Peyton looked at Ava, she seemed to be trying very hard not to grin. A smug grin, too, if he wasn't mistaken. He knew that because she wasn't doing a very good job fighting it.

"Well," she began smugly, "maybe Vicki's not as happily married as ol' Dagbjart would like to think. And ol' Dagbjart is, well, ol'," she added. "He was seventy-six when Vicki married him. He must be pushing ninety by now. The Havertys have always been known for marrying into families even wealthier than they are, but clearly Vicki underestimated that Scandinavian life expectancy. Did you know men in Iceland live longer than men in any other country?"

The matchmaker said nothing in response to that. Neither did Peyton, for that matter. What could he say? Other than, *Hey, Caroline, way to go on the background checks.*

The matchmaker finally seemed to remember she was with a client who was paying her a crapload of money to find him a mate—a mate who wasn't already married, by the way—and returned to the sofa to snatch the folder out of Peyton's hands and replace it with another. "An honest mistake," she said. "I'm sure you'll like this one even better."

He opened that folder to find another sheet of vital statistics affixed to another four-by-six glossy, this time of a woman who wasn't quite as breathtaking, amazing or incredible as the first, but who was still beautiful, gorgeous and dazzling. She, too, had auburn hair, a few shades lighter than the first, and eyes so clear a blue, they could have only been enhanced with Photoshop. Still, even without retouching, the woman was stunning.

"This young woman," Caroline said, "is the absolute cream of Chicago society. One of her ancestors helped found the Chicago Mercantile Exchange and her father is on the Chicago Board of Trade. Her mother's family

are the Lauderdales, who own the Lauderdale department store chain, among other things. She herself has
two college degrees, one in business and one in fashion
design. Her name is…"

The matchmaker hesitated, glancing over at Ava.

As if taking the cue, Ava looked at Peyton and said,
"Roxy Mittendorf. Roxanne," she corrected herself
when Caroline looked as if she would take exception.
"But she went by Roxy when we were kids."

Now Ava was the one to hesitate, as if she were
weighing whether or not to say more. Finally, the weight
fell, and she added, "At least until after that college
spring break trip, when she came home with the clap.
Then people started calling her Doxy. I'm not sure if
that's because they thought she was, you know, a doxy,
or because her doctor prescribed doxycycline to treat
it." She brightened. "But I guess that's really neither
here nor there, is it? I mean, it's not like she still has
the clap. At least, I don't think that's one that flares up
again, is it?"

She traded glances with both Peyton and Caroline,
and when neither of them commented, she evidently
felt it necessary to add, "Well, *I* never called her Doxy.
I didn't even find out about the clap thing until after
graduation."

Peyton closed the file folder and handed it back to
Caroline without comment. Caroline fished for the third
in her lap and exchanged it for the second one. When
he opened this one he found—taa-daa!—another red-
headed beauty, this one with eyes a lighter blue that
might actually occur in nature. Interesting that the
matchmaker was three for three with regard to red hair.

When he glanced back at Caroline, she seemed to
sense his thoughts, because she said, "Well, you did

indicate you had a preference for redheads. And also green eyes, but except for that first, all my other candidates for you have blue eyes. Still, not so very different, right?"

For some reason—Peyton couldn't imagine why—they both looked over at Ava. Ava with her dark red hair and green, green eyes.

"What?" she asked innocently.

"Nothing," Peyton said, grateful she hadn't made the connection.

Had he actually stated on his application that he had a preference for green-eyed redheads? He honestly couldn't remember. Then again, he'd been on the jet heading to Chicago at the time, surrounded by a ton of work he'd wanted to finish before his arrival. He'd only been half paying attention to how he was answering the questions. He thought about several of the women he had dated in the past and was surprised to realize that most of them had been redheads. Odd. He liked all women. He didn't care if their hair was blond, brown, red or purple, or what color eyes they had, or what their ethnic, educational or economic origins were. If they were smart, funny and beautiful, if they made him feel good when he was with them, that was all he cared about. So why had he dated so many redheads? Especially when redheads were such a minority?

Instead of looking where he wanted to look just then, he turned his attention to his third prospective date. Before Caroline had a chance to say a word, he held up the photo to show Ava. "Do you know her?"

Ava looked almost guilty. "I do, actually. But you know her, too. She went to Emerson with us. She was in my grade."

Peyton looked at the photo again. The woman was

in no way familiar. Which was weird, because a girl that pretty he would have remembered. "Are you sure? I don't remember her at all."

"Well, you should," Ava said. "You two played hockey together for three years."

He shook his head. "That's not possible. There weren't any girls on the Emerson hockey team."

"No, there weren't."

Understanding dawned on him then. Dawned like a good, solid blow to the back of the head. He looked at the photo again, shortening the hair and blunting the features a bit. "Oh, my God," he finally said. "Is that Nick Boorman?"

"Nicolette," Ava corrected him. "She goes by Nicolette now."

Peyton closed the folder and handed it back to Caroline. "Not that there's anything wrong with that," he said. "But it would just be kind of, um…"

"Awkward," Ava whispered helpfully.

"Yeah."

Caroline took the folder from him and tucked it under the other two candidates that were a no-go. But she was looking at Ava when she did it. "Who *are* you?" she asked.

Ava shrugged. "I'm just Mr. Moss's *assistant.*"

Caroline didn't look anywhere near convinced. She lifted the last of her folders defiantly. She spoke not to Peyton this time, but to Ava. "*This* candidate has only lived in Chicago for four years. She's originally from Miami. Do you have any friends or family in Miami, Ms. Brenner? Any connection to that city at all?"

Ava shook her head. "No, I don't."

Caroline opened the folder and showed the photo

to Ava before allowing Peyton to look at it. "Do you know this woman?"

Ava shook her head again. "I haven't had the pleasure of meeting her. Yet," she added, seemingly pointedly.

"Good," Caroline said. She turned to Peyton and finally allowed him to view the file. "This is Francesca Stratton. She started off as a software developer but is now the CEO of her own company. Her father is a neurosurgeon in Coral Gables, and her mother is a circuit court judge for the state of Florida. Their lineage in that state goes back six generations. *And* she's a distant cousin to King Juan Carlos of Spain."

Now Caroline looked at Ava, as if daring her to come up with something that might challenge the woman's pedigree. When Ava only smiled benignly, the matchmaker continued, "Peyton, I think you and she would be perfect for each other."

He tried not to think about how Caroline had considered the three candidates ahead of Francesca more perfect, and instead took the file to look over the rest of the woman's particulars. He liked that she had built her own company, the way he had, and her knowledge of computers and software design could definitely come in handy with regard to his own work. She was outdoorsy—she cited a love of scuba diving, rock climbing and horseback riding. She preferred nonfiction over fiction, rock and roll over any other music, eating out over eating in. And she was a fan of both the Florida Panthers and Chicago Blackhawks. There wasn't a single thing in her vitals to dissuade him from agreeing with Caroline. She really did seem perfect for him.

So why wasn't he more excited about the prospect of meeting her?

A movement to his left caught his eye, and he found

Ava trying to read the file from where she sat. Instead of making her work for it, he handed it to her.

"What do you think?" he asked as she turned to the final page.

"Ivy League–educated, accomplished pianist, member of the United States Dressage Federation, one of Chicago's One Hundred Women Making a Difference. What's not to love?"

Funny, but she didn't sound as though she loved Francesca.

"So on the Jackie Kennedy scale," he said, "where do you think she'd fall?"

Ava closed the file and returned it to the matchmaker. "Well, if Jackie Kennedy were a young woman today, I think she'd be a lot like Francesca Stratton."

"So…maybe eight?"

With what sounded like much resignation and little satisfaction, she said, "Ten."

That was exactly what Peyton wanted to hear. So why was he disappointed hearing it?

In spite of his reaction, he turned to Caroline and said, "Sounds like we have a winner. When can you set something up?"

The matchmaker looked both relieved and happy. "Let me contact Francesca to see what works for her, and I'll get back to you. What evenings work best for you?"

"Just about any evening is fi—" Peyton started to say. But the delicate clearing of a throat to his left him kept him from finishing.

He looked over at Ava, who was shaking her head.

"What?" he asked.

"You said you didn't think you were ready to meet any of your prospective dates just yet," she reminded him.

"No, you said that."

"And you agreed. We still have several lessons we need to go over."

He said nothing. He had agreed. And really, he didn't mind that much putting off the meeting. Odd, since he really did want to get out of Chicago and back to San Francisco. Maybe he hadn't felt as antsy over the past few days as he had when he'd first arrived, but he did need to get back to the West Coast soon. So he and Ava needed to wrap things up pronto.

"How long do you think we'll need to get me through them?" he asked. And for some really bizarro reason, he found himself hoping she would tell him it would be weeks and weeks and weeks.

Instead, she told him, "Another week, at least."

"So maybe by the weekend after this one?"

She looked as if she wanted to say, *No, it will be weeks and weeks and weeks.* Instead, she replied, "Um, sure. If we work hard, and if you follow the rules," she added meaningfully, "then we can probably get you where you need to be by then."

Following the rules. Not his favorite thing to do. Still, if it would get him a date with a modern-day Jackie Kennedy…

He turned to Caroline again. "How about next Friday or Saturday if she's available?"

Caroline jotted the dates down on the top of the file folder. "I'm reasonably certain that one of those days will be fine. I'll let you know which one after I've spoken to Francesca."

Great, he thought without much enthusiasm. "Great!" he said with much enthusiasm.

He stood, with Ava quickly following suit, thanked Caroline for all her work, and they both started to make their way to the door. They halted, however, when the matchmaker called Ava's name.

"Ms. Brenner," she said tentatively, "you, ah...you wouldn't happen to be looking for a job, would you? Something part-time that wouldn't interfere with your work as Peyton's assistant? You'd be an enormous asset to us here at Attachments, Inc."

Looking a little startled, Ava replied, "Um, no. But thank you."

Peyton told Caroline, "The reason Ava knew all those women is because she moves in the same social circles they do. Her family is loaded. She doesn't have to work." Unable to help himself, he added, "Never mind that she's bleeding me dry for being my *assistant* at the moment."

Caroline suddenly looked way more interested in Ava than she had when Ava was just a prospective part-timer. Funny, though, how Ava suddenly looked kind of panicky.

"I see," the matchmaker said. "Well then, maybe *I* could help *you*. Introduce you to a nice man who has the same set of values you have?"

In other words, Peyton translated, a nice man who had the same *value* that Ava had. *Cha-ching.* For some reason, he suddenly felt kind of panicky, too.

"What do you say, Ava?" the matchmaker added. And it wasn't lost on Peyton that she had switched to the first-name basis she evidently only used with her clients, not to mention the almost genuinely warm smile. "Would you like to fill out an application while you're here?"

Ava smiled back, but somehow looked even more alarmed. "Thank you, Caroline, but I'm really not in the market right now."

Her response made Peyton wonder again if she was seriously involved with someone, and if that was why she wasn't currently in the market. During the week the two of them had spent together, she had never said anything that made him think there was a significant other in her life, and she seemed to have plenty of time on her hands if she was able to work with him every day. Call him crazy, but he didn't think a guy who had a woman like Ava waiting for him at home—hell, who had *Ava* waiting for him at home—would be too happy about her spending so much time with another guy. If Peyton had Ava waiting at home for him, he'd sure as hell never—

But he didn't have Ava waiting at home for him, he reminded himself. And he didn't want her waiting at home for him. So what was the point of even thinking about it?

"Well, if you change your mind…" Caroline said, leaving the statement incomplete but her intention stated.

"You'll be the first person I call," Ava promised.

Peyton did his best not to wish he could be the first person she'd call. Even though he kind of did.

Dammit, what was wrong with him? He'd just been paired up with a modern-day Jackie Kennedy. He should be over the moon. He was just distracted, that was all—too much going on. The takeover of Montgomery and Sons, massive self-improvement, the hunt for the right woman, the ghost of high school past…it was no wonder his brain was scrambled.

"Are we finished here?" he asked, more irritably than he intended.

Both Caroline and Ava seemed to notice that, too. But it was Ava who replied, "You tell me."

"Yes," he snapped.

Without awaiting a reply, he made his way to the door. Let the women draw whatever conclusion they wanted from his behavior. As far as he was concerned, any lessons Ava might have in store for the rest of the day were canceled. He had work to do. Work that didn't include anything or anyone with more than one X chromosome.

Six

Ava and Peyton sat on a bench at the Chicago Institute of Art studying Edward Hopper's *Nighthawks,* neither saying a word. She had instructed him to spend five minutes in silence taking in the details of several paintings that morning, but none of them had captured his attention the way this one had. It almost seemed as if he wanted to walk right into the painting and join the people sitting at the café bar for a cup of late-night coffee.

As he studied the painting, Ava studied him. He was wearing a different pair of dark-wash jeans today, with another fitted sweater—this one the color of good cognac that set off his amber eyes beautifully. She'd opted for a pair of tobacco-colored trousers and a dark green tailored shirt. She couldn't help thinking that, fashion-wise, they complemented each other perfectly. But that was about the only compatibility the two of them were enjoying today.

He'd barely spoken to her after they left the match-maker's office yesterday, barring one angry outburst that had left her flummoxed. After saying they were finished for the day, he'd offered to have his driver drop her at her house on the way back to his hotel, wherever her house was, since she hadn't told him her address, and why was that, anyway, did she still think he wasn't fit to enter the premises the way she had when they were kids, since he'd had to climb out the window when he left her house that one time he was there, not use the front door like a normal—meaning blue-blooded, filthy-rich—person would?

Ava had been stunned to momentary silence. Until then, they'd seemed to have an unspoken agreement that they would never, under any circumstances, spe-cifically mention that night. Then she'd gathered her-self enough to snap back that he could have used the front door if he'd wanted to, but he'd chosen to go out the window because he'd been too ashamed to be seen with her, reeking of old money as she was, which was at least better than reeking of gasoline and gutter scum.

What followed might have been an explosion of re-sentment and frustration that had been steeping for six-teen years. Instead, both had been too horrified by what they'd said to each other, by what they knew they could never take back, that neither had said another word. Nei-ther had apologized, either. They'd just looked out their respective windows until they reached Talk of the Town. Ava had hopped out of the car with a hastily uttered in-struction for Peyton to meet her at the Art Institute this morning and slammed the door before he could object.

Neither had mentioned the exchange today. Their conversation had focused exclusively on art commen-tary, but it had been civil. In spite of that, a stagnant uneasiness surrounded them, and neither seemed to know what to do to ease it.

She glanced at her watch and saw that the five minutes she'd asked Peyton to give to the painting had become eight. Instead of telling him time was up, she turned her attention to the painting, too. It was one she had responded to immediately the first time she'd seen it, during an Emerson Academy field trip when she was in ninth grade. The people in the painting had always looked to her as if they were displaced and at loose ends, as though they were just biding their time in the diner while they waited for something—anything—to change.

The painting still spoke to her that way. Except that now the people looked lonely, too.

"I like how the light is brightest on the guy behind the counter," Peyton said suddenly, stirring Ava from her thoughts. "It makes him look like some kind of…I don't know…spiritual figure or something. He's the guy providing the sustenance, but maybe that sustenance is more than coffee and pie, you know?"

Ava turned to look at him, surprised at the pithiness of the comment.

Before she could say anything, and still looking at the picture, he added, "What's also interesting is that the only real color on the people is with the woman, and both times, it's warm colors. The red on her dress, and the orange in her hair. Although maybe I only notice that because I've always been partial to redheads."

He'd said the same thing at the matchmaker's, she recalled. Or, at least, Caroline had said that was what he'd stated on his questionnaire. Just as he had yesterday after the comment, he turned to look at Ava…then at Ava's hair. Warmth oozed through her belly, because he looked at her now the way he had that night at her parents' house. The two of them had been sitting on the floor in her bedroom, bleary-eyed from their studies, when Ava had cupped the back of her neck, complaining of an incessant ache. Peyton had uncharacteristically taken pity on her and moved her hand to place his there, rubbing gently to ease the knot. One minute, the two of them had been overtaxed and stressed by their homework, and the next…

"I mean…" he sputtered. "That is…it's just…uh…"

"That's so interesting, what you said about the light and the guy behind the counter," she interrupted, pretending she didn't understand why he suddenly seemed edgy. Pretending she didn't feel edgy herself. "I've never thought about that before."

Instead of turning his attention back to the painting, Peyton continued to look at Ava. Oh, God, that was all she needed. If they followed the pattern from sixteen years ago, the two of them were going to end up horizontal on the bench, fully entwined and half-naked. That was how it had been that night at her parents' house. The first time, anyway—they'd been on each other so fast, so fiercely, that they'd only managed to undo any buttons and zippers that were in their way. The second time had been much more leisurely, much more thorough. Where the first time had been a physical act intended to release pressure, the second time had been much more…

"In fact," Ava hurried on, looking back at the painting herself, "it's the sort of interpretation that might lead to a discussion that could go on for hours."

Her heart was racing, and heat was seeping into her chest and face. So she made herself do what she'd done in high school whenever she started reacting that way to Peyton. She channeled her inner Gold Coast ice princess—who she was dismayed to find still lurked beneath the surface—and forced herself to be distant, methodical…and not a little bitchy. She was Peyton's teacher, not his…not someone who should be experiencing odd, decades-old feelings she never should have felt in the first place. She'd never be able to compete with a modern-day Jackie Kennedy anyway. She was the last sort of woman Peyton wanted or needed to accomplish his goals.

"Which is exactly why," she said frostily, "I don't want you saying things like that."

Sensing his annoyance at her crisp tone, she pressed on. She didn't dwell on how she was behaving exactly the way she had sworn not to—treating him the way she had in high school—but she was starting to feel way too many things she shouldn't be feeling, and she didn't know what else to do.

"What I really want for you to take away from this exercise," she told him coolly, "is something less insightful. That shouldn't be too difficult, should it?"

"*Less* insightful?" he echoed. "I thought the whole point of this museum thing was to teach me how to say something about art that wouldn't make me sound like an idiot."

She nodded. "Which is why I've focused on the works I have today. These are artists and paintings that are familiar to everyone. For your purposes, you only need to master some passing art commentary. Not deep, pithy insight."

"Then tell me, oh great art guru," he said sarcastically, "what do I need to know about this one?"

Looking at the painting, again—since it was better than looking at the angry expression on Peyton's face—Ava said, "You should say how interesting it is that the themes in *Nighthawks* are similar to Hopper's *Sunlight in a Cafeteria,* but that the perspective of time is reversed."

"But I haven't seen *Sunlight in a Cafeteria,*" he pointed out. "Not to mention I don't know what the fu— Uh…what you're talking about."

"No one else you'll be talking to has seen it, either," she assured him. "And you don't have to understand it. The minute you offer some indication that you know more about art than your companion, they'll change the subject." She smiled her cool, disaffected smile and told him, "I think you're good to go with the major players in American art. Tomorrow, we'll take on the Impressionists. Then, if we have time, the Dutch masters."

Peyton groaned. "Oh, come on, Ava. How often is this stuff really going to come up in conversation?"

"More often than you think. And we still have to cover books and music, too."

He eyed her flatly. "There's no way I need to know all this stuff before my date with Francesca. I don't need to know it for moving in business circles, either. I think you're just stalling."

Ava gaped at him. "That's ridiculous. Why would I want to spend more time with you than I have to?"

"Got me," he shot back. "God knows it's not like you need the money I'm sure you'll charge me for overtime. I think I've got all this…stuff…covered. Let's move on."

Well, at least he was abiding by the no-profanity rule, she thought. She decided not to comment on the other part of his charge. "Music," she reiterated instead. "Books."

He expelled an exasperated breath. "Fine. I've been

a huge Charles Dickens fan since high school. How's that?"

She couldn't quite hide her surprise. "You read Charles Dickens for fun?"

He clamped his jaw tight. "Yeah." More icily, he added, "And Camus and Hemingway, too. Guess that comes as a shock to you, doesn't it? That gasoline-reeking gutter scum like me could have understood anything other than the sports stats in the *Sun-Times*."

"Peyton, that wasn't what I was think—"

"The hell it wasn't."

So much for the profanity rule. Not that Ava called him on it, since she was kind of responsible for its being broken. She started to deny her charge, then stopped. "Okay, maybe that was kind of what I was thinking. But you didn't exactly show your brainy side in school. Still, I'm sorry. I shouldn't have assumed that. Especially in light of what you've accomplished since then."

He seemed surprised—and a little confused—by her apology. He didn't let her off the hook, though. "And in light of what I accomplished then, too," he added. "Which was something you never bothered to discover for yourself."

Now it was Ava's turn to be surprised. He still sounded hurt by something that had happened—or, rather, hadn't happened—half a lifetime ago. Nevertheless, she told him, "I wasn't the only one who didn't bother to get to know my classmates. I was more than I appeared to be in high school, too, Peyton, but did you ever notice or care?"

He uttered an incredulous sound. "Right. More than just a beautiful shell filled with nothing but self-interest? I don't think so."

"You don't *think* so?" she echoed. "Present tense?

You still think I'm just a—" She halted herself, thinking it would be best to skirt the whole *beautiful* thing. "I'm just a shell filled with nothing but self-interest?"

He said nothing, only continued to look at her the way the teenage Peyton had.

"You think the reason I'm helping you out like this is all for *myself?*" she asked. "You don't think maybe I'm doing it because it's a nice thing for me to do for an old...for a former classmate?"

Now he barked in disbelief. "You're doing it because I'm paying you a bucket of money. If that isn't self-interest, I don't know what is."

There was no way she could set him straight without revealing the reality of her situation. Of course, she *could* do that. She could tell him about how she had walked in his figurative shoes her senior year. She could tell him how she understood now the battles between pride and shame, and desire and need, and how each day had been filled with wondering how she was going to survive into the next one. She could tell him how she'd listened to her mother crying in the next room every night, and how she had forbidden herself to do the same, because nothing could come from that. She could tell him how she'd stood in the yard of the Milhouse Prewitt School every morning and steeled herself before going in, only to be worn to a nub by day's end by the relentless bullying.

Just do it, Ava. Be honest with him. Maybe then karma really will smile upon you.

But on the heels of that thought came another: *Or maybe Peyton will laugh and say the same things you heard every day at Prewitt, about looking like you live in a box under a bridge, and stealing extra fruit from the lunch line—don't think we haven't seen you do it,*

Ava—and not being fit to clean the houses of your class-
mates because no one wants their house smelling the
way you smell, and maybe you don't live in box under
a bridge, after all, maybe you live in a Dumpster.

She opened her mouth, honestly not sure what would
come out. And she heard herself say, "Right. I forgot.
Money and social standing are more important to me
than anything." Conjuring her before-the-fall high
school self again, she cocked her head to one side and
smiled an icy smile. In a voice that could freeze fire,
she said, "But that's because they *are* more important
than anything, aren't they, Peyton? That's something
you've learned, too, isn't it? That's what you want more
than anything now. Guess that makes us two of a kind."

His mouth dropped open, as if it had never occurred
to him how much he resembled the people for whom
he'd had so much contempt in high school. The two of
them really had switched places. In more than just a social context. In a philosophical one, as well. She understood better than ever now that what defined a person
was their character, not what kind of car was parked in
their garage or what kind of clothes hung in their closet.
She was poor in an economic sense, but she was rich in
other ways—certainly richer than the integrity-starved
girl she'd been in high school.

Peyton, on the other hand, had money to burn, but
was running short on integrity, if what he'd told her
about his business methods were any indication. He'd
thrust plenty of families into the sort of life he'd clawed
his way out of. And he was currently trying to take a
family business away from the last remaining members
of that family, to plunder and dismember it. He'd be putting even more people out of work and more families
on the dole. And he was going to do it under the manu-

factured guise of being a decent, mannerly individual. Really, which one of them had the most to feel guilty about these days?

"I think we've both had enough for today," she said decisively.

"We finally get to escape the museum?" he asked with feigned hopefulness, still looking plenty irritated by her last remark.

"Yes, we've had enough of that, too. Since it looks like you have the literary angle covered, tomorrow we can tackle music."

He looked as if he were going to protest, then the fight seemed to go out of him. "Okay. Fine. Whatever. What time should I pick you up?"

She shook her head, as she did every time he asked that question—and he'd asked it every day. She said the same thing she always said in response. "I'll meet you."

Before he could object—something else he did every day—she gave him the address of a jazz record store on East Illinois and told him to be there when they opened.

"And then I bet we get to have lunch at another pretentious restaurant," he said, sounding as weary as she felt. "Hey, I know. I'll even wear one of my new suits this time."

She knew he meant for the comment to be sarcastic. So she only echoed his ennui back. "Okay. Fine. Whatever."

Ennui. Right. As if the tension and fatigue they were feeling could be ascribed to a lack of interest. Then again, maybe for Peyton, it was. He'd made no secret about his reluctance to be My Fair Gentlemanned to within an inch of his life. He really didn't give a damn about any of this and was only doing it to further his business. Ava wished she could share his disinterest.

The reason for her impatience and irritation this week had nothing to do with not caring.

And it had everything to do with caring too much.

Seven

Peyton gazed at Ava from across the smallest table he'd ever been forced to sit at and did his best to ignore the ruffled lavender tablecloth and flowered china tea set atop it. He tried even harder to ignore the cascade of lace curtains to his right and the elaborately scrolled ironwork tea caddy to his left. And it would be best not to get him started on the little triangular sandwiches with the crusts cut off or the mountain of frothy pastries.

Tea. She was actually making him *take tea* with her. In a tea shop. Full of women in hats and gloves. Hell, even Ava was wearing a hat and gloves. A little white hat with one of those netted veil things that fell over her eyes, and white gloves that went halfway up her arm with a bazillion buttons. Her white dress had even more buttons than her gloves did.

She hadn't been wearing the hat or gloves when she'd

walked into the record store earlier, so he hadn't realized what was in store for him. She'd pulled them out
of her oversize purse as the two of them rode to the
damned *tea* shop—except she hadn't said they were
going to a *tea* shop. She'd said they were going to a
late lunch.

Still, the appearance of a hat and gloves should have
been his first clue that "lunch" was going to be even
worse than something he'd put on a damned suit for.
Something that would, in Ava's words, aid in his edification. He just wished he could believe this was for his
edification instead of being some kind of punishment
for his behavior at the museum yesterday.

He also wished he could think Ava looked ridiculous
in her dainty alabaster frock and habiliments. Which
was the kind of language to use for a getup like that,
even if those were words he had always—before this
week, anyway—manfully avoided. Hell, she looked as
if she was an escapee from an overbudgeted period film
set during the First World War. Unfortunately, there
was something about the getup that was also… Well…
Dammit. Unbelievably hot.

Which was just what he needed. To be turned on
by Ava, the last woman on the planet who should be
turning him on. He'd been so sure he could remain un-
affected by her while they were undertaking this self-
improvement thing. After all, they hadn't gotten along
at all that first morning at her apartment. Instead, with
every passing day, he'd just become more bewitched
by her.

Just as he had in high school.

It was only physical, he told himself. The same way
it had only been physical in high school. There was
just some kind of weird chemistry between them. Her

pheromones talking to his pheromones or something. Talking, hell. More like screaming at the top of their lungs. People didn't have to like each other to be sexually attracted to each other. They just had to have loud, obnoxious pheromones.

Tea, he reminded himself distastefully. *Focus on the fact that she's making you sit in a tearoom drinking—gak—tea and eating the kind of stuff that no self-respecting possessor of a Y chromosome should ingest.* God knew what this was going to do to his testosterone levels.

"Now then," she said in a voice that was every bit as prissy as her outfit. "Taking tea. This will probably be your biggest challenge yet."

Oh, Peyton didn't doubt that for a minute. What he did doubt was that many people actually *took tea*—he just couldn't think that phrase in anything but a snotty tone of voice…tone of mind…whatever—in this country. Not any people with a Y chromosome, anyway.

"A lot of people think the art of tea has fallen by the wayside over the years," she continued, obviously reading his mind. Or maybe his distasteful expression. "But it's actually been rising in popularity. Hence your need to be familiar with it."

"Ava," he said, mustering as much patience as he could, "I think I can safely say that no matter how high in society I go, I will never, ever, ask anyone to—" he could barely get the words out of his mouth "—*take tea* with me."

She smiled a benign smile. "I bet the sisters Montgomery would be charmed by a man who asked them to tea. And I bet not one of your competitors would think to do it."

She was right. Dammit. Two sweet old Southern ladies would find this place enchanting. Crap. *Enchanting*. There was another word he normally avoided manfully. Where the hell had his testosterone gotten off to?

He blew out an exasperated breath. "Fine. Just don't expect me to wear white gloves."

"I suppose we could allow that small concession," she agreed. "Now then. As Henry James wrote in *The Portrait of a Lady,* 'There are few hours in life more agreeable than the hour dedicated to the ceremony known as afternoon tea.'"

Oh, good. At least this wouldn't last more than an hour.

"And I, for one," she continued, "couldn't agree more."

Peyton did his best to look as if he gave a crap. "Yeah, well, ol' Henry obviously never spent an afternoon sharing a case of Anchor Steam with his friends while the Blackhawks trounced the Canucks."

Ava smiled thinly. "No doubt."

She launched into a monologue about the history of afternoon tea—all three centuries of it—then moved on to the etiquette of afternoon tea, then on to the menu selection of afternoon tea. She talked about the differences between cream tea, light tea and full tea—thankfully, they were having full tea, since Peyton was getting hungrier with every word she spoke—then she pointed to the selections on the caddy beside them, categorizing them as savories, scones and pastries, even though they looked to him like sandwiches, biscuits and dessert. By the time she wrapped up her dissertation, his stomach was grumbling so forcefully even his Y chromosome was thinking the little flowery cakes looked good.

Unfortunately, as he reached for one, Ava smacked his hand as if he were a toddler.

"Don't reach," she said. "Ask for them to be passed."

"But they're sitting right there."

"They're closer to me than they are to you."

"Oh, sure, by an inch and a half."

"Nonetheless, whoever is closer should pass to the person who is farther away."

Okay, she was definitely going out of her way to be ornery, deliberately to get a rise out of him. Well, he'd show her. He'd kill her with kindness. He'd be as courteous as he knew how to be. And thanks to her lessons, he'd learned how to be pretty damned courteous.

Sitting up straighter in his tiny chair, he channeled the inner Victorian he didn't even know he possessed and said, "If you please, Miss Brenner, and if it wouldn't trouble you overly, would you pass the…" What had she called them? "The savories?"

She eyed him suspiciously, clearly doubting his sincerity. But what was she going to do? He'd been a perfect effing gentleman. He'd even thought the word *effing,* instead of what he really wanted to think, which was…uh, never mind.

Still looking at him as if she expected him to start a food fight, she asked, "May I suggest the cucumber sandwiches or the crab puffs?"

He unclenched his jaw long enough to reply, "You may."

"Which would you prefer?"

"The cucumber sandwiches," he said. Mostly because he didn't think he could say *crab puffs* with a straight face. Not that *cucumber sandwiches* was exactly easy. "If you please."

Before retrieving the plate, she began to unbutton

her gloves. Evidently good manners precluded wearing such garments whilst one was taking tea.

Dammit, he thought when he played that back in his head. There was no way he was going to last an hour in this place.

When she finally had her gloves off—a good fortnight after initiating their unbuttoning—she reached for the plate of sandwiches and passed it the three inches necessary to place it on the table between them. Then she poured them each a cup of tea from the pot, adding three sugar cubes—jeez, they had flowers on them, too—to her own. Peyton eschewed them—since no one taking tea would ever *blow off* something; they would always *eschew* it—and lifted the cup to his mouth. At Ava's discreetly cleared throat, he looked up, and she tilted her head toward the cup he was holding. Holding by its bowl having grabbed the entire thing in his big paw, because he'd been afraid he'd break off the handle if he tried to pick it up that way. Gah. After a moment of juggling, he managed the proper manipulation of the cup, holding it by its handle, if just barely. Only then did Ava nod her head to let him know he was allowed to continue.

Man, had she actually had to grow up this way? Had her mother sat her down, day after day, and made her memorize all the stuff she was making him memorize? Had she been forced to dress a certain way and unfold her napkin just so, and talk about only approved subjects with other people, the way she was teaching him to do? Or did that just come naturally to people who were born with the bluest blood in the highest income bracket? Was good taste and polite behavior encoded on her DNA the way green eyes and red hair were? Did refinement run in her veins? And if so, did that mean

Peyton's DNA was encoded with garbage-strewn streets and fighting dirty and that transmission fluid flowed through his veins?

It hit him again, even harder, how far apart the two of them were. How far apart they'd been since birth. How far apart they'd be until they died. Even with his income rivaling hers now, even mastering all these lessons that would grant him access to her world, he'd never, ever be her social equal. Because he'd never, ever be as comfortable with this stuff as she was. It would never be second nature to him the way it was to her. He would hate it in her world. All the rules and customs would suffocate him. It would kill everything that made him who he was, the same way taking Ava *out* of her world would doubtless suffocate her and kill everything that made her her.

And why did it bug him so much to realize that? He wasn't a kid anymore. He didn't care what world she lived in or that he'd never be granted citizenship there. Truth be told, now that he was a monster success, he kind of reveled in his mean-streets background. Even as a teenager, he'd taken a perverse sort of pride in where he came from, because where he came from hadn't destroyed his spirit the way it had so many others in the neighborhood. So why had it been such a sticking point with him in high school, the vast socioeconomic chasm between him and Ava? Why was it still a sticking point now, when that chasm had shrunk to a crack? Why did it bother him so much that his and Ava's worlds would never meet? What difference did her presence in the scheme of things—or lack thereof—make anyway?

His cup was nearly to his mouth when an answer to that question exploded in his head. It bothered him, he suddenly knew, because the thing that had sparked his

success, the thing that had made him escape his neighborhood and muscle his way into a top-tier college, the
thing that had kept him from giving up the hundreds
of times he wanted to give up, the thing that had made
him seize the business world with both fists and driven
him to make money, and then more money, and then
more money still…the thing that had done all that was…

Hell. It wasn't a thing at all. It was a person. It was
Ava.

Down went the teacup, landing on the table with a
thump that sent some of its contents spilling onto his
hand. Peyton scarcely felt the burn. He looked at Ava,
who was studying a plate of cakes and cookies, trying
to decide which one she wanted. She was oblivious to
both his spilled tea and tumultuous thoughts, but she
had flipped back the veil from her face, leaving her features in clear profile.

She really hadn't changed since high school. Not just
her looks, but the rest of her, too. She was as beautiful
now as she'd been then, as elegant, as refined. And, he
couldn't help thinking further, as off-limits. When all
was said and done, the Ava of adulthood was no different from the Ava of adolescence. And neither was he.
He was still—and would always be—the basest kind
of interloper in her world.

As if to hammer home their differences, she finally
decided on a frilly little pastry cup filled with berries
and whipped cream and transferred it to her plate with
a pair of dainty little silver tongs. Then she went for one
of the prissy little flowered cakes. Then a couple of the
lacy little cookies. All the fragile little things Peyton
would have been afraid of touching because he would
probably crush them. He was way better suited to a big,
bloody hunk of beef beside a mountain of stiff mashed

potatoes, with a sweaty longneck bottle of beer to wash it all down. The nectar of the working-class male.

When Ava finally looked up to see how he was faring, her brows knitted downward in confusion. He glanced at the plate of sandwiches sitting between them. Although they were heartier than the pastries, those, too, looked just as off-limits as everything else, so small and delicate and pretty were they. He tried to focus on them anyway, pretending to be indecisive about which one he wanted. But his thoughts were still wrapped up in his epiphany. *God. Ava.* It had been Ava all along.

He wasn't trying to master the art of fine living because he wanted to take over another company and add another zero to his bottom line. Not really. Sure, taking over Montgomery and Sons was the impetus, but he wouldn't be trying to do that if it weren't for Ava. He wouldn't have done anything over the past sixteen years if it weren't for Ava. He'd still be in the old neighborhood, working in the garage with his old man. He'd be spending his days under the chassis of a car, then going home at night to an apartment a few blocks away to watch the Hawks, Bulls or Cubs while consuming a carryout value meal and popping open a cold one.

And, hell, he might have even been happy doing that. Provided he'd never met Ava.

But from the moment he'd laid eyes on her in high school, something had pushed him to rise above his lot in life. Not even pushed him. *Driven* him. Yeah, that was a better word. Because after Ava had walked into his life, nothing else had mattered. Nothing except bringing himself up to standards she might approve of. So that maybe, someday, she *would* approve of him. And so that maybe, someday, the two of them…

He didn't allow himself to finish the thought. He

was afraid of what else he might discover about himself. Bad enough he understood what had brought him this far. But he did understand now. Too well. What he didn't understand was why. Why had Ava had that effect on him when nothing else had? Why would he have been satisfied with the blue-collar life for which he had always assumed he was destined until he met her? What was it about her that had taken up residence deep inside him? Why had she been the catalyst for him to escape the mean streets when the mean streets themselves hadn't been enough to do that?

"Is something wrong?" she asked, pulling him out of his musings.

"No," he answered quickly. "Just trying to decide what I want."

Which was true, he realized. He just didn't want anything that was on the plate of sandwiches.

"The petit fours here are delicious," she told him.

He'd just bet they were. If he knew what the hell a petit four was.

"Though you'd probably prefer something a little more substantial."

Oh, no doubt.

"Maybe one of the curried-egg sandwiches? They're not the kind of thing you get every day."

And naturally Peyton didn't want the kind of thing he could get every day. Hell, that was the whole problem.

"Or if you want something sweeter…"

He definitely wanted something sweeter.

"…you might try one of the ginger cakes."

Except not that.

Oh, man, this thing with Ava wasn't turning out the way he'd planned *at all*. She was supposed to be schooling him in the basics of social climbing, not advanced soul-searching. And what man wanted to discover the workings of his inner psyche for the first time in a frickin' tearoom?

"Aaahhh…" he began, stringing the word over several time zones in an effort to stall. Finally, he finished, "Yeah. Gimme one of those curried-egg sandwiches. They sound absolutely…" The word was out of his mouth before he could stop it, so overcome by his surroundings, and so weakened by his musings, had he become. "Scrumptious."

Okay, that did it. With that terrible word, he could feel what little was left of his testosterone oozing out of every pore. A man could only take so much tea and remain, well, manly. And a man could only take so much self-discovery and remain sane. If Peyton didn't get out of this place soon…if he didn't get away from Ava soon…if he didn't get someplace, anyplace, far away from here—far away from *her*—ASAP, someplace where he could look inside himself and figure out what the hell was going on in his brain…

Bottom line, he just had to get outta here. Now.

"Look, Ava, do you mind if we cut this short?" he asked. "I just remembered a conference call I'm supposed to be in on in—" He looked at his watch and pretended to be shocked at the time. "Wow. Thirty minutes. I really need to get back to my hotel."

She looked genuinely crushed. "But the tea…"

"Can we get a doggie bag?"

Judging by the way her expression changed, he might as well have just asked her if he could jump up onto the table, whip off his pants and introduce everyone to Mr. Happy.

"No," she said through gritted teeth. "One does not

ask for a doggie bag for one's afternoon tea. Especially not in a place like this."

"Well, I don't know why the hell not," he snapped.

Oh, yeah. There it was. With even that mild profanity, he sucked some of his retreating testosterone back in. Now if he could just figure out how to reclaim the rest of it…

He glanced around until he saw a waiter—or whatever passed for a waiter in this place, since they were all dressed like maître d's—and waved the guy down in the most obnoxious way he knew how.

"Hey, you! Garson!" he shouted, deliberately mispronouncing the French word for *waiter*. "Could we get a doggie bag over here?"

Everyone in the room turned to stare at him—and Ava—in frank horror. That, Peyton had to admit, helped a lot with his masculine recovery. Okay, so he was acting like a jerk, and doing it at Ava's expense. Sometimes, in case of emergency, a man had to break the glass on his incivility. No, on his crudeness, he corrected himself. His grossness. His bad effin' manners. Those were way better words for what he was tapping into. And wow, did it feel good.

He braved a glance at Ava and saw that she had propped her elbows on the table and dropped her head into her hands.

"Yo, Ava," he said. "Take your elbows off the table. That is so impolite. Everyone is staring at us. Jeez, I can't take you anywhere." He looked back at the waiter, who hadn't budged from the spot where he had been about to serve a couple of elderly matrons from a pile of flowered cakes. "What, am I not speakin' English here?" he yelled. Funny, but he seemed to have suddenly developed a Bronx accent. "Yeah, you in the penguin suit. Could we get a doggie bag for our—" he gestured toward the tea caddy and the plates on the table "—for all this stuff? I mean, at these prices, I don't want it to go to waste. Know what I'm sayin'?"

"Peyton, what are you doing?" Ava asked from behind her hands. "Are you trying to get us thrown out of here?"

Wasn't that obvious? Was he really not speakin' English here?

"Garson!" he shouted again. "Hey, we don't got all day."

Ava groaned softly from behind her hands, then said something about how she would never be able to take tea here again. It was all Peyton could do not to reply, *You're welcome.*

Instead, he continued to channel his inner bad-mannered adolescent—who he wasn't all that surprised to discover lurked just beneath his surface. "The service in this place sucks, Ava. Next time, we should hit Five Guys instead. At least they give you your food in a bag. I don't think this guy's going to bring us one."

He figured he'd said enough now to make her snap up her head and blast him for being such a jerk—as politely as she could, naturally, since they were in a public place. Instead, when she dropped her hands, she just looked tired. Really, really tired. And she didn't say a word. She only stood, gathered her purse and gloves, turned her back, and walked away with all the elegance of a czarina.

Peyton was stunned. She wasn't going to say something combative in response? She wasn't going to call him uncouth? She wasn't going to tell him how it was men like him who gave his entire gender a bad name?

She wasn't going to glare daggers or spit fire? She was just going to walk away without even trying?

When he realized that yep, that was exactly what she was going to do, he bolted after her. He was nearly to the exit when he realized they hadn't paid their bill, so ran back to the table long enough to drop a handful of twenties on top of it. He didn't wait for change. Hell, their server deserved a 100-percent tip for the way he had just behaved.

When he vaulted out of the tearoom onto the street, he found himself drowning in a river of people making the Friday-afternoon jump start from work to weekend. He looked left, then right, but had no idea which way Ava had gone. Remembering her outfit, he searched for a splash of white amid the sullen colors of business suits, driving his gaze in every direction. Finally, he spotted her, in the middle of a crosswalk at the end of the block, buttoning up those damned white gloves, as if she were Queen Elizabeth on her way to address the royal guard.

He hurtled after her, but by the time he made it to the curb, she was on the other side of the street and the light was changing. Not that that deterred him. As he sprinted into the crosswalk against the light, half a dozen drivers honked their displeasure, and he was nearly clipped by more than one bumper. Even when he made it safely to the other side of the street, he kept running, trying to catch up to the wisp of white that was Ava.

Every time he thought he was within arm's reach, someone or something blocked him from touching her, and for every step he took forward, she seemed to take two. Panic welled in him that he would never reach her, until she turned a corner onto a side street that was much less crowded. Still, he had to lengthen his stride to catch up with her, and still, for a moment, it seemed he never would. Finally, he drew near enough to grasp her upper arm and spin her around to face him. She immediately jerked out of his hold, swinging her handbag as she came. Peyton let her go, dodging her bag easily, then lifted both hands in surrender.

"Ava, I'm sorry," he said breathlessly. "But... Stop. Just stop a minute. Please."

For a moment, they stood there on the sidewalk looking at each other, each out of breath, each poised for... something. Peyton had no idea what. Ava should have looked ridiculous in her turn-of-the-century garb, brandishing her handbag in her little white gloves, her netted hat dipping to one side. Instead, she seemed ferocious enough to snap him in two. A passerby jostled him from behind, sending him forward a step, until he was nearly toe to toe with her. She took a step in retreat, never altering her pose.

"Leave me alone," she said without preamble.

"No," he replied just as succinctly.

"Leave me alone, Peyton," she repeated adamantly. "I'm going home."

"No."

He wasn't sure whether he uttered the word in response to her first sentence or the second, but really, it didn't matter. He wasn't going to leave her alone, and he didn't want her to go home. Despite his conviction only moments ago that he needed to be by himself to sort out his thoughts, isolation was suddenly the last thing he wanted. Not that he was sure what the *first* thing was that he wanted, but... Well, okay, maybe he did kind of know what the first thing was that he wanted. He just wasn't sure he knew what to do with it if he got it. Well, okay, maybe he did kind of know that, too, but...

"You said we still have a lot of work to do before I can go out with Francesca," he reminded her, shoving his thoughts to the back of his brain and hoping they stayed there. "That's only a week away."

She relaxed her stance, dropping her purse to her side. It struck him again that she looked tired. He couldn't remember ever seeing her looking like that before. Not since reacquainting himself with her in Chicago. Not when they were kids. It was…unsettling.

Then he remembered that yes, he had seen her that tired once. That night at her parents' house when they'd been up so late studying. It had unsettled him then, too. Enough that he'd wanted to do something to make her less weary. Enough that he'd placed his hands on her shoulders to rub away the knots in her tense muscles. But the moment he'd touched her—

He pushed that thought to the back of his brain, too. He *really* didn't need to be thinking about that right now.

"You should have thought about your date with Francesca before you humiliated us the tearoom," she said.

"Yeah, about that," he began. Not that he had any idea what to say about that, but *about that* seemed like a good start.

Ava spared him, however. "Peyton, we could work for a year, and it wouldn't make any difference. You'll just keep sabotaging us."

He couldn't help noting her use of the word *us*. She hadn't said he was sabotaging himself. She hadn't said he was sabotaging her efforts. She'd said he was sabotaging the two of them. He wondered if she noticed, too, how she'd lumped the two of them together, or if she even realized she'd said it. Even if she did, what did it mean, if anything?

"I only sabotaged us today," he told her. "And only because you were going out of your way to make things harder than they had to be."

Even though that was true, it wasn't why he'd behaved the way he had. He'd done that because he'd needed to get out of that place as fast as he could. The problem now was convincing Ava that he still wanted to move forward after deliberately taking so many giant steps backward.

And the problem was that, suddenly, his wanting to continue with this ridiculous makeover had less to do with winning over the Montgomery sisters in Mississippi…and more to do with winning over Ava right here in Chicago.

Eight

Ava trudged up the stairs to her apartment with Peyton two steps behind, silently willing him to twist his ankle. Not enough to do any permanent damage. Just enough to make him have to sit down and rub it for a few minutes so she could escape him.

In spite of her demands to leave her alone, he had followed her for three blocks, neither of them saying a word. She'd thought he would give up when they reached the door behind the shop that opened onto the stairwell leading up to her apartment. But he'd stuck his foot in it before she had a chance to slam it in his face. At this point, she was too tired to argue with him. If he wanted to follow her all the way up so she could slam her apartment door in his face, then that was his prerogative.

But he was too fast for her there, as well, shoving the toe of his new Gucci loafer between door and jamb before she had a chance to make the two connect. She leaned harder on the door, trying to put enough force into it that he would have to remove his foot or risk having his toes crushed. But his shoe held firm. Damn the excellence of Italian design anyway.

"Ava, let me in," he said, curling his fingers around the door and pushing back.

"Go. Away," she told him. Again.

"Just talk to me for a few minutes. Please?"

She sighed wearily and eased up on the door. Peyton shouldered it harder, gaining enough ground to win access to the apartment. But he halted halfway in, clearly surprised by his success. His face was scant inches from Ava's, and his fingertips on the door skimmed hers. Even though she was still wearing her white gloves, she could feel the warmth of his hand against hers. He was close enough for her to see how the amber of his irises was circled by a thin line of gold. Close enough for her to see a small scar on his chin that hadn't been there in high school. Close enough for her to smell the faint scent of something cool and spicy that clung to him. Close enough for her to feel his heat mingling with her own.

Close enough for her to wish he would move closer still.

Which was why she sprang away from the door and hurried toward the kitchen. Tea, she told herself. That was what she needed. A nice, calming cup of tea. She'd hardly had a chance to taste hers in the shop. She had a particularly soothing chamomile that would be perfect. Anything to take her thoughts off wanting to be close to Peyton. *No!* she quickly corrected herself. Anything to take her thoughts off her lousy afternoon.

Without wasting a moment to remove her gloves or

hat—barely even taking the time to shove the netting of the latter back from her face—she snatched the kettle from the stove, filled it with water and returned it to the burner as she spun the knob to turn it on. Then she busied herself with retrieving the tea canister from the cupboard and searching a drawer for the strainer. She felt Peyton's gaze on her the entire time, so knew he had followed as far as the kitchen, but she pretended not to notice. Instead, after readying the tea and cup, she began sorting through other utensils in the drawer, trying to look as if she were searching for something else that was very important—like her peace of mind, since that had completely fled.

"Ava," he finally said when it became clear she wouldn't continue the conversation.

"What?" she asked, still focused on the contents of the drawer.

"Will you please talk to me?"

"Are we not talking?" she asked, not looking up. "It sounds to me as if we're talking. If we're not talking, then what are we doing?"

"I don't know what you're doing, but I'm trying to get you to look at me so I can explain why I did what I did earlier."

He wasn't going to leave until they'd hashed this out. So she halted her phony search and slammed the drawer shut, turning to face him fully. "You were trying to get us thrown out of there on purpose," she said.

"You're right. I was," he admitted, surprising her.

He stood in the entry to the kitchen, filling it, making the tiny space feel microscopic. During their walk, he had wrestled his necktie free of his collar and unbuttoned his jacket and the top buttons of his shirt, but he still looked uncomfortable in the garments. Truth be told, he hadn't looked comfortable this week in any of his new clothes. He'd always looked as if he wanted to shed the skin of the animal she was trying to change him into. He looked that way now, too.

But he'd asked her to change him, she reminded herself. There was no reason for her to feel this sneaking guilt. She was trying to help him. She *was*. He was the one who had wrecked their afternoon today with his boorish behavior. He even admitted it.

"Why did you do it?" she asked. "We were having such a nice time."

"No, *you* were having a nice time, Ava. *I* was turning into Mary fu—uh... Mary friggin' Poppins."

"But Peyton, if you want to get along in—" somehow, she managed to get the words out "—my world, then you need to know how to—"

"I don't need to know how to *take tea,*" he interrupted her, fairly spitting the last two words. "Admit it, Ava. The only reason you took me to that place was to get even with me for something. For being less than a gentleman—what you consider a gentleman, anyway—at the Art Institute yesterday. Or maybe for something else this week. God knows you're as hard to read now as you were in high school."

Ignoring his suggestion that she'd made him go to the tearoom as a punishment—since, okay, maybe possibly perhaps there was an element of truth in that—and ignoring, too, his charge that she was hard to read since he'd never bothered to see past the superficial—she latched on to his other comment instead. "What *I* consider a gentleman?" she said indignantly. "News flash, Peyton—what I'm teaching you to be is what any woman in her right mind would want a man to be."

He grinned at that. An arrogant grin very like the

ones to which he'd treated her in high school. "Oh, yeah? Funny, but a lot of women who knew me before this week liked me just fine the way I was. *A lot* of women, Ava," he reiterated with much emphasis. "Just *fine*."

She smiled back with what she hoped was the same sort of arrogance. "Note that I said, 'any woman in her *right* mind.' I doubt you've known too many of those, considering the social circle—or whatever it was—you grew up in."

She wanted to slap herself for the comment. Not just because it was so snotty, but because it wasn't true. Right-minded people weren't defined by their social circles. There were plenty of people in Chicago's upper crust who were crass and insufferable, and there were plenty of people living in poverty who were the picture of dignity and decency. But that was the effect Peyton had on her—he made her want to make him feel as small as he made her feel. The same way he had in high school.

He continued to smile, but his eyes went flinty. "Yeah, but these days, I move in the same kind of circle you grew up in. And hell, Ava, at least I *earned* my money. That's more than you can say for yourself. Your daddy gave you everything you ever had. And even Daddy didn't work for what he had. He got it from his old man. Who got it from his old man. Who got it from his old man. Hell, Ava, how long has it been since anyone in your family actually *worked* for all the nice things they own?"

Something in her chest pinched tight at that. Not just because what he said about her father was true—although Jennings Brenner III earned pennies these days working in the prison kitchen, he'd inherited his wealth the same way countless Brenners before him had. But also because Ava still hated the reminder of the way her family used to be, and the way they'd treated people like Peyton. She hated the reminder of the way *she* used to be, and the way *she'd* treated people like Peyton. He was right about her money, too—about the money she'd had back in high school, anyway. It hadn't been hers. She hadn't earned any of it. At least Peyton had had a job after school and paid his own way in the world. In that regard, he'd been richer back then than she. She'd *really* had no right to treat him the way she had when they were kids.

The kettle began to boil, and, grateful for the distraction, she spun around to pour the hot water carefully into her cup. For long moments, she said nothing, just focused on brewing her tea. Peyton's agitation at her silence was almost palpable. He took a few steps into the kitchen, pausing right beside her. Close enough that she could again feel his heat and inhale the savory scent of him. Close enough that she again wanted him to move closer still.

"So that's it?" he asked.

Still fixing her attention on her cup, she replied, "So what's it?"

"You're not going to say anything else?"

"What else am I supposed to say?"

"I don't know. Something about how my money is new money, so it's not worthy of comparison to yours, being as old and moldy as it is, or something like that."

The teenage Ava would have said exactly that. Only she would have delivered the comment in a way that made it sound even worse than Peyton did. Today's Ava wanted no part of it. What today's Ava did want, however…

Well. That was probably best not thought about. Not while Peyton was standing so close, looking and smelling as good as he did.

She sidestepped his question by replying, "Why would I say something like that when you've already said it?"

"Because I didn't mean it."

"Fine. You didn't mean it."

Instead of placating him, her agreement only seemed to irritate him more. "Why aren't you arguing with me?"

"Why do you want me to argue?"

"Stop answering my questions with a question."

"Am I doing that?"

"Dammit, Ava, I—"

She spoke automatically, as she had all week, when she said, "Watch your language."

He hesitated a moment, then said, "No."

That, finally, made her look up. "What?"

He smiled again, but this time it was less arrogant than it was challenging. "I said, 'No,'" he repeated. "I'm not going to watch my language. I'm sick of watching my language."

To prove his point, he followed that announcement with a string of profanity that made Ava wince. Then he fairly rocked back on his heels, as if waiting for her to retaliate. No, as if he was looking forward to her retaliation. As if he would relish it.

So, in retaliation, Ava went back to her tea. She dunked the strainer a few more times, removed it from the brew and set it aside. Then she lifted the cup to her lips and blew softly to cool it. When she braved a glimpse at Peyton, she could see that his annoyance had steeped into anger. She replaced her tea on the counter without tasting it. But she continued to gaze into its pale yellow depths when she spoke.

"No more arguing, Peyton. I'm tired of it, and it gets us nowhere."

He said nothing in response, only stood with his body rigid, glaring at her. Then, gradually, he relented. She could almost feel the fight go out of him, too, as if he were just as tired of the antagonism as she was.

"If I apologize for my behavior this afternoon," he asked, "will you come back to work for me?"

She told herself to say no and assure him that he'd learned enough to manage the rest of the way by himself. But for some reason, she said nothing.

"You said we still have a lot of work to do," he reminded her.

She told herself to admit she'd only said that because she hadn't wanted to end their time together. But for some reason, she said nothing.

"I mean, what if Caroline sets up a date for me and Francesca that involves seafood? I don't know how to eat a lobster that doesn't include slamming it on a picnic table a half dozen times."

She told herself to tell him he should just ask the matchmaker not to send them to Catch Thirty-Five.

"Or what if she makes us go to a wine bar? You and I have barely covered wine, and that's something you rich people always end up talking about at some point."

She told herself to tell him he should just ask the matchmaker not to send them to Avec.

"Or, my God, dancing. I don't know how to do any of that Arthur Murray stuff. I can't even do that 'Gangnam Style' horse thing."

Although that made her smile, Ava told herself to

tell him he should just ask the matchmaker not to send them to Neo.

She told herself to tell him all those things. Then she heard herself say, "All right. I'll teach you about seafood, wine and dancing between now and the end of next week."

"And some other stuff, too," he interjected.

She looked up at that and immediately wished she hadn't. Within the passage of a few moments, he'd somehow become even more attractive than he was before. He looked…gentler. More personable. More approachable. Like the sort of man any woman in her right mind would want…

"What other stuff?" she asked, quelling the thought before it fully formed.

He seemed at a loss for a minute, then said, "I'll make a list."

"Okay," she agreed reluctantly. It was only for another week. Surely she could be around him for one more week without losing her heart. *Mind,* she quickly corrected herself. Without losing her mind.

"Do you promise?" he asked, sounding uncertain.

It was an odd request. Why did he want her to promise? It was as if they were back to being adolescents. Why didn't he trust her to follow through? She'd done her part this week to teach him all the things he'd asked her to help him with. It was only when he'd thrown those lessons out the window and turned into a boor that she'd walked away.

"Yes, I promise."

"You promise to help me with everything I need help with?"

"Yes. I promise. But in return, you have to promise you'll stop challenging me every step of the way."

He grinned at that, but there was nothing arrogant or challenging in the gesture this time. In fact, this time, when Peyton smiled, he looked quite charming. "Oh, come on. You love it when I challenge you."

Oh, sure. About as much as she had loved it in high school.

"Promise me," she insisted.

He lifted his right hand, palm out, as if taking a pledge. "I promise."

"This day's a wash, though," she told him. "It's too late to get started on anything new."

"I'm sorry for the way I behaved at the tearoom," he said, surprising her again.

"And I'm sorry I made you go to a tearoom," she conceded.

The remark reminded her she was still wearing her hat and gloves, and she lifted her hands to inspect the latter. She'd seen them in a vintage clothing store when she was still in college and hadn't been able to resist them. What had possessed her to buy white gloves with more buttons than a lunar module? Oh, right. To match the white dress with more buttons than Cape Canaveral that she'd bought at a different vintage clothing store. She began the task of unfastening each of the pearly little buttons on her left glove.

"No, don't," Peyton said abruptly.

When she looked at him, she saw that his gaze was fixed on her two gloved hands. "Why not?"

Now his gaze flew to her face, and she couldn't help thinking he looked guilty about something. "Uh...it's just...um...I mean...ah..." He swallowed hard. "They just look really nice on you."

His cheeks were tinged with the faintest bit of pink, she noted with astonishment. Was he actually blushing?

Was that possible? Surely it was due to the bad lighting in the kitchen. Even so, something in his eyes made heat spark in her belly, spreading quickly outward, warming parts of her that really shouldn't be warming at the moment.

"Thank you," she said, the words coming out a little unevenly.

When she started to unbutton her glove once more, Peyton lifted a hand halfway to hers, looking as if he wanted to object again. She halted, eyeing him in silent question, and he dropped his hand with clear reluctance. *How odd,* she thought. She went back to the task, but couldn't help noticing how he still pinned his gaze to her hands, and how a muscle in his jaw twitched as his cheeks grew ruddier. Where she normally had no trouble removing the garments, for some reason, suddenly, her hands didn't want to cooperate. When the second button took longer to free than the first, and the third took even longer than the second, Peyton started to lift a hand toward hers again, closer this time, as if he wanted to help. And this time, he didn't drop it.

The more his scrutiny intensified, the more awkward Ava felt, slowing her progress even more. At this rate, he and Francesca would be sending their firstborn off to college before she finished with her first glove. Finally, she surrendered, dropping her right hand to her side and extending the left toward him.

"Could you help me out?" she asked, the question coming out softly and uncertainly.

It seemed to take a moment for her question to sink in, as Peyton was still fixed so intently on her gloved hand. Even when he moved his gaze from her hand to her face, he still looked acutely distracted.

"What?" he asked, sounding distracted, too.

"My glove," she said. "The buttons. I'm having trouble getting them undone. Do you mind?"

Color seeped into his cheeks again. "Uh, no. No, of course I don't mind. I'll be glad to do…ah, *un*do… you…I mean *them*. Help you. Undo them. Of course. No problem."

He moved both of his hands to her left one, but he hesitated before making contact. Instinctively, Ava took a step forward, as if doing so would help him close the hairbreadth of space that hovered between their hands. But all that did was diminish to a hairbreadth the space between their bodies, bringing them close enough that she more keenly felt his heat and more fully enjoyed his scent.

Close enough that, this time, Peyton did move closer, completely erasing any space left between them.

As his torso bumped hers, something at Ava's core caught fire. When he closed his hands over her glove, capturing the fourth button between his thumb and forefinger, that fire exploded, sending rockets of heat through her entire body. It was such an exquisitely tender touch, coming so unexpectedly from a man like him, so unlike anything she'd felt before.

Then she remembered that that wasn't true. Years ago, surrounded by girlish accoutrements in the bedroom of a Gold Coast mansion, she'd felt a touch that was just as tender, just as exquisite. That night, when Peyton had curled the fingers of one hand gingerly over her shoulder and skimmed the others along her nape, the gesture had been so tentative, so gentle, it was as if he were touching a girl for the first time. Which was ridiculous, because everyone at Emerson knew he was already hugely experienced, even at seventeen. With a carefulness no teenage boy should have been able to manage, he had begun to soothe her tense muscles.

The soothing, however, had quickly escalated. His touch did more to agitate than to placate, stirring feelings in Ava she'd spent months—years, even—trying to deny. Each stroke of his fingers over her flesh had made her crave more, until her thoughts became a jumble of desire and want and need. Peyton had been no more immune to the touching than she had. Within moments, what had started as an effort to calm erupted into a demand to incite. They'd been on each other like animals, scarcely breaking apart long enough to breathe.

But they'd been kids, she reminded herself, trying to ignore the heat building in her belly—and elsewhere. They'd been at the mercy of uncontrollable adolescent hormones. They were adults now, and could contain themselves. Yes, she was still physically attracted to Peyton. She suspected he was still physically attracted to her. But they were mature enough and experienced enough to recognize the pointlessness of such an attraction when there was nothing else between them to make it last. Sex was only sex without emotion to enrich it. And she was beyond wanting to have sex with someone when there was no future in it for either of them.

Now the caress of his fingers on her hand began to sway her thinking in that regard. Maybe, just this once, sex without a future wouldn't be such a bad thing…

Then Ava realized Peyton wasn't unbuttoning her glove. He was, in fact, rebuttoning it.

"Peyton, what are you doing?" she asked, surprised by how breathless she sounded. Surprised by how breathless she was. "I need you to help me get my gloves *off*."

He sounded a little breathless himself when he replied, "Oh, I think I like them better on."

"But—"

She wasn't able to complete her objection—she wasn't even able to complete a thought—because he dipped his head to press his mouth against hers. A little gasp of surprise escaped her, and he took advantage of her open mouth to taste her more deeply. With one hand still tangled in her gloved fingers, he pulled her close with the other, opening his hand at the small of her back to hold her in place. Not that Ava necessarily wanted to go anywhere. Not just yet. This was starting to get interesting…

Instinctively, she kissed him back, curving her free hand over his shoulder, tilting her head to facilitate the embrace. When she did, her hat bumped his forehead and tipped to one side. She released his shoulder to pull out the trio of hairpins keeping it in place, but Peyton captured that hand, too, pulling both away from her body.

"Don't," he said softly.

"But it's in the way."

He shook his head. "No. It's perfect where it is."

They were both breathing hard, their gazes locked, neither seeming to know what to do. The whole thing made no sense. Moments ago, they were arguing, and she was telling him to leave her alone. Yes, they'd ultimately arrived at an uneasy truce, but this went beyond every treaty they'd ever studied in World Civ.

Finally, she asked, "Peyton, what are we doing?"

He said nothing for a moment, only continued to hold her hands at her sides and study her face. Then he said, "Something that's been coming for a long time, I think."

"It can't have been that long. You've only been back in Chicago for two weeks."

"Oh, this started long before I came back to Chicago."

That was true. It had probably started her freshman year at Emerson, the first time she'd laid eyes on the bad boy of the sophomore class. The bad boy of every class. Even before she knew what it was to want someone, she'd wanted Peyton. She just hadn't understood how deeply that kind of wanting could run. Now—

Now she understood all too well. And now she wanted it—wanted him—even more.

Nevertheless, she resisted. "It's not a good idea."

"Why not?"

"Because there's no point in it."

"There was no point in it sixteen years ago, either, but that didn't stop us then."

"That's exactly my point."

He smiled at that. "But we were so good together, Ava."

"That one night we were."

He lifted one shoulder and let it drop. "Most people don't get one night like that their entire lives."

Implicit in his statement was that if they let things continue the way they had started, she and Peyton could have not just one but two nights like that. But was it enough? And wanting him more now, would it be even harder to let him go this time?

She didn't have a chance to form an answer to either question, because Peyton lowered his head and kissed her again. He was more careful this time, tilting to avoid her hat, brushing his lips gently over hers once, twice, three times, four. With every stroke of his mouth, Ava's heart raced more wildly, her temperature shot higher, and her thoughts melted away. The next thing she knew, she was framing Peyton's face in her gloved hands and kissing him back with all the tenderness he was showing her.

But just as before, that deliberation quickly escalated. She pushed her hands through his hair to cup one over his nape and the other along his throat. Then both hands were skimming under his lapels to push his jacket from his shoulders. He shrugged the garment off, then moved his hands to the top of her dress, unfastening the first of its many buttons. She wanted to undo the ones on his shirt, but her gloves hindered her once more. She pulled her mouth away from his to attempt their removal again, only to have him stop her.

"I want them off so I can touch you," she said.

"And I want them on," he told her. He grinned in a way that was downright salacious. "At least the first time. And the little hat, too."

Her pulse quickened at the prospect of a second—and perhaps even a third—time. Just as there had been that night when they were teenagers, even if the third time had been thanks to Peyton's gentle touches, because she'd been too tender to accommodate him again. Touching was good. She liked touching. It had been so long since she'd enjoyed such intimacies with anyone. In a way, she supposed she hadn't truly enjoyed them since that night with Peyton—at least not as much as she had with him. When a woman's first time was with someone like him, it left other guys at a disadvantage.

Then the second part of his statement came clear, and she couldn't help but smile back. "Just how long have you been thinking about this?"

"All afternoon."

"But I'm having trouble unbuttoning anything with them on," she told him. She hesitated to add that that was mostly because his touch made her tremble all over.

"Oh, that's okay," he assured her. "I can unbutton anything you—or I—want."

He dropped his fingers to the second button on her dress and deftly slipped it free, then moved on to the third. And the fourth. And the fifth. As he went, he moved his body slowly forward, gently urging her toward the kitchen door. Then into the hallway. Then to her bedroom door. Then into her bedroom. He reached her hem just as they arrived at her bed and, with the release of the final button, he spread her dress open. Beneath it, she wore a white lace demicup bra and matching panties. He hooked his thumbs into the waistband of the latter and eased them down over her hips, then gently pushed her down to a sitting position on the bed.

Ava started to scoot backward to make room for him, too, but he gripped her thighs and halted her.

"Don't get ahead of yourself," he murmured.

He started pulling down her panties again, over her thighs and knees, kneeling to push them along her calves and over her ankles. Instead of rising again, however, he moved between her legs, pushing her thighs apart. When Ava threaded her white-gloved hands through his hair, he gripped one of her wrists to place a kiss at the center of her palm. She closed her eyes, feeling the kiss through the fabric, through her skin, down to her very core. Then she felt his mouth on her naked thigh, and she gasped, her eyes flying open. Instinctively, she tried to close her legs, but he caught one in each hand and opened her wider. Then he moved his mouth higher, and higher, and higher still, until he was tasting her in the most intimate way he could.

Pleasure pooled in her belly as he darted his tongue against her, rippling outward to send ribbons of deli-

ciousness echoing through her. Over and over, he sa-
vored her, relished her, aroused her. Little by little, those
ribbons began to coil tight. Closer and closer they drew,
until she didn't think she would be able to tolerate the
chaos surging through her. Then, just when she thought
she would shatter, those coils sprang free and she fell
back onto the bed, arms spread wide, surrendering as
one wave after another engulfed her.

Delirious, panting for breath, she somehow managed to lift her head enough to see Peyton stand. As
he moved his hands to the buttons of his shirt, his grin
was smug and satisfied. As much as she had enjoyed
the last—how long had she been lying here? Moments?
Months? An eternity?—she enjoyed watching him un-
dress even more. He did it methodically, intently, his
eyes never leaving hers, casting his shirt to the floor
and then reaching for the waistband of his trousers.

He might have been a workaholic, but he clearly also
took time to work out. His torso was roped with muscle
and sinew, and his shoulders and biceps bunched and
flexed as he jerked his belt free and lowered his zipper.
Beneath, he wore a pair of silk boxers Ava had been
in no way instrumental in encouraging him to buy. So
either he cared more about undergarments than he did
about what he wore over them, or else he wanted to impress someone. She remembered he would be meeting
soon with a woman who'd been handpicked for him.
And she pushed the thought away. He was with her
now. That was all that mattered. For now.

When he stepped out of his boxers, he was full and
ready for her. Ava caught her breath at the sight of him,
so confident, so commanding, so very, very male. He
lay alongside her and draped an arm over her waist, then
lowered his head to hers, pushed back the netting on

her hat, and kissed her deeply. She curled her fingers around his neck and pulled him closer, vying momentarily for possession of the kiss before giving herself over to him completely. He covered her breast with one hand, kneading gently. Then he followed the lace of her bra until he found the front closure, unsnapping it easily. After that, his bare hand was on her bare flesh, warm and insistent, his skin exquisitely rough.

He moved his mouth from hers, dragging kisses over her cheek, across her forehead, along her jaw. Then lower still, along her neck and collarbone, between her breasts. Then on her breast, tracing the tip of his tongue along the lower curve before opening wide over the sensitive peak. As he drew her into his mouth, he flattened his tongue against her nipple, tasting her there as intimately as he had everywhere else. Those little coils began to tighten inside her again, eliciting a groan of need.

Peyton seemed to understand, because he levered himself above her and returned his mouth to hers. As he kissed her, he entered her, long and hard and deep. Ava sighed at the feeling of completion that came over her. Never had she felt fuller or more whole. She opened her legs wider to accommodate him and he gave her a moment to adjust. Then he withdrew and bucked his hips forward again. Ava cried out at the second thrust, so perfect was the joining of their bodies. When Peyton braced himself on his forearms, she wrapped her legs around his waist and he propelled himself forward again. She lifted her hips to meet him, and together they set a rhythm that started off leisurely before building to a forceful crescendo.

They came together, both crying out at the fierceness of their release. Peyton rolled onto his back, bringing

Ava with him so that she was the one on top, gazing down at him. His breathing was as rapid and ragged as her own, his skin as slick and hot with perspiration. But he smiled as he looked at her, moving a hand to the back of her head to unpin her hat and free her hair until it tumbled around them both.

He was so beautiful. So intoxicating. Such a generous, powerful lover. She'd been thinking she would be able to handle him better as an adult. She'd thought her hormones had calmed down to the point where she would be in control of herself this time. She'd thought she would be immune to the adolescent repercussions of her first time with Peyton.

Wrong. She had been so wrong. He was more potent now than he had ever been, and she was even more susceptible to him. Her control had evaporated the moment he covered her mouth with his. The repercussions this time would be nothing short of cataclysmic. Because where she had responded to Peyton before as a girl who knew nothing of love and little of the workings of her own body, now she responded to him as a woman who understood those things too well. But it wasn't the physical consequences she might worry about in a situation like this—he had slipped on a condom before entering her. It was her heart. A part of her that was considerably more fragile.

And a part that was far more prone to breaking.

Nine

The second time Peyton awoke in Ava's bedroom, he was just as disoriented as he'd been the first time. Only this time it wasn't due to overindulgence in alcohol. This time, it was due to overindulgence in Ava.

Like that first time, he lay facedown, but today he was under the sheet instead of on top of it. And today he was sharing Ava's pillow, because his, he vaguely recalled, had been thrust under her hips during a particularly passionate moment, only to be cast blindly aside when he turned her over. Her face was barely an inch from his, and her eyes were closed in slumber, one of them obscured by a wayward strand of dark auburn. She was lying on her side, the sheet down around her waist, her arm folded over her naked breasts, her hands burrowed under the pillow. She looked tumbled and voluptuous and sexy as hell, and he swelled to life, just looking at her.

Probably shouldn't bother her with that again, though. Yet. A body did need some kind of refueling before it undertook those kinds of gymnastics a second—third? Fourth? They all got so jumbled together—time.

As carefully as he could, he climbed out of bed, halting before going anywhere to make sure he hadn't woken her up. Coffee. He needed coffee. She doubtless would, too, once she was conscious. He located his boxers and trousers and pulled both on, shrugged into his shirt without buttoning it, then made his way to the kitchen. He still couldn't get over the smallness of this place and wondered again where Ava's main residence was. Wondered again, too, why she was so determined that he not find out where it was. Maybe she would take him home with her, to her real home, now that the two of them had—

He halted the thought right there. There was no reason for him to think today would be any different from yesterday, especially considering the history the two of them shared. The last time he and Ava had spontaneously combusted like that, not a single thing had changed from the day before to the day after. They'd both gone right back to their own worlds and returned to their full-blown antagonism. Nothing had been different. Except that they'd both known just how explosive—and how amazing—things could be between them. Physically, anyway.

Which, now that he thought about it, might have been why they had both been so determined to return to business as usual. It had scared the crap out of him when he was a teenager, the way he and Ava came together that night. Not just because he hadn't understood why it had happened or how it could have been so unbelievably good, but because of how much he'd wanted it to happen again. That had probably scared him most of all. Somehow he'd known he would never have enough of Ava. And talk about forbidden fruit. He'd had to work even harder after that night to make sure he stayed at arm's length.

It hadn't made any sense. He'd still disliked her, even after the two of them made love...ah, he meant had sex. Hadn't he? He'd still thought she was vain, shallow and snotty. Hadn't he? And she'd made clear she still didn't like him, either. Hadn't she? So why had he, every day during the rest of his senior year, fantasized about being with her again? Sometimes he'd even fantasized about being with her in ways that had nothing to do with sex— taking in a midnight showing of *The Rocky Horror Picture Show* at the Patio Theater or sledding in Dan Ryan Woods. Hell, he'd even entertained a brief, lunatic idea about inviting her to the Emerson senior prom.

Sex, he told himself now, just as he'd told himself then. He'd been consumed by thoughts of Ava after that night because he associated her with sex after that night. He hadn't been a virgin then, but he hadn't seen nearly as much action as his reputation at Emerson had made others believe. Adolescent boys in the throes of testosterone overload weren't exactly picky when it came to sex with a willing participant. They didn't have to like the person they hooked up with. They only had to like the physical equipment that person had. Hell, even grown men weren't all that discriminating.

In high school, with Ava, it had just been one of those weird chemical reactions between two people who had nothing in common otherwise. Who would never have anything in common otherwise. Great sex. Bad rapport. There was no reason to think last night had changed that. Yeah, the two of them got along better these days than they had in high school—usually. But that was only because they'd matured and developed skills for dealing with people they didn't want to deal with. Sure, they could burn up the sheets in a sexual arena. But in polite society? Probably still best to stay at arm's length.

Yeah. That had to be why they'd ended up in bed together last night. So it made sense to conclude that today's morning after wouldn't be any different from their morning after sixteen years ago. Except that he and Ava probably wouldn't yell at each other the way they had then, and he was reasonably certain he wouldn't have to climb out the bedroom window to avoid being seen. He was likewise certain that Ava would agree.

A sound behind him made him spin around, and he saw her standing in the doorway looking like a femme fatale from a fabulous '40s film. She was wrapped in a robe made of some flimsy, silky-looking fabric covered with big red flowers, and her hair spilled over her forehead and danced around her shoulders.

"You're still here," she said, sounding surprised.

"Where else would I be?"

She lifted one shoulder and let it drop, a gesture that made the neck of the robe open wider, revealing a deep V of creamy skin. It was with no small effort that Peyton drew his gaze back up to her face.

"I don't know," she said. "When I woke up and you weren't there, I just thought…"

When she didn't finish, he said, "You thought I climbed out your bedroom window and down the rainspout, and that you'd see me at school on Monday?"

He had meant to make her smile. Instead, her brows knitted downward. "Kind of."

In other words, Ava was thinking last night was a repeat of the one sixteen years ago, too. That, once again, nothing had changed between the two of them. That this morning it was indeed back to business as usual. Otherwise, she wouldn't look as somber as she did. Otherwise, the room would have been filled with warmth and relief instead of tension and anxiety. Otherwise, they would both be happy.

"Coffee?" he asked, to change the subject. Then he remembered he hadn't fixed any yet. "I mean, I was going to make coffee, but I don't know where it is."

"In the cabinet to your right."

He opened it and discovered not just coffee, but an assortment of other groceries, as well. He remembered from his previous visit how well stocked the bathroom was, too. Just how often did Ava use this place, anyway?

Neither of them said a word as he went about the motions of setting up the coffeemaker and switching it on. With each passing moment, the silence grew more awkward.

"So," Peyton said, "what's on the agenda for today? It's Saturday. That should leave things wide open."

For a moment, Ava didn't reply. But she looked as if she were thinking very hard about something. "Actually, I'm thinking maybe it's time to make a dry run," she finally said.

The comment confused him. Wasn't that what they'd done last night? And look how it had turned out. All awkward and uncertain this morning. "What do you mean?" he asked, just to be sure.

She hesitated again before speaking. "I mean maybe it's time we launched you into society to see how things go."

He felt strangely panicked. "But you said we still had a lot of stuff to go over."

"No, you said that."

"Oh, yeah. But that's because there is."

Once again she hesitated. "Maybe. But that's another reason to go ahead and wade into the waters of society. To see where there might still be trouble spots that need improvement. Who knows? You might feel right at home and won't need any more instruction."

He doubted that. As much as he'd learned in the last couple of weeks, he wasn't sure he would ever feel comfortable in Ava's world, even if they spent the next ten years studying for it. And why did she sound kind of hopeful about him not needing any more instruction? It was almost as though she wanted to get rid of him.

Oh, right. After last night, she probably did. But then, he wanted to get rid of her, too, right? So why was he digging in?

"What did you have in mind?" he asked.

"There's a fund-raiser for La Rabida Children's Hospital at the Palmer House tonight. It will be perfect. Everyone who's anyone will be there. It's invitation only, but I'm sure if news got around that Peyton Moss, almost billionaire, was in town, you could finagle one."

"Why can't I just be your guest?" No sooner did he ask the question than did it occur to him that she might already be taking someone else. His panic multiplied.

Her gaze skittered away from his. "Because I wasn't invited."

His mouth dropped open at that. Ava Brenner hadn't been invited to an event where everyone who was anyone would be making an appearance?

"Why not?" he asked.

She said nothing for a moment, only pulled the sides of her robe closed and cinched the belt tight. She continued to avoid his gaze when she replied. "I, um…I had kind of a falling-out with the woman who organized it.

Since then, I tend not to show up on any guest list she's associated with." Before he could ask for more details, she hurried on, "But a word in the right ear will put you on the guest list with no problem."

Wow. It took a brave soul—or someone with a death wish—to exclude the queen bee of Chicago's most ruthless rich-kid high school from a major social event. Whoever organized this thing must have come to Chicago recently and didn't realize what kind of danger she was courting, ignoring Ava.

"Then who's going to put that word into the right ear?" he asked.

"A friend of mine who's attending owes me a favor. I'll have her contact the coordinator this morning. You should get a call by this afternoon."

Of course. No doubt Ava had lots of friends attending this thing who owed her favors that could get done at a moment's notice. Favors to pay her back for not walking all over them at Emerson and grinding them into dust.

"But…"

"But what?" she asked. "Either you're ready or you're not. If we can find that out tonight, all the better."

Right. Because if he was ready, then the two of them could part ways sooner rather than later. And that would be for the best. He knew it. Ava knew it. They didn't belong together now any more than they had sixteen years ago.

"Will you come, too?" he asked.

"I told you. I wasn't invited."

"But—"

"You'll be fine going solo."

"But—"

"You can report back to me tomorrow."

"But—"

"But *what?*"

This time, it was Peyton's turn to hesitate. "Couldn't you come with me as my guest or something?"

He'd thought she would jump at the chance. Wouldn't it be the perfect opportunity to stick it to whoever had kept her off the guest list, showing up anyway? Invited, nonetheless, even if by default? She could swoop in with all that imperiousness that was second nature to her and be the center of everything, the same way she'd been in high school. Peyton even found himself kind of looking forward to seeing the old Ava in action.

But she didn't look or sound anything like the old Ava when she replied, "I don't think it's a good idea."

"Then I'm not going."

She drove her gaze back to his, and for an infinitesimal moment, he did indeed see a hint of the old Ava. The flash of her eyes, the ramrod posture and the haughty set to her mouth. But as quickly as she surfaced, the old Ava disappeared.

"Fine," she said wearily. "I'll go. But only as an observer, Peyton. You'll be on your own when it comes to mingling."

"Mingling?" he repeated distastefully. That sounded about as much fun as *taking tea.*

"And anything else that comes up."

He wanted to argue, but backed down. For now. It was enough that he'd convinced her to come with him to this thing. Okay, to *come,* even if it wasn't technically *with him.* They could work on that part later. What was weird was that Peyton discovered he actually did kind of want to work on that part. He wanted to work on that part very much. Which was totally different from how he'd felt on that morning after sixteen years ago. In a word, *hmm...*

So now that he had the *who,* the *when* and the *what,* all he had to do was figure out the *why.* And, most confounding of all, the *how.*

Ava studied her reflection in the mirror of a fitting room at Talk of the Town, feeling the way her clients must. Mostly, she was wondering if she would be able to fool others into thinking this was her dress, not a rental, and that she was rich and glamorous and refined like everyone else at the party, not some poser who was struggling to make payments on the business loan that had bumped her up—barely—to middle class.

That was why most women came to Talk of the Town. To look wealthier and more important than they really were. Sometimes they wanted to impress a potential employer. Sometimes it was for a school reunion where they wanted to show friends and acquaintances—and prom queens and bullies—that they were flourishing. Others simply wanted to move in a level of society they'd never moved in before, even if for one night, to see what it was like.

Fantasies. That was really what they rented at Talk of the Town. And a fantasy was what Ava was trying to create for herself tonight. Because only in a fantasy would she be welcomed in the society where she had once held dominion. And only in a fantasy would she and Peyton walk comfortably in that world together. Sixteen years ago, that would have been because no one moving in her circle wanted to include him at the party. Today, Peyton was welcome, but she wasn't.

Before Peyton's return to Chicago, Ava hadn't given a fig about moving in that world again. But since his arrival two weeks ago—and making love with him last night—she'd begun to feel differently. Not about want-

ing to rule society again. But about at least being welcome there. Because that was Peyton's world now. And
she wanted to be where he was.

Over the past two weeks, she'd begun to feel differently about him. Or maybe she was just finally being
honest with herself about how she'd always felt about
him, even in high school. She'd remembered so many
things about him that she'd forgotten over the years—
things she had consciously ignored back then, but which
had crept into her subconscious anyway. Things that,
for that one night at her parents' house, had allowed
her to let down her guard and feel for him the way she
truly felt and respond to him the way she truly wanted
to respond.

She'd remembered how his smile hooked up more
on one side than the other, making him look roguish
and irreverent. She'd remembered how once, in the library, he had been so engrossed in his reading that she'd
enjoyed five full minutes of just watching him. She'd
remembered how he'd always championed the other
scholarship kids at Emerson and acted as their protec-
tor when the members of her crowd were so cruel. And
she'd remembered seeing him stash his lunch under his
shirt one day to carry it out to a starving stray dog behind the gym.

They were all acts that had revealed his true character. Acts that made her realize he was none of the things
she and her friends had said about him and everything
any normal girl would love in a boy. But Ava had chosen to ignore them. That way she wouldn't have to ac-
knowledge how she really felt about him, for fear that
she would be banished from the only world she knew,
the only world in which she belonged.

Even with the passage of years and the massive reversal in his fortune, Peyton was still that same guy. He still grinned like a rabble-rouser and could still hone his concentration to the exclusion of everything else. He still rooted for the underdog, and he couldn't pass a busker on the street without tossing half the contents of his wallet into the performer's cup. He hadn't changed a bit. Not really. And neither had the feelings she had buried so deep inside her teenage self.

She expelled a soft sound of both surprise and defeat. Sixteen years ago, she and Peyton couldn't have maintained a relationship because their social circles had prohibited it—his as much as hers. No one in his crowd would have accepted her any more than her crowd would have accepted him. And neither of them had had the skill set or maturity to sustain a liaison in secret. Eventually it would have ended, and it would have ended badly. They would have burned hot and fast for a while, but they would have burned out. And they would have burned each other. And that would have stayed with them forever. Now...

Now it was the same, only reversed. Peyton's success had launched him to a place where he wanted and needed the "right" kind of woman for a wife—the kind of woman who would boost his image and raise his status even more. Someone with cachet, who had entrée into every facet of society. Someone whose pedigree and lineage was spotless. He certainly didn't want a woman whose father was a felon and whose mother had succumbed to mental illness, a woman who could barely pay her own way in the world. He'd fought hard to claw his way to the level of success he had—he'd said so himself. He wasn't going to jeopardize that for someone like her. Not when the only thing she had to offer him was a physical release, no matter how explosive.

Maybe there was emotion, even love, on her part, but on Peyton's? Never. There hadn't been when they were teenagers—he hadn't been able to get out of her bedroom fast enough, and his antagonism toward her for the rest of the school year had been worse than ever—and not now, either. This morning he'd said nothing about last night, had only wondered what today's lesson would be, as if their making love hadn't changed anything. Because it *hadn't* changed anything. At least, not for him.

Nerves tumbled through her midsection as she surveyed herself in the mirror one last time. On the upside, the fund-raiser tonight was one of the biggest ones held in Chicago, so there was an excellent chance she and Peyton wouldn't run into anyone from the Emerson Academy. On the downside, the fund-raiser tonight was one of the biggest ones held in Chicago, so there was an excellent chance she and Peyton would run into everyone from the Emerson Academy.

Maybe if she wore a pair of those gorgeous, gemstone-encrusted Chanel sunglasses…

She immediately pushed the idea away. Not only was it déclassé to wear sunglasses to a society function—unless it involved a racetrack or polo match—she couldn't afford to add any more accessories. As it was, the form-fitting gold Marchesa gown, along with the blue velvet Escada pumps, clutch and shawl, and the Bulgari sapphire necklace, were going to set her back enough that she would have to exist on macaroni and cheese until July. Still, she thought as she turned to view the plunging back of the dress and the perfect French twist she'd managed for her hair, she looked pretty smashing if she did say so herself.

When she stepped out of the fitting room to find

Lucy waiting for her, Ava could tell by her look of approval that she agreed.

"You know, I didn't think the blue shoes and clutch were going to work," the salesclerk said, "but with that necklace, it all comes together beautifully. I guess that's why you're the big boss."

Well, you could take the girl out of society, but you couldn't take society out of the girl. Not that some of her former friends hadn't tried.

The thought made her stomach roil. She really, really, really hoped she didn't see anyone she knew tonight.

"I have to go," she said. "Thank you again for working so many hours this week. I'll make it up to you."

"You already have," Lucy told her with a grin. "You've made it up to me time and time and a half again."

Ava grinned back. "Don't spend it frivolously."

Not the way Ava had spent so frivolously with this outfit. She wished she'd had the foresight to charge Peyton for expenses.

"Have fun tonight!" Lucy called as Ava made her way to the door. "Don't do anything I wouldn't do!"

Not to worry, Ava assured her friend silently. She'd already done that. By falling in love with a man who would never, ever love her back.

Ten

Peyton paced in front of the Palmer House Hilton, checking his watch for the tenth time and tugging the black tie of his new tuxedo. Ava had been right about the phone call. That morning, she'd called someone named Violet, who said she would call someone named Catherine, and before he'd even left Ava's apartment, his phone had rung with a call from that same Catherine, who had turned out to be someone from Ava's social circle at Emerson—and someone who had treated him even worse than Ava had—gushing about how much she would love it if he would come to their "little soiree." She'd also made him promise to seek her out as soon as he arrived so the two of them could catch up on old times.

As if he wanted to catch up with anyone from Emerson who wasn't Ava. Jeez.

Where the hell was she? She should have been here

seven and a half minutes ago. He scanned the line of taxis and luxury cars that snaked halfway down Monroe Street. As if his thoughts made it happen, the door of a yellow cab three cars back opened and Ava climbed out. And not just any Ava. But a breathtaking twenty-four-carat-gold Ava.

Holy crap, she looked— He stopped himself. Not just because he couldn't think of an adjective good enough to do her credit, but because there would be no *holy crap* tonight. Tonight he was supposed to be a gentleman. Tonight, he would be a—he tried not to gag—society buck. Guys like that didn't say *Holy crap.* Guys like that didn't even say *Guys like that.* They said... He racked his brain, trying to remember some of the stuff Ava had taught him to say, since even saying stuff like *stuff* was off-limits when it came to presenting a dignified, articulate image.

Aw, screw it. He could think whatever words he wanted, as long as he didn't say them out loud. And what he thought when he saw Ava gliding toward him, covered in gold and sapphire-blue, was...was...

Huh. Even allowing himself to use his usual vocabulary, he still couldn't think of anything. Except maybe about what she was wearing *under* all the gold and sapphires.

Crap.

Okay, so the past couple of weeks had been the best of times and the worst of times. The best of times because he'd been around Ava, and he now knew how to do things that increased his social value to women like her. But the worst of times because, even with his increased social value, Ava still didn't want him. Not the way he wanted her.

Well, okay, she *wanted* him. At least, last night she

had. She had definitely wanted him the way he wanted her last night. She just didn't want him today. Not the way he wanted her. And it was a different kind of wanting he felt today—a way more important kind of wanting—than it had been last night. Which was weird, because last night he'd wanted her in a way that was pretty damned important. What was even worse—in fact, what was the worst part of all—was that she was more firmly entrenched in his head now than ever, and he had no idea how to deal with it. And she wasn't just in his head. She was in other body parts, too. And not just the ones that liked to have sex.

She'd changed since high school. A lot. Yeah, there had been times when she'd tried to shroud herself in the same ice-princess disguise she'd worn in high school, but Peyton had seen past the facade. She was warmer now, more accessible. More fun to be around. Even when the two of them sparred with each other, there was something enjoyable about it.

But then, he'd kind of enjoyed sparring with her in high school, too. Really, now that he thought about it, he realized Ava couldn't have been *that* cold and distant back then. Not all the time. There must have been something about her that attracted him—something only his subconscious had been able to see. Otherwise he wouldn't have been attracted. Since coming back to Chicago, his conscious had started to pick up on it, too. Ava wasn't vain, shallow or snotty. Had she been vain, she wouldn't have thought about anyone but herself, and she never would have helped him out with his self-improvement, even if he was paying her. Why shouldn't he pay her? He was going to pay someone else for their expertise, and hers was even more expert because she'd grown up in the environment he was trying to penetrate. Uh…he meant *enter*. Uh…he meant *join*. Yeah, join.

She wasn't shallow, either, because she knew a lot of stuff about a lot of stuff. Had she been shallow, he could have tallied her interests on one hand. She'd introduced him to things he'd never thought about before, a lot of which wasn't even related to social climbing. And she wasn't snotty, because she'd shared that knowledge with him, knowing he would use it for social climbing, not caring that his new money would mix with old. Not once had she criticized him for being nouveau riche. Only Peyton had done that.

Yep, he definitely knew now what he liked about Ava. And, at the moment, it was all wrapped in gold and walking right toward him.

"What are you doing out here?" she asked by way of a greeting when she came to a halt before him.

"I'm waiting for you."

"You were supposed to leave my name at the door as your plus-one and go in without me to start mingling. We're not together, remember?"

How could he forget? She'd made clear this morning that last night hadn't changed anything between them. "But I don't know anyone in there. How am I supposed to mingle when I don't know anyone?"

"Peyton, that's the whole point of mingling."

But mingling sucked. It sucked as much as having to tame his profanity. It sucked as much as having to pay ten times what he normally did for a haircut. It sucked as much as not being able to wear ten-year-old blue jeans that were finally broken in the way he liked.

Why did he want to join a class of people who had to do so many things that sucked? Oh, yeah. To increase his social standing. Which would increase his business standing. Which would allow him to take over a company that would increase his monetary standing. That was the most important thing, wasn't it? Making money? Increasing his value? At least, that had been the most important thing before he landed back in Chicago. Somehow, over the past couple of weeks, that had fallen a few slots on his most important stuff in the world list.

Huh. Imagine that.

"Just promise me you won't slip out of view," he told Ava.

"I promise. Now get in there and be the status-seeking, name-dropping, social-climbing parvenu I've come to know and lo— Uh…I've come to know."

Peyton's stomach clenched at the way she first stumbled over the word *love,* then discarded it so easily. Instead, he focused on another word. "Parvenu? What the hell is that? That's not one of those upper-crusty words you taught me. See? I told you we still have a lot to do."

"Just give them my name and get in there," she told him, pointing toward the door. "I'll count to twenty and follow." As he started to move away, she hissed under her breath, "And no swearing!"

Peyton forced himself to move forward, ignoring the flutter of nerves in his belly. He had nothing to be nervous about. He'd been entering fancy, expensive places like this for years and had stopped feeling self-conscious in them a long time ago. Even so, it surprised him when a doorman stepped up to open the door for him, welcoming him to the Palmer House Hilton, punctuating the greeting with a respectful *sir.* Because in spite of all that Peyton had achieved since the last time he was in Chicago, tonight he felt like an eighteen-year-old kid who had never left. A kid from the wrong side of town who was trying to sneak into a place he shouldn't be. A place he wasn't welcome. A place he didn't belong.

The feeling was only amplified once he was inside the hotel. The Palmer House was an unassuming enough building on the outside, but inside it looked like a Byzantine cathedral, complete with ornamental columns, gilt arches and a lavishly painted ceiling. The place was packed with people who were dressed as finely as he, the men in black tie and the women in gowns as richly colored as precious gems. Catherine Bellamy, he remembered. That was the name of his former classmate who had asked him to look for her. Except that now her name was Catherine Ellington, because she married Chandler Ellington, who'd been on the Emerson hockey team with Peyton, and who was the biggest...

He tried to think of a word for Chandler that would be socially acceptable but couldn't come up with a single one. That was how badly the guy had always treated Peyton in high school. Suffice it to say Chandler had been a real expletive deleted in high school. So had Catherine. So they were perfect for each other. Anyway, he was pretty sure he'd recognize them if he saw them.

He followed the well-heeled crowd, figuring they were all destined for the same place, and found himself in the grand ballroom, which was every bit as sumptuous—and intimidating—as the lobby. Chandeliers of roped crystal hung from the ceiling above a room that could have been imported from the Palace of Versailles. A gilt-edged mezzanine surrounded it, with people on both levels clutching flutes of champagne and cut-crystal glasses of cocktails. A waiter passed with a tray carrying both, and Peyton automatically went for one of the latter, something brown he concluded would be whiskey of some kind, a spirit he loved in all its forms.

He took a couple of fortifying sips, but they did nothing to dispel his restlessness. So he scanned the crowd for a flash of gold that was splashed with sapphire. He found it immediately. Found her immediately. Ava had just entered the ballroom and was reaching for a glass of champagne herself. He waited until he caught her eye, then lifted his glass in salute. She smiled furtively and did likewise, subtly enough so that only he would see the gesture.

It was enough. Ava had his back. Taking a deep breath, Peyton turned and ventured into the crowd.

Ava managed to make it through the first hour of the fund-raiser without incident, mostly by tucking herself between a couple of potted topiaries on the mezzanine. That way, she could keep an eye on the crowd below and still snatch the occasional glass of champagne or canapé from a passing server. Even if Peyton moved from one place to another, it was easy to keep an eye on him.

It quickly became evident, however, that he didn't need an eye on him. He was a natural. From the moment he flowed into the sea of people, he looked as if he'd been one of them since birth. She kept waiting for him to make a misstep—to untie his tie or ask a waiter for a longneck beer—but he never did. Even now, he was cradling a drink with all the sophistication of James Bond and smiling at a silver-Givenchy-clad Catherine Bellamy as if she were the most fascinating woman he'd ever had the pleasure to meet.

He'd located her within moments of his arrival—or rather, Catherine had located him—and had yet to escape her. Catherine was clearly taking great delight in escorting him through the crowd, reacquainting him with dozens of their former schoolmates. Peyton had greeted each of them with one of his toe-curling smiles, never once hinting at how appallingly they had all treated him in high school.

If he could manage that, there was no way he needed further instruction in etiquette from Ava. After tonight, she could send him on his merry way without her. Off to be the toast of whatever society he might happen to find himself in. Off to his multimillion-dollar estate that was half a continent away. Off to meet the "right" kind of woman his matchmaker had found for him. Off to live his successful life with his blue-blooded wife and his perfectly pedigreed children. Off to launch his business into the stratosphere and line his pockets with even more money. That was the life he wanted. That was the life he had fought so hard, for so long, to achieve. That was the life he wouldn't sacrifice anything for. He was the master of his own destiny now. And that destiny didn't include—

"Ava Brenner. Oh, my God."

It was amazing, Ava thought, how quickly the brain could process information it hadn't accessed in years. She recognized the voice before she turned around, even though she hadn't heard it since high school. Deedee Hale. Of the Hinsdale Hales. At her side was Chelsea Thomerson, another former classmate. Both looked fabulous, of course, blonde Deedee in her signature red— this one a lush Zac Posen—and brunette Chelsea in a clingy strapless black Lagerfeld.

"What on *earth* are you doing here?" Deedee asked. She never could utter a complete sentence without emphasizing at least one word. "Not that I'm not *incredibly* happy to see you, of course. I'm just so *surprised.*"

"What a beautiful dress," Chelsea added. "I don't think I've ever seen a knockoff that looked more genuine."

"Hello, Deedee. Chelsea," Ava said. As politely as she could, she added, "It's not a knockoff. It's from Marchesa's new spring collection." And because she couldn't quite help herself, she also added, even more politely, "You just haven't seen it anywhere else yet. I have the only one in Chicago."

"Ooooh," Chelsea said. "You carry it in that little shop of yours."

"I do," Ava said with almost convincing cheeriness.

"How *is* that little project going, by the way?" Deedee asked. "Are we *still* pulling ourselves up by our little bootstraps, hmm?"

"Actually," Ava said, "tonight, we're pulling ourselves up by our little Escadas."

"Ooooh," Deedee said. "You carry *those* in your little shop, too."

"Yes, indeed."

"Have you *seen* Catherine?" Deedee asked. "I'm guessing she was *very* surprised to find you here."

"I haven't, actually," Ava said. "There are just so many people, and I haven't had a chance to—"

Before she could finish, Deedee and Chelsea were on her like a pack of rabid debutantes. As if they'd choreographed their movements before coming, each positioned herself on one side of Ava and looped an arm through hers.

"But you *must* see Catherine," Deedee said. "She's been so adamant about speaking to *everyone* on the guest list."

Translation, Ava thought, *Catherine will want to know there's a party crasher among us.*

"And since you so rarely attend these things," Chelsea added, "I'm sure Catherine will especially want to see you."

Translation, Ava thought, *You don't belong here, and when Catherine sees you, she's gonna kick your butt from here to Saks Fifth Avenue.*

Ava opened her mouth to say something that might allow her to escape, but to no avail. The women chatted nonstop as they steered her to the stairs and down to the ballroom, barely stopping for breath. Short of breaking free like a panicked Thoroughbred and galloping for the exit, there was little Ava could do but go along for the ride.

The two women located Catherine—and, by extension, Peyton—in no time, and herded Ava in that direction. Peyton looked up about the same time Catherine did, and Ava wasn't sure which of them looked more surprised. Catherine recovered first, however, straightening to a noble posture, plastering a regal smile on her face and lifting an aristocratic hand to brush back a majestic lock of black hair. Honestly, Ava thought, it was a wonder she hadn't donned a tiara for the event. Her gaze skittered from Chelsea to Deedee then back to Ava.

"Well, my goodness," she said flatly. "Ava Brenner, as I live and breathe. It's been years. Where have you been keeping yourself?"

Ava knew better than to reply, because Catherine always answered her own questions. But unlike Deedee and Chelsea, who at least pretended to be polite—kind of—Catherine, having ascended to the queen bee throne the moment Ava was forced to abdicate, saw no reason to pull punches. Especially when she was dealing with peasants.

Sure enough, Catherine barely paused for breath.

"Oh, wait. I know. Visiting your father in the state pen and your mother in the loony bin, and running your little shop for posers. It's amazing you have any time left for barging into events to which you were in no way invited."

Ava had had enough run-ins with her former friends by now that nothing Catherine could say would surprise or rattle her. Or hurt her feelings, for that matter. No, only having Peyton hear what Catherine said could do that. That could hurt quite a lot, actually.

She'd also endured enough encounters with ex-acquaintances to have learned that the best way to deal with them was to look them in the eye and never flinch. Which was good, since doing that meant Ava didn't have to look at Peyton. Imagining his reaction to what Catherine had just revealed was bad enough.

"Actually, Catherine, my father is in a federal correctional institution," she said with all the courtesy she could muster. She lowered her voice to the sort of stage whisper she would have used at parties like this in the past when gossiping about those who weren't quite up to snuff. "Federal institutions are *much* more exclusive than state ones, you know. They don't admit all the posers and wannabes."

Her reply had the hoped-for effect. Catherine was momentarily stunned into silence. Score one for the party crasher. Yay.

Sobering and returning to her normal voice, Ava added, "And my mother passed away three years ago. But it's so kind of you to ask about her, Catherine. I hope your mother is doing well. She and my mother were always such good friends."

Until Ava's father was revealed to be such a cad. Then Mrs. Bellamy had led the charge to have Ava's mother blacklisted everywhere from the Chicago Kennel Club to Kappa Kappa Gamma.

Catherine looked flummoxed by Ava's graciousness. Anyone else might have, if not apologized, at least backed off. But not a queen bee like Catherine. Once again, she recovered her sovereignty quickly.

"And your father?" she asked. "Will he be coming up for parole any time in the near future?"

"Four years," Ava said with equanimity. "Do give my regards to your father as well, won't you?"

Even though Ava had had little regard for Mr. Bellamy since he'd cornered her at Catherine's sweet sixteen party and invited her to his study for a cocktail and God knew what else.

Catherine narrowed her eyes in irritation that Ava was neither rising to the bait nor whittling down to a nub. Really, being polite and matter-of-fact was the perfect antidote to someone so poisonous. It drove Catherine mad when people she was trying to hammer down remained pleasantly upright instead.

"And it sounds like your little shop is just flourishing," she continued tartly. "Why, Sophie Bensinger and I were talking just the other day about how many crass little interlopers we've been seeing at *our* functions lately. Like tonight, for instance," she added pointedly. "All of them dressed in clothes they couldn't possibly afford, so they had to be rented from your pretentious little shop." She scanned Ava up and down. "I had no idea you were one of your own customers. And it *is* nice of you to clothe the needy, Ava, but honestly, couldn't you do it somewhere else?"

"What, and miss running into all my old friends?" Ava replied without missing a beat.

Now Catherine turned to Peyton. Knowing there was

no way to avoid it, Ava did, too. She told herself she was ready for anything when it came to his reaction—confused, angry, smug, even stung. But she wasn't ready for a complete absence of reaction. His expression was utterly blank, as if he were meeting her for the first time and had no idea who she was. She could no more tell what he thought of everything he'd just heard than she could turn back time and start the evening over.

Where Catherine's voice had been acid when she spoke to Ava, it oozed sweetness now. "Peyton, I'm sure you remember Ava Brenner from Emerson." After a telling little chuckle, she added, "I mean, who could forget Ava? She ruled that school with an iron fist. None of us escaped her tyranny. Well, not until her father was arrested for stealing millions from the hedge funds he was supposed to be managing, not to mention the IRS, so that he could pay for his cocaine and his whores. He even gave Ava's mother syphilis, can you imagine? And herpes! Of course they took everything from him to pay his debts, right down to the Tiffany watch Ava's grandmother gave her for her debut, one that had been in the family for generations. After that, Ava had to leave Chicago and go... Well. She went to live with others of her kind. In Milwaukee. You know the kind of people I'm talking about, Peyton, of course."

As if Catherine feared he might not realize she was talking about the very sort of people he'd grown up among—but whom he'd had the good taste and cunningness to rise above—she shivered for effect. And so well had Ava taught him manners, Peyton hesitated only a microsecond before smiling. But his smile never reached his eyes. Then again, neither did Catherine's. Or Chelsea's. Or Deedee's. Wow. Ava really had taught him well.

"Of course I remember Ava," he said as he extended his hand. "It's good to see you again."

Ava tugged her arm free of Chelsea's and placed her hand in his, trying to ignore how even that small touch made her stomach flip-flop. How even that small touch made her remember so many others and made her wish for so many things she knew she would never have. Before she could even get out a hello, Catherine chimed in again.

"Of course you remember Ava," she echoed Peyton's words. "How could you forget someone who treated you as atrociously as she treated you? And have I told you, Peyton, how very much I admire your many accomplishments since you graduated?"

Still looking at Ava, still holding her hand, still making her stomach flip-flop, he replied, "Yes, you have, Catherine. Several times, in fact."

"Well, you have had so many accomplishments," she gushed. "All of them so admirable. All of us at Emerson are so proud of you. Of course, we all saw your potential when you were a student there. We all knew you would rise above your, ah, meager beginnings and become an enormous success." She looked at Ava. "Well, except for Ava. But then, look how she turned out. A criminal father and an unstable mother, and not a dime to her name." She waved a hand negligently. "But there are so many nicer things to talk about. I'm sure she was on her way out. If not, we can find someone who will show her the way."

For one taut, immeasurable moment, Ava thought—hoped—Peyton would come to her rescue and tell Catherine she was here as his guest. She even hoped he would ignore every lesson she'd taught him about manners and tell all of them that furthermore, they could all go do something to themselves that no gentleman would ever tell anyone to do. But she really had taught him well. Because all he did was release her hand and take a step backward, then lift his drink to his mouth for an idle sip.

A small breath of disappointment escaped her. Well, what had she expected? Not only was he behaving exactly the way he was supposed to—the way she had taught him to—but it wasn't as though Ava didn't deserve his dismissal. Back in high school, she would have done the same thing to him. She'd said herself that karma was a really mean schoolgirl. After all, it took one to know one.

Very softly, she said, "I can find my own way out, thank you, Catherine." She turned to Peyton. "It really was nice to see you again, Peyton. Congratulations on your many admirable accomplishments."

She was following her own lesson book, turning to make a polite exit, when she thought, *What the hell?* They weren't in high school anymore. She didn't have to stay on her side of the social line the way she had at Emerson. Nor did she have to silently suffer the barbs of bullies as she had at the Prewitt School. She wasn't part of either society anymore. She was her own woman.

And this society had tossed her out on her keister sixteen years ago. She didn't have to rely on them to further her business or her fortune. On the contrary, any success she saw would be because of people who were like her. People who hoped for something better but were doing their best with what they had in the meantime. People who didn't think they were better than everyone else while behaving worse. Normal people. Real people. People who didn't care about social lines or what might happen when they crossed them. care about social lines or crossing them.

She turned back to the group, willing Peyton to meet her gaze. When he did, she told him, "It isn't true, what Catherine said, Peyton. I knew you were better than all of us at Emerson. You still are. I wouldn't have made love with you in high school if I hadn't known that. And I wouldn't have…I wouldn't have fallen in love with you now if I hadn't known on some level, always, that you were the best there was. That you *are* the best there is."

Catherine had been sipping her champagne when Ava said the part about making love with him, and she must have choked on a gasp she wasn't able to avoid. Because that was when Cristal went spewing all over Chelsea and Deedee, not to mention down the front of Catherine's Givenchy.

"You *slept* with him in high school?" she sputtered. *"Him?"*

That final word dripped with so much contempt and so much revulsion, there was no way to mistake Catherine's meaning. That Ava had sunk to the basest, scummiest level of humanity there was by consorting with someone of Peyton's filthy lower class. That even today, in spite of his *many admirable accomplishments,* he would never be fit for "polite" society like theirs.

Peyton, of course, noticed it, too. As did Catherine, finally. Probably because of the scathing look he shot her.

Immediately, she tried to mask her blunder. "I mean…I'm just so surprised to discover the two of you had a…ah, liaison…in high school. You were both so different from each other."

"It surprised me, too," Ava said, still looking at Peyton. Still unable to tell how he was reacting to what he'd just heard. "That he would lower his standards so much to get involved with a member of our crowd. It's no wonder he didn't want anyone to know about it."

Finally, he reacted. But not with confusion, anger or smugness. Judging by his reaction, he was first startled, then incredulous, then…something that kind of looked like happiness? The flip-flopping in Ava's belly turned into flutters of hopeful little butterflies.

"*I* didn't want anyone to know?" he said. "But you were the one who—"

He halted, looking at the others, who all appeared to be more than a little interested in what he might say next. Gentleman that he was, he closed his mouth and said nothing more about that night in front of them. Nothing else Ava might say was any of their business, either. She'd said what she needed to say for now. What Peyton chose to do with everything he'd learned tonight was up to him—whether he still wanted high society's stamp of approval or whether he wanted anything more to do with her.

If he valued his professional success and the wealth and social standing that came with it more than anything, he would be as courteous as Ava had taught him to be and pretend the last several minutes had never happened. He would watch her leave and continue chatting with his new best friends, even knowing how they truly felt about him. He would collect invitations to more events like this and exchange contact info with like-minded wealthy types. He would field introductions to more members of their tribe, doubtless meeting enough single women that Caroline the matchmaker would no longer be necessary.

In spite of what Catherine had said, and in spite of the way they all felt about him deep down, he was one of them now—provided he didn't screw up. A full-fledged member of the society he'd so eagerly wanted to join. Even if he was nouveau riche instead of moldy old-moneyed, because of his colossal wealth, his membership in this club would never be revoked—provided he didn't screw up. He had his pick of their women and could plant one at his side whenever he wanted, then produce a passel of beautiful, wealthy children to populate schools like Emerson. Except that Peyton's children would enjoy all the benefits he'd been denied in such a place—provided he didn't screw up. Even if Peyton's past was soiled, his present—and future—would be picture-perfect. He was Peyton Moss, gentleman tycoon. No one would ever openly criticize him or treat him like a guttersnipe again.

Provided he didn't screw up.

"If you'll all excuse me," Ava said to the group, "I'll be going. I've been asked to leave."

She had turned and completed two steps when Peyton's voice stopped her.

"The hell you will," he said. Loudly. "You're my—" the profanity he chose for emphasis here really wasn't fit for print "—guest. You're not going anywhere, dammit."

She turned back around and automatically started to call him on his language, then stopped when she saw him smile. Because it was the kind of smile she'd seen from him only twice before. That night at her parents' house sixteen years ago, and last night, in her apartment. A disarming smile that not only rendered Ava defenseless, but stripped him of his armaments, too. A smile that said he didn't give a damn about anything or anybody, as long as he had one moment with her. Only this time, maybe it would last more than a moment.

He started to wrestle his black tie free of its collar, then stopped a passing waiter and asked him what the hell a guy had to do to get a—again with the profane adjective—bottle of beer at this—profane adjective—party. When the waiter assured him he'd be right back with one, Peyton turned not to Ava, but to Catherine.

"You're full of crap, Catherine." Except he chose a different word than *crap*. "I know no one at Emerson, including you, ever thought I would amount to anything. But, hell, I never thought any of you—" now he looked at Ava "—well, except for one of you—would amount to anything, either. It's not my fault I'm the one who turned out to be right. And furthermore…"

At that point, Peyton told them they could all go do something to themselves that no gentleman would ever tell anyone to do. Ava's heart swelled with love.

Catherine sputtered again, but this time managed not to spit on anyone. However, neither Peyton nor Ava stayed around long enough to hear what she had to say. Catherine was a big nobody, after all. Who cared what she had to say?

As they headed for the exit, they passed the server returning with Peyton's longneck bottle of beer, and in one fluid gesture, he snagged both it and a slender flute of champagne for Ava. But when they reached the hotel lobby, they slowed, neither seeming to know what to do next. Ava's heart was racing, both with exhilaration from having stood up to Catherine's bullying and exuberance at having told Peyton how she felt about him. Until she remembered that he hadn't said anything about his feelings for her. Then her heart raced with something else entirely.

Ava looked at Peyton. Peyton looked at Ava.

Then he smiled that disarming—and disarmed—

smile again. "What do you say we blow this joint and find someplace where the people aren't so low-class?"

She released a breath she hadn't been aware of holding. But she still couldn't quite feel relieved. There was still so much she wanted to tell him. So many things she wanted—needed—him to know.

"You were only half-right in there, you know," she said.

He looked puzzled. "What do you mean?"

"What you said about everyone at Emerson. As wrong as Catherine was about you, everything she said about me is true. Every dime my family ever had is gone. My father is a convicted felon and a louse. My mother was a patient in a psychiatric hospital when she died. My car is an eight-year-old compact and my business is struggling. The most stylish clothing I own, I bought at an outlet store. That apartment above the shop? That's been my home for almost eight years, and I'm not going to be able to afford anything nicer anytime soon. I'm not the kind of woman your board of directors wants within fifty feet of you, Peyton."

She knew she was presuming a lot. Peyton hadn't said he wanted her within fifty feet of himself anyway. But he'd just completely sabotaged his entrée into polite society in there. Even if his home base of operation was in San Francisco, word got around fast when notable people behaved badly at high-profile events. He wouldn't have done that if his social standing was more important to him than she was.

He said nothing for a moment, only studied her face as if he were thinking very hard about something. Finally, he lifted his hand to the back of her head and, with one gentle tug, freed her hair from its elegant twist.

"Looks better down," he said. "It makes you look

vain, shallow and snotty when you wear it up. And you're not any of those things. You never were."

"Yeah, I was," she said, smiling. "Well, maybe not shallow. I mean, I did fall in love with you."

There. She'd said it twice. If he didn't take advantage this time, then he wasn't ever going to.

He smiled back. "Okay, maybe you were vain and snotty, but so was I. Maybe that was why we…" He hesitated. "Maybe that was what attracted us to each other. We were so much alike."

She smiled at that, but the giddiness she'd been feeling began to wane. He wasn't going to say it. Because he didn't feel it. Maybe he didn't care about his place in society anymore. Maybe he didn't even care about his image. But he didn't seem to care for her anymore, either. Not the way he once had. Not the way she still did for him.

"Yes, well, we're not alike anymore, are we?" she asked. "You're the prince, and I'm the pauper. You deserve a princess, Peyton. Not someone who'll sully your professional image."

He smiled again, shaking his head. "You've taught me so much over the past couple of weeks. But you haven't learned anything, have you, Ava?"

Something in the way he looked at her made her heart hum happily again. But she ignored it, afraid to hope. She'd forgotten what life was like when everything worked the way it was supposed to. She'd begun to think she would never have a life like that again.

"You tell me," she said. "You went to all the top-tier schools. I could only afford community college."

"See, that's just my point. It doesn't matter where you go to school." He gestured toward the ballroom they'd just left. "Look at all those people whose parents spent a fortune to send them to a tony school like Emerson and what losers they all turned out to be."

"We went to Emerson, too."

"Yeah, but we got an education that had nothing to do with classrooms or the library or homework. The only thing I learned at Emerson that was worth anything… the only thing I learned there that helped me achieve my many admirable accomplishments…" Now he grinned with genuine happiness. "I learned a girl like you could love a guy like me, no matter what—no matter who—I was. You taught me that, Ava. Maybe it took me almost two decades to learn it, but…" He shrugged. "You're the reason for my many admirable accomplishments. You're the reason I went after the gold ring. Hell, you are the gold ring. It doesn't matter what anyone thinks of you or me. Not our old classmates. Not my board of directors. Not anyone I have to do business with. Why would I want a princess when I can have the queen?"

Ava grinned back, feeling her own genuine happiness. "Actually, it does matter what someone thinks of me," she said. "It matters what *you* think."

"No, it doesn't. It only matters what I feel."

"It matters what you think and feel."

He lifted a hand to her hair again, threading it through his fingers. "Okay. Then I think I love you. I think I've always loved you. And I know I always will love you."

Now Ava remembered what life was like when everything worked the way it was supposed to. It was euphoric. It was brilliant. It was sublime. And all it took to make it that way was Peyton.

"We have a lot to talk about," he told her.

She nodded. "Yes. We do."

He tilted his head toward the hotel exit. "No time like the present."

Yeah, the present was pretty profane-adjective good, Ava had to admit. But then, really, their past hadn't been too shabby. And their future? Well, now. That was looking better all the time.

Epilogue

Peyton sat at a table only marginally less tiny than the one in the Chicago tearoom Ava had dragged him to three months ago, watching as she curled her fingers around the little flower-bedecked china teapot. No way was he going to touch that thing, even if it might win him points with the Montgomery sisters, who had joined him and Ava in the favorite tearoom of Oxford, Mississippi. It was one thing to be a gentleman. It was another to spill scalding tea on the little white gloves of his newest business partners.

"Peyton," Miss Helen Montgomery said, "you must have found the only woman worth having north of the Mason-Dixon Line. You'd better keep a close eye on her."

Miss Dorothy Montgomery agreed. "Why, with her manners and fashion sense, she could run the entire Mississippi Junior League."

"Now, Miss Dorothy, Miss Helen," Ava said as she set the teapot back down. "You're going to make me blush."

Wouldn't be the first time, Peyton thought, remembering how radiant Ava's face had been that evening in her apartment when he'd asked her to keep her gloves on while they made love. There had been plenty of evenings—and mornings and afternoons—like that one since then. In fact, now that he thought about it, he couldn't wait to get back to their hotel. She was wearing a pair of those white gloves now, along with a pale gray Jackie Kennedy suit and hat that were driving him nuts.

It was their last day in Mississippi. They'd met that afternoon with the Montgomerys and all the requisite corporate and legal types to fine-tune the deal Peyton had been fine-tuning himself for months. Now all that was left was to draw up the contracts and sign them. Montgomery and Sons would stay Montgomery and Sons, with Helen and Dorothy Montgomery as figureheads, and Peyton planned to keep the company intact. In fact, he was going to invest in it whatever was necessary to make the textile company profitable again, and it would become the flagship for his and Ava's new enterprise. Brenner Moss Incorporated would produce garments for women and men that were American made, from the farm-grown natural fibers to the mills that wove them into fabric to the couturiers who designed the fashions to the workers who pieced them together. Eventually, there would even be Brenner Moss retail outlets. And CEO Ava was chomping at the bit to get it all underway.

Miss Helen moved two sugar cubes to her cup and stirred gently. "Now, remember. You all promised to come back in October for homecoming."

Miss Dorothy nodded. "Helen and I are staunch Ole Miss alumnae. It's a very big deal around here."

"Oh, you bet," Peyton promised. "And you'll both be coming to Chicago for the wedding in September, right?"

"We wouldn't miss it for the world."

For now, Peyton and Ava would be dividing their time between Chicago and San Francisco, but eventually they would merge everything together on the West Coast. She wanted to include Talk of the Town under the Brenner Moss umbrella and open a chain of stores nationwide, but for now had turned the management of the Chicago shop over to her former sales associate, Lucy Mulligan. However, she was grooming Lucy to become her assistant at Brenner Moss once things took off there.

Funny, how Peyton had returned to Chicago for the single-minded purpose of enlarging his business and making money and had ended up enlarging his business and making money…and gaining so much that was way more important—and way more valuable—than any of that.

Who needed high society when everything he'd ever wanted was wherever Ava happened to be?

"By the way," Ava said, darting her attention from one Montgomery to the other, "thank you both so much for the homemade preserves."

"And the socks," Peyton added.

"Well, we know how cold those northern nights can be," Miss Helen said. "We went to Kentucky once. In the fall. It must have gotten down to fifty degrees!"

"In Chicago, it gets down in the teens during the winter," Peyton said. "But I promise it will be nice when you're there in September."

Miss Dorothy shivered, even though here in Mississippi, in July, it was a soggy ninety-five degrees in the shade. "Honestly, how do you people survive up there?"

Peyton and Ava exchanged glances, his dropping momentarily to her white gloves before reconnecting with hers—only to see her eyes spark. "Oh, we find ways to keep the fires going."

Hell, their fires never went out. He could barely remember what his life had been like before reconnecting with Ava. Just days of endless work and nights of endless networking. And yeah, there would still be plenty of that in the future, but he wouldn't be doing it alone, and it wouldn't be endless. It would only be until he and Ava had time to themselves again.

"You two are the perfect power couple, I must say," Miss Dorothy declared. "Intelligent and hardworking and obviously of very good breeding." With a smile, she added, "Why, you remind me of Helen and myself. You were obviously brought up right."

True enough, Peyton thought. They'd just had to wait until they were adults so they could bring each other up right. Still, in a lot of ways, Ava made him feel like a kid again. But the good parts about being a kid. Not the rest of it. The parts with the stolen glances, the secret smiles, the breathless wanting and the nights when everything came together exactly the way it was meant to be. He'd never be too old for any of that.

"When your new business gets going," Miss Helen said, "you two will be the talk of the town."

"That's our plan, Miss Helen," Ava agreed with a grin. But she was looking at Peyton when she said it. "Well, that and living happily ever after, of course."

Peyton grinned, too. Maybe some people thought living well was the best revenge. But he was more of the opinion that living well was the best reward. And it didn't matter where or how he and Ava lived that made it worthwhile. It only mattered that they were together. Talk of the town? Ha. He was happy just being the apple of Ava's eye.

* * * * *

A sneaky peek at next month…

PASSIONATE AND DRAMATIC LOVE STORIES

My wish list for next month's titles…

In stores from 20th June 2014:

☐ Her Pregnancy Secret – Ann Major

& Matched to a Billionaire – Kat Cantrell

☐ Lured by the Rich Rancher – Kathie DeNosky

& The Sheikh's Son – Kristi Gold

☐ A Taste of Temptation – Cat Schield

& When Opposites Attract... – Jules Bennett

2 stories in each book - only £5.49!

Just can't wait?

0614/51

The World of Mills & Boon

There's a Mills & Boon® series that's perfect for you. There are ten different series to choose from and new titles every month, so whether you're looking for glamorous seduction, Regency rakes, homespun heroes or sizzling erotica, we'll give you plenty of inspiration for your next read.

By Request

Back by popular demand!
12 stories every month

Cherish™

Experience the ultimate rush of falling in love.
12 new stories every month

INTRIGUE...

A seductive combination of danger and desire...
7 new stories every month

Desire™

Passionate and dramatic love stories
6 new stories every month

nocturne™

An exhilarating underworld of dark desires
3 new stories every month

For exclusive member offers go to
millsandboon.co.uk/subscribe

Join the Mills & Boon Book Club

Want to read more **Desire**™ books?
We're offering you **2 more** absolutely **FREE!**

We'll also treat you to these fabulous extras:

- **Exclusive offers and much more!**
- **FREE home delivery**
- **FREE books and gifts with our special rewards scheme**

Get your free books now!

visit www.millsandboon.co.uk/bookclub
or call Customer Relations on 020 8288 2888